THE LILY AND THE
DRAGON

The Lily
and the Dragon

A historical novel after Agincourt

by

Dedwydd Jones

ISBN: 0-86381-752-1

Cover design: Sian Parri

Supported by the Arts Council of Wales

First published in 2001 by
Gwasg Carreg Gwalch, 12 Iard yr Orsaf, Llanrwst,
Wales LL26 0EH
☎ 01492 642031   🖷 01492 641502
✆ books@carreg-gwalch.co.uk   Web site: www.carreg-gwalch.co.uk

This book is for Caryl Jones, Peter Kettle,
Danielle Obadia and Gerald Meylan with thanks
for all their wonderful help and encouragement.

✗ Battles	***Dover*** Cinque Ports
◆ Castles	----- Some of the main roads of
✤ Bishoprics	later medieval England
✚ Monasteries	derived from the four-
	teenth-century Gough map

ENGLAND AND WALES 1429

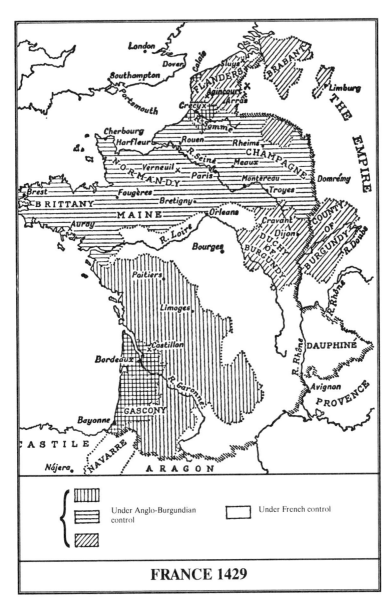

Under Anglo-Burgundian control

Under French control

FRANCE 1429

1

Isabelle of Bavaria galloped into the stable yard of her Château des Bergères, scattering the geese, ducks and chickens feeding around the ornamental pond. She wore her thick, blond hair loose so it streamed in the wind. Peacocks spread their tails in alarm. Pigeons and turtle doves flew from the roofs. Roars and shrieks came from an outhouse. The May sun shone warmly down on the scene of confusion. Only the lambs in the sheep-fold by the pond remained strangely silent. Isabelle leaned down and talked reassuringly to them as if they had just spoken to her.

'Don't be afraid, little ones, Mama's home,' she cooed.

Isabelle jumped to the ground. She disdained the new side-saddle. Like a good Austrian *cuirassier* she rode astride her charger. Nor did she wear a lady's riding habit, just a male shirt and short tunic, hose, a spreading scarlet skirt and boots to the knee. She loved the rippling of the horse's muscle between her thighs. She threw the reins to the groom, and glanced sharply at him a second time.

'Mm, new,' she murmured as he led her horse away. Her eyes ran down his tightly hosed buttocks. 'Why wasn't I told?' she thought, feeling the familiar irresistible itch. 'I'll see to him later.'

Isabelle was short, running to fat but with an underlay of muscle from her love of horses and hunting. Her short thick body with its spreading thighs and powerful rear moved with the assurance of a cart horse. Her broad, rounded face and glittering blue eyes revealed a woman in the prime of life, and a woman determined to enjoy every last drop of it. That itch again.

'Have to have it soon,' she thought. 'Right now in fact.'

Isabelle never employed a valet groom or even scullion without first testing their sexual prowess. She made sure they were ready for her day or night, Sundays and Saints' Days included, in any place from stable loft to royal boudoir. Her aristocratic partners were bound by the same duties, be they grand Dukes or mere chevaliers. All had to be in readiness for her insatiable lust. And now everyone bowed before her, scullion and lord. And why not? Her blazing star was in the ascendant. She bent down among the hissing geese and clucking chickens.

'Chick, chick, chick,' she crooned in her thick Bavarian accent, 'Mama loves you all.' She crossed to the sheep fold and caressed the lambs.

Her Majordomo, oily, pink-cheeked and chubby, stepped out of the rear door of the Château. He approached her warily, bearing a foaming stein of Bavarian beer. It never ceased to amaze him about the lambs. They were all dummies.

Isabelle crossed to the outhouse and threw open the door. Here lived her 'most precious of darlings', five caged snarling black panthers and, next to them behind wooden bars, swinging from the rotten boughs of dead tree chests, a troop of monkeys in gold and grey page suits. They were soiled and they stank, and shrieked at Isabelle as they tried to tear off their braided costumes. Isabelle smiled ecstatically. Yes, her Eden was coming true. How they all loved their mistress.

The Majordomo bowed and proffered the stein. Isabelle emptied the contents in two deep draughts and sighed happily.

'The vines of France are piss compared to the best Bavarian brew, ja.' The Majordomo was only too happy to agree.

'Who was that groom?' asked Isabelle, fixing the fawning flunky with her brilliant, spiteful eyes. The Majordomo was ready.

'A present from the Monk, a surprise,' he said with a leer. 'They're waiting for you in the Shepherdess Salon.' Isabelle nodded impatiently.

'The Cardinal has also arrived,' he added.

'About time, greedy swine,' she replied. 'See up there,' she pointed ecstatically, 'my doves are making love.' She gazed with approval at the bouncing bundles of feathers. She looked around at her latest arboreal creation.

'All so wonderful,' she sighed.

Isabelle's 'Paradise of Eden,' extended for five hundred acres around the small town of Troyes on the Seine south-east of Paris. It was planned as a duplicate Eden before the Fall, a bucolic folly with flocks of fake sheep, sheepcotes, dovecotes, statues of nymphs and shepherds in antique robes, shepherdesses with crooks, swans and geese, doves, owls, pigeons, peacocks, stuffed tigers and lions, dandling artificial lambs, ponds and waterfalls, bowers and hideaways in every shaded nook. And there were other similar estates in different parts of France, each with its own bizarre, distinctive theme. But with Isabelle's unbounded extravagance went unbounded greed. Her follies had to be paid for and she was heavily in debt.

This Paradise was now the centre of all eyes. Apart from Isabelle's Château des Bergères, which backed onto the stable yard, there was the main Château de Beaurevoir ten minutes away which Isabelle never used, and where her daughter Catherine was housed. This was where Henry also had his military headquarters and where the Treaty was to be signed. The charming lesser château in the enclosed parkland opposite, was used by visiting dignitaries, as was the Château de Honnecourt by the barred main gates, kilometre down the road. All were in occupation at the moment, for great events were afoot.

Isabelle pointed across the Park to the lesser château, cool and elegant among the beech trees, its dusky hedges and gardens neatly laid out.

'Any troubles with Humphrey and his whore?' she asked.

'Every minute he insists you perform that special favour for him,' the Majordomo replied indignantly. 'He sends a messenger every morning.'

'*Arseloch*. That is one dog who will never lift his leg at my Court of Good Shepherds. And that Eleanor of his – old sausage fingers! An impossible couple – they should marry. And the Main Hall, my masterpiece of Beaurevoir!' She waved in the direction of a long drive that led away into the woods to the south. 'Any message from Henry the Saint?'

'No, but he has publicly declared that his main conditions to the agreement still stand.' Isabelle's eyes sharpened.

'The greed of the man, all the worse since it's god-inspired, ja? Hypocrite. He needs an abacus, not a bride.' She thought for a second, 'Still stand, do they? We'll see about that.' In spite of appearances, Isabelle knew that priggish Henry had genuinely fallen for Catherine. It was her little secret. And if Henry suspected she knew, all the better. She was confident.

'And the madman?' she asked, her voice hardening. Dangerous ground. The Majordomo shook his head warily.

'Pissed on his own wife, you know that, don't you?' She slapped her chest. 'Me!' The Majordomo held his breath. He gazed at her with a suitable expression of pained sympathy. Isabelle seemed satisfied. 'And the pig, my son?' she demanded. The Majordomo shook his head again and prayed, for this was even more dangerous ground now.

'No *fleur-de-lis* shit in my Paradise.' The Majordomo bowed his agreement. 'Keep your eyes open then.' The Majordomo breathed again. Had he escaped this time? 'Understand? No pigs allowed.'

'The Guard and Captain Owen are on full alert, as ordered, Ma'am,' he said unctuously.

'As ordered, yes. At ease!' She suddenly barked the military command. The Majordomo slumped, pretending to relax. At least there had been no outburst against 'the pig' or 'the madman' or, more importantly, against himself. Perhaps it was the mention of Captain Owen that had mollified her, for he knew she lusted after him.

'And my darling Katty?' The Majordomo took full advantage. This was happy time. He beamed as he said.

'She is on her way here from riding, she instructed me to tell you, Ma'am.' Isabelle looked at the stable where the groom was rubbing down her horse. She couldn't wait, the itch was becoming unbearable.

'My dear Katty will have to wait if she doesn't hurry,' she thought. At that precise moment, as if on cue, Katty cantered into the courtyard.

'My Lady,' announced the Majordomo.

'Katty!' shouted Isabelle, waving.

Catherine smiled at her mother's evident pleasure. She walked her horse over to her. Elegant and straight-backed, Catherine rode on one of the new side-saddles. Beautiful! thought Isabelle with a pang. Was I ever so lovely? The Majordomo bowed as Catherine slid out of the saddle. The two women embraced. They walked together, arms round each other.

'I saw you galloping past in the woods,' said Catherine. 'I couldn't catch you. Don't you ever relax? Your poor horse.'

'It is I who am poor,' Isabelle replied. Catherine looked around.

'I must say Mother, your poverty has excelled itself again. There is no estate as costly as this in the whole of France.'

'The whole of Europe,' boasted Isabelle.

'Aren't the panthers dangerous?' Catherine asked, listening to the snarls and pointing at the locked, barred outhouse.

'Of course they are, that's why they are there. But my sheep, they are the lambs of peace.'

'But they're dolls.'

'So I like dolls, ja?' Catherine shook her head, bemused. There was no discussing Isabelle's extravagances. You either accepted them, condemned them, or avoided ever mentioning them.

'Tell my guests I'm coming,' Isabelle ordered the Majordomo, 'and,' she added in undertones as she approached him, 'bring that new groom'.

The Majordomo bowed and left. He closed the back door with a sigh of relief. He had got off lightly today. That delectable groom had done the trick. Good on the Monk, he managed it every time. He knew how to please the Bavarian boa-constrictor.

Isabelle turned to Catherine.

'Now, my lovely daughter, tell me what is happening, I must go to business in a minute.'

Catherine was short like her mother, but slender and straight like her father in his youth. She had the lustrous black hair of the Valois, a long pale face with delicate features, except for the small mouth with lines as determined as her mother's, a Wittelsbach. Her hazel eyes, soft at first, were steady and knowing, and could shine with gem-hard feeling.

After years of enforced separation, she and Isabelle reconciled. Catherine had longed for her own home with one parent at least, and Isabelle was more than willing, for her own Court. For long periods of her childhood, Catherine had been brought up in a nunnery. This had left a streak of piety which she found hard to reconcile with the realities around her, especially her mother's way of life. But she was learning to be more tolerant, as her mother was learning to be more loving. Catherine now enjoyed her mother's love and lust for life. For her part, the self-centred Isabelle genuinely wanted her daughter's happiness. This was the first unselfish feeling she had had in her life, and she had some difficulty getting used to it.

14

But both were content with the compromise. They were a kind of family again, together every day but lodged separately, retaining their own independence but enjoying each other's company. And most importantly, after such long separations, neither could get too much on the others' nerves.

Catherine sat down at a rustic table by the ornamental pond. Again, she gazed with wonder at the peacocks. What a fabulous idea after all, she thought.

'Do sit down, Mother. You know, I do love your peacocks.' Isabelle clapped her hands with delight at her approval.

'The whole world does, you know.' That itch again. She laid a hand on her daughter's arm. 'I must go now.'

'Mother . . . ' began Catherine.

'What is it, liebling, I have business.'

'The marriage contract, sign it as soon as Henry arrives.'

'I fight for you first. All your French estates, Henry wants. All your revenues. Plus two million in gold crowns, cash. Never.'

'Does it matter? Money! I learned to live without it.'

'Money matters like hell to holy Henry, like it does to me. I mean, why did he come to France in the first place? Because he was penniless, like all his court. The Welsh, Scottish wars. Bloody wastes. Empty Exchequer. A royal pirate, out for loot, that's all. Ask Captain Owen.'

'It was those stupid tennis balls you sent him . . . '

' . . . No! Sent by your stupid brother, Dauphin Louis.'

'Mother, Louis died . . . '

'Just in time, our only excuse.'

'How can you talk about your own flesh and blood like that?'

'No problem. I mean, tennis balls. Silly insult. What a reason for war. And your brother next, Dauphin John, still wanted to fight.'

'Mother, have you forgotten, poor John died just a week after Louis.'

'Thank God.'

'They were both your children, my brothers!'

'Childish fools.' Isabelle was relentless.

'You wanted them dead?'

'They say I poisoned them. I didn't. I just loathed them to death.'

'Mother . . . ' Catherine began, getting angry.

'Want to know why?' Isabelle cut her off.

Catherine briefly saw her father's demented face in her mind's eye and shook her head. But Isabelle was going to tell her, regardless.

'Well then. It's all for money. Holy Henry said he'd return that insult with such a racket, it would be heard all over France. And he promised that it was all for a Crusade to Jerusalem too. Plaster saint! I tell you, this racket and this crusade you are now hearing about, is nothing more than the jingle of coin. But he will not rob you as he's robbed half your father's nobility. Listen,' she went on more calmly, 'I didn't want them to die, not really. Of all my children, you're my last hope, liebling, the only one left.'

Catherine bridled.

'Aren't you forgetting my brother Charles, the new Dauphin.'

'He is not your brother!' Isabelle almost shouted.

Of all her offspring, living or dead, the ungainly Charles was the most detested.

'When we were children, Charles and I, you deserted us.'

'Where did you learn such bitterness?'

'My family, who else?'

'Those nuns . . . ' Isabelle's sarcasm dripped.

'I made good friends at the end. Joséphine, Adéle, Joanna . . . '

'I rescued you. Set up court, our court.'

'Those friends saved me. We keep in touch.'

'Stupid god-hole. What a life.'

'Life? What is life then, mother?'

'Life is . . . business as usual.'

'When we leave this world, we all die in God.'

'Well, don't blame me. And stop talking like a nun.' Catherine was saved from further wrath by the sound of pounding hoofs.

'Look,' Isabelle pointed, smiling now.

Owen Tudor, Captain of the King's Bodyguard cantered through the stable yard at the head of a column of mounted Welsh archers. Owen bent low in the saddle and saluted with a flourish, smiling boldly at the rutting Isabelle. She waved after him as he disappeared into the dusty distance.

'God,' she said, 'he's beautiful. Yes. Special. You think so?'

'I do not think of men in that way, Mother.'

'Don't leave it too late.'

Yes, it's true, thought Catherine with an unwonted pang. He is special. She forced the image of Owen out of her mind.

'Learn to love,' her Mother said. 'In my Bavaria it is healthy to fall in love.'

'With whole regiments?' asked Catherine, remembering the old scandal.

'An exaggeration. Half were on leave.' Isabelle's booming laugh disturbed the pigeons in the loft. Oddly, Catherine found it hard to condemn her mother's amours, however outrageous.

'You can joke about it?'

'Look, I wasted my youth in the arms of a madman, your father. Thirteen *accouchements*, and only you, my lovely, left. I have only funs now. Look around you. Funs.'

'Mother, whatever you say, I'll be married in Troyes in a few days, so sign the contract.'

'I must talk very strict to Henry now. Money matters most. You will not be poor, I promise. Ach!' she exclaimed, rubbing her stomach, 'I'm hungry too. Éclairs. Mountains of them. You like a few éclairs, my Katty?'

'Mother, how can you talk like that? People are starving at your gates.'

'Why share it? Enjoy the day, enjoy life. Go to my bowers and embrace the lambs. Forget sadness. Last time of peace for you.'

Catherine was convinced her mother was sometimes as mad as her father but, whatever they were, however much they might hate each other, she was now sure that she loved them both.

'Well, I must go.' Isabelle's itch was now beyond belief.

'One last thing, Mother, I want Father at the wedding.'

'No!'

'Yes!'

'Can't afford any more lunatics.'

'He is still my father.'

'Don't remind me. Please, Katty, I have work . . . '

' . . . You are selling me.'

'I am selling everything.'

'And my poor brother. I want him at the wedding too.'

'That bastard pig!' Isabelle's face reddened in fury. 'Never! I will renounce him.'

'Not a pig, Mother, my brother.'

With an effort, Isabelle managed to control herself. She didn't want this day marred for Catherine.

'Help yourself then if you want one so badly. Listen. Why all this fuss? Look at the wonderful day, my gorgeous Eden. There is more to life than getting over it. Think of eclairs. Or snails . . . '

'Mother!' Isabelle laughed.

'My lovely, trust me. Break your heart, I never will. Always remember, I take care of my Katty, her happiness, I promise. I must go now.'

'You're impossible.'

'Thank goodness!'

'I love you,' said Isabelle.

The Majordomo reappeared at the back door of the château, bowing to the ladies. Isabelle hugged her daughter. Isabelle mounted up, blowing a kiss to her mother as she trotted her horse out of the yard. Isabelle's lips quivered. So beautiful now. A new wonder, she thought, to be loved by one's child, really loved. She vowed for the hundredth time that her daughter would never again be hurt by anyone.

2

And still, thought Isabelle as she walked along the corridor to her salon, how to explain? That disgusting familiar, Catherine's father, worse than an incubus. She shuddered at the memory of his soiled, demented body on hers, and her loathing of her sole surviving son grew even stronger. How to explain that? A slobbering toad? Never got that bastard by that madman, she swore.

She shivered at the thought of the last ghastly *accouchement*. Her 'precious babe'; 'revolting beast', more like, who squeezed himself out of her body like some swollen, poisonous worm, leaving her bloodied and drained, on the brink of death.

Thirteen *accouchements* had torn her body, and she hadn't forgiven any man for a single one. But she, a woman, was all-powerful now, and all-vengeful too. She would avenge herself on the whole race of men by stripping them, mounting them, pounding them brainless and then discarding them for the world to see what limp pricks they were. They were created for quick pleasure and even quicker rejection. Hadn't she once discarded her brother-in-law, the powerful Duke of Orleans. John the Fearless who was Duke of Burgundy, and her uncle Frederick of Bavaria had both gone the same way. But best of all was the most iniquitous of couplings with her own brother, Prince Lewis of Bavaria, lover and companion of her worst and earliest debauches. Dear Lewis, she thought, you could go on all night too, like me. You understood me. You were worth going to prison for.

She recalled her husband in one of his moments of sanity,

raging at her immoralities. He had then actually had her arrested for 'treason to the King's person', and thrown unceremoniously into a cell in the Castle of Tours. But when the King collapsed again shortly afterwards, Isabelle bribed the prison Governor and escaped. Yes, she decided, Lewis had been worth the enforced stay. She only wished some of the her other lovers were.

'And that madman pissed on me,' she burst out. The Majordomo blinked.

Yet she could now, at the stroke of a pen, make dishcloths or dukes of all her lovers, past or present. The whole world was going to see the uselessness of men now. And which one of them had the guts to raise a single objection to her luxuries and excesses? Not one, apart from her own 'madman'. They would occasionally try rumour, like claiming she was the murderess of her dauphin sons. Typical men-pigs, liars, cowards. Not one of them, she vowed, was ever going to get her down again, except for sex. All her male enemies seemed able to do, she thought, was plan how many more men they could massacre in those endless, open air butchers shops they called 'honourable wars'. Honourable? She shrugged. 'Useless' was a better word. Deserve every death they get.

The Majordomo quickened his step. They were now nearing their destination, the *Shepherdess Salon*, the source of much of the Majordomo's odious earnings. Like the Monk, the Dwarf and the Poet, as well as the more lowly members of her household, he made a fortune out of Isabelle's vices. She had once made him lick her boots after a visit to the stables. He had even managed a smile as he did so. This had earned him two extra louis, and the title of Number One Groveller.

He wondered if he ever dare blackmail her. At once he dismissed the idea. Isabelle would have him torn to pieces by dogs. Life was too sweet now, and too profitable. As they reached the door of the perfumed inner sanctum, he bowed deeply, still with some trepidation.

The fearsome Isabelle was now held in universal awe. Isabelle herself was the only one who never wondered how she had managed it. At the time of her latest debauch, May 10th, 1421 at four in the afternoon, she was at the height of her power. She was the leading Princess of the royal line of Austrian Wittelsbachs, a family wealthier than even the fabulously rich Habsburgs. She was a granddaughter of the amazing Visconti of Milan. She was Queen of France and soon to be Queen Mother of the new Dual Monarchy of England and France and Mother-in-law-to-be of the 'Emperor' Henry V of England. What's more, she was the Regent and Chief Negotiator and Signatory of the Treaty of Troyes, mother of an impotent Dauphin, and the State Guardian of her husband Charles VI, the crazed, pauper King of a shattered nation, whose absolute powers she assumed at every bout of his insanity, which were frequent. Who dared gainsay her?

Well now, she smiled, the whole world was coming to her court, to gape as she manipulated the most powerful potentates in Christendom. They would all bow to her wishes, not that she cared a jot for their ambitions, or for the future of France. Just as long as they paid off her massive debts. And her new estate here at the Château des Bergères, with its train of degenerates, was once the main court of the proud, imperial Capets of France. Infamous, and she loved it. Among all the predators and charlatans around her, only her daughter really meant anything to her now, an angel in Isabelle's eyes. The rest of the players were male, all of them contemptible, mad or dead.

3

Across the park, under a spreading beech, Owen Tudor, Armiger and Captain of the Queen's bodyguard, shifted his gaze from the royal lambs and doves, to Isabelle's figure, departing ahead of the Majordomo.

'Her Majesty's gone humping again,' said Hopcyn in his lilting Welsh voice. No one was shocked by Isabelle's amours any more, just astounded at their number.

Hopcyn was short and rotund, with a soldier's muscled arms. His prematurely white hair grew down over his shoulders. His broad, sun-burnt face was dominated by two huge saucer eyes. They always disconcerted people, for each eye was of a different colour – one brown and flecked with hazel, the other a bright, lambent blue. The old Welsh Druids said that people born with different coloured eyes could see the wind. Hopcyn knew what they really meant, for he had the gift of foretelling the future. He knew too that it was as much a curse as a gift, for he never exactly knew when these disturbing 'visions' would happen. They occurred in the form of mild, epileptic seizures, entirely internal, cerebral. His visions of the future would first form in his mind's eye, then grow in detail to the point of 'warp-spasm', as the old bards called it, the future unfolding in visual implosions of unbelievable vividness. An added curse was that these images never left him, accumulated pictures of the deaths and entrances of many of those about him, like Owen and Catherine.

Owen, or Owain to Hopcyn and his Welsh companions, was one of the Shining ones, like Catherine, whose presence radiated a brilliant external light. Hopcyn was one of the Opalescent Ones, who illuminated the world from an unfathomable source of inner light. It was all a throwback, Hopcyn knew, to the primeval Celtic world of Mysteries and Unities, where the physical, the spiritual and the imagined merged into one, to produce a unitary vision of future time. He was a bearer, a modern survivor. He was an inhabitant of the ancestral dream world and a custodian of prophecy. An ancient himself, though still young, he understood the subtle changes of the intermediate and indeterminate, the shadow point at which life becomes death, twilight becomes night, water becomes dew. He was an antique initiate of the *bardo* state, when a man is neither dead nor alive, neither of this world nor of the next, and yet can behold, however briefly, the bridge between the two, night and light, life and death.

Hopcyn never talked about his visions for he knew he would have been hanged, drawn and quartered as an agent of the devil.

'By Gwydion and the old gods,' he brooded, 'these present-day Christians are the bloodiest and most superstitious savages the earth has ever seen.' How he'd like to tell these Saxons what he really thought of them. What he'd last seen of the armed Yorkist camps reassured him. The *godons* might yet tear each other to pieces.

His ancient soul longed for the truths of the humanity and the poetry of the old druidic days. Yes, he would talk with his new friend, the French poet Eustace Deschamps, one of the few civilised human beings he had met over in France. He knew even the old *La Tene* culture, and had a clear understanding of the Pythagorean beliefs embodied in the stone henges of Brittany and Britain. Eustace revelled in Hopcyn's weird eyes, as Hopcyn revelled in the ugliness of Eustace. They could empty, or fill, a tavern in five seconds. Yes, Eustace had a cosmic sense of humour too, a rare spirit among these Gallic and Saxon barbarians.

Hopcyn looked across at Owen, the man he had been chosen to guide towards his destiny. Owen was a true warrior again out of the early triads, who possessed the 'real awareness of intent', the ability to see the other side of the hill. He was a man of action who understood men of war and could move them on the field of battle like the great Celtic champions of old, to whom war was a chess game bathed in ancestral blood.

Both Owen and Hopcyn had 'been in the world before', as the old saying had it, but Owen never intruded too much on Hopcyn's visions, and Hopcyn, in his turn, left Owen alone to his martial intuitions. The bridge between them was clearly defined, invisible, and immensely old.

Hopcyn played briefly on his smaller, portable harp:

'Man sat under a sycamore tree,

Making love to three,

Three wild women very free,

Under a sycamore tree,' he sang.

'And as for Isabelle,' he added, 'she will be at play, the livelong day.'

'Fate of nations,' said Owen.

'Of fornications.' They laughed.

Twenty years together now, thought Hopcyn. He looked over at Owen; broad shoulders, narrow waist, six feet tall, at thirty-five still an athlete's build. Owen's brilliant, green eyes were set in a broad face pitted with small-pox scars, which seemed only to emphasise the perfectly rounded curve of the lips and the square, cleft chin. Striking in any company, women adored him. Good luck, lad, thought Hopcyn, with looks like that, you need it.

Owen radiated an explosive energy. He had fought in innumerable actions, and was skilled with every infantry and cavalry weapon. The strategies and tactics of battle came to him naturally without the necessity of formal training. He had stood out from the start in his service with Henry as a soldier of cunning, determination and extraordinary foresight. Henry had promoted and rewarded him, but now kept him back within royal beck and call as if sensing a rival. Owen paced restlessly. In the coming campaign, he hadn't yet been promoted to an independent command. Surely, he thought, this royal wardrobe thing was temporary, however prestigious.

Patience, thought Hopcyn, following Owen's restless steps. Owain Tudur came of old Welsh stock out of Penmynydd, Môn. They were descendants of Lord Rhys who was once King of the whole of Wales. His kin had fought at Crecy and Poitiers for the English King, as Owen himself had fought for Henry at Agincourt. This however did nothing to diminish the longing for the old freedoms of the *Cymry*, the people of Wales.

Owen's father had been a Captain in the service of the Bishop of Bangor. In a quarrel over a woman, he had killed one of the Bishop's men and fled into the fastnesses of Snowdonia, where the great Welsh leader, Owain Glyndŵr, had his headquarters. He joined one of Glyndŵr's guerilla columns, and fought against the English until his death in an obscure skirmish. Owain was born in the wild, of the very woman who had joined his father after the fateful quarrel. She, in turn, had died in the Great Hunger after the war. Owen had only the faintest memory of her. His father he remembered as a loving warrior always galloping out from some new hiding place, which served as their home, armed for some fight. Owen had been raised on the field of battle.

Then the young Prince Henry had taken over the command of the Welsh wars from his ailing father, worn out from his campaigns against the great Glyndŵr. But the conflict had exhausted the Welsh too. After twelve years of warfare, there were no replacements for their depleted armies. Remnants of the once great battle arrays of Glyndŵr now retreated into the mountains of Snowdon. Unfed and unsupplied, they finally dispersed to their homes, defeated but defiant, still living in the hope of the *mab darogan*, the 'son of prophecy' who would one day wake and lead them to freedom.

At the end of the Glyndŵr's War of Independence, and the death of his father, the victorious Prince Henry was crowned King in Westminster. As Henry V, he granted the elusive Glyndŵr and his rebellious Welshmen a free pardon. But Glyndŵr responded by simply disappearing. The bards said he had gone to join King Arthur. The growing collection of sons of prophecy slumbered for the time being.

It was not only the Welsh who were exhausted, for Henry's Exchequer was also on the edge of bankruptcy. There were also the other claimants to the throne, and the ever present threat of conspiracy. The Duke of York's claim was strong, even though it was through the bend sinister. Yes, Henry often thought of old King Edward and his eleven children, all at each other's throats, just like their offspring.

Henry had boldly decided to recoup his depleted fortunes on the Continent. Victories would also reinforce his security at home. He promptly made allies out of his former enemies, Welsh, English and Scottish, and promised them rich pickings in France if they would follow him.

Henry had the healthiest respect for the Welsh, who had come so close to defeating him and his father. The Welsh had invented the longbow, and were the most experienced bowmen in Europe. Henry had no hesitation in recruiting them into his armies, Owen Tudor among them. Owen joined the Company of the famous Welsh Captain, one-eyed Dafydd Gam from mid-Wales. With the rest of Henry's host, Gam's Welsh Company embarked for France.

At the decisive battle of Agincourt, Owen had been in the right place at the right time. During a ferocious assault by the redoubtable Duke of Alencon, Owen had saved his Sovereign's life. Henry at once promoted Owen to a battlefield captaincy, and restored his family's confiscated lands in Môn.

Owen had divided his command into three Companies, Dragons One, Two, and Three, under the command of the, by now, late Dafydd Gam's most experienced Captains. Huw was in charge of the bowmen, Ifan in charge of Men-at-Arms, and Idris in charge of Engineers. Owen also persuaded Surgeon Samuel and his wife, the Regiment's chief cook and midwife, to join his command in London. All the other ranks were Welsh, with the express approval of the King himself, and knew each other from many campaigns.

The Tudor clan was recovering its fortunes. Although Dafydd Gam was killed, Henry kept on his Welsh Companies. Owen himself was retained as a personal bodyguard. These favours aroused the envy of other captains and courtiers, especially the King's brother, Duke Humphrey of Gloucester, who saw himself as rightful king, and felt his claims challenged by any promising newcomer, however humble. His old Yorkist enemies, the Duke of York himself, and the Dukes of Somerset and Suffolk, the three 'devil dukes' as they were known, kept themselves out of harm's way. They rarely appeared in person outside their fortifications, preferring to send out their paid and armed retainers. They sent troops to fight with Henry only to gain battle experience for the streets of England. Humphrey often declared all three to be cowards, adding that he'd have them for breakfast yet!

'Is this my fate?' Owen asked himself for the hundredth time, 'stuck out here with these royal eminences and degenerates, a lowly Captain of the King's Bodyguard, a paid onlooker with no real power?'

'Damn, I saved Henry's life!' he said aloud.

'He survived that too,' said Hopcyn. 'Patience, Owain!'

Owen could not understand the envy of those around the throne at his recent elevation to Clerk of the Queen's Wardrobe.

'What's elevated about a woman's wardrobe?' he wondered.

'I want a battle command.'

Hopcyn nudged him as if reading his mind.

'What's the best in Court headgear just now?'

'A headress steeple hat with veil, or a coronet with a surround of plaited hair, again with veil,' Owen replied quickly.

'Brilliant.'

'Thanks to Agnes.'

'Not too boring?'

'Time spent on reconnaissance is never wasted.'

'What about undergarments?'

'Leave that to you, Hopcyn.' They laughed again.

Owen glanced up at the balcony of the lesser Château. Why is royal Humphrey, third in line to the throne of England, so jealous of me, a mere servant? he mused. Me, a sleeping soldier, an underling of the Bedchamber? What challenge do I represent, obscure son of an outlawed Welsh Captain? Duke Humphrey yonder owns half of London. What is my fate? Give me a sign, he pleaded to the skies. Nothing happened. He gave up. He'd talk over the whole thing with Hopcyn later. Bards were never uncertain, whatever destiny had in store for them.

A stooping figure in a leper's heavy white hood and cloak ran lightly from the undergrowth, holding onto a begging cup and bell with stunted fingers, so the metal wouldn't rattle. Owen embraced the hideous apparition, kissing it on both cheeks. Hopcyn shuddered at the brief glimpse of a face rotted to the bone by the ravages of the fearsome disease, leprosy. Owen seemed immune to the leper's touch, and it was just as well, for they had been inseparable since childhood.

Hopcyn remembered what this particular leper had been like in the old days when he was handsome, popular and a sweet singer. He had always been an inseparable companion of Owen. Hopcyn, although he felt the deepest affection for him, for all his magic couldn't quite bring himself to touch him.

Owen or the Leper never minded for their liking was undimmed. After all, they had been boys together. Owen seemed immune to the leper's touch. Inside their colonies, he had close contact with them without any fear of contagion. A part of Owen's destiny, thought Hopcyn, remembering a saying of the old Welsh necromancers: 'He who can kiss the face of death will fly closer to the sun than a mountain eagle.'

'Someone's moving along the outer fences, Owain,' reported the leper in his hoarse, rasping voice, 'and the old mansion by the gates is occupied.' Owen looked questioningly at Hopcyn.

'Could be,' said Hopcyn. 'Could well be.'

'Keep everyone on the alert, King Leper, and don't give the alarm until you're sure. Tell the others to muffle their bells too.' Owen embraced him. 'Go now.'

The leper was soon lost among the trees. He was called King Leper because he led a large troop of wondering lepers, his devoted followers. He was universally respected and much loved by his fellow untouchables. King Leper helped to establish lazariums, and some had even seen the remission of their awful affliction. Owen had recruited them during the Welsh wars and had a special use for them. They were his most reliable source of intelligence. After all, who'd suspect a leper? They moved without hindrance and no one dared search them. Their warning bells were enough to clear the area for miles. They were grateful to Owen for giving them a purpose for which to live. Canny Henry, the King, urged by Owen, had guaranteed King Leper royal protection. Good intelligence, he knew, was half the battle. And it looked charitable at the same time.

'The outer fences? . . . Must be the mad King,' said Hopcyn.

'Yes,' said Owen, 'his daughter's wedding day after all.'

'For her,' said Hopcyn, 'he'd go through sharpened stakes with the whole army on guard. He may be mad, but he's cunning as a fox. And he adores his daughter, whenever he knows who she is. Or who he is, for that matter,' he added.

'Thought we'd get a bit of quiet today.'

'What will he be this time, cobweb or cowbell, crystal or flame?' mused the bard.

'It's beyond me how you recognise his identities, Hopcyn. And bring your harp. Always calms him. Strange how holy Henry loves the harp as well.'

'Best thing he brought out of Wales,' said Hopcyn. 'Catherine and Henry, true love do you think?' Owen shrugged.

'Look,' Hopcyn pointed. A figure muffled in a green cloak flitted towards them, cunningly merging with the branches and bushes like a will o' the wisp. They caught a quick glimpse. Then it was gone.

'There!' exclaimed Hopcyn. Owen started as a figure emerged from under their feet.

'1 could smell you, my Agnes!' laughed Hopcyn.

Agnes embraced Hopcyn, her lover, and kissed Owen. Old friends. Agnes and King Leper worked as a team. They were the most resourceful spies Owen had.

Agnes had been with Hopcyn for fifteen years. Short, with a figure both graceful and sensual, she had flaming red hair and violet eyes. She was a beauty, but reacted impatiently to flattery. She and Hopcyn enjoyed an open marriage, but they never strayed when they were together, both treasuring their enduring affection too much. After a year in France, Agnes had been appointed Chief Demoiselle to Princess Catherine's Bedchamber. They made a striking pair, the flame-haired Celt and the pale aristocratic Valois beauty. Happily too, Catherine had an abiding passion for the harp like her husband-to-be, learned from a Breton nurse in her childhood. Agnes was devoted to her new mistress. She and Agnes had rapidly become confidantes.

'Anything happening?' asked Owen.

31

'He's inside the Park.'

'The Dauphin or the King?' asked Owen.

'Both,' she replied.

Loud voices interrupted them. Hopcyn pointed up at the bedroom balcony of the lesser Château.

The balustrade fluttered with the pennants of the Duke of Gloucester, his crest clearly visible, a falcon with talons extended ready to strike.

Duke Humphrey, the English King's youngest brother and third in line after the Dukes of Clarence and Bedford, strutted out. He was the most heartily disliked of all the Treaty negotiators, making enemies of both French and English impartially. Quarrelsome, vain to the point of megalomania, he was short, bald, paunchy, with legs too short for his body. He wore a variety of badly made wigs.

As he gazed out arrogantly over the Park, he was joined by his mistress, Eleanor Cobham, in her night gown. Her unruly jet black hair stuck out in all directions. Her eyebrows were plucked bare in the current court fashion, but she also plucked the front part of her hair in a half-moon, which gave her a reptilian look. Her face, with its pointed nose and tapering chin, eyes black and shiny as a rodent's, had a kind of repellent beauty. Slender and lithe, she moved restlessly as if never at ease. She leaned against her lover, stroking his arm, then pointed in the direction of Isabelle's stables.

'Eleanor-Turnip-Top,' whispered Agnes in a mock Norfolk burr, 'or She-who-would-be-Queen.'

'Divine right's great floating turd.'

'Ssh, Hopcyn!' admonished Owen.

'The little poison hemlock is sister to the big poison hemlock,' hissed Hopcyn.

Eleanor gripped Humphrey's arm.

'Don't let that whore Isabelle see thee gawpin', love. Come in betimes.'

They disappeared into the spacious bedroom. Eleanor took off her night-dress and lay down on the huge four-poster bed. She stroked her firm upright breasts, and played with her nipples.

'Again?' asked Humphrey.

'I know as how ye wants it thrice on Sundays,' said Eleanor, her voice thickening into her broad native Suffolk as she grew more excited.

'Isabelle,' said Humphrey, 'don't worry, she'll be at it for the rest of the day.'

'Never mind,' said Eleanor. 'Us all fucks like mad 'ere anyway, 'cept Henry, o'course.'

'Saint Henry's at church even now, the hypocrite. While I fight his battles, he's on his knees at the Mount of Olives.'

'And he's tumbled every whore in Eastcheap,' said Eleanor with a fake shudder of disgust.

'And listen, our new English *Emperor of Britain*, as he calls himself, is just an ex-jailbird. Dressed as a highwayman and robbed his own father's tax collectors, didn't he? Got jailed by the King's Bench. And then accuses **me** of feathering my own nest?'

'Whole world knows 'bout that little scandal, too.'

'He should've been passed over for the succession. And that's not all.' Humphrey was now on his favourite hobby horse – the hideous unsuitability of his brother for the kingship. 'Didn't he plan to kill his own father, I mean, my father?'

'Patricide, regicide that be,' echoed Eleanor. This was a favourite, well rehearsed recital. 'With thy uncle Cardinal Beaufort of Winchester ready to cut Henry down too,' Eleanor further fuelled the fire. 'What treacheries.'

'Bastard Beaufort set him up. York and Somerset too. Devil dukes. Had to send my lads onto the streets. Best bully boys in England.'

'Hold 'em back when Henry's about.'

'My iron fist.'

'Not yet.'

'Cannon fodder, who cares?'

'Keep thy opinions under thy hat.'

'Still got Dark's reports on them devils.'

'Use 'em when ye needs 'em,' said Eleanor. 'Concentrate on Isabelle for now.'

'And Beaufort, Cardinal, lives like a bloody pope, the pomp and riches.'

'But we got to oil the palms o' the Church, my lovely.'

'The cost, the percentages . . . '

'Thy divorce is worth every penny,' said Eleanor, lust vanishing now. 'Get thy rightful dues from Isabelle, and thy foxy brother too.'

'To think that German whore controls millions of what's rightfully mine!' burst out the Duke.

'She bargains like a fishwife,' said Eleanor. 'She be no Queen.'

'Damn Henry. Confiscates my prisoners, my booty. Then accuses **me** of stealing his war chests. Me, his own brother. And the titles and offices he's given away to brother Beaufort. As if he isn't rich enough. And Clarence, brother Bedford again, and the rest of the greedy shits. Even my cousin, Edmund of Somerset, a puking brat, gets an estate. And a Yorkist to boot. Shameful. They won't get away with it. But we true Lancastrians will conquer.' He pounded the bed in fury. His face began to turn purple, like a child's in a tantrum. Eleanor gently sat him down. He mustn't get too demented to manipulate.

'Calm now, me darlin'.'

'Sometimes, I think I should give Captain Dark the final order.'

Humphrey used the scar-faced, cashiered ex-soldier Dark to get rid of his more awkward opponents. Eleanor was alarmed. Such actions were too dangerous, and the real seat of power, that of Henry the King, too close.

'Forget thy brothers, my lovely,' she advised. 'We have means of dealing with them, remember. Look, and take comfort.'

She slid back a long panel set in an extended, wooden travelling chest. Humphrey stared. He was hypnotised whenever Eleanor revealed the accoutrements of her black arts. Inside the chest was a row of life-size wax heads. They were scored and stuck with needles, like pin cushions.

The first head was a likeness of Henry the King; the second of Clarence, his brother, first in line; next Bedford, the middle brother; next Beaufort, uncle of the royal brothers; then Catherine's crowned head. The last was the head of a baby, the future firstborn of Catherine. Eleanor plunged another needle into the tiny skull. Humphrey shuddered. Eleanor slid the panel shut.

'The Witch of Eye, Suffolk's best, be at work on thy behalf, so, no worries. Thy brothers be for the devil's piss-pot. Listen now, 'tis that tame Roman Cardinal of Isabelle's we wants.'

From under the bed, she pulled out an iron-bound chest, and lifted the heavy lid. It was filled to the brim with shining louis, nobles, rings of silver and gold, small unminted nuggets mixed with brooches of brilliants, necklaces of pearl and altar vessels encrusted with rubies. Fair French booty, and all Humphrey's, one of a dozen such 'private' chests stored in the cellars below. Eleanor lifted out a walnut-sized diamond pendant on a gold chain.

'This be for the Cardinal,' she said.

'It's a beauty,' Humphrey groaned.

'Exactly,' replied Eleanor, 'the price of thy divorce. Why'd thee ever marry that leaking Dutch barge?'

'She had half of Holland in her hands.'

'And that's where it stayed.'

'Not my fault.'

'Must squeeze more information out of that Agnes.' said Eleanor. 'A sly one there, late with our news on purpose . . . '

'Just for more money,' growled Humphrey. Humphrey wanted to bed their paid spy, Agnes, and Eleanor realised this. In revenge she played on Humphrey's envy of Owen's good looks and success.

'Agnes, the slut, be head of Catherine's bedchamber. Good luck for us, but suppose Owen gets her 'tween the sheets?' Eleanor was goading and Humphrey fell for it.

'God what a freak,' he said. 'Pads himself out, you know, down there. Cod pieces like a bull, everyone knows.'

'And the women . . . '

' . . . like whores when he's around . . . '

' . . . I was goin to say, my love, women fall for **thee** when he's around.' She lied easily. He believed completely, preening like one of Isabelle's peacocks. She continued. 'What Agnes sees in that mad Hopcyn, I never knows. Owen's a fine figure, whole court agrees, but not that white-haired ape.'

At the mention of Owen, Humphrey bristled again, as Eleanor had meant him to.

'Welsh clothes peg. Back to the bogs. Bloody savage. And that Davy Gam. Blind as a bat. At least he's dead. Henry toasts him, you saw, with his last arrow on the table. Devil stuff. Will it point to all Henry's enemies?'

'No, just leave it to me.'

'Mad-eyed bard's put a spell on him, the Treaty, too. And my booty. All I want . . . '

' . . . is thy fair due. And,' Eleanor went on, 'thy fair due be – the crown!'

'Ah! Ssh, the servants . . . ' said Humphrey, glorying at the thought.

'Thy common soldiers, and the folk of London, didn't they all hail thee – true victor of Agincourt, royal giver of gifts?'

'Yes, they did. I have to say it. Only thing is, they smell.'

'Ssh! Just stand up for 'em in public.'

'And these plots against me . . . '

' . . . thy mission be to free thy English people from their curse.'

'I know. Damn Yorkists started it.'

'O' course. But thy white rose of destiny will conquer!'

'Give me a straight battle any day. I tell you, if I had one foot in heaven, I'd pull it right back for an honest, decent English fight with my lads. How could Henry leave 'em in arrears, I fought for their pay.'

'After the battle, didn't they shout – Humphrey for King!'

'Ssh . . . '

' . . . from the roof tops.'

'Please, my love.'

'It be the truth.'

'Aye, it is! Their fathers smashed 'em at Crecy, their sons smashed 'em at Agincourt. One of your ordinary English yeomen's worth ten of your frog-eating Frenchies.'

'Let 'em hear that! St George be Emperor, and St George be here!' shouted Eleanor, saluting her puffed up lover, Roman style. 'See thyself, my lovely, as Caesar!'

She pulled back the velvet curtains of a wide alcove by the bed, revealing a huge wooden model of an antique pillared Roman temple, Duke Humphrey's 'Temple of the Caesars', a folly he planned to build in his Palace of Placentia on his vast estate at Greenwich, paid for out of the 'secret' profits of the French wars. The model travelled everywhere with him, at considerable expense. Set between each pillar were pedestals with figures of various Roman Emperors. On the far side of the Temple, the statues, although still in imperial togas, wore recognisably English crowns. The last niche remained empty. Humphrey stood in front of it, in regal pose.

'Here be thy rightful place, here in the pantheon of Kings,' declared Eleanor. Humphrey affected a noble look. 'My Witch of Eye dreams it,' she went on. 'My Witch of Eye sees it. I see it. Thee, in the Temple of Caesars. When has the Witch been wrong? God save the true King,' she yelled, raising her arm again in the Roman salute.

Down below, Hopcyn, Agnes and Owen exchanged grins. They'd heard this almost daily, Eleanor's afternoon performance – usually after she'd exhausted her stunted ducal partner.

Eleanor picked up a hand mirror from the dressing table, approached Humphrey and curtsied. 'Your Majesty,' she held up the mirror, 'salute the image of thy royal power.' Humphrey saluted himself, moaning with pleasure at his coming omnipotence.

'And I'll see those devil brothers dead, from the first seat of the Cathedral. I'll be there out in front, with ye! And don't ye ever forget it, my lovely.'

Humphrey pulled Eleanor onto the bed.

'Now sing to me, my nightingale,' he urged, caressing her thighs.

Eleanor marvelled once again at the simplicity of men. She played every day with Humphrey, like a cat with a mouse, and never once did he suspect it. He lapped up her poison like milk. Now the game was ending, with Eleanor the victor once again. She always made her exit with a song. She began an old folk tune. Down below, Agnes, Owen and Hopcyn covered their ears. Every note of the lovely old tune was off key. Humphrey was in raptures for he was tone deaf. The caterwauling wound down to its discordant finale, and the Witch and the Moron made love again.

Eleanor was the daughter of the wealthiest wool merchant in England. Humphrey had met her when he went to beg her father for a huge loan to pay off his debts. Eleanor's father was quite prepared to see his daughter become the mistress of one of the most powerful men in England. But the Duke would have to pay for it, and his payment was a promise of marriage. But first the divorce. He felt he could leave this to his daughter. Eleanor had rapidly replaced the Duke's legal wife, the miserly heiress, Jacqueline of Hainault, in his affections. Her father also let her keep the loan accounts and she turned out to be brilliant at this. But the old wool merchant had never taught her the airs and graces of the court, or the 'proper' voice, and Eleanor never shook off her native brogue. Courtiers and servants alike never ceased mimicking her broad Norfolk accents. To make matters worse, her father had made her work like any common apprentice in his baling warehouses, 'to learn the real business of business,' he said. This, to his great present regret, had left her hands coarsened and callused, and she was now mocked both as 'turnip-top' for her manners, and 'sausage-fingers' for her hands. She swore a terrible vengeance every time, but her mockers proved as elusive as eels. In one fell swoop, she would now take care of the lot. Her marriage to Humphrey would do the trick. She would be at the head of the royal festivities.

First, the Cardinal. He had already been diplomatically approached for an annulment with gifts of gold and silver plate. He was at once most sympathetic, and had promised a Papal dispensation. He prayed for them to have patience, and to understand his adoration of large gems was for pious purposes only. Eleanor's were to be set in his pastoral staff, for the good of the congregation. But this might take a little time. Eleanor became patience herself. She knew the jewels under her bed would more than take care of the greedy, unholy Cardinal. They were her guarantee to majesty.

'Get on top of me, lovely, and tell me 'bout when ye be King,' she said, grabbing Humphrey.

'*Vanity rules the world,*
in gold and silver and in pearl,' sang Hopcyn below. 'And

39

thank God she's stopped singing. I'll finish with a little triad. Three things the less of them the better for Wales – poverty, low instincts, and the word of an Englishman.' Hopcyn's gaze turned abruptly into the interior distance.

'I see . . . ' His friends kept silence, ' . . . yes, the Duke . . . ' The warp-spasm came, the vision fell clear. 'Humphrey . . . burning like a candle . . . drowning in wax . . . '

'Wake up then,' said Agnes as the vision faded. 'Don't want to get singed, do you?' Hopcyn's eyes re-focused. He kissed Agnes. She had brought him back safely again from his other worldly trip. Owen clapped him on the shoulder, but asked no further questions.

'Well, Owen,' said Agnes, 'what is Catherine wearing tonight?'

'Please . . . '

'Come on.'

'Full length blue velvet outer dress, tight to the body, gipon cut low . . . '

'Turned back at the wrist?'

'Yes, or furred, reaching the ground.'

'This boy'll go far,' laughed Agnes.

'The Dauphin and the King,' said Owen, 'find them, Agnes.'

Agnes wrapped her cloak about her. With a kiss and a smile, she flitted away into the shifting shadows of the undergrowth. Abruptly, Hopcyn looked up. He peered at the tops of the trees around them. The warp-spasm was still working. He gripped his brows. With a shiver, he felt the presence of an unseen threat.

'What do you see?' asked Owen. The answering words came slowly.

'Beware of the sign of the three suns.'

'Tell me Hopcyn, is my destiny there?' Hopcyn pushed the ominous sign to the back of his mind. His gaze focused on the height of a towering beech. Behind his eyes the image shimmered, then he had a positive shape. He knew who was out there, high in the trees, watching their every move.

'No,' he said, 'these are mere distractions. Be patient.'

4

Catherine looked out of the window of her room in the Château de Beaurevoir. Her mother had excelled herself again. The new wing which she'd had built was another monument to extravagance. It was twice as large as the original building. Isabelle intended to show them what a Wittelsbach meant by 'a little extra space for the occasion', for the new banqueting hall measured fifteen metres by sixty metres. It was called the Salle des Preux, being full of the heroes of history that Henry and the French court most admired including King Arthur, Charlemagne and the crusader Geoffrey de Bouillon. A host of female worthies occupied other niches, from Athena to Ceres, Semiramis to Mary, Mother of God. The hall also boasted an immense new mantled chimney, high vaulted ceilings, and wide arched windows to bathe the whole space in bright sunlight. The walls were hung with new tapestries from Bayeux, and the floor was laid from wall to wall in red Cordovan leather, instead of the usual perfumed rushes. Twice the usual number of candelabras and torch sockets would transform night into day. A raised dais at one end would enable the grandees at the signing to view all those present at a single glance.

Off the Hall, a new boudoir for the ladies had been constructed. A third interior tennis court had been added, with a new wooden ceiling decorated with carved leaves, fruits and grapes in the most intricate detail. New stables had also been built to accommodate the hundreds of extra horses, and more rows of kennels for the hunting hounds. New marble parapets for the spacious terraces were set in place. A series of water tanks, six metres by six metres and the largest ever seen, were installed in the attics. They supplied the kitchens by four water conduits. Metal workers had welded in new copper kitchen sinks. The roofs had been re-covered and the guttering replaced. Still more gargoyles adorned the eaves.

To make more space for the carriages, wider iron-barred gates had been designed, forged and installed. Locksmiths had replaced the old keys, locks, bolts and hinges. On Isabelle's personal orders, they had oiled them so that not a squeak would disturb the proceedings.

Isabelle made sure the whole world knew exactly the cost of the refurbishments, in excess of two million louis in gold, and that she alone, a Wittelsbach first and foremost, had met the entire expense. She would show those penniless English Plantagenets and threadbare French Capets how to spend in style.

Catherine thought of her coming marriage. Yes, in her heart of hearts, she did desire it. But she also longed for the elusive happiness that marriage was supposed to bring, a happiness she had never found in her family, or in the marriages of Christ she had seen in the Convent. But she knew such content existed. She had glimpsed it in her new love for her mother, and in the enduring affection for her father, both before and during his terrible illness. She had seen the warmth too in the friendships between Owen and Hopcyn, and Hopcyn and Agnes, her new Head Demoiselle and First Companion, and now, dear friend.

She looked up to her future husband, Henry. Was she being given a chance for happiness? Perhaps her heart wasn't brimming with love, but she felt deep gratitude and affection for him. She had learned Henry did nothing unless the ground had been thoroughly prepared. But Catherine realised his attitude to their match was different. He had become

43

increasingly caring of her feelings, and consulted her when it was not really necessary. Had he really fallen for her? The thought made her dizzy. Was this more than just a dynastic alliance? Was it a love match as well? She had a feeling he would be an ardent lover, whatever he thought about God. She wondered at this little burst of irreverence. Was her mother's example getting through to her? In spite of the delays, Catherine was sure her mother would sign the contract. The delays, bless her, were merely to make Henry pay the best price for her dowry to assure Catherine of some kind of independence.

Catherine recalled the misery of her childhood, the pawned silver, the paper windows, the unswept dirt in the rooms, the cold hearth, the greasy scraps of left over food. But now at last, she realised, her mother was fighting like a champion.

She fingered the little crucifix on the gold chain round her neck. Her father had given it to her when she was ten. She remembered embracing and kissing him. She had loved him, like many of his court. The ordinary people outside the palace gates adored him for his generosity, which had often saved them from starvation, and earned him the name 'the Well Beloved'.

Father and daughter had always been close. After the King's attacks of insanity, he always asked for Catherine, and usually knew her at once. Owen's bard, Hopcyn, she thought, also communes with him. Did the inspired harpist and the mad King inhabit the same strange recesses of the mind? She was more at ease with her father when Hopcyn was there, for she knew Hopcyn could help him. Owen too she felt at ease with, but wondered why before sleep she would sometimes turn away from thoughts of him. Why did this stir such uncomfortable feelings? She shrugged them off again. Owen, she had often seen, also had empathetic contact with her father. He was always first with news of any sightings. Agnes knew about what was going on, too, and in the most astonishing detail. Catherine wondered about the Welsh, they seemed to see right to the heart of things. Little wonder Henry, and indeed herself, so often consulted them, in spite of their queerness.

5

Isabelle personally supervised the menus for her intimate suppers with her cronies. She examined the dishes in the huge kitchen with an eagle eye. The cooks trembled at the inspection. But today she was hungry. The Majordomo also knew she was randy as a she goat. Shouldn't be any trouble with her in the kitchens or salon, he thought. It was her lovers who'd better watch out.

Isabelle sampled a dish. She nodded, pleased. The cooks and servers relaxed. Isabelle always insisted on multiple choices of dishes, whether they were eaten or not. The cooks encouraged her mania for exotic menus, for it fed them too. The staff had nothing but praise for their nymphomaniac Queen and her bizarre gluttonous entourage. Famine might rage outside the gates, but Isabelle kept their families alive.

Tonight they had roast swan and peacock, decked out in their feathers with beaks gilded and standing upright in a natural landscape of lawns, flowers and hedges made out of spun sugar and painted pastry. The Monk had the brilliant idea of adding a few lambs and some doves in the act of love. The birds seemed alive, the lambs picked out in tender detail. Isabelle clapped her hands in delight. Wonderful! The whole staff beamed.

She sampled suckling pig and fresh crab in its shell. She sniffed the jugged hare, the roasted pike and the basted snails which were a favourite. She popped one into her mouth and smacked her lips. Perfect. Herons and carp had been done to a turn. There were lark pasties and rissoles of beef marrow; white leeks with plover laid out beside roasted kids and pickled ox-tongue; eel pies and carp in lemon sauce with frizzled beans, meat gelatines and lampreys.

To finish the banquet, there were junkets, tarts jellies, wafers, comfits, medlars, and her beloved éclairs. Resisting the impulse to cram a few into her mouth, she crunched on peeled nuts. She preferred to devour her éclairs while she was making love.

Finally, there were twenty different sorts of cheeses laid out in fresh greenery amid coloured fruit in glowing bowls of silver. The only floral decoration for the main table were Isabelle's favourite flowers, wild violets. Crystal dishes of these adorned every banquet, floating purple petals glistening in fresh water. 'My everlasting sweeteners,' she crooned as she sniffed their familiar fragrance. Isabelle was satisfied. At last this was up to Wittelsbach standards. It was a good omen.

As a reward for their success, Isabelle called for a barrel of the best imported Bavarian beer. The cooks gave three resounding cheers. Sometimes, if well pleased, she permitted a little spiced wine for those whose weak taste buds had become attached to the grape. So, for her chef, she called for a bottle of the best Claret. The chef grovelled in thanks.

Isabelle herself disdained the wines of France. When she made love, hunted, or cornered a well-favoured scullion, she worked up such a thirst that small glasses of wine never sufficed. Isabelle liked her drink in gallons. In her cellars were huge tuns of German beer. At her private table, only the best Bavarian brews were served. She sampled the stein her Majordomo now handed to her, drained it, nodded final approval, and swept out of the kitchen with a happy smile. Everyone cheered again. They had won another culinary victory against the Great Whore. Fresh tankards were poured, more bottles opened. The kitchen maids did a wild dance of celebration on the tables, throwing up their skirts. In

47

anticipation, they wore nothing underneath. As if at a signal, the entire staff of cooks, servers, carvers and scullions joined in a riotous orgy of their own. It was going to be an exciting night. Why not? Didn't Isabelle expect everyone at her Court of Good Shepherds to enjoy life's pleasures to the fullest? The world outside, the world of pain, death and poverty, could go and bugger itself.

Isabelle lay back on a couch piled with cushions and silken coverlets. Like her guests, she was sated for the moment, and was taking a little pause before the fun began. Isabelle had changed into her most elaborate shepherdess costume, and lay with one hand resting on her gold-embossed crook. She looked around at the dimly-lit inner sanctum and the boon companions of her febrile lust. She knew every private detail of their bodies, minds and characters, their every failure and failing, and manipulated them at will.

The chamber was divided into alcoves with the new Persian divans piled with damask pillows and swans' down cushions. The walls were hung with tapestries depicting the pleasures of love. The sometimes near miraculous positions that were depicted had been discovered in the brothels of ancient Pompeii by her tame Cardinal. At enormous expense, he had had exact copies woven into these wall coverings. He sent them with his undying love to his adored mistress, the Queen of France.

Set into each wall were niches, each with its own distinctive figure, all conforming to antique Greek archetypes. The only difference was that the male statues boasted huge erections, in white veined marble. The fauns, satyrs, Mercuries, cupids and Eroses were in advanced stages of sexual excitement. Even the eternally poised discus thrower had a screwed on phallus of extreme proportions. The pudenda of the Venuses and nymphs were graphically displayed, open as full-blown roses, the 'petals' rendered lovingly and unblushingly, just as the mistress of ceremonies liked her loving, in full view, without any embarrassment or constraint whatever.

'All ye who enter here, abandon modesty,' were her welcoming words to newcomers. After giving them a tour of the tapestries, she would follow her own advice with enthusiasm and great expertise. Her partners always followed suit. They had no choice. Woe betide any holding back on the part of the initiate, male or female, for wasn't Isabelle now the premier power in the land? Couldn't she have any of them dragged off to the cells with a mere nod? So everyone pounded away as if their lives depended on it, as indeed it did, in total, carefree abandon, intent on proving their devotion to this tyrant Bavarian goddess of love. The only vice in this secret sanctum of unbridled lust was fake orgasm.

At her side squatted her pet dwarf, dressed in extravagant black velvet, his thick squat face and bulging lips resting in his mistress's lap, his tongue ready to work at the first signal. Behind her stood Eustace Deschamps, the leading poet of the day. Hideously disfigured at birth, he called himself 'the King of Ugliness', which he was with the skin of a boar and the face of a monkey. He turned out verses to order, and boasted he had at least sixteen hundred and seventy-five *ballades* to his credit. Their publication had made his modest fortune. He despised only one thing. Not the venery or the brutality of the times or the vanity and butchery, but the hypocrisy of those who perpetrated the continuing outrages against his beloved country. Henry he regarded as the devil in human form. He longed to see the vile *godons*, as the English were called, hurled out of his *belle France* into the sea. Only here in his Lady of Eden's secret court could he express his hatred openly, for the besetting sin of hypocrisy was absent, and his ugliness went unremarked.

Deschamps now recited his latest poem, an elegantly

worded ode to love in the open air. As he recited, he paused from time to time, to suck on his lady's nipple. She moaned with pleasure both at the sucking and the recitation, for she loved both. She ran a hand fondly over Eustace's face, as hairy as any ape's, and luxuriated in the silken covers trimmed with ermine rippling under her arched back. The feather-light tassels caressed her naked shoulders, mingling with the soft, urgent fondlings of her lovers' hands. She cuddled down deeper into the soft pillows. At a nod from Isabelle, the dwarf began raising her wide-skirted, embroidered petticoats.

On her left was Isabelle's Monk, a renegade soprano jewel thief on the run from the Papal eunuch choir. His pale skin and piping voice resembled that of a twelve year old virgin. In an effort to cultivate more masculine tones, he spoke in rasping whispers. The Monk had a rare gift for foretelling Isabelle's pleasures, and always found the right lover for them. He knew her body more intimately than anyone, but had never had any kind of sensual gratification from her. As he bent down to talk piggy sex in her ear, Isabelle asked,

'You thought of those sugar love doves round the roasts, ya?' He nodded, anticipating his reward. She clouted his head affectionately. The Monk moaned pleasurably. But she had no desire for revenge on this grotesque, dispossessed male. That had already been taken.

Isabelle went for the well endowed, and it was the Monk's job to find experienced outsize members wherever he could, from the Court to the stables. But she also enjoyed the open-eyed defencelessness of horny youth. She loved to put a fourteen year old through his paces, strip him of innocence, then turn him out without a hope or a sou. She made a point of never seeing these victims again.

It was the Monk who had found this fresh adolescent groom. She gazed at him, moistening her lips. He was reclining naked on a couch, holding a flimsy kerchief over his crotch. The

Monk had made sure that he had adopted Isabelle's favourite posture, looking upwards to Venus on Parnassus on the Cardinal's tapestry. The groom gazed round wide-eyed and tense. In spite of his jitters, he seemed to know what to do, massaging his prick, getting ready for action. Isabelle eyed the kerchief as it rose in the air. The kerchief was transparent. Perfect, thought Isabelle.

On a gilded, padded throne close to her couch, sat her gorgeously arrayed tame Cardinal, hot-foot from Avignon. That city was now the seat of a schismatic Papacy, the centre of the most brazen system of corruption in the Christian world. The stooping, wrinkled Cardinal Piero della Rovere leaned forward, gazing at the youth. His drooping eyelids gave nothing away, except devouring lust. He ran a hand over the flake-dry skin of his face, making a dry, rasping sound. His liver-spotted hands moved rhythmically under the spacious purple of his Cardinal's cassock.

Isabelle's skirt rode up into her lap. The dwarf buried his head in her dripping crotch, tongue in frantic motion on the glistening bud he found there. As the dwarf got more and more frantic, Isabelle ripped off her clothes. This was going to be more than just good. She nodded to the youth. The Cardinal, quivering with excitement, extended his ringed finger. The groom rose, arched his back so his member stuck out, giving it added dimension. Ignoring the holy ring, he took the Cardinal's middle finger into his mouth, as instructed, and sucked and rimmed the tip of the old man's middle finger. The Cardinal, moaning with pleasure, caressed the boy's erection with his free hand.

Isabelle, now quite naked, turned, with the help of Eustace and the dwarf, and knelt on her 'throne,' presenting her muscular, perfectly rounded rear to her courtiers. At a nod, the Groom rose, bent over her hunched back, shining lightly with pre-coital sweat, and slipped into her with the ease and force of a well trained ram. Now, as Isabelle thought she had planned, he was to lose all innocence in a frenzy of copulation. Yes, Louis, like a lamb to the slaughter. She reached under her crotch and caressed his swinging testicles. Yes, I'll name him, 'Louis the Lamb', she thought. The Lamb now spread open her buttocks to get an even deeper thrust, gripped her hips. She yelled with unbounded pleasure until, shouting as loudly as the Lamb, her whole lower body erupted in a shuddering orgasm. Gasping, she slumped back onto the divan.

From the darkness of a corner, behind a drooping arras, a figure was watching. His arms were pinioned at his side, folded shut like those of a bat. A long hooded cloak covered the rest of his body. His sharp pointed features were set in a flour-white face, pasty as a corpse's. He chittered briefly as the groom dismounted from the panting Isabelle. Such filthiness, such moral grime, such mortal sin. He felt he could eat it all up, feast on the morass of depravity there. But his aims were more elevated, he wanted to devour the sin of a king, or of a king-maker at least. He wanted his sin-eating to be royal and on display for the ages, like a reign. He lusted after immortality as a lover lusts after love. With a brief subdued chitter, he moved back into the little door behind the arras. Light from one of the candles briefly lit his face. His eyes snapped shut. They hated light. He slowly opened them in the returning gloom. They were as shiny and solid as black marbles. With metallic claws, he wrapped his cloak about his scaly body and slipped into the shadows of the cellars below. He had spent the last few days resting there, plotting his next move.

6

Hopcyn woke again to his surroundings. He had just had a series of miniature implosions, brief images which came effortlessly in sequence, without the disturbing impact of a major vision. He shook himself out of it. A white kerchief was waving from the top of one of the distant beeches, then another and another, along the whole line of trees. Owen had placed watchers in the tallest, forming a gigantic circle of eyes around the entire estate. Any suspicious movement was immediately spotted and relayed to Owen within minutes.

'He'll be at the bowers for Isabelle,' said Hopcyn. 'Can't keep away from the original serpent.'

'Better get Catherine,' said Owen. I'm sure you will, thought Hopcyn, just give it time. Owen urged his horse into a gallop. But no hurry. Hopcyn had just had a vision of Owen which he dared not yet tell Owen. There were traps in the path of his destiny, deadly ones.

Hopcyn moved through the trees towards the bower he had visualised, as if guided by an invisible hand.

7

With languorous kisses and embraces, Isabelle dismissed her 'court'. The Monk, Dwarf, Cardinal and Poet departed for their private chambers, drained and replete. They were assured of rich rewards for the day's work. And Louis the Lamb with his sweet limbs, tufted pubes, gasping thrusts and purring gratitude, she had mothered him even as he climaxed deep inside her.

'Glorious,' smiled Isabelle. As Louis made to leave, Isabelle hauled him back with her crook. His testicles ached. Did he have to deliver again?

'Hold your hands out,' she ordered. Isabelle poured a stream of golden louis into them. The Lamb gasped. Staring at the gold he realised he had enough to buy back his father's farm, and keep the family in bread for years. And Isabelle had not spotted it. As a chorister, he had been the catamite of the local priest since childhood. He fell on his knees, sobbing with gratitude and relief. He was now also free of the priest. He was blessed indeed.

'Bless you, ma'am, bless you . . . ' was all he could mumble. Isabelle stared, then stroked his damp hair. To her astonishment she found she had grown quite fond of the youth. What was happening to her?

'Be at the stables when I call,' she ordered. He left, eyes still brimming with tears of thanks.

'Well,' she thought, 'never had a pet lamb since kindergarten. And what a splendid session, four climaxes in four new Pompeian positions.' She glanced at the tapestries they had followed. 'With four different men,' from anal thrills to vaginal climaxes, to simultaneous penetrations to endless clitoral orgasms by tongue, lips and touch – luscious! She recalled the trio she'd had with the Doge of Venice and her nephew Galeazzo Visconti in a closed gondola on the Grand Canal. It had become an international scandal, but that session too had been short and, like this one, of exceptional quality. The Doge had been terrified by the gossip, the limp prick, which made him all the easier to discard. Pity, he had been slung like a stallion. Isabelle loved her savage, sweet little revenges. But what about this time? It was true. She **had** grown fond of the boy.

8

Owen was listening attentively to Catherine as she made final preparations to leave the main Château. They were in Isabelle's great hall. Owen stood at one of the arched windows looking out at the tall, swaying elms, on the alert for any signal.

'Yes,' said Catherine, 'all I wanted was a happy family. What everyone wants in their hearts, don't you think? To be caressed and comforted, like my father before his illness.' She thought how the Welsh always touched and embraced each other as out of some well of human fondness she had never tasted. She hurried on,

'Afterwards, with Mother all over the place, and us children alone most of the time, we were in rags you see. Even the urchins in the streets pelted us with garbage. A happy family. I feel I can tell you this, Owen. You don't mind?' Owen shook his head, transfixed by the new warmth in her voice.

'I feel that's what Henry wants too. Poor mother, thirteen *accouchements*, she didn't have much of a chance, did she? All she ever wanted was a happy life. *Funs* as she calls it. And her marriage was so wonderful at the start, she says so herself. You can't blame her, can you?'

'No, my Lady. And your father, he'll be alright with us, don't worry.'

'Call me Catherine when we're alone, Owen.' Owen nodded wordlessly.

'I do love mother now,' said Catherine. 'Strange, I know. I think she really has my happiness at heart.'

Owen felt his sympathy turn into affection. He nearly

reached out to stroke her arm. Of anyone he knew, Catherine was the first who most deserved a little real happiness. He felt frustration rise again. What could he do, a mere tame warrior of the wardrobe?

'I'm glad you see it, Owen, I will be happy once in my life. I am determined. A family is all. But why all these quarrels? Yorkists, Lancastrians? Who started it?'

'King Edward, Henry's grandfather. Eleven children. And each thought they should have the crown. Their children think so too. That's all, really.'

'But who are *they*?'

'Now its the three Dukes, York, Somerset and Suffolk.'

'I've never seen one of them.'

'Their homes are now their castles. They direct their wars from there.'

'Just like over here. The Dauphinists. Who will win?'

'The strongest.'

'And who is the strongest?'

'House of Lancaster. Henry, Clarence, Bedford, Humphrey. Three Dukes against the four. White rose against the red. Henry's bound to win.'

'I hate it. My mother hates wars too. I still think a family's everything. And yours, Owen?'

'Lost them early in the Welsh wars. My father to an Englishman's lance. My mother to an Englishman's famine.'

'So you never had a family either?'

'Yes, but for the years one can't quite remember.'

'How sad.'

'Yes.'

'I'm sorry.'

'Thank you.'

The evening sun streamed through the coloured panes, giving Owen's silhouette a golden, halo-like glow. As his tall, commanding figure turned to her again, his features appeared lit by some inner light. His green eyes, afire now, seemed to probe into her very being. Catherine felt tingles rising along her spine and spread over her whole body. She blushed furiously at the thought she'd just had. Looking at the blazing, green-eyed Captain, she had wondered who was the most attractive, her husband-to-be, a King, or the unknown Welsh squire before her. Owen again checked a burning desire to touch her. The fires died down. He was in control.

Catherine tossed her black hair, trying to subdue the breathlessness rising in her. Owen or Henry? She thrust the question aside and picked up her cloak.

'We'd better be off, Owen,' she said, scarcely able to look at him.

'Yes, Catherine, of course.' He realised he had used her first name, and it had seemed the most natural thing in the world. As they left the Hall for their horses, Owen's confusion turned into desire for action. They mounted and Owen spurred his charger into a gallop. Catherine responded, keeping up with him. Together, they were soon lost in the shadows of the dense woodland.

9

Drowsily, Isabelle emptied her sixth stein. She hadn't moved from her divan. Her mind wondered drowsily. Terrific orgasms. When was her first? She groaned. Yes, it had to be. Her cursed husband, Charles. Her first man, her first climax. And a virgin. She could hardly recall it. She had been examined by the ladies of the court, as was the custom, who had publicly declared her *virgo intacta*. What a first night it had been. Six times. By the seventh, she had fallen in love, not only with her royal husband, but with this breathless new thing called lust. Hadn't she swooned over the man who had first revealed the heavenly nature of physical love? Then the curse fell. Madness. But despite the pitiful, terrifying dementia, Charles still raged with lust after her. Her love meanwhile was soon replaced by disgust, which then hardened into hatred. During the course of his attacks, the King lost all control of his bowels. He fouled her again and again, and each repulsive coupling only seemed to lead to these terrible, unwanted pregnancies. Thirteen years of dynastic duty! Thirteen years of hell! Well, it was her turn now. It was she alone who decided when to take her pleasure, and with whom. But in his ruined mind, the King still brooded over their early passion. In his clear moments, he became frenzied at the seeming beast he had unleashed on that first night, and raged to punish Isabelle's many 'treasons' against him.

In spite of the pain, she recalled the day. What a wedding, what a coronation. Wonderful! She had been thrilled, taken out of herself, a dream fulfilled. She re-lived it again, the procession into Paris passing under the huge arch of the Porte de St Denis.

Stretched above the gate was a vast cloth, sprinkled with gold-foil stars. Children dressed as angels sang sweetly from the battlements. Two of the 'angels' then descended in silver chariots and placed a coronet of gold on her brows.

When the procession arrived at the royal rostrum that had been set up on the banks of the Seine, Isabelle beheld a tightrope stretched from the high tower of Notre Dame to the turret of a towering palace by the bridge. An acrobat with a candle in each hand, wearing the coat of arms of the Wittelsbachs, walked along the taut cord to the roof-top opposite, singing the new Queen's praises. What marvels! And all for her. Then she was escorted the rest of the way to the Palace of St Pol on a richly decorated litter carried by members of the royal family, dressed as ancient sages. The horses of an escort of the leading nobility of France were caparisoned to the ground in cloth of gold. But her own robe had outdone them all in magnificence. It was embroidered with two-and-a-half thousand pearls, sprinkled with diamonds. The city squares they passed through were hung with colourful tapestries. Artificial fountains ran with free milk and wine for the populace. In one elegant square, the adoring crowds on one side wore green, on the other, the imperial purple in honour of Queen Isabelle.

Isabelle mistily recalled the coronation feast. The adulation, the universal adoration had made her too excited to eat. And then, the lewd but regal procession to the bed chamber. Charles had disrobed at once, displaying a muscled, athletic body. He too loved the chase and the new royal game of tennis. His shoulder-length blond hair was as long as his bride's. The splendours of the day had inflamed his passions. In the light of three carved ivory candle-holders, they first ate strawberries with crystal picks mounted in silver and gold. Then they had made love on a bed smothered in fresh red and white rose petals. And what loving it was! Ecstatic. Was that dim unforgettable dream really her wedding night? Was the madman lurking out there anything to do with her? No, she decided, it was all a young girl's dream, a dream to be re-lived time and again during the deaths and disappointments that soon crowded her life. She wept bitter tears as she again bade *auf wiedersehen* to the bright visions of her youth.

10

Henry spurred his horse into a canter. He had to get to Beaurevoir in the shortest possible time. He was planning his favourite military tactic – surprise. No one expected him to ride straight from a dawn confession on a Sunday to parley with the French and Burgundian emissaries. They were still supposed to be in Paris, leisurely going over the details of the Treaty. These same emissaries now rode with the King's entourage, the brassy, boastful, splendidly attired Duke of Burgundy at their head. He was still irritated by Henry's sudden decision for negotiations had gone ahead even as they rode along.

Burgundy glanced at Henry, riding upright and silent in the saddle. Henry the Saint, he thought, is as much a miser over time as money. But the unpredictable Duke was determined to squeeze more territorial concessions out of Henry the Conqueror, the 'grasping, slippery English brigand', as he called him behind his back. Burgundy had insisted that Northern and Eastern France were his own special sphere of influence. Why, he thought, without my armies, the English alliance would founder. The short-sighted Duke little understood that without the English, he also would be lost.

With grim satisfaction, the Duke gazed around at the landscape. It was shattered by the continuing civil war between his own semi-independent state of Burgundy and the royal, warring factions of France. Henry's booty-laden war bands had added to the desolation. Burgundy's hatred was fuelled by the recent Dauphinist-Orleanist conspiracy. This royal alliance had succeeded in murdering his well-protected father. The Duke would have happily hanged every subject of the King of France along the route. The mad King's dominions couldn't be torn apart enough for his liking. But Henry would have to share more of the spoils with him. After the recent assassination, the Duke saw it as a moral retribution and a reward, God's punishment for murder most foul. It was the Lord's wish, as he often reminded holy Henry, for the powers of Burgundy and England to rule France, though privately (and mistakenly) he believed that he was the pivot of the alliance.

Yes, thought the Duke, perhaps I should favour the Dauphinist party, just for a bit. That would bring Henry to his senses. And why keep my temper, as they all advise? I am the High Duke of Burgundy, the equal of any power in Europe, and I have a murdered father to avenge.

'To hell with the milksops, I'll say what I please,' he muttered. In his more violent furies, Burgundy turned a faint alarming tinge of blue. This presaged savage, indiscriminate punishments on his nearest underlings.

Henry had reason to feel satisfied. After the amazing victory of Agincourt, he had personally arranged the wedding, the coronation, the Treaty and the Alliance, adding to his security by the minute. He had then wrested the initiative from Burgundy and circumvented the outrageous but formidable Isabelle by judicious bribery. The Dauphin he had tamed, the French nobility he had humiliated, but with the mad King he had been surprisingly merciful. But Henry knew well that, mad or sane, Charles was to be his new father-in-law, and he was all too aware of his nickname among the people, 'the Well Beloved'. He had planned the marriage alliance with Catherine long before the others had even suspected. And he also had his reputation as a saint to keep up, especially in the eyes of his bride-to-be whom he knew loved her poor, deranged father.

Every decision was now Henry's, down to the last detail, even to the menu of the wedding feast. He had taken this out of

Isabelle's hands. After seeing her menu, he realised it could bankrupt him. He was certain Isabelle would acquiesce on every point of the Treaty. He had approved most of her lists of expenses, including her private debt accounts. Not that he had told her immediately. She'd had to work for it. Surprisingly, she fought tooth and nail for her daughter. The great whore of Babylon, he thought, an international scandal, from her panthers and lovers to her chained monkeys, but she was also brilliant, powerful and calculating. Did she suspect he had more than just diplomatic feelings for 'Katty'? As he considered the millions coming in, he made the sign of the cross – wasn't every *centime* meant for his Crusade of European Powers against the Infidel? Henry's eyes were fixed on Jerusalem. Astonishingly, he planned to redeem the Holy City for Christendom.

Henry had decided on the final details of the Treaty of Troyes. He was equally determined the agreement would be signed in the next twenty-four hours, come what may. The wedding would take place immediately after that, also at Troyes. The reception would be at Beaurevoir and the honeymoon at Sens, or Melun, or even Montereau. Wherever, it would be a honeymoon of battles, depending on the resistance of the Dauphinist towns. Once these towns had been tamed, the pacification of the vast lands to the south could begin. What better way to spend a honeymoon than gathering harvests of booty? What better time to balance the books.

Riding with the King were his main officers of state, all seasoned generals. His favourite brother, the Duke of Bedford, formerly Lord High Admiral was big, blond, fleshy, with a huge beak of a nose and a curiously receding chin, and never far from his side. And woe betide anyone who mistook that lack of chin for weakness. In battle, he was feared for his extraordinary physical courage. He had sworn fealty to Henry, an oath to be kept to the death, his own as well as his brother's.

Bedford was the only member of Henry's English entourage who had a genuine love for the French nation. Not only was he was fluent in French, he also encouraged French scholarship and, after the victory of Agincourt, founded a University at Caen. He was popular with the native, aristocratic families Henry had slaughtered, and was respected for his learning. Bedford also knew how to keep the Parisians happy, in spite of the heavy taxes he was forced to levy for the English Exchequer. He was fair and just in his administration of the law. In the present peace, he had proved himself a patient and skilled diplomat. It was due to Bedford that the powers of Burgundy, France – in the person of Queen Isabelle – and England, managed to remain united, if sometimes only by a thread.

It was Bedford too, being second in line, who managed to keep the jealous and combative brothers in order. They often came to blows, even in public. Henry, in person, had cause to part them on more than one occasion.

Clarence, the next in line, was as ambitious and impetuous as his younger brother, the jealous, foul-tempered, imperious and greedy Humphrey, who was third in line. Their personal retainers, more like private armies, were constantly at each other's throats. Henry sometimes felt his brothers posed more of a menace than the French. Dangerously, they fought on their own home ground in England, both of them threatening Henry's communications and his rear. He had for the moment scotched the Yorkist conspirators, but knew that they would pounce if he put a foot wrong. The three 'devil Dukes' were bad enough, but add the brothers to them and the danger could be mortal. But for now, he was experiencing triumph after triumph. Thank God for Bedford, he thought. Johnny, his childhood name, had always been his favourite. Henry again prayed for the health of his only really steadfast, truly gifted brother.

At Bedford's side rode the Earl of Salisbury, Lieutenant Governor of the despoiled Duchy of Normandy. This occupation by English forces reversed the English triumphs of William the Conqueror centuries earlier, and was to last for over thirty years. Salisbury was a skilful, forceful imaginative strategist, respected by friend and foe alike for his chivalry in war. Like Henry, he had foreseen the future importance of the use of the new-fangled firearms, and was one of the first of Henry's generals to become a gunnery and artillery expert. He was proficient in siege as well as in set piece field infantry assaults, and led from the front. His muscular, squat figure resembled one of his new mortars, but he was just as destructive in hand-to-hand combat. He saw eye to eye with Bedford and Henry on practically every major issue. Working in concert, the trio were irresistible.

Behind Salisbury rode the patrician Earl of Warwick, descended from the Beauchamps, an old Norman-French family. Immensely wealthy in his own right, he was a fine-boned, graceful, arrogant man who was also fluent in French, but wholeheartedly pledged to the English cause. For all his aristocratic elegance, he was a ferocious adversary. Henry had promoted him to First Captain and Regent in the Field. Warwick found further favour in Henry's eyes because he had made the arduous and dangerous pilgrimage to Jerusalem.

Henry's uncle, Bishop of Winchester and Cardinal of Rome, was absent in England. He was another of Henry's brilliant officers of state. Winchester had become the special object of Humphrey's hatred. It was Humphrey who launched the rumour that Henry, goaded by Winchester, had plotted the murder of his own father in Westminster Cathedral. Humphrey had come to believe this lie, and still bruited it abroad. Winchester was perfectly aware of this. He blocked Humphrey's every move for high office, and headed off Humphrey's retainers in the streets of London. Winchester also possessed a golden touch. To display his ever accumulating wealth, he put on costly tournaments, feasts and fairs for the populace. This goaded his nephew to even greater fury. Humphrey spent more money for spies on Winchester than on his enemies in France.

Henry pushed the column into a gallop. Wake them up a bit, he thought. Henry himself was tall, muscular and carried armour like a light summer cloak. He had a military pudding-basin crop, brown eyes, a long nose and a high complexion. After his coronation, among other traits, he found royal hauteur could be a devastating weapon. One disdainful look down his long nose brought cowering silence in seconds. It was now part of his diplomatic armoury, but many accused him of arrogance and intimidation.

Henry's claim to the throne was as weak as his father's. Both were descended only from the third son of the old king, Edward III. There were others with stronger claims, although he would never concede to this fact. But to compensate for this weakness, Henry acted with utter ruthlessness against any dynastic threat. Bedford was one of the few who understood that Henry meant above everything to establish his line once and for all on the throne of England, whatever the cost.

Henry, after a dissolute youth, had experienced a road-to-Damascus conversion. He deserted his old habits and haunts and became dedicated to Christian chivalric ideals. He believed his recent victories had been won with the direct intervention of God. He became convinced it was his destiny to recover the holy places, including Jerusalem. But his faith tended to bigotry and his frugality to greed. He never shared ransoms. He 'confiscated' all the noblest prisoners. He insisted on more that fifty per cent of all booty, instead of the usual thirty per cent. He knew that France was far wealthier than England for France had three times the population, and therefore three times the revenue, even when despoiled. Henry became a master of pillage, 'robbing a treasury whose vaults are never exhausted,' as he described it. Immense quantities of his French booty was for sale all over England. But he was, of course, doing it for the Prince of Heaven and for St George, never himself.

Similarly, his ruthlessness tended to cruelty. He ordered the death of his prisoners at Agincourt on the basis of the rumour of a thrust to the rear behind the baggage wagons, where the prisoners were coralled. But their deaths were gruesome – throats were slit, brains were bashed out with poleaxes whilst others were burnt alive on pyres. Nor did he spare the badly wounded. He also ordered the hanging of a twelve-year old page for parading a donkey dressed as the King of England. After Agincourt he had the noblest French survivors serve him at table like common servants. His cruelty to heretics mounted. A local Lollard, a new breed of puritan Christian, publicly denied transubstantiation. Henry had him boiled in oil before being hauled out and promised a free pardon if he recanted. The intrepid Lollard refused so Henry had him plunged back into the pot and boiled to death. Henry, after all, was the Lord's newly anointed, God's agent carrying out His chastisement.

Henry also felt blessed in his choice of bride. Bright, undemanding, frugal, Catherine cost very little. And the financial returns were enormous. Added to that, she was beautiful. The old desires of his youth stirred in him. He crossed himself against temptation, but without much conviction. He really did desire her. All the more reason to hurry the wedding. She would be exquisite in bed, virginal yet sensual, he could feel it. But once again he felt that rare tenderness towards her. Was he really falling in love? Best keep that side of things in the dark. He felt lucky having Isabelle as the principal French negotiator. She was as willing an accomplice in the dismemberment of France as his most rapacious Captain. With Isabelle so amenable, he would soon secure his new Kingdom, the price of his great Crusade. Yes, he thought piously, however unholy Isabelle may be, God has a purpose even for the greatest of whores.

He glanced back at his followers, dedicated to a man to Saint George and Saint Booty. The English nobility enjoyed a prosperity they had never known in England, and certainly not in Wales. Every soldier in the column, noble squire to humble carrier, had benefited. They had no intention of letting it slip through their fingers. Henry was obeyed unquestioningly. They fought like lions for it meant more and more coin. Henry muttered his favourite saying, 'Out of diversity, unity'. He clasped his hands briefly. 'Yes, Thy will be done!'

He ordered the column to close up. They were passing through a region noted for brigands with deserters from both sides, gangs of robbers, dispossessed peasantry, criminal soldiery, all of them bent on plunder. Throughout this county, manors had been seized, convents sacked, nuns raped. Crop failures and famine were endemic. Villages became blackened ruins. Disused roads vanished into nowhere and paths disappeared under brambles and weeds. Cattle moaned unmilked in the fields and slaughtered beasts littered the farmyards. In many villages no cocks crowed. It was the same through huge areas of the northern provinces.

They came to a crossroads. Henry signalled the column to halt. From a gibbet on the side of the road hung a naked corpse dangling by a cord round its genitals. Smoke wafted across from a burning farm. Even as they watched, a gust of wind swung the corpse. The weight of the body tore the scrotum from its cord and it crashed to the ground. An audible moan rose from the troops. Further along, they saw the decapitated bodies of children in ditches. Next, in a field, were piles of smouldering faggots. The stink of burning flesh testified to even more hideous work. Around the flickering flames lay lumps of half-roasted meat, and across the grass fluttered flaps of a curious parchment-like material. On closer inspection it proved to be human skin. The evil *Ecorcheurs*, the Flayers who were specialists in kidnap and ransom, had again been at their butchery. These reeking victims had fought back and had paid the ultimate price. Impaled on stakes, their skins had literally been torn from their bodies. What remained of them was torched. It was said the Ecorcheurs feasted on the burned flesh of their victims. Henry regarded these monsters of war as a biblical plague, a foul pest which had to be exterminated without quarter.

He knew the terrain, and quickly devised a plan. He called up his company of *gallowglasses* – all of them long-haired, moustachioed, saffron-cloaked, barefoot, axe and claymore wielding berserkers from the bogs of Ireland. They often returned from their expeditions with decapitated heads, knotted together by the hair, hanging from their saddles.

Henry pointed to a trail of hoofs in the soft, cindered, bloodied soil. They led up to a wooded hill. This route had to be secured once and for all. He would return along this very way with his betrothed, the fair Catherine, and as Henry the Conqueror he could not allow his future Queen to be confronted by such horrors. God was calling to him again to cleanse this evil.

'No prisoners,' he ordered, and urged the column towards the woods, swords drawn, *galloglasses* in the van.

11

Hopcyn and Agnes crouched behind a bush watching the open area in front of one of Isabelle's sylvan bowers canopied with trellises of intertwining hazel boughs. Wild honeysuckle had been trained over the structure. It made a fretted roof of leaves and sweet-smelling blossoms. Rustic tables of rough-hewn timbers and benches stood in the centre. On the table were earthenware pots and jars. At the back hung the Wittelsbach coat of arms and *fleur-de-lis* pennants of France. The ground was covered with a profusion of wild violets. It was to such bowers that Isabelle sometimes retired on balmy afternoons with her lovers.

'Sweet violets make the best bed,' she always said. Beside the bower was a sheep-cote with the usual weird, static lambs and stationary, stuffed tigers. Hopcyn put his finger to his lips and pointed.

To the left of the bower, the bushes parted and a half naked figure with glaring eyes peered out. Seeing no one in the bower, the King of France emerged. His face was smeared with dirt, his wispy blond-greyish hair clotted with mud and leaves. His lips were green from chewing grass. Wisps still clung from his mouth. His only clothing was a ragged, soiled, loin-cloth. The upper part of the body was roughly daubed with wavy blue lines. He stood for a moment, his head unnaturally still, as if afraid of moving it. He began weaving to and fro, arms extended sideways, imitating the action of seaweed in the tide. Charles, the sixth of that name, spotted the standards with the Wittelsbach coat-of-arms. With a shriek he attacked them, tore

71

them down, ripped them to pieces with his teeth, and then stamped on them. The King's rage mounted. He tore and stamped, stamped and tore.

Hopcyn plucked the strings of his harp. The King paused, pricked up his ears. Hopcyn played a few phrases of an ancient Welsh melody. The King calmed, then seemed to disintegrate from within. His legs folded and he fell limply onto his hands and knees onto the leafy soil, weeping as if his heart would break. He clutched at the dead leaves, seeking for something to cling to. Hopcyn approached him. The King started back like an animal surprised. His gaze fixed on Hopcyn. He smiled radiantly, pointing at Hopcyn's single, brilliant, blue eye, as strangely made on the outside as he surely was on the inside. As Hopcyn played, the King began the waving motion again, holding his head tightly upright.

Behind him Hopcyn heard hoofs. They slowed to a halt. Catherine and Owen dismounted and ran over. Catherine stared down at her father, tears in her eyes. She gripped Owen's shoulder and sobbed softly. Owen pressed her hand. She stifled her tears. They watched as Hopcyn began to imitate the King's waving motions. Charles smiled, nodding in time to Hopcyn's movements.

'Don't move,' warned Hopcyn softly. 'He thinks he is a wine glass, and might spill.'

The King slid forward again, collapsing completely. Catherine cradled the stricken head in her arms and stroked his brow. The King's red-rimmed eyes widened in recognition.

'My . . . daughter, lovely Catherine. A . . . kiss.' Catherine gently kissed the grimed, furrowed forehead. The King's eyes clouded in anguish.

'My darling,' he begged, 'please find who's doing this terrible thing to me, find them and tell them to stop this agony . . . or kill me. Please, my darling.'

Hopcyn soothed him again with strains from the harp.

Catherine brushed the leaves from his hair. The King's eyes slowly registered on his surroundings. The music was doing its work.

'Back in the real world,' murmured Hopcyn, 'if it can be said to be real.' But for how long, he wondered?

Catherine and Owen, their arms around the King and each other, did not notice Hopcyn's sudden searching gaze into the underbrush. Yes, there scuttled the dark bat-like form, getting bolder each time. Hopcyn had felt its presence for days. The Sin Eater had come to France to devour Owen, son of princes and father-to-be of princes. Hopcyn would need all his druid arts to confound the deadly Sin Eater. And both Sin Eater and Bard knew it. It was war over Owen's destiny, war to the death. He looked tenderly at his two charges and resumed playing. Neither would know of this evil until later.

12

Abruptly, Isabelle came out of her reverie. What had disturbed her? She got up in the half light. Something shifted in the far corner. With complete assurance she marched towards it, sniffed, and bellowed with rage. It was the pig, her son, half concealed by the arras. Stunted, knock-kneed, long-nosed, the Dauphin's shifty eyes peered up timidly at his mother.

'So you escaped from your sty, pig. How did you get in?'

'The cellars,' muttered the Dauphin. He drooled as he spoke.

'I thought you were terrified of houses.' Charles looked up fearfully at the ceiling. His most recent phobia was that he would be killed by collapsing masonry.

'*Arseloch.* I only wish a gargoyle would fall on you. Mad as your father. And he mad as his mother, Jeanne. Remember your loony old grandma? All crazy. You're no different. Never forget that. Come to Mama, my little bastard loony.' Charles the Dauphin, later to be Charles the VII of France, slunk hesitatingly forward.

'And wipe your snout before your Queen, you dripping piglet.' Charles hastily did so, on his sleeve.

'Ugh!' again interjected Isabelle.

Charles looked around, wrinkling his nose at the perfumed flesh of his mother. He trembled. The sight of all the nudity and erotic statuary merely intimidated him. He shrank back.

'Don't sit there, pig,' she said as he was about to sit on her couch. 'You'll defile it.' She pushed him onto the floor.

'Now what are you doing here and what you want?

'I want to see my sister.'

74

'Your sister she is not, ja. I will denounce you. Don't you know I'm a whore. Look around you. How many cocks do you see? You didn't spurt from any, certainly not the King's. Listen, you drained out scum, a bedtime story now. Once the King locked me up in a brothel for being a whore. Know what? I loved it. That's where I got you up my belly.' Charles heaved, trying to be sick.

'Ha,' jeered Isabelle, 'can't even puke right.'

The Dauphin, however, quickly recovered.

'She is my sister and I'm still Dauphin. All the signs say so.'

'You knock-kneed cretin, how did you manage to get a sister as beautiful as Katty?'

'I am your flesh too.'

'Fat chance,' exclaimed Isabelle. 'And leave my flesh out of this.'

'My father has clear moments, he acknowledges me.'

Isabelle grabbed him round the neck, and pulled his face close to hers.

'You came with him, didn't you? He is here, isn't he?'

'Yes, and much better,' Charles said triumphantly, wriggling free and rubbing his neck.

'Too late. My Treaty is assured.'

'The shame of France!' Isabelle ignored the remark and spat, 'Better is he? We'll see about that.'

But if the King got better, she knew her powers were threatened.

'We've set up court in Honnecourt.'

'You've what?' exclaimed Isabelle.

Charles looked pleased. He'd surprised his awful mother for once. None of her spies had reported any movement on the long road or in Honnecourt.

'With whom, you piece of snot?'

'Old retainers, courtiers, faithful attendants.'

'Who?'

'Le Camus, Gilles de Rais, Yvaine de Foix, Huguet de Guisay, La Tremouille . . . '

'Courtiers! Parasites, rats and murderers. Le Camus I know from my own bed, a poisoner who murdered his wife. Gilles' brother was clubbed to death for sodomy. They chopped off his prick when he was dead so he couldn't bugger the devil from the grave. Yvaine and de Rais are Satanists. Don't blame them for that, but they murdered their children for funs. Huguet's a fake astrologer . . . ' Charles broke across his mothers diatribe.

'Nothing wrong with astrology. Stars say I am the real Dauphin.'

'Never, knock-kneed bastard.'

'We only want what is rightfully ours.'

'As for La Tremouille,' Isabelle pressed on, 'just a pox ridden witch.'

'Like that Odette of yours.'

Isabelle often distracted her husband's lust with buxom peasant wenches from the cow-sheds. Odette, for a change, was a horse trader's daughter.

'That sow hasn't throttled anyone. And wipe yourself, you drop of dripping phlegm, I'm really a sister of mercy. Know why Odette's called "the Second Queen?" – because she looks like me, and you know why? Because that loon fucks her till he drops because he thinks she's me, thank God.'

Charles looked around for a way out but his mother was still in full flow.

'Now you piece of puppy puke, I warn you, if you get in my way . . . '

'All the filth here,' he said at last, 'will be punished by God.'

Isabelle laughed uproariously.

'Watch your language,' she said. 'There's a Cardinal in the house.'

'My father wants your punishment, too,' said Charles. Isabelle was surprised again. She knew only too well her husband could be extremely nasty in his saner moments.

'He is still King. The Well-Beloved.'

'The shite! He is not your father.'

'He could strip you of all this. By royal prerogative. And he wants to be at the wedding. With me as Dauphin. That *godon* Henry's still marrying a sister of mine, isn't he?'

Isabelle glanced sharply at him. Perhaps the pig did have a spark of the Wittelsbachs after all. It was true. As brother-in-law he had every right to attend the wedding. The bastard.

'Get out,' she yelled, gripping her crook. As he turned to flee, she thwacked him across his spindly buttocks. He yelped in pain and raced down the corridor to the back door. Outside, he smiled and wiped his drooling nose. He had stood up to her, yes, even shaken her. At last he felt like a man. He didn't feel so helpless, so nerveless any longer. He had fire in his veins, too, and he'd do it again.

His father had returned much better from the woods. That weird poet had bathed him and he had been almost normal. He, the true Dauphin, had chosen the right time to establish the Court at Honnecourt. And his father, his recovered father, was going to give a Ball tonight. The great Harlot couldn't stop that, even if she was Regent. Many of his father's old courtiers would be there, however much she vilified them. Perhaps this time his father would recover permanently. He felt disturbed about going to the wedding, although he wanted Catherine's happiness, they had shared such misery together. Deschamps had said the marriage was a national humiliation. He shrugged. Tonight they would have fun too. The first royal ball of the new court, and a new age! He prayed his father to stay well. Marvellous to be treated as the true heir apparent at last, the true royal Dauphin of France. And he had won the last round against the Great Whore. He shuddered to think of her in his father's bed. There would be more victories for himself, he swore.

Isabelle dropped the crook and slumped on the couch. So the madman was around, and far too close for comfort. Well, she thought, the devil himself was not going to get in the way of hard cash. But suppose he was cured? Hell, she swore, when everything was going so well, and after such a gorgeous session. But she knew Henry wouldn't permit the King or Dauphin to threaten a single detail of his plans. It was another question of coin and that mad crusade of his. She had quadrupled the expenses of her final demands. She knew Henry would milk the French Exchequer dry. If that was the price of happiness, well, so be it. But she would stick to her own figures until Henry agreed.

Yes, with the mad King so much in evidence, Henry would want to get the Treaty and the wedding out of the way as rapidly as possible. However insane, or sane, come to that, her dire husband and gross son would not get in the way. Henry would settle in gold, just as it ought to be between opportunists, she thought. Except that Henry, incomprehensibly, believed in the Saviour. The saviour of what? she wondered.

Hell. Again the thought returned to torment her. What if the madman did come round permanently? Her eyes narrowed as she recalled the terrible day he'd had his first attack. They had been out hunting with Louis, Duc d'Orleans, the King's brother and an old lover of Isabelle's, along with the frightful courtier de Guisay and other attendants. They were riding along the edge of a wood when a frenzied barefoot beggar in a torn smock darted forward and seized the bridle of the King's horse, yelling, 'Ride no more, noble King, you are betrayed!' Charles ordered his bodyguard not to harm the poor wretch, for he was clearly mad. However, the lunatic pursued them for miles crying out his insane warnings. Yes, she wiped her forehead, the sun blazed down like a furnace, she could feel the heat now. The King seemed unaffected at first. Then a page dozing in the saddle next to him let his lance fall onto the head of the King's horse. At once, the King drew his sword and screamed,

'They want to deliver me to the enemy! We are betrayed!' He struck out in all directions, severely wounding two attendants. He then tumbled from his horse and laid into his nearest followers. Everyone drew back, afraid to lay hands on an anointed monarch. They let the King rage on until he was exhausted. As they finally approached him, he caught a glimpse of his faithless wife, now keeping a safe distance. He fell into a further frenzy, pointing at her, yelling,

'Treason! Treason!' then charged at her and tried to run her through. He was overpowered just in time by his Chamberlain, Michel de Freye, a massive man and redoubtable soldier. The King then collapsed into a wide-eyed coma. He was laid out in a passing oxcart and taken home to the Palais de St Pol.

He remained in the coma for four days. When he finally came out of it, he seemed normal enough. He asked to see Isabelle. When she approached his sickbed, he sprang out, dagger in hand, and made her kneel in front of him. He then proceeded to piss all over her. The abominable scene filled her mind with nausea. But to her rage, even after this filthy act, the people and many courtiers had sympathised with their mad King. The common folk said a hundred masses for him and burned thousands of candles at the altar. They paraded effigies of their 'Well Beloved' through the villages and prayed four times a day for his recovery. Mocking verses began circulating, penned some said, by a new surpassingly ugly poet called Eustace Deschamps. They first pilloried the vile habits and mindless excesses of some of the poor King's favourites, then the 'foreigners' in court – which was a thinly veiled attack on Bavarian Isabelle herself. One poem directly blamed her for the King's condition. But the illness did not stop the King from exercising his marital rights. He was still King, mad or sane. After these episodes, she ended up praying for his demise whilst plotting the humiliation of the accursed French nation. And Henry and Catherine fitted neatly into her plans.

Strengthened by the familiar comforts of her inner sanctum, she called for more beer, and ordered the Cardinal to present himself at her chamber. She had pressing cash matters to discuss with him.

First, she thought, let's have a look at that familiar of the Witch of Eye, Eleanor 'Sausage Fingers', ja. She opened a jewel box and lifted up a pendant with a walnut-sized brilliant. It shimmered in the candle-light. A beauty that was delivered by that cunning minx, Agnes, along with copies of the Duke's military accounts, both secret and official. There was a list of Captain Dark's murders, letters to and from the Witch, and copies of letters from Eleanor to Isabelle, sometimes signed by Eleanor herself, or initialled by her commissary clerk. Significantly, there were no letters from Isabelle to Eleanor.

Agnes, Isabelle thought, must be in the pay of every faction at court. Well, why not, so was she when she was broke. Yes, she decided, gazing at the sparkling stone, what to do about the Duke this time? She re-read the letters. What fools, all signed and dated. Eleanor offered still more gifts for an annulment, but now promised the aid of The Dark One. Witchcraft. What stupidity. She could be burned at the stake. She should stick to the point – and pay hard cash. As for vainglorious Humphrey, his actions were as predictable as a clown's. Yes, squeeze every penny out of the *godons* now, before the tide of war turned, as those pointless abattoirs always did.

But her tastes were costing her fortune after fortune. Henry would pay up this time as he had paid up before. The marriage was essential. Without it, Henry's claim to the French throne was legally untenable. He had to ensure his grip on the two crowns, plan his crusade, strip France of its wealth to pay for it, and pray that Catherine would present him with an heir within nine months. He would agree to Isabelle's terms. And Isabelle had an inkling of his real feelings for Catherine, too.

The Majordomo ushered the Cardinal into the salon. The Cardinal, surprisingly, looked perky and relaxed. Isabelle gave him a quick peck. They had much more important business to transact.

'I have just received a communication directly from the Papal Court at Avignon,' he said, piously making the sign of the cross. 'From Pope Benedict's principal secretary himself. Here, my dear one.'

'Thank you, Piero, love. Perfect.' She settled down to read the latest news from the Holy City.

Her pet Cardinal was in the business of absolution. He peddled salvation like selling ribbons from a tray. He was licensed to sell absolution for any sin, however bizarre, from gluttony to blasphemy, to buggery with mules. He could annul vows of chastity, remit penances for theft, incest, murder. He could legitimise children and allow cousins to marry (on a sliding scale depending on propinquity). He could also raise money for funerals, births, deaths and holy crusades, all for hard cash – most of which went into his own pocket.

Piero's clothes of the day revealed nothing of his clerical state. He was dressed in the height of fashion – a checkerboard short coat with a jewelled girdle and tight multi-coloured hose, like any young lover. He had on the modish slashed boots, with the tips curved back and attached below the knee. Piero ignored the tonsure and wore his hair shoulder length. With his wrinkled face, scrawny neck and spotted hands, he was a parody of both old age and youth. But in Isabelle's Court of Good Sheperds, no one noticed. The grotesque was the norm.

Isabelle looked up from the letter, smiling. Just what she had requested. Incredibly, she felt the itch mounting. She wondered if Piero could manage a bit.

'Well done, Piero, darling,' she said, giving him a long moist kiss. She reached down, stroking his codpiece. The Cardinal wriggled his hose to his knees, revealing a surprisingly solid erection. He solemnly made the sign of the cross over his swollen prick. Humans, thought Isabelle, you can't beat them, and that includes me.

She lowered her mouth onto his throbbing, gluttonous member. Sweet reward for an annulment, she thought, and it costs nothing.

13

Charles VI made one of his miraculous one-day recoveries. He knew who he was, and had already begun assuming some of the lighter duties of his exalted state. He had called in his old confidantes, including Huguet de Guisay. Huguet's astrological talents had blossomed. He now deflowered children of both sexes before telling their horoscope. Yvaine, the satanist, had also branched out. He had developed a healthy loathing for the masses, especially his servants, whom he called, Dog One, Dog Two, Dog Three, and so on. He rode them on their hands and knees, raking them with his spurs, yelling,

'Bark dog, bark!'

At his funeral a few days later, his servants followed his coffin, themselves yelling,

'Bark, dog, bark!'

Yvaine and Huguet had brought in crowds of hangers on and parasites. In the flickering rushlight of the main hall, they now gathered round Charles's makeshift throne, ingratiating themselves with their still half-mad monarch. Charles had little recollection of Huguet or Yvaine, except that they were pleasingly familiar. Huguet made a special fuss over the Dauphin. Just as well to keep in with the Court, he thought, even if the heir is a drivelling idiot and a bastard to boot. They were preparing special 'funs' for their Seigneur, which the Dauphin had devised. He would show the tormenting Isabelle that he could have just as much 'funs' as she.

Huguet and Yvaine had decided, at the Dauphin's insistence, to recreate one of their most famous early spectacles, the *Bal des Ardents* with the King himself leading the fake cannibals. The courtiers were now formed into a wide circle, with a space in the middle for the dancers. While the audience waited, Charles, Huguet and Yvaine donned their make up and costumes. First, they were sewn into skin-tight costumes of leopard skins, then tarred and feathered, their faces blackened. To complete their transformation into authentic savages, they were armed with leather shields and short spears. They were ready now, waiting in the wings like any nervous actors. The King's eyes gleamed with delight. He hadn't had so much fun since he could remember. And the terrible agony in the bower had faded. What had really happened there, he wondered? Or anywhere else come to that?

The Dauphin banged the floor three times with his staff, signalling for the Dance to begin.

Charles, Yvaine and Huguet rushed into the main hall, leaping grotesquely, stamping their naked feet, howling like baboons. The assembled hangers on bellowed along with them. The trio now danced in circles like demented dervishes. No doubt, the 'fun' was succeeding beyond their wildest dreams. Just like the old days, thought Huguet, yelling and stamping in time with his ecstatic monarch.

Then it happened. The revelry attracted late gate-crashers and at the height of the dance, a group of drunken guests burst in, carrying torches. A shower of sparks flew up with the draft. They settled in clusters on the three cannibals. In an instant they were transformed into human torches. The King was, fortunately, immediately seized by his medical attendants and plunged into a vat of wine. He suffered only minor burns. For Huguet and Yvaine there was no escape. Their sewed on costumes were too tight. The King's two friends died in agony the next morning.

The King was carried to his chamber and cut out of his charred costume before being put to bed with a glass of mulled wine. He had light burns on his hands. Five minutes later, he had forgotten the incident. The Dauphin administered the usual tincture of poppy and his father slept peacefully all night.

News of the disaster broke with the announcement of the deaths of Huguet and Yvaine. Isabelle pounced on the disaster like a lynx. At once she publicly condemned the irresponsible Dauphin. Hadn't he reduced the royal court to scandal and outrage again? She accused him of deliberately trying to destroy his father to get to the throne. She blamed him for aggravating her husband's malady, thus exonerating herself. She played on the mob's sympathies by expressing heartfelt thanks that God had spared their 'Well Beloved'. She prayed that His Majesty would be well enough to attend the signing ceremony as well as the wedding, but was certain that his condition would prevent it.

Thoroughly cast down and feeling his enemies gathering around him, especially his gloating, devilish mother, the Dauphin slunk out of Honnecourt at dawn with a few of his last, subdued hangers on. He made his way to Paris where he set up court in the deserted, half-ruined Palais de St Pol, although he hated the memory of his miserable childhood there. There he sat in the small draughty dining room in front of a guttering fire, served by one half-blind servant of seventy. He was penniless and alone for the last 'courtiers' had disappeared as soon as they had seen their apartments.

Charles shivered and clenched his fists. How had the whore done it again? Was there no end to her tortures? I'll make her pay one day, he swore for the hundredth time, remembering his late little victory. But when he began listing his enemies, he gave up.

'I am the rightful heir,' he exclaimed out loud, sobbing in an agony of doubt. The wind whistled through the paper panes of the window and the fire went out. The Dauphin of France wiped his nose on his sleeve.

85

His lone servant took his cloak and bundle, crept out of the hall, and walked down the road to the warm auberge there, ironically named The Happy Shepherdess.

14

Humphrey stood blinking in the light of the flaming torches in the antechamber of the great hall of Beaurevoir. He was enraged at being summoned so early from the warmth of his mistress's arms. He'd not even had time to don one of his wigs. He squirmed every time Henry glanced at his gleaming pate. Hell, he thought, it's nearly dawn. Why had Henry kept him waiting? Something about the mad King. He dismissed the thought. He had himself to think about.

Humphrey glanced at his royal brother's impassive face. What unpleasantness had Henry in store for him now? He'd been pacing about for over an hour as his brother silently signed and sealed piles of documents. Secretaries came and went, laying out copies of the Treaties on the main table of the great hall. At every attempt at conversation, Henry just looked down his nose and 'shushed' him, as if he was a child. For Humphrey, this merely confirmed his brother's unfitness for the English crown, for he was now as much a tyrant as any Turkish Sultan. He looked covertly at him again. Henry appeared unfatigued. He'd been in a recent fight, Humphrey knew, but he was freshly shaved.

'So you think Captain Owen wears padded codpieces?'

Humphrey's mouth dropped open. The words, let alone the question they contained, fell like a loud clang in the silence. How in the hell did Henry know?

'Just a joke,' he muttered. Henry laid an arrow on the table.

'At the signing, we will toast this.'

'What? Well, if you say so, Henry.'

'Sire, if you please. For our subjects.'

'Yes... Sire.' Typical tyranny! Henry picked up the arrow. He pointed at the notched, feathered, end.

'You see the notch here, Captain Gam's idea, to make the notch too narrow for the thicker French bow strings, so they couldn't re-use the arrows fired at them. So Captain Gam developed a new thinner string for our bows, but we could re-use all the arrows fired at us. Hence we never ran out of arrows. The French did. The 'V' shaped notch here, we commemorate with this sign.'

Henry held up two fingers, palm inward, in a 'V' sign and continued.

'Means – damn you! Up your arse! Troops love it. Use it all the time now. Reminds them of victory. My victory.'

What in the hell was this leading up to, thought Humphrey? But Henry broke the silence with a snappy question of his own.

'We do present a united front, don't we?'

'Yes, I mean . . . '

'Isabelle, Burgundy . . . '

'Of course, Henry . . . '

' . . . Our Yorkist cousins . . . '

'I'll have their guts for garters!'

'And us, the royal brothers?'

'Don't know about the others. But you have my word – to the death.'

'What about this plot to murder my . . . our late father?'

So that was it.

'They say it was I who planned it,' snapped Henry and Humphrey hastily answered.

'That's our uncle of Winchester, he'd say anything . . . '

'But Winchester is supposed to be part of the plot.'

'The assassin was arrested . . . ' blustered Humphrey, his heart knocking against his ribs.

'He was thrown into the Thames before my agents could

interrogate him.'

'That was not my fault.'

'His throat cut by a certain Captain Dark.' Humphrey was by now sweating freely.

'Nothing to do with me.'

'Then see to it that this rumour is knocked on the head forthwith.'

'You have my word, Henry.'

'And that includes Captain Dark.' Humphrey blinked. 'Did you hear?'

'Yes . . . right . . . as you say.'

Humphrey bowed, giving an inward sigh of relief. The plot had indeed been engineered by himself. But a guard dog had disturbed the hired assassin as he crept through the gardens towards the King's bedchamber. The alarm was given. Captain Dark had killed the assassin and escaped, just in time. Bless Captain Dark! As for the target, his own father, Humphrey saw both his brother and his father as evil influences destructive of the throne, a curse on the nation. He felt no conscience. It was he, Humphrey, whom God had selected to lead the English people back to their rightful place in the sun, and to smash all England's enemies, from Yorkists to Dauphinists. Humphrey knew his position in the Pantheon of Heroes. Not now perhaps. But soon. He passed a hand over his damp scalp. Henry smiled. Damn! His day would come!

'So, let's have a look,' Henry put down the arrow. 'When we salute this arrow, we salute Captain Gam. Clear? Captain Tudor is hereby confirmed in his offices, whether he pads his codpieces or not. We salute him for saving my life. Our uncle of Winchester is also confirmed in his titles and offices. We salute him too. And if I hear again of any word against the Welsh or against our uncle, before or after this treaty, or of any trumped up conspiracy, which might get in my way on the road to Jerusalem, I will strip you of every office, of every piece of booty in your cellars, and post you back to govern your London rabble from the stews.'

For a second Humphrey comforted himself with the image of a steel needle being thrust into his brother's brain.

'Now, about Eleanor.'

'What about Eleanor?' Humphrey bridled.

'You are still married to Jacqueline of Hainault, brother.'

'In name only.'

'Eleanor is not to be present at any of the ceremonies.'

'I must object.'

'No, you mustn't. Now, Humphrey,' Henry put an arm around his brother. Humphrey stiffened but dared not shake him off. What further humiliation was coming now?

'To show our public solidarity, I am appointing you Chief Overseer of the Treaty, the wedding at Troyes, and the Coronation ceremonies in Paris and London.'

Humphrey paused in astonishment. Then his chest swelled up. So it was this recognition and honour that Henry had really been leading up to. It had all been a sort of stupid test.

'Chief Overseer,' he repeated.

'It puts you at the centre of things . . . '

'I understand.'

' . . . So I'm afraid Eleanor . . . '

' . . . Of course, Henry, I see.' Yes, the eyes of Europe would be on him. A kind of Emperor after all. He would have his pedestal. He glowed in anticipation.

'Here are the schedules.' He gave Humphrey a thick wad of papers. 'Go to it, brother.'

'Sire, a great honour.' Humphrey bowed himself out, his earlier mortifications lost in a cloud of self glory.

The glittering, empty baubles of authority, thought Henry. How people fall for them. All is vanity. His crusade would show that there was more to this world than vanity and power.

He picked up the arrow. Yes, he decided on a rare impulse,

when his day came, he would be buried with this arrow.

15

An hour later, another group stood before Henry in the ante-room. He had given strict orders that they were not to be interrupted. He was reviewing the latest intelligence with Owen, Agnes, Hopcyn and King Leper. King Leper's face was muffled in his hood.

'Mustn't cause offence,' he explained to Owen, with a laugh.

'Now this Dance of the Cannibals,' Henry was saying. 'Never heard of such madness. Reports still coming in. King survived. Leper, be on call for all messages. But it will not affect the ceremonies today in any way.'

Henry began telling Owen about his 'little skirmish' on his journey through the scorched countryside.

'We flayed the flayers, then torched them.' He paused. 'War without fire is like sausage without mustard.'

They nodded. The royal *bon mot* was well known but Hopcyn shifted uneasily. What had death to do with mustard, he thought, or sausages? Images should be left to poets, and fighting to warriors. Agnes raised her eyebrows warningly. Hopcyn's attention returned to Henry.

Under all the camaraderie, Hopcyn knew that Henry was as ruthless as any *ecorcheur*. Henry sensed his feelings.

'If you live next door to a graveyard, you can't feel sorry for everyone.' Not bad, thought Hopcyn, nodding diplomatically as he had been instructed to do by Agnes. But where was Jesus meek and mild in all this? He stared with mounting intensity into Henry's eyes, an old tactic which always worked. Henry looked at the two different eyes, then blinked and looked away.

The multi-coloured gaze put him off. Most unnatural. Agnes glared at Hopcyn.

'Further pacifications are overdue. Our troops are ready.' Henry insisted before turning to King Leper. 'My brothers, King Leper?'

'Humphrey and Clarence mainly, Sire,' replied the leper in his hoarse voice. 'Not only in the court here, as reported, but on their estates in England now. In the towns the Yorkists are also out in force, and their retainers are openly wearing the white and red roses. If my Lord Beaufort of Winchester's troops hadn't intervened . . . '

'What a waste of resources!' said Henry, banging his fist on the table.

' . . . And my Lord Bedford sent troops too.'

'Good for brother Bedford,' said Henry. 'He understands. If I'm ever killed, he will be Regent. Now to this business at the French court last night. A scene out of hell. A punishment. God be thanked, the Dauphin's disappeared. Queen Isabelle of course gloried in the carnage. Princess Catherine must be protected from their madness. So Charles still insists on being present?'

'Dressed and ready in the tennis court. Remembers nothing, Sire. Quite calm, though he doesn't know where he is. But what he'll do if he sees Queen Isabelle . . . '

'Hopcyn, have your harp ready. And my Lady of the Bedchamber, Agnes, stay close to the Princess Catherine at all times. She has become . . . she must not be hurt.'

Abruptly, he turned to the papers on the table.

'These copies, again well done, Lady Agnes. Isabelle's accounts, most useful. And the other lady? Signed. Excellent. More if you can get them. But be careful. So Piero's in her pay as well as her bed.' Henry came to another of his *bon mots*. 'When dealing with holy orders, remember one thing – plunder is sacred.' Hopcyn nodded emphatically. This was right.

'Hopcyn, the Dauphinists call us *godons*. What does that mean?'

'*Godons* Sire, means God damns,' replied Hopcyn. 'The English are named after their favourite oath.'

'Really? We are not a nation of blasphemers.'

'Your Crusade to Jerusalem proves that, Sire.'

Henry nodded approvingly. Agnes smiled. Her bard was doing well today.

'Now what about this Deschamps, Hopcyn. Look what he's saying about us English.'

'A mere poet, Sire, a wart hog embittered by his own ugliness.'

'I should arrest him for treason.'

'Why not just let him sing his silly songs, Sire?'

'What!? Why?'

'Because, Sire, they are timely reminders of French defeat.' Hopcyn made the 'V' sign.

'I see,' agreed Henry. 'Good, Hopcyn.'

'The people will approve of your mercy, too, Sire.'

'So be it. Let him sing on – for the time being.'

Hopcyn relaxed. He had got wicked old Eustace off the hook again.

'Now, Captain Owen, I am confirming you as Captain of my personal bodyguard, and as my Clerk of the Queen's Wardrobe.'

'I am honoured indeed, Sire, but I was hoping for a fighting command.'

'With you here I feel Princess Catherine is in safe hands. We'll see about a command later. Here are copies of the arrangements for the wedding and coronations. Be sure to keep a close eye on Duke Humphrey. He will undoubtedly try to change the schedules. Let me know if he does. And on no account is that "turnip top" to be near any part of this.' They all smiled at Henry's use of the nick name.

94

'To the last matter now, King Leper, the Dauphin's legitimacy. Your report.' King Leper took out a paper from his cloak. He read without lifting his head.

'The Dauphin, Charles, was born on February 22nd, 1403. Therefore he must have been conceived towards the middle of the month of the preceding May. Now, we know that his father had a period of insanity just before Whitsuntide on May 14th, although before that time he appeared to be in good health. The attack of madness happened on May 12th or 13th and we know it lasted until the middle of June. Also, Sire, it is fair to add that Isabelle spent the whole of May in their Palace of St Pol in Paris. We know that she had her usual string of lovers in the first two weeks. Because of the King's madness, she was left free for the rest of the month. But she may have had relations with him nevertheless – a matter of proximity.' He paused. 'Just an outside chance . . . '

' . . . But still a chance.' Henry was insistent.

'Yes, Sire.'

'That's the only copy of the report?'

'Yes, Sire.'

'Burn it.' King Leper lit it from one of the wall torches.

'Bastard or not, this isn't the end of it. Thanks King Leper. And all of you, watch out for the poor King. Right, you can go, by the back door. My thanks.'

16

The grandees of the Triple Alliance from England, France and Burgundy were now gathering. Henry's victories and diplomacy had brought them together but, wondered the Duke of Bedford as he glumly surveyed the groups, would they stay together – including his own family? The elusive Yorkists were always breathing down their necks whenever there were reverses. His beak of a nose sniffed the air, yes – trouble. And news of the deaths at the *Bal des Ardents* had dampened everyone's spirits.

Humphrey had even managed to find a faded throne which he had placed at the head of the table. With his accustomed pomposity, he now welcomed the guests into the hall, glorying in his hollow prominence and his best wig. His manner prompted more ridicule than hostility, as Henry had calculated. Humphrey still worried that he had not yet told Eleanor of her real role in the proceedings, or rather, her lack of any role. But she would see reason, now he was so firmly back in the saddle. Chief Overseer!

The secretaries entered with large maps of France spread tight over wide frames, which they set up behind Henry's chair. The details were well known but everyone awaited Henry's final endorsement. A glance at the map revived Humphrey's bile against his brothers.

The divisions of the new English empire in France were clearly marked in red. England now possessed direct rule of over one third of the territory of France including Normandy, which Henry had once called 'the milch cow of the

Lancastrians', Acquitaine, Anjou, Touraine, Poitou, Maine and Ponthieu. The Duke of Burgundy had appropriated huge swathes of northern and eastern France. These lands, he felt, still only partially revenged him for his father's death. The Dauphin and Charles, God be blessed, were reduced to a patchwork of lands around Paris surrounded by hostile areas. The main royal support was in the south and west, well away from the capital and the real seat of power. France lay at the feet of its wolfish victors, and it was Henry alone who was now the sole dispenser of France's destiny. But recently, everyone had noticed, he had begun to lord it over the French with unrestrained arrogance. Without Bedford's wiser counsel, the populace might well have risen in universal revolt.

Normandy was a model of how the spoils had been divided. This enormous Dukedom was one of Humphrey's main bones of contention. The governorship of Normandy should have been his. Henry had set about the 'pacification' of this rich, ancient province with his usual efficiency. The French nobility had been dispossessed wholesale, and their estates redistributed. Clarence, for example, had been granted three Viscountancies, six estates and three counties. Even the fabulously wealthy Warwick had been made Count of Aumale, one of the richest pickings. Humphrey raged with envy. Bedford had been granted plums too, the Dukedoms of Alencon and Anjou. He was also Count of Mortain, Count of Beaumont and many more.

It was Salisbury who had been appointed Lord Governor of Normandy. Humphrey groaned, for Salisbury wasn't even a member of the royal family. And it was Salisbury who appointed all the main officers of state in Normandy, the Treasurers, the Lords High Admirals, the ten Governors and Seneschals, all handed to Englishmen, of course. But Humphrey had received nothing. Another insult. He looked from Burgundy to Salisbury. He hoped their little quarrel would again get out of hand.

To recoup his investment in men and material, he, the King's own brother, had been reduced with his Captains to employ the methods of brigands and freebooters. They had been caused to use extortion, blackmail, 'indemnities' for safe conducts, protection rackets and kidnap and ransom. They had clipped the coinage and watered the wine, withheld pay, and even employed petty larceny. He had even raided his royal brothers' war booty.

'Slim pickings,' he fumed impotently. And now Henry was squeezing huge concessions for himself out of Isabelle right under their noses.

'Ignore me again at your peril!' he thought. Humphrey, although still basking in his new 'promotion', was by now writhing anew in the grudges prompted by the appearance of the map.

The aristocratic Warwick had been appointed to watch over the warring brothers. Warwick regarded their vulgar brawls with disdain. As a Beauchamp of immense inherited wealth, he was richer than anyone present except, perhaps, the king himself. He was therefore neutral, uninterested in self-aggrandisement. Everyone recognised and respected this. As the King's watchdog, he had special powers of arrest. The brothers knew he would have no hesitation in using them.

Henry was still closeted with Isabelle. No one doubted Henry would come to a 'diplomatic settlement', the polite term for haggling over cash. But everyone was impatient for the pair of royal rag-pickers to hurry it up.

The various factions shifted uneasily as they awaited the entrance of King Henry. The accord, fragile at the best of times, was stretched to breaking point. Bedford knew the ceremony had got off to an exceptionally bad start. There had already been two disputes of a potentially disastrous kind.

First there had been the quarrel over the Earl of Salisbury's daughter, Anne, an acknowledged court beauty. One of the

Duke of Burgundy's main brags was that he had available at any given moment, thirty-two mistresses of noble birth. But due to Henry's abrupt descent on Troyes, he now had none. When he had first met Anne in the hallway, he promptly propositioned her, roundly inviting her upstairs for 'a quick romp'. Bad as this was, it had been said in the hearing of the fiery Earl himself, her father. The Earl had at once, in accordance with chivalric practice, called out the flabbergasted Burgundy. Bedford and Warwick had managed to wring an apology out of Burgundy, who as mulish and self-righteous as any of the royal brothers, now glowered defiantly at the Salisbury faction. Lady Anne had been hurried off to one of the upstairs chambers and would take no further part in the ceremonies, thus further infuriating the Earl for he had given his favourite daughter his word that she would be there.

Then there was the matter of the Duke of Clarence. He was piqued when he heard his younger brother would be master of ceremonies, and at once arranged to arrive last, still wearing his fighting armour. When Humphrey remonstrated, he had ignored him. When he had indicated Clarence's assigned seat, Clarence simply walked off. Another toad to swallow, fumed Humphrey. Wish I had my London lads here, my St George crusaders. They'd soon have the Gloucester crest of talons streaming from every flagpole.

The Duke of Clarence was the physical replica of the King, but without either his intelligence or strength of character. His chief boast was that he had never backed out of a fight, whatever the odds. This meant his companies suffered the highest casualty rate in the army. Henry constantly upraided Clarence for this 'wastage', but Clarence took no notice for, as he said, he had never shied away from a royal fight either – though he had lost nearly every battle. This thick-headed loser was now about to confront Humphrey, the vainglorious.

But Clarence knew who was responsible for the recent

rumours of conspiracy and murder. He also knew where large portions of the war booty ended up, exactly how the paymaster's wagons got 'lost', and other shameful extortions. It was dangerous knowledge. And above all he loathed the witch-like Eleanor, and made it known at every opportunity.

As Humphrey insistently directed Clarence to his place, Clarence, who was by now irritated beyond measure, declared in a loud voice so the whole hall could hear,

'Not now, me lovely. Betimes later!' And he blew Humphrey a kiss.

At this seemingly quite gratuitous mockery, Humphrey lost all control and went for his brother. Warwick, who had been closely watching the developing quarrel, with the speed of rapier stepped between the two antagonists. He coolly pushed them apart, as he had so often done before. The brothers moved off reluctantly for no one opposed the King's personal Constable, especially when he had a dagger in his hands.

A loud rustle of unease again passed through the hall. Was the Peace Treaty to open with a knife fight between two of the royal signatories? And where was the man who could settle it all in seconds with a few words of command? Even Bedford's powerful presence did little to alleviate the situation. The tension continued to mount.

It was at this point that the prudent Bedford committed an inadvertent error. He had politely requested Humphrey to remove his hat.

'After all, he explained, 'one always goes uncovered before the sovereign, even if he happens to be one's brother.' Humphrey at once interpreted this as a deliberate slight on his baldness, calculated to add further insult to injury. He strutted around checking things for the umpteenth time, seething and hatless, with his wig askew. For a second, in his mind's eye, he had a fleeting glimpse of a whole row of pierced heads. Yes, he knew his mission. Let them do their worst, his day would come.

And there was still Captain Dark as a last resort.

The groups stiffened every time there was an unwonted noise. Burgundy looked pointedly at the floor and scuffed his shoes. The startled onlookers looked up, as he intended. He was the centre of attention again. Burgundy peered with approval at the leather coverings under his feet, for it was precisely the kind of pointless luxury he revelled in. Obviously Queen Isabelle's work. Queen Isabelle? He paused. If not the stupid virgin, he thought, then why not the old whore? Holy Henry and his greedy brothers, and that stupid pious Earl. That would set the cat among the pigeons. He, Burgundy, rutting with Isabelle. Perfect. How in hell was he to know whose daughter the wench was anyway? She should have been honoured by his proposals, like the thirty-two others. He regretted his apology and stared sulkily at Salisbury, who icily ignored him.

The French faction was represented by three of the mad King's cronies, Michel and Gilbert de Senneville, and Antoine de Mornay, minor squires with reputations for debt and profligacy. Their main claim to fame was that they had been too drunk to escape with the rest of courtiers. After the King had been rescued and the Dauphin had slunk away, Isabelle had sent in her retainers. They had dragged these three from the blackened ruins. To humiliate the French even further, Isabelle had declared them the official delegates of the French court and had them haled off to her great hall under guard. She posted troopers at the main entrance with orders to throw the three back into the hall should they make any effort to escape. Still half drunk, they dozed on benches set against the wall, too fuddled to think and still stinking of burned tar and sour wine. In their clear moments they were totally subdued by their surroundings and the grandees gathered there. Gilbert held his stomach and groaned. Michel snored softly. Antoine was burning up with hangover thirst. Bedford regarded these dregs of ancient nobility with pity. How had they sunk so low? He still loved and respected *la belle France*, but as long as Isabelle held the upper hand and the King was deranged, the nation had little chance of recovering. Bedford vowed to continue helping the common folk of France.

The three, as if suddenly sensing the increasingly hostile atmosphere, struggled to sit up. They looked around blearily. They were studiously ignored. They still had no idea where their King was or what exactly they had to sign. The only thing they understood was that they were there on Queen Isabelle's orders, and that to disobey her was extremely dangerous. Their Dauphin had fled like a frightened rabbit. Their King was mad. What could they do?

17

Not far from the great hall, in the interior tennis court, Catherine, Agnes, Hopcyn and Owen were in attendance on Charles VI, King of the French.

'Mother's keeping the whole world waiting, as usual,' Catherine whispered to Agnes. The presence of her three closest attendants reassured her. She glanced at Owen thankfully. She felt safer when he was close.

Charles wondered around the chamber, blinking vacantly, unnaturally calm. Miraculously, he had suffered no serious burns, but wore bandages around his slightly scorched hands. From time to time he smiled at his daughter, and his eyes lit up whenever he spied Hopcyn's harp. He had no recollection of the previous night. His mind guttered like a fading candle. He knew there was to be a wedding ceremony. That was why he was here, to give away his lovely daughter. It was his duty. He would do it, however painful it was to say goodbye to a loved one. He smiled affectionately at her as she took her Well Beloved's arm for another turn around the court.

18

Henry and Isabelle were standing over the coffers on the table in Henry's anteroom. Guards had been placed at the entrances.

This is really just bargaining between two ex-jailbirds, however royal, thought Isabelle.

She had just learned of the presence of her husband, and cursed the blaze which seemed to have temporarily restored his sanity. Damn dancing cannibals! But her own delegates were in place. They alone would act as the French signatories. Charles, though monarch, had no place in the proceedings.

Henry and Isabelle were now going over the veritable heart of the Treaty, the finances.

'No,' said Isabelle, 'pay this and pay that. Does such beauty need a dowry, ja?'

'Yes,' said Henry. 'Half a million in gold crowns, at least. There are the expenses of the two coronations to consider as well.'

'One for the winners in Westminster,' replied Isabelle with a wicked grin, 'and one for the losers in Paris, ja?'

'One for my people, one for Catherine's.'

'Nothing could be fairer, my son. But all her hereditary revenues on top of this?' asked Isabelle looking at Henry's list. 'Outrageous.' Henry looked loftily down his nose.

'She will lack for nothing,' he said.

'You will make her the poorest Queen in Europe. She has had enough of poverty and unhappiness.'

'All your debts will of course be honoured.'

'All of them?' she asked suspiciously.

'As I promised.'

'To be paid directly in gold?'

'These two chests here are ready for your collection, dear mother-in-law,' said Henry lifting the lids. They were filled to the brim with gold crowns. Isabelle picked up a handful. She dropped one onto the table. It rang true.

'Do you want to count them?'

'Of course. But later. Now, Catherine's income from the royal estates. Hereditary, for the Queens of France alone. Can't be touched. Forty thousand golden Louis per annum. You confirm this?'

'You promised to disown the Dauphin.'

'You confirm it? Forty thousand?'

'Where is your official statement?'

'Here.' Isabelle handed Henry her prepared statement rejecting the legitimacy of her only surviving son. '

'Excellent. This of course will be incorporated into the Treaty.'

'Now, the forty thousand Louis?'

'In instalments, over ten years.'

'Five years. Instalments in advance. Lump sums.'

Henry was not surprised. But lump sums. How he hated parting with those. He looked regretfully at the brimming chests.

'Catherine would be grateful, Henry. I'll tell her you did it for her.'

Henry knew this was bait. Dammit, he thought, she knows I've fallen for her daughter. Costing me already. Better the other way – no emotion, no blackmail. But he found again that he couldn't refuse Catherine, just as the old whore had anticipated. Well, so be it.

'Done then. You will receive the first instalment in two weeks.'

'Two days.'

'I never break my word.' Isabelle smiled sweetly and said with a touch of sarcasm,

'That's because you never give it. Ja?' Henry shrugged.

'Two days then. You have fallen in love with gold, Isabelle.'

'With you as my son-in-law, I can see my reputation is intact,' Isabelle smiled. 'Did you really cut off your mother's allowance to pay off some of my debts last time?'

'With her agreement, of course.'

'Of course,' Isabelle was all smiles again. 'A sacrifice your new mother here really understands.'

Henry hurried on to the next point.

'Now your crown of France, if you please, Madam.'

Isabelle opened a leather box stamped with the royal arms of France. She lifted out an object wrapped in purple silk. She pulled back the folds, revealing a magnificent arched crown with a circlet of *fleur-de-lis*, all in pure gold, set with pearls and diamonds. Henry tried not to appear enraptured. He already had a Florentine banker who would pay a king's ransom for such a bauble.

'Your own coronation crown, wasn't it?' asked Henry.

'It no longer fits anyone in the house.'

'How much?'

'Twenty thousand crowns, in gold.'

Henry couldn't take his eyes off it.

'Done,' he said too quickly.

'Shit,' thought Isabelle, 'he's got a buyer already. Asked too low.'

But still, she had got what she wanted, her debts cleared, guarantees of her daughter's income, and a ton of freshly minted gold in her treasury.

The secret agreement was signed and sealed, a copy for each. But with the accidents of time and tide, both knew that the agreement wasn't worth the parchment it was written on. It would serve for now, however. They had both got what they wanted. And Henry knew that the crown was an unexpected bonus.

'And now,' said Henry handing Isabelle her copy, 'let's see what we can do about the Dauphin.'

'My pleasure,' said Isabelle. Her eyes glittered savagely. The *Bal des Ardents* had been a gift, but her renunciation would be a blessing. Such funs.

19

As Isabelle and Henry entered, a palpable feeling of relief swept through the hall. A murmur of expectation arose. In unison, the assembled grandees stood and bowed. Even the French delegates swayed briefly to their feet before collapsing again. One will now overrode all others – Henry's. Jealousies became muted and hostilities momentarily faded as a seeming unity was imposed. Together, the three brothers conducted Henry and Isabelle to the raised thrones at the head of the table. Before the throne lay a solitary arrow.

Isabelle was to sit at Henry's right hand. Looking at her future son-in-law, all she could see was an abacus, a ruthless prig, a greedy swine and, worst of all, a God lover. How they all bow and scrape to him, the flunkies! Henry was one of the very few men she had never had a sexual thought about.

At the same time, Isabelle had instantly become the object of intense scrutiny. The lecherous Burgundy was enjoying her in a variety of fantasies. Even young Clarence felt stirrings of lust. The French delegates gaped at the 'the Greatest Whore in Christendom', so long the deadliest enemy of their sick master. Isabelle looked around. She couldn't see her crazed husband. She nodded at the French delegates, who quailed. Bedford and Salisbury looked warily at her. She responded to the universal stares with a beaming, fleshy smile.

Unannounced, the main door opened again. The mad King and his group entered in a rush with the bewildered King leading, followed by Agnes, Owen and, last of all, his lovely pale-faced daughter. As the whole room turned towards him, the King stopped dead. Everyone had heard of the deadly *Bal des Ardents*. How had the lunatic escaped? Only his hands were lightly bandaged. The King was trying to focus. He clearly had no idea where he was. He peered at Henry.

'Who is that man at the head of the table?' he asked.

'My husband to be, father, Henry of England.'

Charles pointed uncertainly at Isabelle. Everyone tensed.

'And that woman?'

'Never mind now, father. Here, sit down.' Catherine and her father sat side by side. Owen, Agnes and Hopcyn stood behind them.

Isabelle felt a faint twinge of disappointment that he had not recognized her. She had hoped her presence might liven things up. She looked at Humphrey, Bedford, Clarence, Warwick, Burgundy and their respective cattendants. Henry seemed to have them under control. She sniffed. But the atmosphere. Yes, there might be some fun yet. Burgundy was truculent, Bedford wary, Salisbury simmering, the French delegates drunk. But in Henry's presence, they all deferred.

Burgundy decided against a flirtation with Isabelle. She smelled of trouble and he had had enough for one day. Anyway, he was pleased with his pickings. The 'brigand' hadn't had it all his own way. Humphrey meanwhile wondered how much extra cash Isabelle had squeezed out of Henry. She looked too satisfied. With a quick glance at the map, Isabelle was calculating Henry's revenues from his new possessions. Yes, she decided, she had made a good bargain.

The various representatives took their assigned seats. The secretaries hurried into position, helping the two French signatories, Michel and Gilbert, to sit. Antoine lay like a log on the bench. Nothing could stir him from his oblivion. The meeting settled down to business. Even Clarence took his assigned place quietly, though pointedly ignoring Humphrey. Bedford and Warwick watched every move. Henry had devised a plan in case of emergencies.

Henry signed the document and gestured to Bedford. The Duke read out the formal Treaty agreements. The contents were well known, the maps self-explanatory. The air was at once filled with the scratching of pens. Henry sat back and watched. It was all working out. It was done! Everyone relaxed. The secretaries collected the signed documents. Henry now motioned to Isabelle. The question of the legitimacy of the Dauphin's claim to the French throne would now be settled once and for all in favour of Henry's dynastic line.

Isabelle rose. In her thick Bavarian accent, she read out, with biting gusto, the article relating to her son, the 'so called' Dauphin. Her final revenge against the Capets had begun. Leaning forward, she directed each word at her wilting husband.

'We hereby recognise Henry of England as Regent and as the true heir of France. We confirm the union of Henry with our daughter Catherine and recognise their children as being the sole heirs and future monarchs of France. I hereby formally exclude the so-called Dauphin, Charles, from any inheritance on the grounds of his illegitimacy, his heinous and unforgivable crimes, including the recent near death of his own father, and of consorting with thieves and murderers. I confirm that no treaty or concord can ever be concluded with, or by, this so-called Dauphin!' The last part was delivered with a lifetime's accumulated venom. Catherine was stunned at first, like the others. But her mother had warned her. Owen glanced at Catherine. Her face was set. She would see this humiliation through with some remnant of dignity for her family. The room remained silent, waiting for a word from Henry. Hell, thought Isabelle, what else can I do to restore some enmity?

So, thought Bedford, the Queen of France has declared before the world, her daughter and her husband, that her son was a bastard, that she, the Queen, was an adulteress, and the

King a mere crazed cuckold, 'Well Beloved' or not. What a family! But, Bedford reflected ruefully, is ours any better? He nodded at Henry. The final stage now.

Henry raised his voice.

'To Agincourt! To Captain Davy Gam, who saved the day with this!' He held up the arrow.

Humphrey couldn't resist. Sneering at the inert French delegation, he raised his fingers in the two-fingered sign. A roar of triumph came from the English delegates. Bedford winced. Don't rub their noses in it, he thought. Burgundy shrugged. The gesture meant nothing to him. Mad these English, he thought, to be watched at all times. Cunning Albion. Henry frowned at Humphrey, who sat at once, subdued again. Well, he had shown his brother. He, too, could lead from the front.

Henry rapped the table. The murmur of conversation subsided.

'Beyond all this, we now declare to all present and to the world outside, that after this glorious Treaty and our coming marriage and coronation, we intend to set out, with the whole of Christendom . . . ' he paused for effect ' . . . to re-edify the walls of Jerusalem!'

The whole hall was stilled. This was beyond the understanding of them all – except Isabelle who thought, 'More honourable slaughter. Even God is not spared.'

A sudden scuffling came from the door. It burst open and a frightening figure with Hopcyn hanging round its neck, thrust its way into the hall, staggering drunk and shrieking curses. Henry, who had been half expecting a scene like this, motioned everyone back. Eustace swayed drunkenly in front of him. Again, he found himself confronted by the ugliest being he had ever beheld, the poet Eustace Deschamps. His face was that of a chimpanzee's, but covered with warts and sprouting bristles. His skin had the texture of beaten leather. His long arms trailed the floor behind him. Eustace, his chest covered with stinking,

111

congealed vomit, pointed accusingly at Henry.

'The war you wage is false, treacherous, damnable,' yelled Eustace. 'You are an accursed race, you *godons* here, opposed to all good reason, justice, and civilisation.'

'Sire, he is drunk,' soothed Hopcyn, trying to drag his friend away. The hulking Eustace shook him off like a puppy. In turn, Eustace now pointed at Humphrey, Clarence, Burgundy and Henry.

'You are proud, arrogant, crooked, hypocritical wolves without conscience. You gorge on human blood, ours and your own. You are the cannibals! You have the nature of vultures, you unchained demons, you destroyers of peace . . . '

'Perfect,' thought Isabelle, applauding loudly. Choice words. Worth every ducat. She'd toast Eustace tonight.

'He's drunk, Sire,' Hopcyn went on. 'He doesn't know what he's saying.'

' . . . This is the bloodiest, blackest day in the history of France!'

'Arrest the dog,' roared Humphrey. Everyone ignored him.

Hopcyn groaned inwardly. Surely this was the end for his friend. But he had laid the seeds of royal leniency all too well.

'Let him be,' Henry ordered. 'Deschamps, we have need of your songs.' Eustace stopped in mid-flow as Henry continued. 'So you may sing on. Go on. You understand?'

Eustace understood only too well. He had lost this round, although Hopcyn had saved his life again. A sigh of admiration went round the room. This was a wise and merciful monarch indeed.

Henry motioned to Bedford, the only *godon* who had been left out of Eustace's curses. Bedford poured out a glass of wine, and offered it to the poet.

'You may not like the Treaty, Eustace, but go in peace anyway,' he said quietly. 'You are the best balladeer in France.'

'Vive la France. A bas l'Angleterre!' toasted Eustace. 'You

may be King of England, Henry Five . . . ' he drained the glass and tossed it over his shoulder, ' . . . but I am the King of Ugliness. History will forgive me, because I can't help what I am. But never . . . Never will it forgive you, for you know exactly what you're doing.' Eustace staggered past the grandees, leaning on Hopcyn's shoulder. They recoiled in turn at the stench of the hideous, human ape. At the door, Eustace held up his hand in the new two fingered salute.

'Up your arses, death to you *godons*!' he shouted. And before anyone could react, he fell out of the door, dragged by Hopcyn. Everyone awaited Henry's order. Surely this meant a hanging. Unexpectedly, Henry slumped onto his knees.

'Let us all kneel . . . and pray for forgiveness.' Everyone followed suit.

Some wondered who was the madder, the French or the English king.

But before prayers could commence, there was a loud thump. Everyone looked up, startled. Antoine de Mornay had fallen off the bench onto the floor, still asleep. And Isabelle looked on with mounting rage a wide, wet stain was spreading from under Antoine. He was pissing himself – right on Isabelle's brand new leather floor.

'Not in my house!' She whooped in rage, and started forward to the snoring, peeing Antoine. At the sound of Isabelle's whoop, the mad king turned sharply. Some hellish memory had risen to the surface. He pointed a shaking finger at Isabelle. Everyone rose in alarm.

'Arrest that woman, we are betrayed!' he shouted hoarsely, and hurled himself down the table at her. Owen caught him a foot from Isabelle.

'You filthy shit,' Isabelle hissed, shaking her fist under his nose. The King stared back with black, mad, naked, hatred in his eyes. Catherine hurried to her father's rescue.

Henry had been prepared for this. At a nod, Bedford

113

signalled to the guards at the door. The doors were at once flung open and a band of heralds marched in. They stood in line, each giving a royal salute on horn, trumpet and sackbuts, drowning out all other sounds. Owen, as arranged, at once began leading out the King, Catherine and Agnes. The sound of galloping hoofs and carriages from the driveway filled the hall.

'To your carriages,' ordered Henry. 'Go with God's blessings.'

Warwick, Salisbury, Clarence, Humphrey and Burgundy with their retainers, obeyed to the letter, as if on a military manoeuvre. Isabelle departed, led by her Majordomo whom Henry had ordered to be ready. He had expected her to celebrate after her double triumph. The French delegates were lugged out, Antoine between two troopers. The secretaries cleared away the last of the papers and maps, as arranged. The room emptied in minutes. Only Bedford and Henry remained.

Another battle won. Henry gripped his brother's arm.

'Thank you, brother Johnny.'

'Anytime, brother Henry,' smiled Bedford.

Of all who had been in the hall, only between these two was there a perfect accord – except, reflected Bedford, this business about Jerusalem.. He'd have to have a serious talk with Henry about that. But now a quiet toast, between brothers.

A distant, unearthly howl rose from the chambers above. The King of France was baying at the moon. And it was only midday.

20

As the last carriage clattered away, two figures rose above a clipped hedge in the discreet shadows of the garden. At once they fell to clapping each other on the back, laughing uproariously. Miraculously, Hopcyn and Eustace showed no trace of their recent drunkenness.

Eustace reached down behind the bench and retrieved the bottles of wine they had left there before their dramatic entrance into the hall. It had been doubtful for a moment whether the friends would ever return to drink it. Hopcyn also retrieved copies of Eustace's spontaneous 'outburst', ready for distribution to friend and foe alike. The speech· had been penned, and the entrance rehearsed by the two, the night before. They had been moved by the same simple desire, to tell the truth of what they really felt.

'You think Isabelle rumbled us?'

'Watch the ducats roll in.' He brushed the fake puke off on his chest. 'My ugliness and your eyes did the trick. Santé!'

'Yours too!'

'The truth against the world . . . ' toasted Hopcyn.

' . . . in the eye of the light, in the face of the sun.'

'First rule of the bards. *Iechyd*, Eustace.'

'*Santé*, Hopcyn.' They emptied the first bottle in gulps.

'Treacherous!' Hopcyn made the 'V' sign.

'Arrogant!' Eustace followed suit.

'Damnable!'

'Accursed'

'Uncivilised!'

115

'The blackest . . . '

' . . . and the bloodiest day!'

'Today I have struck a blow for France!'

'Which will never be forgotten!'

'France groans under the shame of this marriage.'

'Catherine's light will shine longer than you think.'

Eustace didn't quite see what Hopcyn meant, but he would. He always did. They looked over the speech again.

'*Wolves without conscience*, well put, Hopcyn.'

'*Unchained demons*, well said, Eustace.' They drank deeply.

'A triad to celebrate.'

'Three Things that Dwindle Continuously, The Dark, The False and The Dead.'

'All present in there,' said Eustace. 'They divide the world up as if apples grew in halves, the ripe bits for them, the rotten bits for us.'

'While an apple, like the world, is one.'

'The henges say it. Pythagoras reveals it.'

The warp-spasm hovered behind Hopcyn's eyes.

'France will be delivered by flame.'

'A flame of hope?'

'A flame of faggots.' Eustace knew he would see it. He remained silent before saying.

'But the *godons* will stay in Cymru for . . . Don't like that! Another bottle!'

'*Iechyd*!'

'*Santé*! Another triad Hopcyn?'

'Three places where poetry is most found.'

'Yes?'

'Where it is most sought; where it is most loved; where there is the least of self.'

' . . . The least of self. Perfect.'

'From the Isle Abounding with Beauty, Eustace, namely, Cymru.'

'And what is it we do?'

'Our business as poets, Eustace, is to merge our little soul-light with the endless communion of spirits in eternity, through the medium of poetry.'

'I'll write a ballade to that.'

'But there is a sin-bound one abroad, Eustace, who spews the filth of Self over the land. But the Shining Ones needn't worry, for I have the beast in my sights. I think, Eustace, this wine is getting to me.'

'Me too. The Life of man, Hopcyn, is bound to death by way of reproduction, and is only relieved by a good story.'

'I'll write a triad to that.'

'Say it now.'

'Three Things that Grow Continuously, my friend: Light, Truth and Love.'

'*Santé*, Hopcyn!'

'*Iechyd*, Eustace! And may great Gwydion spare us, if just for a second, from the Three Grisly Mechanics of Life; Birth, Fornication and Death!'

The King of Ugliness and his wide-eyed comrade sang to the harp long past midnight, the triumph of the Opalescent Ones over the Dark Ones.

21

Isabelle was well pleased with her day. After victory over the victor of Agincourt, she had plenty to celebrate. She lay half clothed on thick horse blankets in the hay loft above the stable stalls. By her side lay Louis, her new 'lamb,' naked from top to toe, purring, grateful as ever, ready to try anything for his royal mistress. His family had been overjoyed with the gold. He was a hero. He smiled happily.

Isabelle enjoyed making love in the hay. Underneath she could hear the stallions snorting and kicking at the doors. They could smell the mares in the field outside. Their steam rose through the loose floor boards, stinking of dung and fresh urine. It excited Isabelle immeasurably. I love it all, she thought, the smell, the juices, the drippings, the comings. She shivered with pleasure. She stroked Louis' white breast tenderly, lowering her head over his aching crotch. He had to put in a top performance again, he knew, although in truth his weapon of love was sorely pressed, indeed practically raw.

A sudden rustling came from the rafters above.

'What was that, little one?'

Louis merely gazed adoringly at her through half-closed eyes. Look at me, he thought, riding in the hay with the Queen of France. Me, Louis the Lamb, family hero and stud. If they could only see me.

She raised her legs high, pulling him towards her. Just as he was about to thrust into her, the main doors of the stables burst open. There was a clattering of swords on scabbards, the clanking of armour and the rapid tread of heavy feet. A ladder thwacked against the loft ledge. They both sat up in alarm, scrabbling for their clothes. Men-at-arms with the royal *fleur-de-lis* of France, clambered up into the loft and moved in on them. Isabelle gave one shriek of rage before she was pinioned from behind, roughly gagged with her own petticoats, and bundled down the ladder. Louis, also gagged with his hands bound behind his back, was lowered down. He was given no time to cover himself, and his testicles swung and banged as he was pushed from soldier to soldier on the stable floor.

The stable was now lit with torches. In cloth of gold from shoulders to feet, a glittering coronet on his head, stood Charles VI of France, regal, icy calm, quite sane for once and with a savage look in his eye. A smithy with his anvil stood behind him.

'*In flagrante*,' he declared. 'Treason against the King's person. Again.' There was no doubt. The King was back, and with a vengeance. Isabelle tensed. This was dangerous. The King scarcely glanced at Louis. Even more dangerous.

'This time, madam, you will both pay.'

He motioned to the smithy. The smithy grabbed Isabelle's left hand and brutally tore off her wedding ring. Two troopers manacled her wrists with a long chain, looping it through an iron hook high on the wall.

'Now haul,' ordered the King. He nodded to the smithy. The smithy laid Isabelle's gold wedding ring on the anvil. Isabelle's arms rose higher and higher until she was on tip-toe, her breasts exposed and her furry, gold pubic patch gleaming in the torchlight. The smithy pounded the ring flat. Isabelle started struggling furiously. The King watched calmly. Isabelle's wrists began chaffing and a trickle of blood ran down her forearms. Charles nodded, satisfied. He had evidently planned all this beforehand.

'Bury that symbol of treachery in the dung heap outside,' he ordered. The smithy left with the ring. The King turned to the terrified groom.

'Madame,' he ground out, 'let the manner of this fool's execution serve as a warning.'

He motioned, and a trooper threw the hide of a recently skinned pig onto the ground, and rolled it out with his foot. Louis, mad with fear, was forced to his knees, laid flat out, and wrapped tightly inside the hide, the pig's head lolling to and fro with his frantic squirming. The pig's trotters were tied into a knot across the body. Two troopers with thick needles proceeded to sew up the unstitched belly. As Louis' grunts became more muffled, Isabelle ceased struggling. Was it her turn next?

'Into the river with him,' ordered Charles. The troopers obeyed instantly. The Well Beloved was back in complete control. As Charles approached her, a shiver ran down her spine. He was more terrifying sane than mad.

'Madam, you will stay here until some passing beggar releases you. And that might take time since your wild animals are released. Who knows, your panthers might find you first. I might meet you later at the wedding – that depends on fate, but I promise you one thing. That shameful Treaty of yours will be utterly revoked. Don't worry, I will leave the doors open, so you have a royal chance of escaping. Now, madam, let me wish you a very good night.' Charles VI bowed to his Queen Consort and withdrew.

As Charles led out his troopers, darkness enclosed the stables. The moon was a distant fading lamp. Isabelle, the all powerful Princess of Austria, Queen Regent of France, Mother-in-law and wife of Kings, was left strung up in chains, bleeding and terrified. Why had the monster released the panthers? That was a demonic touch.

22

Again that rustling sound. Isabelle stared around. The moon faded in and out. High in the cobwebbed rafters, she made out a shape. Her eyes focused on it. She recoiled in horror. Was it the devil himself? The figure was poised, crouching on one of the beams. Bat-like chittering sounds came from it. It was Hopcyn's deadliest enemy, the Sin Eater. He raised his arms high over the Queen. A hooded black cloak spread outwards, attached from the wrists, like a bat's. A skull tight head-covering left the paste-white face exposed. A thin-lipped leer twisted the mouth, like a lizard in heat. His eyes snapped open. Isabelle shrieked into her gag. Eyes solid black, the Sin Eater could see perfectly in the dark. He began climbing down to the half naked woman, chittering and emitting out little dry gasps. He reached out and caressed Isabelle's naked breast. As his fingers spread out, she nearly fainted. The hand was webbed like a toad's, yet his fingers felt like scrabbling, withered twigs. Isabelle twisted violently away. The caresses became more and more urgent, the gasps louder. The creature seemed to possess unnatural strength, its stick-thin arms stiff as steel rods. The Sin Eater raised her up bodily in her chains and turned her as if she was a bundle of straw. He bent her over, ripping away the shreds of her petticoat, exposing her trembling buttocks. Isabelle gave a muffled yell. She felt a penetration so deep that it at first terrified, but then of course thrilled her. Up, up, up higher inside her. And then she felt it coiling in ever expanding whorls, until her whole vagina was filled to bursting point. The coil itself now whirled around and around in a mounting

121

climax. Isabelle felt hers beginning too. As she came, she gave a muted howl of ecstasy all the more intense for being mingled with terror. The coil thing within her seemed to explode, then withdraw at lightening speed, like a whip. Isabelle slumped down. If this is the devil, she thought dazedly, then more of it. This was the most amazing fuck of her life, worth every drop of the blood now pouring from her torn wrists. Without a second look at the woman, the Sin Eater, his breath still rasping and rapid, folded his wings and backed away. He promised himself a further feast of her sins after her corpse was laid out in her coffin. His marble-black eyes peered out of the doorway. The moon clouded over. The Sin Eater, satisfied as the body he had just tasted, flitted over to the nearest beech and melted into the shadows of its upper branches.

Dazed, Isabelle slowly opened her eyes. An incubus, the devil itself. Amazing. This Wittelsbach had excelled herself. She looked over at the doorway. She stiffened again, but this time in far deadlier shock. There, not ten feet from her naked body, crouched a panther preparing to spring, its blazing, yellow eyes fixed terribly on her.

23

Owen, followed by King Leper and Hopcyn and two archers, cantered down one of the winding paths of the wood. Ghostly shapes of shepherds, shepherdesses, Greek heroes, lambs and panthers loomed up in various bowers, unsleeping sentinels of peace frozen into postures of eternal rest. They passed the spot where they had last confronted the King of Crystal. Now the King was well again. After his wolfish rage had subsided he had, with no prior sign, suddenly snapped out of his dementia, and with the full use of his faculties. Owen knew the King had donned cloth of gold and a coronet. This meant royal retribution of some kind. Owen had at once ordered a sweep and search operation to locate Isabelle. They had visited her living quarters, the cellars, even searched the Court of Good Shepherds, much to the ribaldry of the troopers. The stables, outhouses, bowers yielded nothing. No one had thought of the stable loft. What would a Queen be doing there, especially on the night before her own daughter's wedding? The Monk had also apparently gone into hiding. When Isabelle's pet Cardinal had seen the troopers, he had taken up his pastoral staff, donned his Cardinal's red cape and hat, and decamped poste haste for his palace in Avignon where any rumours of his doings could be scotched without questions. Isabelle's entire staff, from scullion to secretaries, professed ignorance of their Queen's whereabouts. Even the Majordomo turned down a bribe for information. The household remained remarkably faithful to their faithless mistress.

Owen knew that the King had left the Great Hall at

midnight with a force of thirty guards. They had been observed galloping along the road to the main gate, the horses' hoofs muffled. They had re-grouped at Honnecourt, divided into four squadrons, one going north, another to the south, another to the east and the last to the west. It was an obvious tactic, Owen saw, to conceal the King's real direction. The ruse had worked. Cunning! – Hopcyn as always was right. Owen divided his men into four groups and sent them in pursuit. Owen's own little force now cantered rather aimlessly along the track, waiting for further reports. Two of the King's groups had been located well away from the châteaux, and had disbanded, but where were the other two? The skies were clearer now, and moonlight bathed the tops of the woods with a greenish glow.

Hopcyn was unusually silent. He had been summoned from a deep alcoholic sleep and was now nursing a monumental hangover.

'Had too much to dream last night,' he groaned to King Leper. The leper offered him his flask of pure water. Hopcyn nearly gagged on it, but it cleared his head a little.

'What do you see of the King?' asked King Leper.

'He leads a charmed life,' Hopcyn replied, 'in the middle of a nightmare. Hush!' He looked upwards.

'What is it?' asked Owen, reining in. Hopcyn listened intently. Yes, the Sin Eater. But something else as well.

'Something not quite right.'

'What?' persisted Owen.

'Bats,' said Hopcyn.

'Hate those things,' muttered Owen.

'Leave them to me,' said King Leper in his hoarse whisper. 'Lepers have a way with bats.'

Owen was thinking of Catherine. By God, she had looked beautiful in the hall.

'They should let me do the honours!' he blurted out. There. That was it. He had let it slip out. Hopcyn seemed to know at

124

once what he meant.

'Not going to be the happiest day of her life,' said Hopcyn, surprisingly. He abruptly looked up again. What in the hell was it? A child's page surcoat suddenly flapped through the branches and landed on Hopcyn's upturned face.

'Ugh!' he exclaimed, throwing it off. 'It's covered with shit.'

Then it happened. The tops of the trees were suddenly alive with shrieking monkeys, swinging from branch to branch, intent on tearing off their hated uniforms. Hopcyn pointed at the tree tops farther off. They were covered with discarded page boy uniforms. The boughs bent under their weight. The troup paused, then shrieked in chorus again and were off at high speed. They were running in panic from something.

The horses neighed and reared in fright. What was it?

'There!' said King Leper. A huge cat-shape slunk from trunk to trunk just below the troop of simians, evidently on the hunt for food, with monkey high up on the menu.

'Be ready to shoot,' ordered Owen, unsheathing his sword. The two bowmen fitted arrows into their bows. Before they could shoot, the beast disappeared into the undergrowth.

'Bloody panthers!' said Hopcyn. Owen got it.

'The King's revenge. To the stables!'

As they spurred forward, a messenger galloped up to Owen, and gasped out his report.

'What's this?' thought Owen as he listened. 'Cloth of gold, a pig's hide, something in the dungheap, troopers searching the river.' He'd heard enough.

'Let's go!' he ordered. The horses leapt forward at the signal, relieved to get away from the place of panthers. With the sound of shrieking monkeys in their ears, they rode out to the aid of the ravished Queen of France.

As they were about to enter the courtyard, Owen held up his hand. They dismounted and continued on foot. The panther house lay open to the night. The bars of the monkey house had

125

been wrenched apart. Page uniforms littered the area. The dummy lambs, birds and Wittelsbach penants had been cut to pieces. Owen froze, and pointed. They all saw it at the same time, a black panther at the entrance to the stables, crouching, preparing to spring.

'Shoot!' Owen ordered at once. Both archers fired. The first arrow was a hit, passing under the panther's jaw. It cut through the windpipe and severed the jugular before striking the dust on the other side. The second arrow missed.

'A torch.' The bowman lit one with tinder and flint. Owen ordered King Leper and the second bowman to rally the scattered troops at the stables. As they galloped off, Owen and Hopcyn moved warily towards the stables.

At the sudden whirring hit of the arrow, Isabelle nearly peed herself. The panther grunted, reared up, then fell with blood frothing from its mouth. Still it dragged itself determinedly towards its intended prey. Just a foot from Isabelle, its rear legs jerked convulsively as it died. Isabelle whimpered weakly.

Owen lifted the torch. With unsheathed swords, they entered the stable. As the light hit her eyes, Isabelle strained at the chains and grunted furiously against the gag. Her eyes signalled ferociously to Owen.

'Alive and kicking,' said Hopcyn.

'Thank God,' thought Owen, 'for Catherine's sake.'

Hopcyn sniffed the unmucked dung and horse piss. Poetic justice. He looked at Isabelle. Her rippling body was a bit on the generous side, but that was how he liked it.

Isabelle was entirely naked, the remains of her garments lay in shreds at her feet. Owen fetched a horse blanket from the stall, and wrapped it around her. Her body, he observed, was quite unmarked, except for some strange twig-shaped scratches in the pubic area. Congealed blood covered her wrists and forearms. Owen unhooked the chains. Isabelle slumped down, tearing the gag from her mouth.

'Tried to murder me!' she yelled, pointing at the dead panther. She gave it a kick.

'The King was here?'

'You know it,' she replied, shaking the chains. 'But he won't last.' She paused. 'You took your time.'

'So did you,' Owen replied.

She decided to overlook the riposte.

'You're not hurt?' Owen pointed at the dried blood and the strange scratches.

'No.' She looked down at her wrists, smiling secretly. She could still feel the incubus aching inside her. She took in Owen's martial figure and striking face. She let the blanket slip.

'There's my favourite Captain.'

Owen and Hopcyn looked on wonderingly. In those glittering blue eyes did they detect, yes, the last vestiges of a huge, recently satisfied lust? Was she, bloody and an inch from being torn to pieces, could she still be 'ripe'? Her shining eyes shifted and probed the rafters.

'My men are coming in. I'll post a special guard for the rest of the night.'

'Stop drooling, One Eye,' she said to Hopcyn. Hopcyn's hangover vanished without trace. Perhaps later, then. No. What would Agnes say?

Isabelle abruptly pointed at the ground.

'My Louis! The swine killed my Louis! There. Dressed him as a pig and threw him in the river.'

More troopers entered the courtyard.

'My men are combing the banks,' said Owen.

'Poor Louis, poor panther. Not their fault. Now, take the beast to my kitchens. I will have the skin for my salon. Yes, My victory! Now get me home, I have to dress for the wedding.'

Owen and Hopcyn were momentarily transfixed.

'Wake up! My Katty's marriage day? I, the proud mother.

127

Listen, both of you. My Katty I will never let down. I have planned. Now, come on.'

At the doors she spotted the dung heap. Without hesitation, she plunged her bloodied fingers into it and carefully groped around.

'Got it!' With a shout of triumph, she held up the ring and kissed it. 'I win. He will be mad, not too late, you'll see. And this,' she flourished the ring, 'I will re-make for my next lover, ja!? And . . . ' she yelled at the trees outside, 'every lost pet replaced, madman. Every Louis, every lamb, every panther, do you hear.' She motioned to Owen. 'Come on, now greet the day.'

The half naked Queen Regent of France swept past the steaming dunghill and through the ranks of astonished cavalry towards her Court of Good Shepherds, followed by Owen and Hopcyn, and a dead black panther swinging between two troopers.

24

Next morning, at precisely half past ten as laid down by Henry, the Archbishop of Sens accompanied by Humphrey, Duke of Gloucester, led the royal wedding procession from the Great Hall to the Church of St Michel in the nearby town of Troyes. At first it had been difficult for Henry to find a pliable French cleric. But Henry's winning ways would not be denied. He had earlier noted that the Bishop of Sens had risen in revolt against his superior, the Archbishop, and had gone over to the Dauphinist party. Henry sent out two of his best regiments, subdued the town in short order and returned it to the authority of the Archbishop. His full revenues were restored, which was the whole point of the operation. After that, the Archbishop was only too grateful to fall in with the wishes of his new sovereign, however English. But Henry was more than just that, he was a conqueror.

The day was dry and bright, the ground hard. A perfect day for a battle, thought Henry in the covered royal carriage. Side by side, Catherine's arm rested lightly on his. Yes, he thought, ravishing. He was relieved that Captain Owen had contained the actions of the French King and had spared Catherine any direct involvement in it. Towards dawn, the King had again disappeared from his bed chamber. This boded ill, for he had deserted his most trusted counsellors. Owen had at once been placed in command of security. Again he had sent out search parties. He had checked and cleared the roads to prevent any unfortunate incidents. Owen's troopers, discreetly concealed with lookouts perched in the tallest trees, formed a wide circle around the church. Owen would be personally scouting the countryside during the wedding and the banquet afterwards. Henry was making certain of no more 'embarrassments' for Catherine. Owen had reassured her that both the Dauphin and King were safe, though absent. She had fought hard to have them there, and it was through no fault of her own they weren't. Her heart had warmed to him.

The procession arrived at the wide porch of the church. The whole cavalcade dismounted and lined up, in orders of precedence worked out by Henry himself. There were no disputes. The royal brothers and Burgundy still bent to one will.

Catherine and Henry paused until the line was ready to move into the church. They looked directly into each other's eyes. Yes, there it was. Catherine was certain. He did love her. Her whole face glowed in response. Yes, thought Henry, I do love you. But what about your love?

'Beautiful,' he heard a voice murmur. It was Isabelle standing directly behind them. She looked as fresh and rested as one of her painted shepherdesses. Diplomatically, for once, she had chosen a long-sleeved gown which covered the bandages on her wrists. Her gown and crown outshone all others, except her daughter's. Isabelle had made sure of that. After all, it was Catherine's day. When Isabelle had woken that morning, she had shrugged off the torment and the torture of the previous night. But the pleasure of it she recalled with an ever present thrill. That would never leave her. And the King, her 'curse'? Vanquished. Vanished. She had been right! So, *carpe diem*. Isabelle was ready for the day. No, she was ready for anything.

Catherine wore the arched crown (already in hock to Henry's Florentine banker), a white veil trimmed on both sides with ermine reaching down to her shoulders. Her mantle lay over a close-fitting purple gown, tight up to her throat. Another strip of ermine with golden tassels studded with jewels girdled her waist and hung down in front.

Henry was dressed from head to foot in burnished armour, as if at the head of one of his regiments, with a fox's tail ornamented with precious stones in his helm. He looked readier for the field than the altar. There was no denying that he was a commanding sight. They were a brilliant, striking couple.

Henry nodded. The Archbishop and Humphrey took their places before the royal couple. The whole procession moved off. Henry paced briskly down the aisle. He had instructed the Archbishop and Humphrey not to delay. The spacious church filled rapidly. Apart from the French delegates, all the signatories were present as were all of Henry's leading generals. Isabelle seemed to have wiped, or repelled, the opposition off the face of the earth. There was enough room for everyone. It had all gone off with the precision of a military parade.

At the high altar, before the Archbishop, Henry repeated the vows in a strong, clear voice. Without hesitating, Catherine followed suit. The Archbishop finally blessed them and Henry with his new bride at his side retreated a little. To everyone's surprise, the Archbishop then led Isabelle to the top steps in front of the high alter. Humphrey wondered what it was all about, for he had not been told. Queen Isabelle confidentially faced the whispering congregation. Now she would show the madman and the weaklings of the *fleur-de-lis* of France! What she had to say would be all the more devastating since it would become public knowledge, and with the Conqueror's consent.

The Archbishop now ceremoniously presented Isabelle with an illuminated copy of the Treaty, inscribed on parchment. He raised it high, so the congregation could see. For the occasion, the Treaty had been re-named "The Accord of Peace Perpetual". The Archbishop announced this in a loud voice.

Isabelle opened the sheets to the first pages. She intended to read out only the new peroration, her own contribution. This she declared in ringing tones so that the awed locals outside could hear:

'To Henry of England, we cede the crown and realm of France with all its rights and appertenances, which shall remain and abide and be of his imperial Majesty's and Queen Catherine's heirs for evermore! Amen, ja!'

Her eyes swept over "the leaders of men" in the congregation, the fully qualified butchers – Bedford, Clarence and the rest. Men! She was revenged on the pack of them! Any lingering affection for Louis the Lamb vanished. And still she was left with a beautiful daughter. She beamed lovingly at her. Catherine couldn't gainsay her. What a performer! She smiled back.

Bedford groaned inwardly. Was there no controlling Henry and Isabelle's arrogance?

'Be straight, not superior,' Bedford had advised, but Henry seemed in a cloud these days. Perhaps he really was in love. No! Perish the thought. Bedford knew he would again have to introduce measures to quell the hostility which this new insult would undoubtedly rouse.

Humphrey, however, looked delighted. The "froggies" deserved to have their noses rubbed in it. They had lost. Woe to the defeated! No chivalric code, and definitely no political wisdom, ever entered into it. Henry's other generals looked uncomfortable. Milksops, thought Humphrey. He had managed to convince Eleanor that she had to stay away for security reasons. But this excuse was wearing thin. God, he prayed for the hundredth time, let the final curse of the Witch of Eye fall on the lot of them.

25

After the ceremony, the cavalcade resumed its place in the mile-long procession of carriages. Only Isabelle demurred. She had decided to go on directly to Paris, whatever the danger. To the general astonishment of all she mounted her favourite stallion, which was waiting in readiness outside the church. With only a small retinue and four mounted guards, she blew a kiss to her daughter as Catherine walked out of the porch, her arm resting on Henry's. Isabelle had warned them in advance. She didn't want to witness the bedding. For once she'd had enough. With a smile, Catherine returned the kiss. Isabelle wheeled her horse round and urged it into a wild gallop. Catherine wondered what her mother was really up to in Paris.

Injury to insult, thought Bedford as he watched Isabelle disappearing into the distance, already outdistancing her followers. Henry heaved a sigh of relief. Isabelle was a very expensive woman to have around.

Still headed by the Archbishop, the huge wedding party set off for the banquet laid out in the main Hall of Beaurevoir. The guests dismounted, still maintaining the correct order. They assembled in lines, awaiting their new Queen. The Archbishop led in the royal couple, again blessed their union with holy water and, according to custom, solemnly led them upstairs to the royal bed-chamber. The guests followed. The royal brothers crowded round the door, but did not enter. They were to witness the fact that the King had indeed bedded the new Queen. The Archbishop finally blessed the bed, prayed for fruitful issue, and then called for the ritual hot soup and wine to sustain the lovers. The marriage would now be consummated, and the sheets and linen later examined by the ladies of the court. Isabelle had warned Catherine of all this. Henry had also warned her that at the end of the short afternoon, he would be leaving at the head of his troops to complete the conquest of the adjacent territories, and make the way clear for their coronation in Paris. She had found the prospect of two coronations daunting. But it was her duty for both her peoples. As the heralds below blew the royal salute, the bedroom doors were closed and guards posted.

The guests returned to the mountains of dishes piled on the refectory tables in the main hall, and took their assigned places under the jealous eye of the pompous, bewigged Humphrey. They proceeded to eat and drink noisily, making bold, bawdy jokes about the pair upstairs. They laughed uproariously, intent that Henry and his bride could hear their celebrations. Bedford regarded them dourly. He exchanged glances with the equally sceptical Salisbury. There was a long way to go yet. Still, the wedding had gone off without serious upset, except for that perilous insult of Isabelle's.

The generals knew they were marching directly on Sens after Henry had performed his dynastic, marital duties. The army was already drawn up in regiments of the line along the road to Sens, and thereafter to Paris. More 'pacifications' could be expected within the hour.

After a non-stop marathon of feasting the heralds, on a pre-arranged signal, suddenly sounded the royal salute. Henry at once appeared at the top of the stairs in full fighting armour, with the Archbishop behind him smiling serenely. Henry raised his arm in military salute. Loud acclamations broke out. Their King had done his duty. They were assured of an heir! No one doubted Henry's victory in this field either. Henry had strapped on his favourite battle sword. There was no use in wasting the dress armour in the coming campaign, for it had cost a fortune.

Bedford, Clarence, Salisbury, Warwick and Burgundy filed outside, leading their retinues to the waiting horses. Henry was the last to settle into the saddle. As his army waited, he looked up towards Catherine. She was there standing at the window, as promised. She waved. Roars and cheers broke out from the assembled troops. Henry smiled. Yes, his dynasty would last. The way to Jerusalem was studded with notable victories but, under the convenient mask of love, this was the vital one.

From the upper window of their room, a frowning Catherine watched the long lines of troops and cavalry move out. Henry had been tender, passionate and unrushed. Using the considerable expertise he had gained from the London stews, he had drawn her close to orgasm. Now she wanted more of what she felt was just beneath the surface of her being. Why had he gone just at this moment? There was always time for war, as bloody as it was pointless. Isabelle was right about that, she thought. She looked at the empty bed now that her husband was gone. Her mother had departed, her father had disappeared, her brother was absent, Agnes and Hopcyn were away and Owen was on duty. Was it an omen? Did this point the way to an ever present circle of warm friends and a happy family life, the things she most longed for on earth. The new Queen of England and France sat on the edge of the bed and found the unexpected solitude as sad and silent as the distant cloisters of her childhood. She shivered.

The town of Sens, which had momentarily attempted another rebellion, surrendered to Henry after token resistance. Before nightfall on his wedding day, Henry was able to plant the banners of St George and the Holy Trinity on the Tower over the main gate. Henry handed over the keys to the town to the satisfied Archbishop:

'You gave me the jewel of my life this morning, Archbishop.

135

Tonight I give you yours.'

Henry had then set up camp and sent out a reconnoitring force to Corbeil, Montereau and Melun, the next towns on his list for pacification. He then settled down to write a note to his wife and Queen, Catherine. Among more tender sentiments, Henry "commanded" her to be "in attendance" at Corbeil close to Melun. Henry was certain the towns would fold as rapidly as Sens. After the few days necessary for their defeat, the couple would make a royal progress to Paris for the coronation in Notre Dame. Catherine was somewhat relieved. Henry had written at once. Perhaps, after all, this was the beginning of the family she longed for. As she made preparations, she wished she didn't have to use that word "perhaps" so often. Was he playing with her or did he really love her? She knew he wasn't the cold fish people believed him to be. But was she really his "jewel". Or was she just another "matter of state"?

26

Agnes and Hopcyn had been granted leave to go on ahead. Alone together at last, they cantered along the route to Paris, revelling in their freedom and the open spaces of Eustace's *la belle France*. The confines of Court and protocol were soon left behind. Eustace would meet them in Paris. He had promised to be their guide before the coronation took over the city. Preparations had already begun.

The sun had been shining when they left. The blue skies were now fast disappearing. The last reflections of the sun faded and were replaced by gathering inky clouds. From a grassy knoll, they watched a thunderstorm raging over the next line of hills. The jagged lightening illuminating the scene seemed to pause and turn in their direction. Gusts suddenly whipped the trees around them. They would have to find shelter. Hopcyn pointed. Behind them rose the slopes of a hill, broken by scrub oak and huge boulders. They would have to find shelter among those outcrops. They spurred their horses forward. Thunder crashed directly overhead and the skies opened. A solid deluge hit them. The horses abruptly reared and came to a halt, quivering with fear. They were engulfed in billows of swirling smoke. They dismounted and stroked the muzzles of their frightened horses. Hopcyn sniffed. Charcoal burners, was it? Above the din of thunder, a discordant chanting reached their ears. It rose and fell in the raging wind, harsh but not unpleasing. Agnes and Hopcyn exchanged puzzled glances. Hopcyn coughed and peered into the smoke. He pointed. On the far side of the rocks, they could make out the flames of a giant bonfire of felled trees. As they moved towards it, in a single movement the bushes around them parted and a throng of chanting figures emerged, many armed with scythes and sickles, to surround both of them. The smoke lifted. Hopcyn and Agnes held their breaths. Were they seeing right? Yes, the entire mob was naked, except for the packs and bundles that some were carrying. Their bodies were daubed with mud and the men had long, untrimmed beards and matted hair whilst the women sported locks down to their waists. Garlands of wild flowers and crowns of ivy adorned their heads. The mud on their limbs was rapidly melting in the lashing rain.

'Don't move!' shouted Hopcyn to Agnes in Welsh, recognising the mob from a warning of Eustace. 'God inspired innocents or murdering devils, take your pick – but stay clear of them.'

Hearing a strange language, the mob lowered their weapons. Hopcyn and Agnes had passed the first test. They were not the loathed *godons*. Had they spoken in English, they would by now be dead.

'Do as I do,' shouted Hopcyn, again in Welsh. To Agnes's amazement, he began undressing. When he was as naked as the rest, he smeared himself with mud.

'Hurry' he yelled. Agnes stripped rapidly. Hopcyn raised his wet harp high. The crowd drew nearer, intrigued. Hopcyn stared intensely into their eyes. They fell silent, giving a collective sigh of awe. Who was this being with multi-coloured eyes? Who was his flame-haired fellow spirit? It was a sign, yes, a sign. Hopcyn played. The mob swayed in time. The chanting increased again. Yes, God had sent two saints to lead them in worship.

Hopcyn by now knew that they were among the crazed sect known as the Brethren of the True Cross, who were roving fanatics driven half mad by famine and slaughter. In their enforced fasting, they experienced visions of heaven and hell and the Day of Judgement. They were enacting their new law. Christ's Second Coming, they knew, was imminent. They, the chosen Brethren, were to clear the way for his glorious reign. But the Earth had to be cleansed. The riches of the corrupt clergy were to go first. Then the nobles and their murderous greed. Afterwards, this new plague of bloody *godons* – the "scorpions of the anti-Christ". All were for the knife, and the Brethren's murders were legion. Thank God for Eustace and his advice and knowledge, thought Hopcyn, for he saved our lives. As Hopcyn played, the mob began a whooping, stamping dance.

The Brethren pursued their aims with mad logic. Since all money and gold were tainted, they were empowered by God to enter any tavern or household or manor and strip it bare. If they were opposed, they were empowered to kill, also by divine right. They never bathed, shaved, wore clothes, or slept in beds. These earthly habits only masked the view of Christ from His children. Marriage was also a barrier so it was abolished. Procreation had to be seen to be true. It was therefore freed from the artificial bonds of marriage. Virginity was condemned. Sex was had by all, with all, whenever the 'holy spirit' so moved them. In the early days, priests unwise enough to try and part these indiscriminate couplings had been torn limb from limb, on the spot. Now, no cleric went anywhere near them.

'Dance!' Hopcyn yelled. Agnes demonstrated one of the wilder reels of her youth, her flaming hair swirling about her shoulders, her breasts rising and falling rhythmically. The Brethren cheered, they had indeed been blessed by the Lord this day, two saints and both soon ready for the fray. Agnes saw that many of the Brethren now sported full erections, even in the driving rain. The women moved around, caressing and nibbling the pricks they took a fancy to. Even the children joined in.

'Fuck,' roared Hopcyn. 'Fuck Agnes fach, 'cos your life depends on it.'

With one wheeling movement, the crowd bore Agnes and Hopcyn towards the fire. On the far side, the entrance of an enormous cavern opened out. Tuns of broached wine stood on trestles. Stolen loaves and provisions were stacked in corners. Smaller fires had suckling pigs sizzling on spits. Deeper inside the cave were layers of dried hay and straw. There, everyone went to their 'devotions' as they saw fit, eating, drinking and fornicating, at the same time if need be. Gluttony abounded. Copulation thrived. And why not when it was all in the eyes of God.

Agnes and Hopcyn were gently laid down amongst a group of writhing, panting bodies. Agnes surrendered herself to a muscular mud-besmeared giant. With a deft movement, she mounted him. Tightening her vagina in time with her thrusts, she rode her charge into his seventh heaven. Hopcyn mounted his second holy sister, who was now praying in a frenzy with her knees upwards. They were fucking for their lives alright! As Hopcyn looked over, he blew a kiss to Agnes. Agnes caught the kiss and blew it back. The holy celebrants cheered. At once, the cavern was full of blowing kisses and ecstatic comings. The Gods indeed had landed among them!

Yes, thought Hopcyn, the whole unbelievable race is at it. No one escapes – thank God. He blew another kiss to Agnes.

27

Henry had established his battle lines round the town of Montereau. He did not expect to stay for more than a few days. Montereau and the other recalcitrant towns would soon be brought to heel. Pacification would be brisk. After a pleasant progress with a disciplined army, he felt at ease. His bride would be joining him soon, then on to Paris for another triumph, the coronation. Clarence he had dispatched on an inspection tour of the coastal forts. Humphrey was in Paris brooding over plans for the coronation, with his frightful mistress. Bedford had established his massive and authoritative presence in Paris. Henry had retained Warwick and Salisbury as his principal captains. With these two at his side he knew the new campaign would soon be over.

Isabelle, too, had not upset the royal apple cart over much. No doubt she was up to some expensive mischief at the Palace of St Pol, but she had done her job and she was well out of the way. The Dauphin was discredited, the old King had disappeared in a show of perfect timing for the coronation. The Lady Agnes and Hopcyn had been ordered to prepare the Palace of the Louvre for the royal couple. King Leper and Owen meanwhile were ordered by Bedford to widen the allied intelligence network. Henry had granted Owen a roving commission. Soon, he had promised the chagrined Owen, a battle command would ensue. Owen was reassured. He would keep the Clerkship of the Wardrobe only until the Coronation was over.

'Yes', thought Henry, 'things are neat and tidy. And Montereau is a ripe plum.'

28

King Leper and Owen now rode along the pacified route to Paris.

'Don't worry,' he reassured King Leper as they had left the encampment. 'After this, a field command, as promised. And you with me, as promised too.'

In the hot sun, the blackened ruins of farms and cottages lay on every side. The road was badly rutted and little wider than a pathway. Brambles and creepers grew across the road, uncared for in the wars, offering perfect ambush spots to brigands and robbers. Henry the Saint? More like the Dark Horse of the Apocalypse, thought Owen, as he surveyed the devastation. But Owen knew that France held vast reserves of people and revenue. Losses could easily be made up. Henry seemed too cocky. He had let his respect for his enemy lapse since Agincourt. He wondered how long Henry could hold onto France. Without a line of faithful towns to the coastal ports, he would be cut off. Henry seemed to know this well enough, but still clung to his dream of Jerusalem. Owen thought that Warwick and Salisbury knew what they were doing. But would Henry listen to them? he wondered. Henry, Owen was convinced, could well run out of men and supplies, very much as Wales had done during Glyndŵr's war. France was too big to garrison, and far too rich to impoverish. It was simply a matter of time.

'Any trouble along the way?' he asked King Leper.

'Only at nunneries,' grinned the leper.

'No one caught on to you yet?'

'Don't worry, my ailment brings rapid advancement.'

'And the others?'

'On alert.'

'The spy money?'

'At the Lazarium outside the north gate.'

'The untouchables. Bless you, brother!'

Owen reached over and hugged the leper. They had been together since they were babies in the same cot. Their other brothers and sisters had died in the wilderness like their mother, after the last Welsh war. Owen and King Leper were the sole survivors, and brothers to the end. Together they would restore the family estates in far off Ynys Môn. What is my destiny? wondered Owen again. Is it in France?

The two secret guardians of his fate, Hopcyn and King Leper, knew the answer. Yes, it was in France. But there was still one real danger, that great black bat of the devil, the Sin Eater. Hopcyn had warned the Leper that the bat had already arrived in Paris. The whole network was watching over Owen as well as the King.

29

Five weeks later Henry stood, furious and frustrated, at the entrance of his war tent. Salisbury and Warwick watched with apprehension. Corbeil had fallen readily enough but Montereau and, particularly, Melun under the redoubtable Arnaud de Brabazon, had raised the *fleur-de-lis* banner and still stoutly resisted the hated *godons*. Salisbury knew that the recent insult of the Treaty, along with the near death of the Well-Beloved and Henry's increasing cruelties, had rallied the populace. Salisbury wished Bedford was with him. Together they might have restrained Henry's more extreme 'pacifications'.

Salisbury knew his bombardments were weakening Montereau. He had just called up his reserve cannon, including a monster called 'London' that was donated by the wealthier merchants of the City. He gave the word. Another hail of steel exploded inside the walls. Breaches appeared down to the water line. Just right for an assault by boats, thought Salisbury. Henry watched the scene closely, biting his lip. Where were his allies?

During this prolonged crisis, Catherine had been installed in the battle zone at Corbeil. She was becoming increasingly anxious to get on to Paris, to be with her mother and friends. Henry spent little enough time with her. He was rarely away from the front lines. Henry suspected she might be pregnant and knew that, if such was true, then a pregnancy and coronation would seal his grip on the dual Monarchy. Henry was in a fever to know the truth. But Catherine said little. She seemed indifferent to the alarms and excursions. Henry utterly failed to understand that it was her own people, after all, he was slaughtering and pillaging, and in front of her very eyes. Indifference was her only defence. She was now as sick of war as Isabelle had been. And yes, she was pregnant, but she would talk to Henry in Paris about that, away from the explosions and the blood and the death. Thoughts of love had flown out of the windows of war.

The last thing Henry wanted were protracted sieges. Yet all the towns around Paris had to be kept under strict control. Henry especially needed a freeway to and from the Channel ports for supplies and reinforcements. At least, he thought, his rear was well-secured under the firm governorship of Bedford. And Paris was only one day's hard ride away!

He cursed the enemy again as Salisbury's artillery sent another cannonade into the walls of Montereau. It was at this point that the exhausted town unexpectedly ran down its *fleur-de-lis* flags, and asked for honourable terms. As it turned out, the town had surrendered more out of lack of provisions than the will to fight. This augured ill for the siege of Melun farther down the river.

Before Salisbury could advise against it, Henry ordered the first twenty-four prisoners to be strung up from the battlements. Warwick remonstrated. It was simply not chivalric but, more importantly, it would enrage the survivors. Henry took no notice. But Burgundy at once rode over to Henry's lines, embraced his ally and applauded the hangings. This was the town where the assassins had buried his beloved father. He asked Henry's permission to bear off his father's remains. Henry, again against the advice of Salisbury and Warwick who knew Burgundy only too well, granted the request. To ingratiate his ally still further, Henry winked at the massacre of the inhabitants which followed. Both were mistakes.

Burgundy proceeded to dig up his father's remains. Without a thought for his hard-pressed allies, he at once formed up a sumptuous cortege with almost his whole army of seven thousand as escort. The procession made off for the ancient Burgundian town of Dijon for the entombment in the Charterhouse, the mausoleum of the House of Burgundy.

This unexpected departure wasted still more precious weeks, and the sieges dragged on. Henry now turned his attention to the next disobedient town, Melun, on the Seine. It straddled the broad river on a strategic, defensive bend. The fortified town centre and citadel stood on an island in the middle, the waters forming a natural moat around it.

At first, the town showed no sign of surrendering. Henry ordered mining operations. Saps were driven under the walls and tunnels pushed under the battlements. The defenders counter-mined. Bloody hand-to-hand struggles took place in the infested warrens under the river. In one such fight Henry himself encountered the garrison commander, the stubborn Arnaud himself. After exchanging fierce blows, both had retired before blood was drawn.

Salisbury's cannon continued to tear huge gaps in the fortifications, but Henry lacked troops to exploit the situation, and the breaches were soon plugged with earth-filled barrels and bags of sand. Henry tried amphibian assaults, but the boats bogged down in the muddy shallows of the river. Henry's efforts once again ground to a halt.

To make matters worse, the summer was the hottest for years. Under the blazing sun, a drought had set in. Dysentery and malaria rapidly thinned his ranks. Soon, Henry was losing more troops to sickness than battle. With their battle commanders so far away, the few remaining Burgundian troops, robbed they thought of further booty, began deserting in droves. Henry's armies were melting away. The dual alliance was under extreme pressure.

Salisbury and Warwick wrote urgently to Bedford begging for support and advice. Henry was getting out of control.

Bedford decided to try diplomatic means. He tracked down the Dauphin, treated him with royal respect and told him his help was needed at the front. The Dauphin at once fell in with Bedford's plan. He was dispatched to the front with a suitable escort. Bedford's plan was for the Dauphin, from the discreet safety of Henry's war tent, to order General Arnaud to obey his feudal overlord, the Dauphin, and thereafter his superior the King, Henry himself. Arnaud could therefore surrender quite honourably. The plan might have worked but Henry, with his dismayed commanders looking helplessly on, paraded the pitiful Dauphin below the battlements for all to see, the very last thing that Bedford had advised. The humiliation merely resolved the defenders to fight to the end 'for the honour of France and their real King, the Well-Beloved'! Arnaud was therefore able to utterly reject the surrender demand, and in no uncertain terms. He declared he would only ever give in when the hated *godons* were on the 'right side of the channel', having been chased back to England. He also announced that the Dauphin was probably an impostor and nothing more than yet another example of Henry's savage and dishonourable tricks. The crafty Arnaud had blackened Henry's reputation while adding to his own. Again Henry was furious. He threatened dire punishment on the town, and on Arnaud in particular. He returned the weeping Dauphin to Paris, but kept his escort as an addition to his garrison.

After this final humiliation among all the others, the Dauphin was now convinced his only salvation lay in lunacy or death, or in the direct intervention of God. But a worse fate than any of these awaited him in Paris – his dreaded mother, Isabelle.

But the pause had given time for Clarence's reinforcements to come up from the coast. Scraping together all available troops, Henry prepared for an all out assault. And God help the defeated, he thought, for they would pay for all this.

Unknown to Henry, the garrison and townspeople had been starving for weeks. The last cat and dog had been devoured. Arnaud had known the end was in sight, but it would be a brave end. Before Henry could attack, the flags were lowered and Arnaud sued for terms before surrendering in person to Henry and his staff, at his war tent. The presence of his intrepid enemy infuriated Henry. He promptly ordered his execution, but Arnaud had foreseen this possibility. He cited a law of chivalry which protected any chief commander who had met in personal combat on the field of battle, as he and Henry had. This was confirmed by Warwick, who knew the old laws of chivalry. Salisbury backed Warwick. Before his assembled court, Henry was forced to give in. But to spite the old warrior, Henry at once ordered the resourceful Arnaud to be suspended in a cage from the battlements. However, Artaud merely became a focus for the general cheers of the defeated but still defiant town. Henry was again forced to bring him down, and set at liberty.

In fury, Henry vented his rage on the small Scottish contingent he had captured in the town. He would teach them to stab him in the back! He had every last kilted Scot hanged from the towers. Still not satisfied, Henry ordered the lands around Melun and Montereau to be laid waste for up to twenty leagues. This would be his final monument to victory.

When the tardy Duke of Burgundy finally arrived back from the entombment to share in Henry's 'triumph,' the armies of the assembled Allies numbered fifteen thousand. The garrison of Melun had been a mere seven hundred.

God, Jerusalem and Empire were Henry's constant companions. God forgave him, his Empire sustained him and Jerusalem blessed him. But Henry knew that God could ill afford any more such 'victories' for him. Only now could he turn to his silent bride, wearied, frustrated and humiliated as she was, for the delayed honeymoon and the final triumphal march on Paris.

30

Humphrey was frantic with the preparations. He had just received urgent orders to have them completed in twenty-four hours and was sweating with apprehension. One specific order had been – no more humiliations. He stood in the central aisle of Notre Dame, fists on hips, looking at yet another banner with his crest being raised. Yes, he thought, this cathedral just about fits my size. Not bad. The massive columns, the serried seats, the huge expanse of carved ceiling, all were his to do with as he wished. In the glorious centre window, within a wide halo, sat the throned virgin, in double divinity. The portal sculptures were as abundant within as without, from archangels and saints to demons and gargoyles. The rose windows, with their iridescent glass, were aflame with colour, red, blue, gold, and sunbursts of jewels in the air. Just below the ceiling, a panoply of streaming banners hung the whole length of the aisle. The walls were covered with the arms of the royal brothers, red and white roses everywhere. Humphrey had decorated the walls with lozenge shaped panels showing the lion of England, red in tooth and claw, a golden crown around its neck. There were crests of boars, bulls, new moons, silver lilies, a Saracen woman's head, a bloody hand severed at the wrist. Here and there, Humphrey had condescended to display the royal *fleur-de-lis* of France. From floor to ceiling Humphrey's own crest, a falcon with outstretched talons, seemed to float down from every direction to seize up the onlookers. A massive altar triptych had almost been completed, concealed behind huge linen curtains. Humphrey had not yet inspected it, but his crowning surprise would be unveiled at the last moment.

Humphrey stepped back to get a better view and tripped over a pulley. The workmen guffawed. Humphrey glared at them and there was instant silence. Humphrey was deadly when in a vicious mood. Already he had ordered a dozen lashes for three of the carpenters for insolence, real or imagined.

'Get smaller pulleys!' he roared, readjusting his wig.

'Damn,' he thought, 'what am I going to say to Eleanor?' He still hadn't told her of Henry's ban.

Through the huge main portals, with a loud clatter of footsteps, strode Eleanor herself. The workmen redoubled their efforts. This woman was real, evil trouble.

In the echoing aisle, she confronted Humphrey with the new outrage.

'I am not to be invited with thee.' She thrust a parchment at him. 'Thy official lists of guests.' Damn, she knew. Must have been going through his papers again.

'Those are matters of state, my love.'

'These are matters of ME. Get Bedford to put me in the second row with thee.'

'Can't you see, if all of us were to have our mistresses there, it would need four bloody cathedrals.'

'Ha bloody ha!' There was that special, nasty, ring to her voice. What in the hell was she up to now?

'Keep your voice down. Someone might hear.'

'I dang well hope so, they be jealous of thee.'

'I will still go down in history.'

'But what about me?'

'Be patient, my songbird.'

'Ye knew all along.'

'It's Henry. He insists that we wait till the annulment's through.'

'I waits no more.'

'Not my fault.'

'I will be with ye.'

'No, ye . . . you will not.'

So she wouldn't share in the glory, the crowning, the acclamation, any of it. Her eyes glittered dangerously.

'I be the light of thy life or be I not?'

'Wait till you're my wife.'

'No, I will not,' she shouted, ignoring the listening workmen. Humphrey writhed in embarrassment.

'Why didn't ye tell me?'

'Didn't want to upset you, my love.'

'I be no one's fool.'

'Of course not, my songbird.'

'Don't ye 'songbird' me.'

'Can't you see I'm up to my neck . . . '

'Did ye hear . . . ?'

' . . . Have to do everything myself. My last orders. Now let me get on with it.'

But she was not finished. Eleanor upended the bag she was carrying. She knew this would get through to her most unsubtle Caesar. Turnip tops of various sizes thumped onto the floor. Humphrey gaped.

'Found 'em after ye left.'

'Where . . . ?'

'In our bed, my love.'

'Hell and damnation, an insult to my person!'

'What are ye goin' to do about it?'

'Heads will roll!'

'Ye said that last time, an' the time before . . . '

'I swear, this time, I'll have their guts.' She raised her hands as if holding a needle and hissed.

'The Witch. I'll send a message.'

'Then tell her to hurry up,' ordered Humphrey.

As if in response to their words, a flurry of wings came from the rafters. The Cathedral ravens took off and flew through the open doors and landed, flapping, on the lawns of the graveyard outside, their beady black eyes and voracious beaks pecking for worms. But Eleanor and Humphrey continued to stare fixedly upwards at the cavernous, arching roof. Must have been the shadow of one of the gargoyles. Yes, that was it. For a moment, they could have sworn they'd caught a glimpse of a strange bat-shaped creature flitting among the roof beams.

31

Owen approached the walls of Paris alone. He wanted to see for himself how things were going. He had ordered King Leper to go on ahead to the Louvre. Henry had sent a message to get everything in readiness for the coronation. He intended to go straight to the Cathedral after his own triumphal entry.

He looked up. Flags of St George and the *fleur-de-lis* fluttered side by side on poles above the city walls, immediate evidence of Bedford's good work. At first Owen was shocked by what he had seen. The gates were open and unguarded. As he passed under the archway, he was mobbed by gaunt, deformed, skeletal beggars of all ages, living on the swill thrown out for the pigs. The gigantic city rubbish tip was dotted with the corpses of little children who had died of starvation while looking for scraps to eat. On the gibbet close by hung the body of a woman who had murdered her three children and salted them down for food during the winter. Wolves had swum the Seine, dragged bodies out of their graves and devoured them, leaving their remains to rot in the sun.

But even as Owen watched, Bedford's cleaning up squads arrived to tidy up this last gate. Bedford now policed the capital with his most disciplined troops. They wheeled on a line of carts, set up guards at the gate, cut down the hanging woman, began removing the bodies of the children and herded the beggars into the carts. They would be driven to convents and centres for food and medical care. Bedford was clearing the mendicants off the streets. Bedford's new laws were simple, fair, and strictly enforced. The price of bread had tripled in a month. Bedford stabilised it for a year. Crime was instantly punished. After years of warfare and corruption, the unruly Parisians now welcomed Bedford's troops in an amazing change of heart, and a measure of the sufferings they had undergone. Bedford intended to hand over a law-abiding, prosperous, clean city to his sovereign for the coming week of royal festivities.

Bedford had also reinforced the power of the leading Bishops. Their coffers were now brimming with recently collected ecclesiastical taxes. Bedford's share was considerable, but he was never greedy, and the Bishops had come to trust him. They had even agreed to post priests along the royal route chanting *te deums* for Henry and Catherine, and choristers to sing Henry's favourite psalms. Food, wheat and wine were to be distributed free. Bedford's diplomacy had been so successful that he had even obtained ratification of the hated Treaty of Troyes from the city's Estates General and had, astonishingly, wrested a denunciation of the Dauphin from the Dauphin's own *Parlement*. They had also renewed the Dauphin's proscription from the crown, as read out by the feared Isabelle. For a moment the people seemed to have forgotten their 'Well-Beloved'. But it was Bedford's genuine love for France and things French which had been his greatest ally. Bedford now prayed that the good will he had built up would not be jeopardised by the arrogance, insolence and ignorance of his brothers. And that included Henry himself, especially after Warwick and Salisbury's disturbing reports. Bedford also thought Henry's plans for such a rapid coronation were too hasty. After so much bloodshed, this was a moment for the people to enjoy for as long as they possibly could. But he duly ordered Humphrey to speed up the final plans.

As Owen made his way through the narrow streets, he noticed a new bustle and purpose everywhere. Stall holders yelled out their wares and invited him inside. Street vendors with their trays stood at every corner. Peddlers, merchants and packhorses, clerics and retinues, royal officials, government messengers and couriers, friars, jongleurs and pardoners crowded the streets. Prostitutes strolled by in their distinctive striped dresses, or with their garments inside out, both being uniforms of their profession. Porters bent low under loads of wood and charcoal. The gigantic tavern and shop signs had been repainted, at royal expense. Above his stall entrance, a tooth puller was painting a gigantic tooth. A glover was redecorating a massive glove, the fingers big enough for a child to stand in. A huge chamber pot advertised an apothecary who 'read' people's urine. The sinister bellman passed through the crowds, shouting so all could hear,

'Wake, ye sleepers, now pray for the new dead this day, for they cannot pray for themselves! Wake, wake!' Dogs and passers-by alike quailed as he sounded his fatal bell. But life went on. For the great capital, it was again business as usual. And the credit was entirely Bedford's. Everyone knew it and everyone respected it. One thing the English can do really well in a country that is not their own, thought Owen, is organise – especially things that don't belong to them.

32

'Please Lord send a sign,' had been the Dauphin's prayer for the last few months.

Instead, God sent him Isabelle. She descended like a plague of locusts ready to pick him bare. She promptly packed him off to the humblest quarters in the gardens. She took over the small Palace of St Pol with a regiment of architects and builders to re-design her new Court in the capital. With his father howling at the moon and his mother in the arms of scullions and dwarves, the Dauphin felt both guilt and relief to be out of the way. Apart from Bedford, no one expressed any wish to see him.

Isabelle settled her creatures into the style they were accustomed. Her Majordomo and the Monk were combing the city for new lovers. The Monk sighed sadly. It was hard work. Louis the Lamb would never be replaced. Isabelle had planned to ride out to join her daughter at Corbeil, but the Monk had reported murmurings against her for her rejection of the Dauphin. He also warned her that it was too risky to join the triumphal entry into Paris. Henry had agreed. He distrusted the volatile capital as much as he did Isabelle. But the Monk knew that Isabelle wanted to shine at the coronation. And when she wanted to shine, eclipses were out of the question.

In a pantry next to the kitchen in the gardener's cottage of the Palace, Eustace and the Dauphin looked down at the mad King. He lay comatose under grimy blankets on a military cot. The Dauphin was becoming more and more frantic. His father had agreed to swear to his son's legitimacy before the high justices. He said he possessed dates proving his son's conception. But he then lapsed into madness, and afterwards a coma. The Dauphin wept in frustration.

Eustace was as popular with the King as he was with Isabelle. Even after his recent scandalous behaviour with the mad Welsh bard at Troyes, his standing remained high. He could move between the two royal courts with no hindrance. Eustace, for all his bulk, had proved a tender nurse, and he was concerned about the condition of the King. Charles was sweating it out. Eustace gently wiped his sovereign's brows with a cool, damp cloth. Yes. The fever was subsiding.

Eustace now had even more reason for rallying to Charles. In the recent clear period at Troyes, Charles had made him Steward of Forests and Water and appointed him Supervisor of the Household Exchequer. Eustace was fast becoming the scourge of the cheats and frauds who preyed on the King. His ugliness alone was enough to repel them, but he also revelled in casting out the spoliators of France with the tip of his boot. Those who refused to pay their debts to the King, he pilloried in brilliant *ballades*. Nor did Isabelle begrudge her favourite poet his new source of loot. In fact, she respected his obvious cunning in obtaining it, and it helped to soak up the slender resources of the King.

The Dauphin wiped his nose on the back of his hand. He looked shoddy and clownish as ever. His old tunics were mended, new sleeves sewed on, his hose darned by the housemaid. His thinning hair was never combed and he rarely shaved. He had lost his terror of falling masonry, but had now developed a fear of crossing bridges, a phobia that severely curtailed his movements in a city so dominated by a huge river. His few servants had a new nickname for him, *le Falot* meaning 'the clown' and also 'grotesque'. His father remained the 'Well-Beloved', especially after a recent visit to a nearby farm during a clear moment. He had accidentally kicked over a pailful of milk in the cowshed. He had apologised at once and insisted that the milkmaid be paid in full for it on the spot. The story of this little human courtesy had won him still more popularity.

Eustace was worried. He glanced at the multi-coloured bottles of medicine, powders and ointments by the King's bed. The Dauphin had called in a pseudo-mystic so called 'surgeon' he had met in a brothel, a charlatan called Grandison. Grandison, as unkempt as the Dauphin himself, claimed he possessed tablets given by God to Adam which guaranteed cures for all the world's ailments, especially those caused by original sin, including lunacy. Behind Eustace's back, Grandison had administered a medicine of powdered pearls, sweat of toads and urine of mink. Somehow, Charles had survived.

Grandison now appeared at the door, holding a box of saws, drills and primitive surgical instruments. When he saw Eustace, he paused uncertainly.

'Now to the next stage of his Majesty's cure,' he announced. 'Incisions to the cranium, to permit the furies to escape.' He held up a rusty once sharp tool.

'Permit the King of Ugliness to introduce daylight into your cranium,' said Eustace, sweeping the box out of Grandison's hands. He followed this up with savage kicks from his huge feet to the 'surgeon's' rear.

'Don't let me find you near the poor man again,' he roared as Grandison took to his heels.

Tears began rolling down the Dauphin's face.

'Don't worry, Sire, he won't be back,' Eustace reassured him.

'Sire? Yes, Sire. I am the true heir,' the Dauphin sobbed. He looked up. 'It's Catherine's coronation, not that *godon* Henry. But we won't be there anyway. Not her fault.' He wiped his drooling nose on the blanket. 'Thank you Eustace. I'm sorry, I was desperate. What do we do?'

'Let the King sleep off this "medicine". Then send for Odette.'

'The Little Queen? Will that do any good?'

'As long as he can fuck, he can still be your good father.'

'Yes. I'll send for her now.'

'And you will be our King one day, you'll see.'

'Thank you, Eustace. You're not only a great poet, you're a great friend as well.'

The future King of France embraced the present King of Ugliness. Their fate, too, was sealed. With the sleeping King and the weeping Dauphin, Eustace felt he had struck another blow for the whole of his bruised and beloved people. The Dauphin gazed at the astrological charts on the wall. There had to be a sign soon.

33

The broad, mile-long avenue up to the main doors of the grand Palace of the Louvre was lined with royal standards, St George banners, the Flags of the Holy Trinity and of Mary, Mother of God. Pennants of the Capet and Valois also fluttered here and there, on equal terms. Bedford had seen to that. Owen saluted his Welsh guard, stationed at intervals up to the Palace entrance. As the main Cathedral guard, they had their orders. They now knew their duties down to the last drill movement.

Owen marvelled at the elegance and precision of the gardens. They were miracles of geometry with green squares, rectangles, and curving borders of circles, laid out with close-cropped box-hedges. There was an air of order and calm about them. In the recent bread riots, put down in short order by Bedford's troops, the mob had carefully avoided trampling on them.

The Duke of Bedford gazed down from an upper window. He used a separate wing of the Palace as his administrative and military headquarters. He had requisitioned the magnificent Hotel des Tourelles close by as his private residence. The royal apartments, under the supervision of the efficient Demoiselle Agnes, had long been ready for the Queen. The Queen's courtiers had also completed the preparations for the coronation.

The intelligence network was working smoothly, providing information from York, Somerset and Suffolk; from Troyes, Orleans and Paris. King Leper had organised new couriers and agents everywhere. All were in place, as expected, placing

Bedford's administration in control, and ensuring that his administrators were the most efficient. He had never been afraid of talent, or of delegating, except to the brothers. He also knew that great events were afoot, but kept discreetly in the background. He would leave this to the Queen and to her Bedchamber. He had to show his trust in her, and early in her reign too.

'Well begun is half done,' he thought, echoing one of the old Welsh sayings he had heard Hopcyn quoting.

34

Bedford watched the approaching Owen. What a waste to stick a natural fighter in a woman's wardrobe, he thought. He knew what Owen had come to report. Bedford had assured Henry that, after his reforms, it was safe to enter Paris, but Henry still insisted on entering at the head of a large force of fighting troops, separately from Catherine. She had travelled to the Palace at the dead of night, and not even the gardeners had witnessed her arrival. It was not a sign of great trust in the citizens, Bedford sighed. An ominous start indeed. Peace for the time being was the most he could now expect, in spite of the ratification of the Treaty. He had managed to keep his brothers from each other's throats. But how long would that last? They would all be there for the coronation. They had accepted Bedford's ban on the new two-fingered 'V' gesture. The Parisians soon learned the deadly insult it represented. But again, how long would it last? Things had a way of bursting at the seams when the brothers were present. Burgundy was right. What a bunch of brigands we are. He remembered his brother as Prince Hal, in highwayman's outfit, rifling through the pockets of his father's tax officials. Typical of the whole army, always rifling through someone's pockets. But look at the ruffian Prince Hal now. He'd come a long way to be Emperor of Britain and France. Yes, concluded Bedford, it was the Welsh wars that made the Prince into a King, while the infernal Yorkists had turned him into a watchtower, on perpetual alert.

In the Queen's apartments, anticipation was mounting. Catherine had made the final selection of her Demoiselles of the

Bedchamber. All had been her last friends at the Convent school. First was the brilliant Adéle de Coucy, and then there were two of the half-French half-English members of the nobility, the clever Countess Joséphine Belknap and the vivacious Joanna de Marle. With Agnes, they would in future be in attendance on the Queen wherever she went.

Catherine had at last told her assembled friends the tremendous news. Yes, she was pregnant. She had done her duty impeccably and with extraordinary punctuality. Henry would like that, she knew. If love was not yet in the air, Catherine revelled in the thought of motherhood. She had not yet told Isabelle. But with her uncanny instincts and her spies, she probably knew already. But no public announcement yet. That would have to wait for Henry.

The Demoiselles, now joined by Agnes, looked down from the adjoining windows. The Welsh Commander of the Guard, Captain Owen, was approaching. They had heard much of him from Agnes. Even from this distance, Owen seemed to shine. What was it? Health, vigour, beauty? The Ladies craned to get a closer look.

'So you're back with us, you lovely man,' thought Agnes. 'Haven't seen you since before . . . the Brethren!' She smiled at the legendary epic of lust she and Hopcyn had shared. Amazing. They had been archangels, released after three days to ascend back to heaven. And what a price – delicious!

Catherine sent her down to greet Owen at the main doors.

35

On the first of September 1421, through the Porte de St Denis, Henry, in full fighting armour, made his triumphal entry into Paris with the perpetually truculent Burgundy at his side. Henry had ordered the naked sword of sovereignty to be borne at the head of the procession. This the waiting crowds found somewhat upsetting. They were already angry that their own beloved French Queen, Catherine, was not in Henry's military train. They were even angrier to discover that she was already in their city. This had denied them the traditional royal welcome and the usual public holiday. Burgundy was universally detested. His wild rages against the Dauphinists was reciprocated in full. The people lapsed into sullen silence as Henry and Burgundy passed, exactly as Henry had expected. What he little realised was that he was the cause of it.

On the far side of the gateway, Henry was greeted by the senior Marshal of France, Jehan de Lisle. Behind him were the leading citizens and nobility of Paris. The Marshal strictly observed the orders of chivalry. Two Counts of Paris presented Henry with a silver tray covered with a fine silk gauze. Through the gauze, in thick piles, glittered gifts of jewels and gold. Henry's eyes narrowed. He would accept the gifts, but not the demand for remittance of taxes that usually came with them. The Marshal stepped forward and bowed.

'Your Majesty,' he said. 'Please accept our humble gifts.' Henry nodded. An attendant rapidly disappeared with the expensive tray. The Marshal bowed again, and asked,

'May we now beg the honour of escorting you to the Palace

of the Louvre?' Henry was taken by surprise. This high handedness had to be answered.

'We much admire you respect for chivalry, Marshall,' he said, 'but please note that in future you make all such requests to your sovereign with eyes averted, as has been the custom for centuries past.' The Marshall reddened in embarrassment. This was perfectly true, but had long fallen out of use.

'But on this occasion you may join the procession at the rear.' A murmur of anger came with the insult, the more so because it had to be obeyed. Henry spurred his mount forward, leaving the Marshal and his entourage fuming.

So began the fifteen-year English occupation of Paris. But Henry, after this inauspicious start, would not be there to see much of it.

36

Henry had arrived at the Louvre in black mood. Burgundy had insisted on staying near the Cathedral in the barracks with his troops. The sullen populace had been anything but respectful. But Henry noticed as he got closer to the Louvre that their attitude changed. It was only when Bedford appeared on the steps that Henry knew why. For the first time loud cheers came from the crowds.

After a brief interview with Catherine, Henry re-emerged. His whole bearing was transformed for he was now a proud and happy father-to-be. Moreover, his royal line was assured. He knew it would be a boy. God was on his side. Jerusalem was growing ever closer. He had not been mistaken in his bride. He announced the pregnancy himself from the balcony. The assembled troops and Parisians joined in the cheers. Their conqueror had done it again. The Christian King Emperor, Henry V of England and France, now prepared to move out to his coronation with his lovely, fruitful consort.

37

Owen made a last inspection tour of the Cathedral. He and Hopcyn had been re-united at the Louvre. Hopcyn had greeted him with a disturbing prophecy.

'Henry born at Monmouth shall short time reign and gain all. Henry born at Windsor shall long time reign and lose all.'

'Are you sure this isn't something put out by Eustace?'

'Eustace uses it, but it's not his.'

'Is it yours?' asked Owen.

'Yes, Hopcyn confessed, 'but I'm buggered if I know what it means – yet.'

'Henry was born at Monmouth,' said Owen. 'But Henry is here, Henry is young, and Henry is king.'

'And Catherine is pregnant,' said Hopcyn.

'Then she must avoid Windsor, mustn't she?'

Owen's heart thumped. What was going on? What was fate trying to say? Even his bard couldn't tell. Or could he?

King Leper and his followers watched from the shadows of the nearby parks. Owen had placed bowmen on the buttresses, and lookouts on the roof and in the twin towers. From these vantage points nothing was missed.

Humphrey pushed his way out for one last check on the square. In front of the Cathedral, new fountains with conduits and brass stop-cocks had been installed. At the end of the ceremony, at the King's touch, from the mouths of the carved stone lions and marble stags, sparkling Rhenish wine would gush; Malmsey and the best Beaune would pour from the magic horns of the unicorn fountains. The left overs of the huge

..ion feast would be for the populace, too, a miracle of
..y after the recent famine. A towering Russian dancing bear
..od chained to a post by the entrance to the banqueting hall
opposite the Cathedral. After the feasting, the bear would first
dance to the balalaika, then to the tune of roaring mastiffs as
they baited him. The bear keeper, Humphrey noticed, drained a
bottle in salute to the bear. The crowd cheered. Damn these
foreigners, thought Humphrey, they never wait.

To outdo his popular brother, Humphrey had rashly
promised a remission of taxes. This kept the crowds in a
cheerful mood, and Owen's guards kept the Cathedral entrance
clear without any trouble.

All in order then, thought Humphrey. That puffed up Welsh
Captain had done his job at least. The only odd note was the
unusually large numbers of prostitutes behind the barriers,
easily recognisable by their striped dresses. Some were holding
up likenesses of the hideous poet, Deschamps. What barbarism,
he thought. He also heard, with a tick of anger, one of
Deschamps more crude ballades against the *godons* being
chanted. And the wine had been turned on early. That would
all have to be stopped. He looked around for Captain Owen,
but the troops just laughed and joined in the choruses. No one
knew what the stupid words mean and anyway, the men
would be up their skirts afterwards. So keep in with the girls
now, the brutes. The guards had long given up trying to
quieten anyone.

Humphrey was also apprehensive about Eleanor. After
renewing her curse over the wax heads, she had been far too
calm. But it was his day in the palace of the worthies. He would
lead the royal couple down to the high altar. But he vowed
Eleanor's day would come too, as his lawfully wedded wife
and, dare he say it, his Queen.

The engineer foreman hurried from the work banqueting
hall,

'Would your Grace please come?' he asked. Humphrey followed him impatiently into the vast hall.

'Well?' he demanded. 'What is it? I'm a busy man.'

The foreman pointed. Elaborate pulleys and hoists had lifted painted theatrical sets almost to the rafters. They represented the turrets and walls of the Holy City. They were to be lowered onto specially constructed stages at the given moment. The premiere spectacle was *The First Crusade* and the second was *The Fall of Jerusalem*, all in honour of Henry's holy dream. More cut-outs of archangels and heavenly choruses swayed over the central area. Huge stitched sheets of dyed blue linen provided a covering sky, studded with stars and the gates of paradise. Fixed onto the turrets of Jerusalem were chests of holy relics, from thigh bones of the saints to sacred prepuces. After the spectacle, a light aromatic drizzle of rose water from tanks and nozzles in the roof would refreshen the guests below. The finale was *manna from heaven* indeed, with showers of sweetmeats and newly minted coins from Bedford's reformed currency. This would keep the people happy for a few days.

'We need more pulleys up there, your Grace.'

'Is that all?' snarled Humphrey. 'Look at the plans, it's been worked out.'

'But some of the pulleys have gone missing,' protested the engineer.

'Bloody bunch of froggies. Typical.' In the distance came the blare of the heralds' salute.

'Just carry on!'

Humphrey dashed back to the Cathedral and took up his post at the door just in time. In spite of the crises and the general stupidity of those around him, Humphrey felt that he had organised a brave show. There had to be more titles and promotions in it. He stiffened to attention. The first of the royal carriages turned into the cheering square. Sitting beside Henry and Catherine was the stately Queen Mother, Isabelle. The whores gave her the loudest cheer of the day. Bedford had been kept at his headquarters by urgent news from more rebellious towns. He would come on later.

38

As Owen turned into the graveyard behind the Cathedral, he saw Hopcyn release an arrow into the shadows of a yew tree.

'What are you doing, my friend, shooting at shadows?'

'I never shoot at shadows, Owen, I know the shades only too well.'

'Tell me what is the matter, Hopcyn?'

'There's a Sin Eater about.'

'Go on?'

'He's come to kill you.'

'Hate those things. Remember them from the famine at home. What do we do?'

'Sin Eater's set snares, from Notre Dame to the Vale of Glamor, our Vale of Enchantment. It lies directly in our path.'

'So?'

'We must hunt him down and destroy him.'

'Then let us do it.'

Yes, thought Hopcyn, *y mab darogan*, the man of destiny, can do it.

39

Things began to go wrong at the altar. As Henry mounted the steps a golden spur came loose and clattered on the stone. In the world of chivalry, to lose one's spurs was to lose one's *raison d'etre*. It was a bad omen indeed. The royal couple were duly anointed and the crowns placed on their brows. But when it came to putting the King's purse on the offertory plate, the purse had gone missing. Humphrey tried to pass Henry a gold louis, but it slipped from his grasp and was lost on the floor. Worse was to come. The crowned couple came forward for the general acclamation. Humphrey gave the signal for the triptych drapes to be drawn. There was a shudder of horror. The triptych represented the Triumph of Death. The Man with the Scythe on a skeletal horse surrounded by serried ranks of grinning skulls. He was driving the damned into hell. In front of him, sinners dangled above the flames by their tongues or were boiled in steaming cauldrons; others were being gnawed by monstrous fish or devoured head first by hideous serpents, whilst yet more melted in fiery sulphur. At the bottom of the central panel lay the effigy of a corpse on a tombstone, its innards spilled open in a mass of writhing maggots. Catherine clutched her belly, swayed and nearly fainted. Henry, in suppressed rage, supported her down the aisle. In the fresh air outside, she recovered and insisted on being escorted to the banqueting hall. She would not let down her faithful subjects. She was their Queen and their blood. Henry did not deign to glance at his Chief Overseer. He was anxious to get the banquet over and done with so he could get on with the conquest of his host nation.

After ecstatically embracing her beautiful Katty and promising to visit her later at the Louvre, Isabelle was driven away by the waiting Monk and Majordomo, again to a rousing chorus from the tarts. Had she known it, she was going to miss the best of the fun.

Humphrey was faint with rage and humiliation. The hellish triptych was his fault. The submitted design had been *The Virgin Crowned*. He should have checked it. He at once ordered *The Triumph of Death* burned in the graveyard. The apprentices who had set it in place each received twenty lashes. When Humphrey was finished, not a charred fragment of the triptych remained. Hence, no one could trace who was responsible for the actual painting of it.

As Humphrey hurried to join the royal party in the hall opposite, he was drawn by shouts of alarm. Guards hurried forward, dragging the masked figure of a woman with them. She had been hiding in one of the confessional boxes. What next? groaned Humphrey. The figure seemed vaguely familiar. He motioned to the guard, who ripped the veil off the woman's face. The guards recoiled, releasing her as if she was hot pitch. It was Eleanor. Humphrey dumbly motioned the guards to return to their posts.

'I seed it all,' said Eleanor, hissing like a viper. 'The Witch of Eye, her curse be on 'em all.' Her eyes widened and she made the sign of the evil one, curving her fingers into talons. Unceremoniously, Humphrey fled from his implacable, demented mistress. He prayed for the banquet to provide some escape.

40

Catherine's 'people' had pressed in through the guards before the royal party had arrived. Humphrey had arranged for all the dishes to be laid out on the table at the same time in the English fashion, not after the sloppy French who only ate a single course at a time. The odour of steaming tureens, teeming roasts, casseroles, hot soups, and freshly baked loaves whetted the appetites of the onlookers. Henry and the royal party now entered, the guards scarcely able to hold back the throng. Burgundy had grumpily refused to leave the barracks. Such was the crush, the brothers could not dispute over order and precedence, nor did they have time to gloat over Humphrey's discomfiture. They were only too glad to find a safe seat. Fights broke out at the entrance. Things were getting out of hand. Hell, what was going on now? Humphrey felt a pang of fear. No one could trust these foreigners.

Catherine remained composed. She had been pleased and amazed by the acclamations. The cheers had not only been for herself but also for her 'Well-Beloved'. It was almost as if the spirit of her father had been at the coronation too. The people loved them both. There was so much comfort in that knowledge. Henry looked uneasily at the growing mob. He leaned forward solicitously.

'Are you alright?'

'Don't worry,' replied Catherine.

'That damned triptych.'

'We were reminded we are only mortal.'

'Not at our coronation.'

174

'I don't think I can eat much,' said Catherine sipping a glass of water. 'But their welcome has made me happy.' Henry wished he could say the same thing for himself.

The crowds sent up another cheer for her from the end of the hall.

'Send for Captains Owen's men,' Henry ordered a guard.

'Captain Owen?' murmured Catherine, as if the name was from another world.

Before the royal party could begin eating, still more people crammed in behind the retaining chain at the entrance. Some had clambered up onto the broad window sills. Still more climbed in from outside, only to be pushed backwards through the windows onto the cobble stones below. Humphrey was getting more and more alarmed. The rabble needed something to distract them. He now had his brightest idea of the day and signalled for the spectacle to begin. The artificers and engineers began lowering the sets of the Holy City. At first they descended smoothly enough, but the ropes suddenly shuddered and jammed. The sets were still twenty feet from the ground. One rope suddenly snapped. In slow motion Jerusalem tilted over. Boxes of holy relics slid off and burst open on the floor scattering bones, fragments of the true ark, the rods of Moses, bits of John the Baptist's skull, the foreskins of saints, flasks of the Virgin's milk and strips of the swaddling clothes of Jesus over the excited crowd. They watched the creaking swaying sets with terrified mirth. Was it going to fall on them? Or fall at all. A pulley hurtled down from the roof and smashed into a soup tureen. Cries of dismay and alarm were added to the hilarity. The royal party jumped to their feet. The entire set now keeled over and collapsed with a crash onto the waiting stage, which also gave way. Fortunately the set settled, half leaning against the far wall. The heavenly clouds fell next followed by the sky and the gates of paradise, dragged down time the tanks of rose water in the rafters decided to release their contents in one mighty rush, half drowning those directly underneath. Like some burst of mad artillery, this was followed by a hail of sweetmeats and wrapped coins, which nearly brained some of the uplookers. The coronation now lay in ruins about Humphrey's feet. The whores burst into one of Eustace's songs, shrieking with laughter. To this din were added howls of terror from outside. The drunken keeper had released the bear which had promptly gone berserk. It cleared the square quicker than a troop of *Ecorcheurs*. Henry herded his party towards the rear entrance. The feast could be left to the mercy of the mob. Owen's guard now poured into the Hall, driving everyone before it. The royal party was escorted through a rear entrance, Owen bringing up the rear. As he paused, the whole of Jerusalem took a final plunge, falling among the gorging celebrants around the long table, who shrieked, thinking the Day of Judgement was at hand. Owen burst into laughter. He heard someone ahead join in. He looked up to find he was gazing into the most beautiful laughing eyes he had ever seen. Yes, Catherine's.

Not everyone took the debacle as lightly. Once under the safety of his guard, Humphrey retaliated with a burst of blind spite. He ordered the wine conduits and the stop-cocks in the square turned off. He cleared the floors and tables of the discarded food and dispatched it to the royal piggeries. He pressed Henry to suspend all remission of taxes, which Henry was only too pleased to do. Humphrey also urged the suspension of the fourpenny coins, the staple currency. This would release a mountain of money for the tax gatherers. Bedford tried to veto the plan but, on this occasion, Humphrey won. The populace responded with a drunken rampage, invaded Humphrey's apartments and destroying his store of wigs. Before they could do further damage, they were driven off. Eleanor he found cowering in her chest of wax heads. He liked to think that he, her champion, had saved her from a fate worse than death. Humphrey determined to leave this place of barbarism at the first opportunity. In Paris, his chances of further honours, he now saw, were doomed. But he was wrong. That very night Henry ordered him to Westminster, again as Chief Overseer. Humphrey had, as ever, triumphed against the odds. He woke Eleanor, her spectral appearance at the Coronation now forgotten. She must go ahead, poste haste, and urge the Witch in person to effect her final cure. Their star was in the ascendant. The prophecies were against Henry. Humphrey's heroic age was about to begin.

41

It was full moon and the gardens of St Pol were light as day. Hopcyn and Eustace were searching the hen houses, dovecotes, pigeon lofts, piggeries and refuse tips for Charles VI of France. After his unorthodox medicament, he had awakened to a clear period. Then he had vanished again among the flower beds. They had been searching, and drinking, all evening. It was now midnight. The Dauphin himself had taken to the cellars, the only place Isabelle permitted him.

They settled down for a drink by a hay wain full of straw.

'King Leper tracked him back somewhere here,' said Eustace, handing the bottle to Hopcyn.

'Cunning as a fox,' said Hopcyn. 'Take my hat off to him. *Iechyd.*'

'*Santé!*'

'To coronations!'

'To the walls of Jerusalem!' Both whooped delightedly.

'Your vestal virgins were magnificent,' said Hopcyn. They drank to the whores.

'Your cracked pulleys were superb,' replied Eustace. They toasted the pulleys.

'Your turnip tops were fantastic.' They drank to the turnip tops.

'Your bear was magnificent.' They drank to the bear.

'What did you give him?'

'Ginger and mustard.' They drank to ginger and mustard.

'The deluge was your masterpiece.'

'Undoubtedly.'

'Our triptych, divine.'

'*Iechyd!*'
'*Salut!*'

From an upper window of a brothel in the Cathedral square – a prepared and very well-stocked vantage point – Eustace and Hopcyn had witnessed the entire scenes of chaos and confusion. With the help of the whores, the bear keeper and the bear, they had engineered the ensuing riot with all the skill of the antique Lords of Misrule. First the missing pulleys and the cracked ones; then the frayed ropes and the missing plans and the the the free booze; and finally the substitute design for the triptych. They felt some guilt that Catherine had been upset by that, but she had finally rewarded their labours with peals of the most splendid laughter, and in front of Henry too. They were celebrating the victory of poetry and inspiration over law and order. Isabelle was going to be disappointed that she had missed such glorious routs.

'Bless your Shining Ones, Hopcyn, they were certainly happy today.'

'Curse these solemn Christians,' Hopcyn said. 'Give me the Brethren any day.'

'We are the most creative poets this century has produced,' said Eustace. 'We are works of art in ourselves. Me, the King of Ugliness and you, Muse of the Uncanny.'

'Here's to your France Abounding with Liberty.'

'Yours too.'

'You know, Eustace, I exist only in the dreadful breakfast of my imagination.'

'I love it.'

'There's a good triad in all this,' said Hopcyn, 'but I can't remember it.'

'Play your harp,' said Eustace, 'for your friend here, the God of Warts.'

Hopcyn played. There was a rustling in the straw. Both turned as Charles, the King, struggled to his feet above them in the cart, his body painted this time in curved, leaping red and black flames. He crackled and hissed, leaping upwards again and again, as if trying to rise up into the sky.

'Ssh,' whispered Hopcyn, 'he is . . . a torch.' Hopcyn bowed to him. The King bowed back.

'Sire,' said Hopcyn, 'all red and black. You become the night, a true flame.' The King leapt upwards, pointing.

'He wants to join his friends up there,' explained Hopcyn.

'The *Bal des Ardents*. Poor little man,' sighed Eustace. Hopcyn bowed again and said.

'We thank you, Sire, your agony is the whole world's.'

Hopcyn then played as if he had been born only to do that, and with every note the three beings in the moonlight warmed to the maddest of all dreams, the dream of being happy in this life. Charles lay in the straw, eyes wide in wonder at the music, sucking his thumb like a child entranced in his own heaven.

42

In Henry's apartments, a mild post mortem was in progress between the King and Bedford. Campaign maps and documents lay on the table before them.

'Worms,' said Henry, 'are about the last thing a pregnant woman wants to see.'

'I heard the bear chased the whores up the flag poles,' chuckled Bedford.

'No laughing matter, brother.'

'Made the Queen laugh, brother. Look, no harm done in the end.'

Bedford wished that more people could see Henry like this. No arrogance, open to suggestion, unvengeful even if disapproving. He had hardly mentioned Humphrey. More reports were coming in of the disquiet the new taxes and the fourpenny ban were causing. Perhaps he could get them rescinded.

'Did you find the author of this awful prophecy?'

'Eustace Deschamps, but no proof.' Bedford had not dug too deep, and had no intention of doing so.

'I'll see the baby's not born at Windsor. And the "incidents", the spur, I mean. I intend to take no notice of them.' Henry's superstition always surprised his favourite brother. 'But to more pressing matters. What do we do about our regiments, here, and here. Three months in arrears. How did that happen?'

'Apart from the obvious milking by the contractors as well as the commanders, our basic problem, Henry, is to raise ever more revenue. The cost of your campaigns now exceeds their profits.'

'And the solution?'

'Peace. A long period of peace. Only that will increase your revenues.'

'But there is a mountain of booty out there.'

'If you confiscate any more of the troops' share, they will not re-enlist. Either way, Henry, you are left without an army. But there is nothing, brother, that cannot be solved with strong, fair administration.'

'Do you think I am sometimes too cruel?'

'It is sometimes not necessary.'

'Then I shall leave the governorship of Paris entirely in your capable hands. Now here, a petition from my faithful burgesses of London. They beg me to come "to comfort, support and refresh them by my presence." So, now to finalise the details of our Westminster coronation.'

'Done. Here.' Bedford handed Henry the plans.

'Splendid.'

'Afterwards, a royal progress.'

'But your campaigns out here?'

'The people want to greet their new Queen.'

Bedford understood. A fund raising progress as well. Their lovely Queen, pregnant with a sixth Henry on the way. The pleas of a young mother for her country? Foxy and manipulative as always. What would Catherine think?

'You will be Regent of France in my absence.'

'And Isabelle?'

'I have made a generous private donation to her renovations.'

Bedford smiled. Clever. Apart from sex, spending money was the only thing that kept Isabelle out of the way.

Now to their brothers, Humphrey and Clarence.

'I've confirmed Humphrey as Overseer of our Westminster coronation. I've ordered him to leave at once.' That particular order was not too difficult to understand.

'So Clarence is to stay in France?'

'Yes.'

'Our Clarence is a very expensive general.'

'Clarence would follow me to hell.'

'That's what I'm afraid of.'

'But under the direct supervision of Salisbury.'

'That will do it then. Stop these brawls.' But who are the worst, reflected Bedford, our bloody retainers, or theirs? However he continued,

'And if we can keep the three Dukes quiet at home . . . '

'And the Duke over here.'

'Then, Henry . . . '

'We might look forward to a little period of peace,' Henry's reasoning as always was sound when it came to planning ahead.

'And lots of full coffers,' added Bedford.

Henry poured out a glass to toast their new battle orders.

43

Owen had been ordered to lead his Household Guard in the advance party commanded by Duke Humphrey. Humphrey rode with his pack horses loaded to the maximum. His secret, closed wagons were weighted down to the axles. But they were well provided with changes of mounts and would ride with all speed to Calais.

Catherine was now making the last arrangements to her wardrobe for her Westminster coronation. To her astonishment, her Clerk of the Wardrobe seemed to know the finer points of dress and style.

'The Lady Agnes has been teaching me, your Majesty.'

'Just my name, Owen.'

'Catherine.'

'I like to feel I have my friends about me.'

After all, he did know more of her private life than most of her royal brothers, or her mother, come to that. Owen felt awkward in her presence now. There was her beauty. She glowed in her pregnancy. There was her yearning for a family. She seemed another person altogether. Yet there was still that indefinable thread connecting them. They laughed again over the rose water flood and the fall of Jerusalem. It seemed to be one of God's better jokes. Yet he was more than aware that her husband held his own life in the palm of his hands. Not to put a finger wrong, he thought, Hopcyn is right. He wanted to get back to his beloved Wales to re-establish the family estates. He had come far. He didn't complain so openly now about a fighting command.

Catherine and her three Demoiselles of the Bedchamber, Joanna, Adéle and Joséphine had finished the seemingly endless packing. They were all in their travelling habits. Agnes was in the courtyard supervising the Queen's immense baggage train. Everything had to be just right for Henry. They were waiting for the order to move out. Bedford had provided an escort of two thousand troops. There would be further pacifications along the route, if necessary – the mailed fist inside the velvet glove.

'What about this prophecy?' Catherine asked unexpectedly.

'Henry wants you to avoid Windsor.'

'That's for the baby to decide.'

Owen paused. He had to ask.

'And my leave for Wales?'

'Two months. The best I could do.'

'My thanks.'

'You will return to your duties with me, in London.'

'Why does His Majesty so much request my presence?' He used diplomatic language.

'He's a bit superstitious. You saved his life. You're his lucky charm.'

Well I'm damned, he thought, I'd never have thought of that in a hundred years.

'We'll miss you. Thank you for everything you've done for my father. What will he do when I'm gone?'

'Eustace will take care of him. He's doing a good job running your father's Household. He'll keep an eye on your brother too.'

'I feel that Charles is my brother.'

'Your father believes it too.'

'Why does my mother provoke him so?'

'Her *accouchements*.'

'She told me.'

'He was often not in his right mind.'

'I know. Thank goodness we can talk like this. We will meet again in London, won't we?'

'I'll be leaving directly after the ceremony.'

'You're still upset about not having a command?'

'Not so much.'

Catherine hesitated.

'Agnes had these made for me. As a token of thanks for my father, my brother, my friends.' Catherine held out a silk handkerchief embroidered with the white *fleur-de-lis*.

'And Agnes had these made for me . . . ' smiled Owen, 'the minx.' He held out a similar kerchief, this one bordered with red dragons.

'Bless you and Hopcyn and Agnes. My true friends.' They exchanged kerchiefs, smiling. They heard distant shouts of commands and trumpets. Humphrey's vanguard was preparing to move out. Owen took the kerchief, saluted and hurried out. Before he thrust the kerchief into his tunic, he pressed it briefly to his lips.

44

Humphrey rode at the head of the column so all could see just who was Chief Overseer of this most royal progress. Thank God his troublesome brothers were out of the way for once, and Salisbury and Warwick on inspection tours. He prayed he wouldn't encounter his arrogant Cardinal uncle, Winchester, on this triumphal journey.

To his surprise, the whole column made rapid progress. No pacification was needed. Along the entire route, in towns and countryside, the populace turned out to cheer their beautiful Queen and her court of lovely Demoiselles. The royal party were often held up by lavish welcomes, gifts and freedoms of towns. Catherine felt relieved after all the bloodshed. This was the peace her spirit longed for. She did her duty tenderly, firmly and with evident pleasure. Yes, they thought, she comes after her father, the 'Well Beloved', and cheered all the more loudly.

Humphrey's dislike of Owen – the 'Welsh clothes peg' as he called him – intensified. But he was careful to keep his remarks to himself. Owen had the ear of the Queen. How or why Humphrey had no idea, but it was best that he be careful. And Owen was often in the company of that disgusting leper. There was some pact with the devil there, and it was best not be tarred with that brush. As a result of all his reasoning, Humphrey decided to keep strictly out of the way with the consequence that things went much more smoothly than expected. The royal train arrived in time and in good order at the port of Calais. The transport ships rode on a gentle swell in the bay, their sails unfurled in readiness. To the cheers of the townspeople crowding the quay, the radiant Queen and her Court departed on a bright, sunny day with a fair wind for the English shore.

45

The royal party was unable to get in close to the quay at Dover. Unusually low ebb tides exposed sands which had never before seen the light of day. The royal vessels were forced to stand off shore.

Catherine was able to see in close detail her first sight of her new country. She was suitably impressed by the towering white cliffs, a difficult obstacle for any invader. But what about those who wanted to get out? A long swim, she thought. This island is indeed a fortress.

Ships' boats were lowered and the Queen and her companions were rowed ashore. On the beach waited a welcoming deputation. The Barons of the Cinque Ports were there as were the commanders of the local forts, the leading gentry and citizens of the towns and counties, all dressed in white cloaks trimmed with the imperial purple as a sign of respect. Henry Chichele, the Archbishop of Canterbury himself, stood on the shale higher up, pastoral staff in hand, proud to greet his pregnant Queen before her people.

It was at once evident that even the boat couldn't reach dry land. The Archbishop pointed his staff to the Barons and motioned to the boats. The five Barons immediately pushed through the waves. To shrieks and giggles, they lifted out the bemused ladies, chaired between their arms, and waded back to deposited them safely on the high tide mark. Catherine loved this little adventure, and laughingly waved to the waiting crowds. It was already well known that she was carrying the heir. Loud cheers of genuine admiration and affection rose on all sides. This was a lady who could take things in her stride! The Archbishop, with the aid of the angels, had turned an embarrassing problem into a diplomatic triumph. It was an auspicious start for the royal progress.

Henry and Owen and his escort landed farther up the coast. Owen was ordered on to London with Humphrey and his troops. Henry joined his bride ten miles inland from Dover to still more declarations of loyalty, declarations that Henry knew could soon be changed into donations. This was better than he had ever expected. The progress would at least pay for itself, and maybe even show a profit. The whole magnificent three-mile long procession continued its stately progress to Westminster, and beyond.

Humphrey gloried in being back and playing such a prominent role again. He would shine as brightly as any bauble on display. He had conveniently forgotten the banquet debacle in Paris, although a second banquet would be held in the White Hall of the Abbey. Humphrey had ordered Owen to carry on with this job, although Humphrey still interfered. Owen noticed the Duke's retainers always turned out in force. They mobbed and cheered him in the streets, often provoking Clarence's or Winchester's retainers to savage brawls. The Yorkist mobs were also much in evidence, determined not to be outdone. These factions within factions often fought without being sure who they were fighting. Owen learned that Eleanor had made free distributions of bread and beer to the populace, who succeeded in being half drunk most of the day. These were Humphrey's own 'brave lads' who loudly shouted *Humphrey for King*. He wouldn't let them down, and greeted them with the two fingered 'V' sign, which provoked instant cheers that led to assaults on the French in the capital. Owen was constrained to remind his Commander that the gesture was banned, and the wearing of the white or red rose disallowed.

Angrily, Humphrey desisted. Looking at Owen's retreating figure, he decided that Owen too should receive the attentions of the waiting Witch. Humphrey fretted over Eleanor's return. Was his annulment through? Who would be the first of the wax heads to melt? Who would be the first to feel his sword sweeping through the land – his brothers or the three devil Dukes? Whatever, they would all fall before it.

The King-in-Waiting was getting impatient with destiny. He was ready. Why then wasn't fate, the sluggard!

46

Humphrey surveyed the expanse of the famous White Hall of Westminster Abbey. This was the banqueting Hall and Assembly Rooms for the cream of the land. The high vaulted ceiling gave the impression of immense height, and the width created an astonishing sense of space. When empty, the echoes sometimes returned to drown out the very voice that created them. When full, the Hall sounded like a town square on Market Day. Just off the Hall were the royal apartments, known as the Green Rooms, where the Kings and Queens of England traditionally entertained their personal friends. Even the royal bedchamber opened directly onto the Hall. Catherine and her Ladies approved of the arrangement for it gave them privacy and also easy access to the Court and the City.

The procession would start off from the Hall and move along the cloisters of the Abbey directly to the high altar, where the Archbishop, bishops and nobility were in attendance. Once there, the procedure was identical to that at St Michel, in Troyes. Even the Latin prayers were the same. When the coronation was over, they would return by the same route, and after a short interval, settle down for the evening banquet.

There was little complaint from the royal brothers or Henry's generals. The high table seating had been arranged by Henry. Those below the salt had been given their appointed places by him. Henry made certain his spur was firmly strapped on, and that the money for the offertory was safe inside his breastplate. Outside and inside, Owen's guards were deployed in the same fashion as in Paris. Everyone knew their parts and positions. There was no chance of error this time. Henry was in full command.

Humphrey as Chief Overseer moved around freely and, though nothing more than a royal husk, could still draw the attention of all eyes. He knew his retainers would be awed by his public prominence, however powerless. But he was satisfied – for the moment. Wait till Eleanor arrived back!

While the ceremony was in progress, hundred of cooks and servers would load the long refectory tables with a sumptuous feast, again in the English fashion, every course on the table at the same time. There were however some concessions to French cuisine, at the request of the Queen herself. Provision was made for the poor at the doors. Free bread and beer would be distributed all day. There would be no hunger riot this time.

Though the principal players were nervous and the clerics sometimes gabbled their words – they had been warned by Henry not to be tardy – this coronation passed without a single mishap or evil presentiment. Once settled in the White Hall again, the atmosphere was as relaxed and good natured as anyone could remember. Perhaps, Catherine thought, her coming really did presage more peaceful times.

Amid a cheerful buzz of anticipation and excitement, the hundreds of guests settled into their seats. The augurs had been favourable indeed. Henry and Catherine sat side by side under regal canopies with their royal brothers. Also on Catherine's right sat the captured King of Scotland, James I, taken in battle and imprisoned in the Tower. To commemorate the coronation, Catherine begged for James's release. As royalty himself, James had the right of chivalry to sit at the high table. Henry was reluctant, remembering the Scots' 'treacheries' at Montereau, but Catherine prevailed and James was invited to the banquet. He now sat, relieved and somewhat dazed, under his own special, carved canopy. This gesture of royal clemency was greeted with cheers. Maternal tenderness had won the day, the best of omens. Was Henry changing, and for the better? Later, as a condition of his release, James promised never again to oppose his feudal superior, Henry. This promise was directly due to Catherine's show of mercy, a lesson learned by very few at the banquet.

A huge fire blazed in the great fireplace. A vast stone canopy over it channelled the smoke and fumes up a high chimney. A hundred torches blazed from new wall brackets, which were replenished as they burned out. The high tables were lit by candelabras of the longest burning tallow candles from the Abbey. A royal display of solid silver and gold plate on a side table was on permanent view.

Gifts of miniature table ornaments, or *subtleties*, were laid out on the table before each guest, concealed at first under coloured silk gauzes. These miniatures were variously made of silver, gold, marzipan, icing or spun sugar, pastry, or any moulded material. They could take any shape, usually one which meant something special to the individual – a heraldic beast, the battlements of a famous town, weapons, a musical instrument, angels, a royal crest, a coats of arm, a portrait or a likeness. Some were valuable, others worth no more than a sweetmeat in a shop. When Henry lifted his gauze, before him lay a tiny, near perfect replica of the walls of Jerusalem, with his favourite Trinity banner flying from a tower. This was greeted with wild cheers. Next, the Archbishop. Under his silk lay sculptured marchpanes of angels with Gabriel announcing a hymn to *the prince of peace*, Henry himself, from a silver trumpet. This, too, was greeted with roars of approval.

Around Catherine now stood her special attendants. First, King James himself. Catherine had presented him with a silver chalice. His chivalric duty for the evening was to pour wine for Catherine whenever she called for it. On her right stood the rising star, the Earl of March, who was a direct descendant of the old King, and close by was the weasel-faced young

Somerset. Both were present as a gesture of reconciliation. The Earl's duty was to hold Catherine's sceptre at all times. Catherine's pantlers and almoners were all drawn from old families, the Beauchamps and Salisburys, to show that in the feudal hierarchy she, a royal, stood far above them. At Catherine's feet, much to her amusement at first, sat the Countess of Warwick, her special task to clear away any spilled food or wine. Catherine at once invited the Countess to stand behind her with the Earl. This again brought general approval. The banquet was off to a marvellous start.

Since it was a Friday, it was a feast of fish. There were steaming dishes of bream of the sea in cream of almonds, conger roasted with lamprey, fresh carp and sturgeon, boiled porpoise and crabfish, some served a single dish at a time to honour the cuisine of France. Strained jellies of different colours had one of Henrys favourite mottoes, in raised icing, *Out of diversity, unity*, all with a surround of delicate columbine blossoms. The wines were the best that France could provide, much of it being booty taken on many a successful campaign.

There was only one blot on the splendid evening. When Humphrey sat down late in the evening, after his duties were completed, and removed the silk from his subtlety, he paled in alarm. There before him lay a model of St George with a golden lance pinning a snarling cur to the ground. The cur resembled the Dauphin, and wore a *fleur-de-lis* crown. The legend read, *St George of English fame, beasts like this doth ever tame*. Before any other guests could glimpse it, Humphrey swept it under the table, but not before Catherine had taken in every detail. She started, paled, and fingered the crucifix her father had given her. It was strange, but she had been thinking of him at that very moment. With quiet determination, she smilingly carried on. No one was going to spoil this special, peaceful evening of hers. Henry glared at his brother, who shrivelled up. Who had done it? Not on his orders. One of his London retainers no doubt, stupid bastards. He'd see to them tomorrow. He ground his teeth in rage and was scarcely able to eat. The rest of the guests studiously ignored him and his crushed subtlety, until they dispersed for bed. Apart from Humphrey, the evening went down as one of the most agreeable ever enjoyed in the annals of the great White Hall of the Abbey, and all agreed it had mainly been due to the grace and tenderness of the new Queen.

47

The revelry in the White Hall floating on the night air, was now drawing to a close. The mood was triumphant. A great victor come home with his lovely bride. Owen could feel it. Joy, success. At last Catherine had a real taste of it. Owen felt a warm glow at the thought. For once, *Triumphs of Death* were dead and gone.

He was making his last inspection of the ring of guards around the Abbey. The light was fitful, with occasional gleams of moon. He could make out the silhouettes of his men along the far side of the Abbey, some sheltering under the huge arches of the flying buttresses. Owen passed under them probing the darkness with his eyes. They formed perfect cover for anyone to slip unseen into the Abbey precincts.

King Leper prowled the old cemetery, investigating a report of movements there. Yes, thought Owen, King Leper – the Great Hearted, that would be his new name. The best of brothers, the last and only. He looked up at the soaring buttresses, wondering at the faith that raised such mighty monuments. Christians he found were mostly mean-spirited, superstitious and intolerant. But not like this. He sighed. The Welsh, he mused, were throwbacks. Odd to be Welsh in this day and age. Mystic Pythagorean poets trying to drink or fornicate themselves to death, often at the same time.

'What am I doing here,' he asked for the hundredth time. Was his star rising. Was Hopcyn right? Hopcyn. He smiled in the gloom. By God, Hopcyn and Eustace had excelled themselves. Their antics beyond compare. They gave one hope.

Tall tales between life and death. Poetic justice is the only justice he thought, the other sort is just luck.

'Yes, we Welsh, superannuated clowns,' he decided. 'But with great hearts, like King Leper.'

A sudden scratching came from the top of the buttress. He stared upwards. What was that? He was instantly flattened by a hurtling body, the wind knocked out of him. At once he felt himself enfolded in a spreading leathery cloak which pressed down over his face, cutting off his air. Owen gasped, fighting for breath. Chittering bat sounds came from the beast. Strange stick-like fingers gouged his hands, tore at his breast, slicing open his tunic with scissor-like cuts. Owen kept his senses, holding off suffocation, tensing for a supreme effort. The hands were over his heart now. An appalling stench rose to his nostrils. He heaved with all his strength. The force pinning him down was immovable. In desperation, he heaved again. Useless. More chittering. The beast scrabbled to break through to Owen's skin. Then a shout close by; peals of a leper's bell; a bobbing light. An arrow sped overhead, splintered on the stonework. The Sin Eater paused, his marble-black eyes giving him perfect night vision. King Leper was charging out of the graveyard, torch in hand, bell sounding madly. Two bowmen and Hopcyn followed behind him. The Sin Eater sprang onto the curve of the buttress, scrambled upwards like an escaping rat. At the top, he paused, staring furiously down at King Leper. At once an arrow thunked through one raised wing. Chittering with rage, the Sin Eater melted into the lengthening shadows of the upper masonry.

Hopcyn and King Leper helped Owen to his feet.

'Sin Eaters, a cloud of them,' said King Leper.

'What?'

'Among the tombstones. One got away.' King Leper rang his bell. 'Scattered the rest. You alright?'

Owen looked down at the shreds of his tunic. Underneath,

the chain-mail shone dully in the light, scored and discoloured. Hopcyn pointed at the scratches on the back of Owen's hands.

'Just like Isabelle's,' he said. The three paused, thinking as one,

'Not with the devil?'

'Ah, the stink!' Owen said, pulling at the gluttonous mass on his chest. It stuck to his fingers. 'Ugh!?' He wiped it off on the stonework. 'What is it?'

'A little bit of hell, Owen,' said King Leper. 'Poultice, to draw the sins out of your heart and soul.'

Hopcyn sniffed and recoiled.

'Used that bit over and over.'

'Owen,' said King Leper, 'with this unleavened dough, the Sin Eater eats the risen sins of our people. Now he's after yours, too, the immortal ones.'

'Immortal?'

'Your destiny, Owen.'

'Haven't lived long enough.'

'Your future sins,' Hopcyn said.

'Why?'

'*Y mab darogan*, the son of prophecy.'

'Me?'

'Your destiny is now in play.'

'To what end, Hopcyn?'

'To leave for Ynys Môn in the morning.'

'And wear chain mail at all times,' warned King Leper.

Hopcyn stared at King Leper. A sense of somewhere else. The tremors of the warp-spasm. The image formed, clear as a rose, then vanished in a second, like petals in a storm. Hopcyn shook himself. Abruptly, he embraced King Leper and kissed him full on both wasted, rotted cheeks.

'Ha!' smiled King Leper. 'Welcome, Hopcyn!'

They embraced again. But it was not a welcome kiss. Hopcyn had seen King Leper impaled on black talons. It was a farewell kiss, and both knew it. The vision of the three suns had also flashed closer. Hopcyn thrust it away. The mists over those deadly suns could stay in place.

48

The next morning, Hopcyn, Owen and King Leper set off for Wales. Henry in the meantime had decided to celebrate what was left of summer and possibly autumn with his bride. Her Progress must now not only be seen, it must also be seen to be paying. The saints would do the trick. They travelled northwards. At St Albans, the royal train stopped at the shrine of St John the Evangelist, famous for pilgrimages. They sat in state in the spacious main chamber of the town hall, receiving vows of fidelity. Henry had invited the most powerful nobles, landowners, Mayor and aldermen of the town corporation. There were representatives from the clergy, from bishop to humble clerk, as well as artisans. He also insisted on seing the apprentices – for he never forgot his perpetual need for recruits. Many present had benefited from the French wars, but they now complained that the profits had dwindled to nothing and that they were a poor investment. Henry was determined to reverse this trend. Piracy on the high shires, he thought with a smile. He would do it. Henry's final meeting with his parliament in Westminster had to be backed with supplies from the north, in advance and in abundance. The Yorkist threat had melted away before him.

The King now addressed his faithful subjects of St Albans.

'My Lords, Aldermen, commoners, all of you joined in unity, you see before you not only your sovereign, but the leader of the faithful of St George, patron of our wars in France, blessed of Jesus, protector of saints. On our march to Jerusalem, St George has indeed blessed our arms. I need mention only Agincourt.'

Wild cheers greeted the famous name.

'We urge you again to give your wholehearted support. We are now established in Paris, one of the richest cities in Christendom.'

The crowd pricked up its ears.

'My brother, the Duke of Bedford, has just informed me by special messenger that the coffers of state in the capital are now full!'

Even greater cheers greeted this news.

'We know that profits rise and fall as in any trade, but the whole of France is now part of our dominions. And let me remind you, the supplies will not only be going in the direction of the Holy City, they will also reach here, into your very borough of St Albans!'

The crowd was now on its feet.

'Crecy! Agincourt! Paris. Where next!?

Henry knew at once that his appeal had worked. 'Greed and patriotism,' he thought. 'God bless them.' He continued aloud, however, in more tender tones.

'You see before you the true queen of the dominions we have won in France. And within Her Majesty at this very moment, there moves before you here the rightful heir to the dual crowns of France and England.'

He paused, and then shouted,

'Will you fight for your Queen?' Huge hurrahs went up.

'Will you fight to the end?' was followed by another gigantic acclamation. Catherine inclined her head; so lovely, so maternal, so vulnerable. It inspired generosity as well as trust. 'Bless her,' thought Henry. 'Whatever love is, she is the best recruiting officer I've ever had.'

At a prearranged signal, the royal commissioners threw open the doors, revealing tables outside loaded with documents and open war chests. Officers of Henry's guard stood by to sign on new recruits. With Henry placing a bag of gold in the first box, and Catherine dropping her diamond necklace into the second – to be retrieved later, as arranged by Henry – the whole assembly queued up with donations, vying in amounts with each other, now happy to sign the promissory notes placed before them. Henry's coffers clinked to the sound of coin. Henry beamed and made the sign of the cross.

The same scene was repeated in a dozen towns northwards. After St Alban's came Leicester, Lincoln and York. From there back to Westminster and the final stop. After a second visit to St Albans, where the response had exceeded his wildest expectations, Henry went ahead to London, leaving Catherine to follow on at a more leisurely pace. She deserved it, brave girl!

Catherine mostly kept her mouth shut, as she had planned from the beginning. She wanted some peace. Yes, during the strenuous tour, she often thought as she grew bigger and bigger that she had something of the tough Wittelsbach constitution.

In spite of the adoration, she felt out of things. Like an ornament on a shelf, she was admired by everyone, but only from a distance. She longed for the human contact of her Demoiselles waiting in London, and her friends far off in Wales. She had now reconciled herself however, whether love was there or not, to her royal duty. Resting in her closed litter on the road to London, she had a feeling that the baby would arrive when least expected. But, she reflected, that was always the way. Nonetheless, she was ready to do her duty there too. But, she reflected, was this all there was to her life – just duty?

49

Henry left the great Hall of Westminster in high spirits. Parliament had granted the supplies. They had complained of 'the constant drain of resources' – without mentioning those seeping in. But with reinforcements and revenues arriving daily from the north, the Londoners would not be outdone. They granted the customary fifteenths from every borough and county in the country. The royal tax gatherers were on their way. The clergy had granted a solid tenth of their tithes. Henry now met his officials of the Exchequer to tot up the final sums. Seventy thousand in cash, not bad, eighteen thousand alone from his faithful uncle of Winchester. Not a penny came from Humphrey, of course. They now calculated the expenses of the present and coming campaigns. Henry leaned back in dismay. However much they checked and re-checked, the net figures showed only a small, negligible profit, even after the recent donations and supplies. Even those feathering their own nests made little difference to the final sums. 'Blast,' thought Henry, 'I must have another Agincourt.' The English empire overseas was beginning to drain the homeland dry.

50

The evening was close and sticky. Pillars of greasy smoke rose into the lowering sky. Strange sights and sighs exhaled from all sides. The three had arrived on the sinister day of *Samhain*, when the spirits of the dead rise from *Annwn*, the Celtic Otherworld, to meet the quick in this world. Giant bonfires lit to fend off the visitations, would burn all night. The local inhabitants huddled together, drinking, singing, dancing, all sleepless in their frantic, drunken revelries trying to drive out the fear of the unknown.

Leper and Hopcyn walked their weary horses in the rapidly fading twilight. They were following a path up *Mynydd Myrddin*, Merlin's mountain, to the craggy height of Arthur's Seat. The great Glyndŵr himself was said to have retired here after his final defeat. He now slept in the immemorial cave, awaiting the call to return. Hopcyn remembered the Sin Eaters gathering to feast off Glyndŵr. They had been driven off by the bards and Glyndŵr's legend was freed, as Owen's would be.

Shouts of fear came from straight ahead.

'Stop, we're right in the middle of it,' said Hopcyn. The cries of the hideous Messengers of the Dead came clear to their straining ears:

Food for the Messengers of the Dead,
Food for shades long since fled.

Darkness fell with appalling suddenness, the path ahead instantly shrouded in impenetrable gloom. The inky coverlet of night came down over the entire mountain. At once a thousand glittering candle flames dotted the slopes. The outlines of hollowed out pumpkins, carved into demon grins to drive off the spirits, sprang into view. The eye-gleaming heads seemed to float and bob above the undergrowth. The cry came again:

Food for the Messengers of the Dead.
Food to keep the spirits from your bed.

'If we get separated,' warned Owen, 'we meet at Arthur's Seat, by the dragon-headed rock. Watch for the smoke.'

Hopcyn saw the spirits rise in the hollows of his vision.

'What do you see?' asked Owen and Hopcyn pointed,

'The crimson-eared white-haired hounds of *Annwn*.' His multi-coloured eyes followed the pack from hell as it loped by, invisible to King Leper and Owen. Hopcyn pointed still,

'With eyes red as after weeping. Many deaths here. Listen! Tolling trees and rings of blood, howling bells in every wood. And – there! Get down!'

They shrank lower among the roots of the tree. Tall, feathered, stick-like shapes rose above the branches, their long, dripping beaks sharp as daggers.

'Lantern Birds,' whispered Hopcyn. 'Foul, one-legged familiars of Sin Eaters. Look now, picking pale entrails in red mires. Sin Eaters first, then those.' The spectral birds faded and dissolved, leaving hissing, knife-like sounds in the air.

'Friends, I must go.'

'Where?'

'To stare down the fates,'

'Tell us.'

'Great Heart, King of Lepers, brother of Owain,' Hopcyn motioned to the topmost crags. 'Up there, there's a hidden ruin known only to bards, called the Dolmen of Unease. That ruin is the haunt of a blood-eyed, red-cloaked fury which flits like a giant crimson bat among the blocks. This fury, which rises on Samhain night, is guarded by a lizard, and when that fury yearns to travel, she curls herself into a wheel, and flickers like a thousand funeral candles, and whirls, onwards and downwards, onwards and downwards . . . '

he felt the spasm come,

' . . . here to join the Lantern birds, the Sin Eaters, to fall among us. Do as I do. I know. We must go alone now, yes, all of us. Fates demand it. I go first. You, Owain, that direction. King Leper, straight ahead.' The hissing, sweeping blade sounds grew closer until they seemed to hover directly over the ash tree.

'One, two three – go!'

The neighing horses bolted the way they had come. The three broke away from the path and dashed separately for the distant underbrush. Owen saw King Leper disappearing ahead. Owen jumped the ditch but as he landed on the other side, his legs were swept from under him and he fell in a tumbling, uncontrollable rush into the blackness.

51

Thomas, Duke of Clarence, sat down to dinner in the great hall of his requisitioned Château de Pont de l'Arche, close to the border of Normandy. He was bursting with pride. He had, at last, surpassed his brother in battle. In the absence of the Earl of Salisbury he, the second in line, had led a sortie over the Loire into the province of Maine, defeating the large Dauphinist force sent against him, and won his spurs. He kept on his golden coronet, and exulted. Victory at last. And cheap. What would his brother say to that? He had returned laden with booty and numerous nobles for ransom. Clarence's dinner guests, his brother's new Marshal of France, Sir Gilbert Umfraville, and the doughty Earl of Huntingdon, exchanged worried glances. Clarence was lucky to be alive. It had been a trap. A strong French force had failed to come up in time. The Dauphinists were merely bait. Clarence dismissed this as pure fantasy, or jealousy. Clarence, the hot head, thought Gilbert, was even worse than the rash Burgundy. Salisbury had ordered no offensive action until his return. He would be furious.

The Earl groaned as Clarence made the 'V' sign of contempt.

'I will sweep them away like chaff!' He shouted for more wine. Instead of the Wine Server, a muddy archer uniform burst in. He paused for breath.

'Get on with it,' ordered Clarence. 'I'm thirsty.'

'The French. Advancing on Bauge. In force.' He held out a message.

'But Bauge is mine! Muster for an immediate attack!' Gilbert took the message.

'Clarence,' said Huntingdon, 'we have been ordered not to go over to the offensive.'

'This is my command!'

'There are five thousand of them.' Sir Gilbert pointed at the message. 'Not counting their cavalry.'

'Another Agincourt then. We'll take them from the rear.'

'That's exactly what they'll expect.'

'And I'll lead the victory parade this time.'

'We do not have the Men-at-Arms.'

'The Men-at-Arms have me.'

'You have only eight hundred men.'

'Each worth ten froggies.'

'At least wait 'til the reserve archers come up.'

'Go home, then. You are good only to tend the graveyards of heroes!' With this parting prophetic shot, the half drunk Duke strapped on his sword. He ignored his heavy breast plate and clattered out of the hall calling for his horse. The Marshall and Huntingdon followed in trepidation.

An hour later Clarence was surveying the enemy from the edge of a wood on the far side of the river. Beauge stood below them. The French were strongly entrenched on a hill overlooking the town. An open meadow stretched down from the hill to the unguarded bridge. Clarence's depleted garrison was desperately manning the ramparts. They had beaten off three assaults, but had suffered heavy casualties. They stood and yelled to their compatriots. French scouts had spotted Clarence coming up. Any element of surprise had been lost. Clarence rejected all the advice of the experienced Gilbert and Huntingdon. He had concentrated his small force of cavalry just back from the bridge.

'Straight over,' he ordered. 'Up the meadow, into the heights. Clear them out. I'll follow with the infantry.'

The cavalry clattered across the wooden bridge, spread out and charged. At once things went seriously wrong. The horses bogged down and were soon floundering up to their knees in mud. The French had diverted a stream and flooded the meadow. Without considering the obvious fact that the mud would hinder his infantry as much as his horses, Clarence, ordered his men to advance, urging them on from the front. The French could scarcely believe their luck. They waited for the right moment. When Clarence reached the struggling cavalry, the Dauphinists launched an all-out counter attack from their fortifications, using cross-bowmen and light artillery on the closely packed masses. It was slaughter. The Scottish Earl of Buchan, leading the Scottish contingent, recognised his royal enemy by the golden coronet he still wore. Thirsting for revenge for his hanged Scots, he charged Clarence. Clarence was thrown into the mud. As he staggered to his feet, the Earl ran him through with his lance. A breast-plate would have diverted the blow. The Earl finished off the Duke with his poleaxe. When Buchan held up the smashed coronet, an almighty cheer went up. The King's own brother, defeated in battle and dispatched by a hated Scot.

It was now the Dauphinists' turn. The garrison lost heart. Beauge surrendered, and was picked bare of its booty. English knights were now held for ransom. The remaining forces retreated under Gilbert to the Château de l'Arche, which was itself now threatened. The bard of the Earl of Buchan wrote:

Buchan laid his wicked lance at rest,
Having tamed the bloody crest
Of royal Clarence, once Plantagenet.

The Earl of Salisbury galloped in four hours later. The French had released the body, even returning the twisted coronet. Salisbury dreaded the task of telling Henry. Henry had loved his brother in spite of his foolhardiness. But it was Clarence's command. Only Henry could have countermanded his order. Looking at the broken body of the Duke, Salisbury knew that such rash actions could well lose them the war.

52

Only two others, apart from the enemy, gloried in the loss. They were royals too, and were now gloating over a line of wax heads.

'Done,' said Eleanor triumphantly. She plunged the final needle into Clarence's head and draped a black shroud over it. That the dead man had been her soon to be husband's brother scarcely entered her mind. She simply said to Humphrey.

'Raise high thy talons, love, ye be second in line now.

They stood in the Long Room of their Palace of Placentia at Greenwich, panelled with solid oak and decorated with a myriad of rose carvings. They practically lived in these quarters, acting out their glorious roles as Emperor and Empress. To please the mob Henry had ordered a mystery play on the life of St George, clearly seen as himself, to be performed on all feast days with free beer. The mob went on another rampage, shouting 'Humphrey for King'. This added to his present delight.

At the end of the room, on a raised dais, was a replica of the Abbey throne. Humphrey installed himself in it. Eleanor unveiled the Temple of Heroes on Humphrey's right. She placed a model orb and sceptre in his hands and pointed dramatically at the empty niche.

'Thy place in history be here!' And so was hers. In the niche was a second pedestal. On it rested a coronet. She raised it high, passed it over to Humphrey and knelt before him. Humphrey did as he had been instructed. So simple! He ceremoniously crowned her, and she took her place behind the throne. Soon, she thought, I will be sitting beside him. The annulment had come through. Humphrey was marrying her in two days. Humphrey put on his regal look. Yes, the world was finally coming round to his point of view. It had moved over and made room for him. And high time, too! He swelled so he filled the whole room, a mighty Caesar indeed. He nodded graciously to Eleanor. Raising her voice to breaking point, Eleanor began caterwauling a song, which even a cat could not have recognised. The giggling serving wenches, scullions and clerks listening at the door, cringed at the noise. Later, one of them tip-toed into Humphrey's bedchamber carrying a handful of turnip tops.

53

Catherine sat alone on the canopied four-poster bed in the Green Rooms off the White Hall. She had given Agnes permission to visit Wales. Hopcyn, King Leper and Owen seemed to have disappeared from the face of the earth. Agnes would track them down. Her Clerk of the Wardrobe had been away for too long. Henry might get angry, but Catherine only longed for their honest, friendly company. Her father's absence weighed on her. Nothing had been seen of him for months either. The thought of Isabelle brought a nostalgic pang. Isabelle was a life force, in spite of her life style. And what was the Dauphin doing? His supporters seemed to have taken matters into their own hands for opposition to Henry was growing.

Catherine had no truck with the revenge her husband was planning. War and more war, while she was burgeoning with new life. And all against her own people? She wondered how many more of her compatriots would be slaughtered before her husband felt secure in his God-appointed kingship.

The Palace of Westminster had been thrown into turmoil when the news of Clarence's death arrived. Salisbury himself had announced it. After the first shock of grief, Henry became white-hot with rage. First was the loss of revenue, but just as important was the loss of face. And by a Scot. He should never have had King James at his table. He should have had him at the block. He would teach them a lesson. Catherine could hear his shouted orders in the Assembly room. He was organising a punitive expedition across the Channel. His uncle, the Cardinal of Winchester, was with him filling in for the departed royal.

This calmed Henry somewhat. His formidable uncle knew how to set about things. With the Cardinal and the Church's money at his side, Henry knew he could retrieve the situation. But the detested Humphrey was now suddenly only second in line, after Bedford. Henry and his entourage knew that Henry's direct involvement was needed to plug the royal gap. Humphrey was again getting out of control, and so was his consort to be. Humphrey's retainers were again rioting in the streets. A major victory would restore family unity. At the big table covered with the familiar military maps of France and Normandy, Salisbury now awaited Henry's final orders.

'At the next encounter, my *gallowglasses* will take on the Scots.'

'They are cousins,' observed Warwick, 'being Irish.'

'It takes a Celt to catch a Celt,' said Henry. 'I learned that in the Welsh wars.'

'It was a fair fight,' Warwick said, determined not to be intimidated.

'It was not. I will not hear otherwise.' Henry shouted as he paced up and down furiously. 'My brother's head was crushed in as he lay on the ground, England's next in line. My order of the day – in future, all Scots taken in battle will be executed on the spot.'

'There are nobles in the Scottish army,' objected Warwick.

'Not any more. King James, my prisoner, has sworn never to take up arms against me. If the Scots do, then they are traitors. That too is chivalric law. See that my order is carried out, Warwick.'

Warwick bowed courteously and left for the barrack lines. Henry had a presentiment that, unlike the devoted Warwick, he would never make the pilgrimage to Jerusalem. He tried to shake off a feeling of foreboding. The Yorkists had also resumed hostilities after his departure. They seemed to sit on his brows like a cold sweat. He had never had such a feeling before.

The whole army was now ready to leave at notice, Salisbury at their head. With him and W; side, and Winchester and Bedford behind him, was surely his.

Henry had already taken leave of Catherine. She had done so much for him and for his royal line. He did love her. Or did he? That most private of emotions, love, had been submerged under a sea of public duties. He had no time to think of such things. But above all, he had the heir to consider. He had ordered Catherine not to have the baby at Windsor. She must be accompanied at all times by her Ladies and her physicians. The *accouchement* must be at Westminster. The bardic rhyme about the two Henrys haunted him. He had told the Archbishop to baptise the babe as sixth in the line of Henrys, a true Lancastrian. Catherine's preference for a name was not even considered. But Henry had officially nominated Cardinal Winchester as Chief Sponsor at the baptism. That should settle any doubters. But the Cardinal was more worried about Humphrey. His nephew, he knew, was the very incarnation of vanity and foolishness. But his stupidity made him dangerously unpredictable. What would happen if Henry the King was suddenly killed, like his brother Clarence?

54

With Adéle, Joséphine and Joanna at her side once again, Catherine felt restored. But her condition now gave rise to increasing bouts of restlessness. She couldn't relax unless she was on the move. She was suddenly drawn to vistas of flowing water. On impulse, she decided on a journey down the Thames. Why not? The royal barge was moored at Westminster. They would wait for good weather first and make a leisurely, easy day of it. Nothing could go wrong. The physicians and the Demoiselles would accompany them everywhere, as Henry had ordered. Delighted at the prospect, the Ladies prepared a travelling picnic on the Thames, under silken awnings, without the fuss and bustle of the Court. Delightful! Their destination was to be Richmond, just a few hours sail from Westminster. A lazy day. Catherine felt she deserved it. Henry was pleased. Henry was busy. Duty was done.

55

Owen woke. His eyes slowly registered his surroundings, faint moonlight reflected off the surface of a sluggishly flowing river. He lay on a wooded river bank, his face resting on mud-coloured sand. He raised himself on his hands. He felt his body. No blood, no wounds. He was bruised but unhurt. What was it? He looked up. The moon moved in and out of lowering, blood-streaked clouds, yet he could observe no setting sun. The winds seemed muffled and the stars indistinct. The bobbing, unnatural white lights of the distant bonfires and candles were even stranger. What was it? He abruptly looked down. In the shallows at the water's edge, the clear outlines of fallen warriors were slowly taking form on the sandy bottom. The water surged forward and the shapes were washed out. He stared for a moment. Again the shapes re-emerged to be swept away again. That was it! Hopcyn had warned him. The shades of Samhain veterans rising from antique slaughters. They wanted to rise again in him, a living warrior. Once more the shapes came into being, the lines getting stronger, and a deep, agonising groan seemed to rise from the depths of the river. An accursed spot! Owen turned and ran.

He stopped at last to get his breath. Where was he? He turned full circle but still couldn't get his bearings. He pressed on along the bank. Around the next bend, he paused in alarm. In a burst of moonlight, not a few feet from him, squatted a figure scrubbing clothes on a broad stone in the river. From the back Owen made out the form of a lithe and lovely young girl. Alone? Among all these dangers? He stretched out a protective hand. Suddenly he saw the garment she was holding. It was his own russet army tunic! And from a deep rent in the cloth, as one made by a blade, oozed a continuous stream of blood, discolouring the waters. Owen clutched his breast and staggered back. Hearing the movement, the 'girl' turned. Suddenly her face seemed an inch from his, the face of a withered, leering hag. From her reptilian lips, the quick forked tongue of a snake licked out, spitting at his eyes. Half-blinded and shouting in terror, Owen plunged back into the dense underbrush and ran until he fell panting against a tree. He wiped his eyes. Thank God, he could still see. Would the hellish night never end? And where were his companions?

He pressed onwards, away from the damned river. Soon he found himself climbing a wild, wooded, rock-strewn hillside. Pushing through chest high ferns, he stumbled into a small clearing. In the misty darkness, he could make out upright slabs of stone. Their shapes seemed familiar. Yes. Headstones. All around. An ancient Celtic burial ground, the stones carved with the dead man's head on both sides – facing both ways to represent life and death, departing and arriving, and the middle stage between the heads representing the body becoming spirit. Dozens of such tombstones rose up to the looming uprights of a towering henge. Owen knew at once that he had arrived at the fearsome Dolmen of Unease. At the same moment, the discordant tinkling of tiny black bells and the shivering clashes of miniature cymbals filled his ears. The sound hovered like an evil, metallic choir over the topmost branches displacing the peaceful, daytime murmuring of winds in the leaves.

Owen collapsed weakly under the capstone. He listened. What now? Where were his companions? He suddenly realised that the only help against this was destiny itself. Yes. There it was. Horses hoofs, approaching fast. The interior of the henge stones began to hum and glow with an unearthly, blue light. The hideous bells and cymbals sounded again as the horses crashed towards him, Owen's heart seemed to stop. Not a dozen paces away loomed the frightful silhouette of *Yr Arglwydd Angau*, the Grim Reaper of the Otherworld. On his emaciated horse, hour glass in one hand with a scythe in the other, a sable hood pulled over a grinning skull, cloak floating behind him, he held up a skeletal hand. His phantom troupe, mounted on black chargers, reined in. The scythe hissed out over the tombstones in broad sweeps, as if searching for a target. Owen shrank back. Those rimless sockets seemed to stare straight at him. A dense chittering arose. The apparition looked up. It beheld rows of Sin Eaters crouched on the upper branches above him, like hungry crows. The fiend-like figure raised the hour-glass in salute. Marble-black eyes gleamed in the foliage. The true Lord of the Universe still had need of them. Around Owen, the blue light streamed out in increasing intensity, the locked spirits straining to join the ghastly troupe. As the phantom cavalcade turned away, Owen felt himself splashed with a steaming liquid. He tasted it, and shuddered. Then he saw the fetlocks of the disappearing horses were streaming with blood.

The evil chorus of bat, bell, cymbal, scythe, hoof and spirit rose to a brief, shocking climax. Then universal silence smothered all, and Owen lapsed into merciful unconsciousness.

56

Catherine was borne on a closed litter from the royal barge. So enjoyable was the trip, she had ordered the Captain to sail on. It was only when she fainted that her Demoiselles realised what was happening. Her time was due. Just at that moment the Captain hailed them, as instructed, and pointed to the rounded towers and turrets of Windsor castle coming up dead ahead. The barge at once put in to shore. Without hesitation, the physicians carried Catherine, still in a faint, up the road to the castle. She would soon be lying in the comfort of the royal chambers. What better place for the heir to the English throne to be born? As they moved up to the gates, Catherine through half-closed eyes could just make out the faint outline of high towers. As expected, the labour passed without complications. Catherine fell into an exhausted sleep. Only when she awoke, a mother for the first time, did she discover the towers were those of Windsor Castle.

57

The Dauphinist town of Meaux lay on both banks of the Seine. Between its two halves rose a heavily fortified island connected to the far bank by a bridge. This effectively blocked the direct route to Paris. Henry had counted on a rapid march to the capital, the way having already been cleared by his previous savage sieges, to link up with his brother, Bedford. But he was again bogged down in a protracted, profitless, expensive siege. The French seemed not to have learned their lesson. It never occured to Henry that he hadn't either.

The stubborn garrison was commanded by a hated local tyrant, popularly known as the Bastard of Vaurus. No one suspected that the cruel bastard would turn into a national hero. No, thought Henry, there was to be no mercy this time.

Henry's only consolation, early in the siege, was the news that Catherine had borne him a son and heir. The babe had been safely christened, as instructed. As the future Henry VI, surely the Lancastrian line was now assured. Every Church in the occupied areas welcomed the news with masses, prayers, bell ringing and feasting. Henry celebrated with a cannonade against the faithful subjects of his new son's mother. But even these festivities had been tempered by the fact that the boy had, after all, been born at Windsor. Henry wondered about the explanation he was given of 'a craving for water voyages?' He had summoned Catherine to re-join him at Corbeil close by after the surrender of the town. The royal babe was to stay in the care of the Demoiselles. Her mother would also visit Corbeil, eager to have firsthand news of her first grandchild.

Henry now often felt too fatigued to give in to his continuing forebodings.

The siege dragged on, week after week, month after month, season after season. The troops had to endure the hardships of a static campaign in all weather conditions. They had inadequate supplies of food, clothing, munitions, fuel and medical care. But worst of all was the lack of proper living quarters. Henry's war chests were rapidly emptying. He would be bankrupt before he ever got to Paris. To add to his troubles, an epidemic of deadly cholera and dysentery struck his army. He was soon losing more troops to sickness than to his desperate assaults on the town. Henry insisted on personally staying in the battle lines. This was interpreted as the sign of a caring commander who shared all the privations of his men. But Salisbury knew it was a last desperate effort to stem the ever increasing desertions among the severely disaffected army. Salisbury contacted Bedford and Henry's other leading commanders. The situation was grave. He set up a military conference to be held at Corbeil.

Reinforcements finally arrived in the middle of a snowstorm. With them came fifty of Salisbury's heavy new-fangled cannon, with plenty of spare ammunition. Once the guns were in place, Salisbury directed a furious bombardment against the enemy fortifications. The gunners were ordered to concentrate on the huge flour mills which were still operating on the bridge. Without them, Henry and Salisbury knew, the town would soon run out of flour. No flour meant no bread. It was only their supplies of winter grain that had kept the town and garrison from starvation. With the last of his men, Henry ordered a final amphibious assault. It took both the island and the remains of the splintered bridge. Salisbury was now able to bring up his devastating cannon and pound the town from two sides. After one day, the town capitulated. Henry at once ordered the confiscation of all the silver and gold plate, the surrender of the jewellery of the women and the entire specie of the merchants, their working currency. Again Salisbury knew that this was to inform the troops that he had, at last, the wherewithal to pay them. In a body, the patriotic yeomen decided to stay with their victorious and now solvent commander.

The Bastard was not so lucky. Like a true son of chivalry, Henry kept his word. He spread out the Bastard's bend sinister coat of arms just below the battlements. Henry then had him hanged by his feet directly above it, so that when the blood began pouring out of the Bastard's nose and mouth, it drenched every inch of the detested banner. Henry ordered the Bastard to be left in place until the very last drop had drained out of his corpse.

Henry then ordered a second execution, that of a fourteen year old cornet player. The boy had daily paraded an ass on the battlements, crowned it as King of England and, when the ass brayed, pretended it was the King and brayed back even louder. When he finished each daily performance, he gave the 'V' sign to the furious English troops and pissed on them from above. The foolish boy was hanged next to the intrepid Bastard.

58

Henry abruptly gave up further pacifications. He felt an urge to move on at once to Corbeil to consolidate his gains and reunite with his family. Salisbury helped him onto his war horse and, still in his heavy fighting armour, Henry set out at the head of his depleted but still conquering army. He was soon shaking with fever. When the columns arrived at Corbeil, Henry was no longer able to bear the weight of his armour, and suddenly pulled up. Before his aides could reach him, he toppled out of the saddle and lay still on the ground, an ominous stain spreading under him. It had been the same for thousands of his troops. He had contracted the deadly dehydrating dysentery, for which there was no known cure. He was taken to the chateau of Vincennes nearby, seat of the ancient Kings of France. Ironically, chambers were always kept ready for visiting French Kings. Henry was conveyed into these chambers and laid down on the comfortable bed. He was in great pain, but still in full command of his faculties.

Henry knew the symptoms only too well. He ordered the physicians to tell him the truth.

'Only two to three hours at the most,' one of them had the courage to reply. Henry rewarded him with five gold nobles.

Henry called his personal Confessor.

'Have my priests sing these penitential psalms until I am dead.' He gave the priest the Psalter. Henry next ordered his generals and counsellors of state to attend his last hours. He had to set his house in order. Bedford and Warwick had already arrived in response to Salisbury's call. Cardinal Winchester would soon be on the way. They were waiting outside the bed chamber, stunned and silent, Bedford still shaken and grieving over the heedless, needless death of brave young Clarence. And now his favourite brother was stricken. That loss would be irreparable. But he vowed to himself he would serve his brother in death as in life. Salisbury and Bedford had taken pains not to send messengers in the vicinity of the household of Duke Humphrey at his Palace of Placentia, however preoccupied the pair were with their supposedly 'secret' marriage. Chichele was put on the alert. If Humphrey made a move, the Archbishop was to block him with the dead King's dispositions, and the role he was to play. Chichele waited in readiness at his Palace in Lambeth. All aimed at keeping Humphrey out of the way as long as possible, knowing that Henry would do the right thing by everyone, especially his most dangerous brother. But best to let him do it in peace.

They were ushered into the dying presence. Speechless, they grouped around the death bed. A solitary arrow lay at Henry's feet. Priests and notaries stood ready close by. The chant of plainsong came from the side chapel. Bedford felt tears. He could hardly recognise his vital, brilliant, shining brother, so shrunken and gaunt. Henry had not eaten for days, and his once athletic body was wasted to a bundle of bones. He was only thirty-five years of age. All this had happened in one short week. But there was still time to speak to their 'dread sovereign', or 'dear brother', whichever way their allegiance lay.

'Hello, Johnny,' whispered Henry, using Bedford's childhood name.

'All. Come closer. Listen. Above all, unity. Secure the nation. Together. Our alliance with Burgundy. Honour him. Keep the alliance. Make Burgundy understand. Without us . . . Salisbury, never surrender Calais. Normandy. Our base, our last redoubt,' he smiled bleakly, 'our war chest.'

They knew their Commander-in-Chief's final assessment was accurate, as always.

'The minority. Never permit York, Somerset, Suffolk to walk the streets of London. Wolves. Watch . . . our rear? Clear? Follow it, unity.'

Warwick, Salisbury, Bedford and Winchester nodded.

'We will do it,' Bedford spoke for them all. But, he thought, would Humphrey?

'Your son,' Bedford asked, 'my nephew. What are your orders?'

'Waiting, yes.' He motioned to the notaries. 'Take this down. Johnny . . . Duke of Bedford, confirmed as Regent of France. France, for Henry until he is seven. His Regent here. Understood?' Bedford nodded, eyes glistening. The scratching of the scribes' pens filled the room.

'I also appoint you, Bedford, as the child's personal guardian. Take every step, protect his person. Warwick, you and Lady Warwick, my son's upbringing, in your hands. After seven, normal duties of state, under your guidance, Warwick, and Johnny. Clear?'

His voice was beginning to fade. He beckoned the notaries.

'The seal.' The notaries affixed the royal seal. 'And the copies.' The copies were done.

'Humphrey. Tell him, unity, not self. Johnny, you never wanted the crown?' Bedford shook his head.

'So I leave France and my son to your keeping. Henry must be crowned in Paris.'

'My word on it. Henry, a question . . . ', but Henry already knew what it was.

' . . . Our brother Humphrey? Listen. Hereby, set up supreme Council of State. I appoint you, Bedford, you Warwick, Winchester as co-equal members, majority decisions. Humphrey, I appoint Regent of England, with title, "Lord Protector of the Realm".' He paused, breathless. The notaries came forward. The royal seal was again affixed to the documents.

Bedford and his group saw at once what Henry was doing. Humphrey again held the grandest title, and a seat on the highest council. He had not been excluded, so his followers could not rise in rebellion. But Humphrey had no say in the care of the next in line or in his education – and whoever had control of the heir also had control of the Kingdom. Moreover Bedford, Warwick and Winchester were granted equal conciliar powers. During the minority of the baby King, majorities were to decide policy. The triumvirate now standing in front of Henry would have full control while Humphrey, as in the past, had nothing more than the outward trappings of authority. They all knew that Humphrey would swallow the bait. Cunning Albion! But when Humphrey learned how impotent he was, aye, thought, Bedford, and what then? A devil's alliance with the Yorkists? Over Bedford's dead body!

'Give me the crucifix,' Henry asked. His Confessor pressed one into his hands.

'Now, my dear wife . . . find comfort for her. Chief mourner. I grant her Baynard's Castle, her Court. Her revenues of France.' The pens of the scribes scratched across the parchment. Warwick and Bedford exchanged glances. Baynard's, well out of the City, was a gloomy pile that no one much wanted, but it had extensive wooded gardens, and was close to the Thames. Henry obviously didn't want Catherine embroiled in politics. But the revenues. They would be hard to collect. Henry's breath rasped.

'My feet are cold.' Henry's feet were wrapped in two thick blankets.

'Now,' he struggled on. 'My army. I thank it for its faith and valour, every one. My Welsh archers. Confirm Captain Owen as Clerk of the Wardrobe, until the Queen might relinquish . . . ' His breath became laboured. ' . . . Assure repayment of all our

227

borrowings.' The priests were chanting Henry's favourite psalm, *Build thou the walls of Jerusalem* . . .

' . . . Yes,' he whispered, 'my desire.' He rallied.

'Lastly, my bones buried at the Abbey of Westminster . . . '
Henry pointed at the arrow at the foot of the bed.

'That arrow . . . my Welsh wars, in my coffin.' His lids fluttered shut. The assembled company crossed themselves. The end. A moment later, Henry suddenly sat bolt upright, eyes open for the last time. He pointed an accusing, trembling finger into the air.

'You lie,' he thundered, as at some invisible accuser. 'I am no murderer. My portion is with Jesus Christ.' Henry fell back onto the pillow. The last psalm faded. Henry the Conqueror was dead.

59

Catherine was closeted with Bedford. It was he who had led her in to view her dead husband. She hadn't recognised him at first. She shuddered again. *The Triumph of Death*, that hideous triptych. Bedford held her by the arm and gently sat her in a chair by the bed. Henry's body had been taken below. It now rested on trestles in the huge kitchen next to the stables.

'Henry, the man I almost loved,' she thought, looking at the ruffled bed. 'And who almost loved me.'

'He did love you,' said Bedford softly. Catherine realised she had spoken aloud.

'In his own way.'

'You were the only one.'

'And you loved him, John?'

'Always, Catherine.' Bedford was the only brother-in-law whose first name she felt comfortable using.

'So Lady Warwick is to have the upbringing.'

'As Queen Dowager, you have access at all times.'

'So you will be guardian to my son?'

'Yes.'

'And have effective control over the Council.'

'Yes.'

'To keep Humphrey at a distance.'

'Yes.'

She remembered Humphrey's subtlety. *Wild beasts like this . . .* It was the Duke himself who was the most 'beastly' of all the *godons*.

'Thank God for that.'

'To be frank, he is powerless.'

'Will that stop him?'

'No. But every barrier has been placed in his path.'

'He is now second in line.'

'And I am first, Catherine.'

'Happy families. What about this business with the Yorkists?'

'Leave them to me.'

'My mother was held up. My father ill again.'

'I have ordered the best physicians for him.'

'My mother is bored with St Pol. She misses her Court of Good Shepherds. Don't laugh.'

'I am one of the very few who does not underestimate your mother.'

'I know, John. Will you be able to stay on here? These recent revolts . . . this peasant girl from Domremy . . . '

'Militarily she is no danger. In other ways though . . . '

' . . . And my brother, the Dauphinists?'

'Burgundy is still solidly with us.'

'He is rash, not to be trusted.'

'Whatever, Catherine, I have given my word. Paris I shall keep for you and your son.'

'I know you love *la belle France* as much as I do. But, John, both our families are tearing each other to pieces.'

'Not while I'm here.'

'And my little family, my first and only, is truly broken up. First death, now theft.'

'The heir is not stolen from you.'

'No, but my son is.'

'Like Henry, he belongs to the nation.'

'England or France?'

'Both.' Yes, she thought, Henry has seen to that. What's in a family? Henry had thought of everything, she saw now, except her own feelings.

'Am I ever to have a family of my own?'

'Henry will be absent only during the minority.'

'Seven years. My firstborn. And why Baynard's?'

'To keep you out of harm's way.'

'Was he really thinking of me?'

'You are the future King's mother.'

'That's something, I suppose. Listen John, I am sent into exile from the grave. Baynard's – Henry's departing gift.'

Bedford was struck again by her maturity, clear-headedness and absence of bitterness.

'It is for the good of all. And, Catherine, you are Queen Mother.'

'Will I be allowed to travel freely to my home here, in France?'

Bedford did not answer.

'Baynard's castle is my gilded cage.'

'Baynard's may be better than you think. And I will always be here for you.'

'And what happens when you are gone? Thank God for my friends, Agnes, Joanna . . . '

'Captain Owen is confirmed as Clerk of your Wardrobe. Do you want to retain him?'

She felt an unexpected glow at the question.

'Yes.'

'A damn good fighting man. Where is he?'

'Buying back the family lands in Wales.'

'Glad someone's making an honest penny out of all this.'

'It was Henry who took it in the first place.'

'Now, Catherine, do you want a last view of your husband?'

Catherine thought of the boiling cauldrons with horror.

'Do you?'

'No. Is all . . . that . . . downstairs . . . really necessary?'

'It is the custom, sanctioned by the church. The Archbishop of Sens, Henry's greatest admirer, will supervise the prayers.'

231

'It's still . . . awful.'

'I know. His bones will be interred at the Abbey, his last wishes.'

'As Chief Mourner, what would you have me do?'

'Lead the cortege on the funerary route back to England.'

'Another progress to Calais?'

'There will be a considerable escort.' Even in death, she thought, Henry displays his power on earth.

'What are the arrangements then?'

'If you'll come to the stables . . . '

Ten minutes later, Catherine entered the cavernous royal stables that were capable of housing one-hundred-and-twenty horses at a time. The stalls, she noted, were full. Bedford motioned to sixteen jet black chargers, their coats curried till they shone like coal.

'This is all too much in my opinion,' said Bedford wearily, 'but the people expect it, and Henry ordered it. The funerary chariot.'

He pointed to the immense six-wheeled chariot. It was painted in differing shades of black. On it rested the bier, dressed out in black crêpe. On the bier was the coffin, of black-painted oak. A tapestry with the royal coat of arms in black and gold covered it. The canopy was of silk, again in black.

'There will be an escort of four hundred of Henry's cavalry, all in black armour, black lances, riding chargers like these. Henry's officers will bear torches as the light fails. Behind the bier, Henry's attendants and generals, chargers caparisoned in black. His household servants, in black capes. The cortège, about three miles long. You will bring up the rear, so the last thing the people see of the cortège will be . . . '

' . . . Their brave and sorrowful queen. Don't worry, I know what I am to do. And it will be over soon enough.'

Bedford marvelled at her determination and self-possession.

'We have arranged perpetual masses in every town along

the route to Calais. At Dover and on the road to London, the aldermen and mayors of every town will meet you at the gates, in heavy mourning. Every apprentice and craftsman will wear black gowns with black hoods. And,' Bedford couldn't help adding, 'they will share fifty per cent of the costs.'

'Henry would have approved of that,'

'Henry thought of it,' said Bedford 'including the cost of the torches. First stop, the Tower. Next, the Abbey. The final requiem mass. The lying in state.'

'How long is the mourning?'

'At least a year.'

'Six months for Henry. And six for my son. And your last request?'

'Prepare yourself.'

He drew back a curtain which separated the bier from the driving seat of the chariot. Catherine nearly fainted.

Before her, on a dais at the head of the coffin, sitting on his gilded throne draped in black silk, was a life-size effigy of Henry, fashioned in boiled leather The likeness was uncanny. The skin glowed as if it still had life. Catherine found herself looking up at the familiar long nose, the pudding basin cut and the sharp, now lifeless eyes. She stepped back, breathing hard.

'I'm all right,' she murmured. She forced herself to look again. She would have to get used to it. The effigy wore a diadem of gold and diamonds, a sceptre in its right hand, a golden cross and ball in the left. The whole chest was shrouded in a state mantle of imperial purple bordered with sable. The effect in the subdued light of the stables was ghoulish but overpowering. Even as a phantom, Henry retained his majesty. Yes, she thought, whatever else, you do adorn the gates of your own Jerusalem.

233

60

The military butchers were busy in the kitchens. Overseeing the gruesome work was Henry's old clerical Gallic ally, the Archbishop of Sens. Henry's body was rapidly decomposing, and wouldn't last the long journey back. His body had to be re-arranged in a more acceptable manner. The principal cause of the embarrassment, the royal flesh, would be boiled down, and the bones, the pristine, royal bones, extracted and laid out in the bier for the last, odourless interment in Henry's massive Abbey tomb.

The Head Chef and the Overseer of the Army Abattoir had been appointed to supervise the final solemn work. The Chef and Overseer had at first been too awed to touch the royal corpse. To encourage them, the Archbishop had blessed two tuns of the best Bordeaux wine. Holy wine for holy work.

'Your health, zur,' they both toasted.

The two butchers said their prayers and set to sharpening their cleavers, brimming flagons of wine at their side.

Two immense cauldrons were suspended over the main fire in the chimney piece. They bubbled away merrily giving off odours of rosemary and thyme. One cauldron was for cleansing, the second for boiling. Perforated ladles lay in a row ready for use. The trestle with Henry's draped body lay next to a butcher's block. The Chef now removed the covering, lifted up Henry's leg at the hip. The Overseer, with his butcher's saw, sawed away at the hip joint. It was then scalded in the clean boiling water, scraped of all body hair, the hair burnt on a glowing brasier, and the limb finally dropped into the second aromatic cauldron for boiling down. First the fat, then the sinew and lastly the remaining meat were scraped off the bone until only the bone remained. The Archbishop paled at the first leg. At the second, he vomited over his cassock and hurried outside to the fountain. There was not a soul about. The area had been cleared for the pious gory labour.

The two experts grinned and emptied their flagons. It was a privileged job. It wasn't every day one skinned the hide off a monarch. Pity the corpse was practically all bones. It wouldn't take long. More's the pity, thought the Chef, a story for a lifetime. Plus a prime hangover at the army's expense. What more could a soldier ask? They drank deeply again. They were well on the way, happy with their lot. When the Archbishop returned, the two stood swaying over the boiling cauldrons, flagons in hand.

'Plantagenet soup!' shouted the Abattoir Overseer, pretending to drink from the stirring ladle.

'Enough!' ordered the Archbishop. 'This is a holy duty.'

'Aye, zur,' replied the Chef. 'That's why we be so pissed. Your health!'

'Your health!' echoed his friend.

The Archbishop looked into the tureen, now spitting with grease, and decided not to argue.

'Too many lumps,' declared the Overseer, lifting up bits on the end of a flesh hook.

'Always was a stringy bugger.'

'Please hurry,' begged the Archbishop.

'They takes their own time a'coming into this world, and they takes their own time a'going out, zur,' said the Chef thickly.

'To St George!' cried the Overseer, lifting Henry's head by the locks and plunging it into the scummy waters.

'Cheers!' roared his friend, giving the 'V' sign.

The Overseer thrust his hand inside the rib cage, and held

up a blood clot as big as a knuckle bone.

'Into the pot!'

'Cheers!'

Three hours later a mound of whitened bones, from vertebrae to tibia, lay on the block, surmounted by the skull, picked clean of the all-conquering Plantagenet. Almost as white as the bones, the Archbishop made a last trembling sign of the cross over the royal pile. But Henry's apotheosis was not quite complete.

The two butchers had been dismissed with ten gold nobles each and the rest of the wine, again with the Archbishop's blessing. They now presided over the last stage of Henry's earthly pilgrimage. The two tureens rested on a hand cart in the yard, with the last of the wine. The staggering Chef and Overseer trundled the cart out of the gates. When they reached the royal sties, they crashed the gates open, kicked aside the squealing sows and hauled in the slopping tureens which they tipped into the grease-encrusted pig toughs. The last Henry's army butchers saw of their warrior King-Emperor was oozing between the chops of two fat, shit-soiled porkers. The Archbishop had declined to give a final blessing over the piggery. He was busy finishing off the rest of the Bordeaux. Again he thanked his Maker for not having being born royal. What a way to go – in the overflowing muck of a nasty, grunting, fly-blown sty.

61

The King of France had got used to his womb-like little pantry in the gardener's cottage. He could curl up there when he wished, suck his thumb contentedly, and weep. Few visited the poor loon in the pantry. People merely waited for God to bless, or curse, him with a clear moment.

The moonlight filtered in through the unshuttered window space. The shimmering shadows of the ivy leaves outside fell onto the bottom of his blanket. The King slept in torment. He moaned and jerked like one on a wrack, sometimes giving terrified squeals like a rabbit between a fox's teeth. A thousand hideous imps, devils and gargoyles teemed in his brain, stabbing and thrusting with their pitchforks. Through half-closed eyes he saw them there at his feet, glimmering and grinning, crawling up towards his face. He cowered into the pillows. Through his terrors, he heard the door open with a loud rattle. He opened his eyes to the greater horror, a human visitor. He shivered. Grandison's bulk filled the doorway. He stealthily crossed over and sat on the side of the bed. He had a small wooden box. Grandison raised his hands and pressed his finger tips against his temples. He bounced up and down pointing upwards. Yes, get the demons out! The King, grinning in hope, followed suit. He knew. Yes, not a monstrous human at all, but an angel from heaven come to stop the agony, to help him re-join his friends up there. Grandison opened the box and took out a knife. He mimicked making an incision on his temple, and indicated devils escaping. Yes, this was the way. The King stretched his hands high, waving to and fro like a bird in flight. Grandison pressed the knife into the King's hand, and raised it to the throbbing vein in his temple. He mimed a cut. The King pressed the blade. Blood gushed from the wound, easing the pressure on his fevered brain. The King moaned in relief. Grandison raised the hand to the other temple. This time, the King made a slower cut. A heavenly feeling of release again. He leaned back. Yes, the demons were sliding, flowing wetly out, incised and exorcised by this shining angel. With a feeling of immense satisfaction, Grandison watched the King slipping away. Let them insult the greatest physician since Hippocrates at their peril! As the blood began drip-dripping onto the floor, Grandison quietly let himself out, his revenge complete.

The Monk was unquiet. He couldn't sleep and was prowling the gardens. Strange things were abroad. Isabelle was in an unaccustomed drooping mood. She could feel menace in the air and had refused every lover. She was alarmed at the vacuum created by the demise of her son-in-law, and dispirited by the sudden access of hope the Dauphinists received from this ridiculous so-called virgin of Domremy. The Dauphin was a bastard and, God notwithstanding, he would stay a bastard. But Henry, man of iron, what would happen to her daughter and grandson now? She longed to see them. On both sides of her family, all she saw was chaos and blood. Business, as usual, I suppose, she thought. But she knew that this time she would have to be more watchful than ever.

The Monk looked up as he saw a shadow flit by the door of the gardener's cottage. As he quietly crept through the underbrush, he heard a startled cry from inside. A few seconds later, the door was thrust open and a figure rushed out, running towards the rear entrance of the Palace. The Monk recognised one of the Dauphin's new attendants, another returned fugitive from the dance of the cannibals.

Within minutes, the Monk was hammering on Isabelle's bedroom door. Hoarsely, he gasped out the news. Isabelle at once grasped the gravity of the situation. The Dauphin was no longer just the Dauphin. He was her new King, Lord and Master. Her feelings of unease vanished. This was a time for action.

'Get my carriage ready at once. And join me at the cottage.'

As Isabelle looked down at the emaciated, marble-white face of her former lover, husband and sovereign, she unaccountably burst into tears. Was it for herself? she wondered. Behold the monarch! How would she end? She, a queen. Or was there still a mortal bit of longing left for him. Isabelle kissed the ice cold forehead. The blood, she observed, was congealing fast, and for one so thin, she noted with surprise the vast amount the corpse had yielded. The Monk entered hurriedly, a bundle of hessian sacking under his arm.

'I can see lights in the Dauphin's rooms, we'd better . . . '

'Right now! Come on.'

They laid out the body on the sackcloth, washed it hurriedly with the water from a bucket in the corner, and wrapped the waif-like corpse in fold after fold of rough, smelly hessian. Outside, the Monk lowered the body into a sitting position in the large wooden garden wheelbarrow. With the moonlight still bright on the ivy leaves and shining on the pools of blood, Isabelle, Queen of France, wheeled the dead monarch, Charles VI, like a pile of mouldy autumn leaves destined for the compost pit, to her waiting curtained carriage, and fled into the night.

62

The word arrived from Bedford. The cortege had set off. The Archbishop of Canterbury, Henry Chichele, was to inform Duke Humphrey of the death of his brother. Copies of Henry's dispositions were included, with the royal seals and various batons of office. The Archbishop knew the contents. He wondered if he shouldn't take an armed guard. He settled for two of his Deans, both of whom were seasoned chaplains who knew how to use a sword. With these two clerical stalwarts, he made the short trip to Humphrey's Palace at Greenwich. He had been fully informed of Humphrey's secret marriage and knew too of Eleanor's reputation for witchcraft. Poor Henry, he thought, of all his brothers, he had only one on whom he could rely. And this one, Humphrey, was married to the devil's dam. He wondered what awaited him within.

It was the enormous scale of the palace that struck the Archbishop as the carriage trotted up the interminable drive to the huge doors at the top of the steep steps. But his knockings failed to arouse anyone, not even a flunky. Finally the chaplains, on a hunt in the stables, collared two half-drunk grooms. They said that the Duke and Duchess were receiving no visitors, and that they were at their devotions in the Long Room.

'Tell them the Archbishop of Canterbury is here, and that his brother, the King, is dead.'

In three minutes, the Archbishop and his Deans were ushered up the wide marble staircase. The doors to the Long Room were flung open. The Archbishop looked around. He had forgotten how grand the room was. He saw the oak panelling was now teeming with wooden roses. More bizarre than ostentatious, he thought. Apart from new tapestries of Roman heroes, the room was bare of decoration or furniture. His eyes focused on the far end. A single long carpet in imperial purple ran up to it. On the raised dais were two thrones. Who were the figures there? The Archbishop stared. Yes, it was Humphrey. In the heavy armour of kings, a small crown on his plumed helm. His consort, the Duchess Eleanor of Cobham, was as strikingly dressed in a sky-blue full-length gown trimmed with fur. She also sported voluminous double-skinned pelts of ermine that hung to the floor; and her surcoat was held by a jewelled girdle. Around her throat was a golden necklace studded with rubies. On her head, she wore a horned head-dress hung with white veils. What shook the Archbishop was, surmounting the head-dress, a crown that was not the ducal coronet to which Eleanor was perfectly entitled to wear, but a replica of the royal coronet of the queens of England. So this was to be a royal audience. The Archbishop and his Deans lapsed into astonished silence. Humphrey took this as awe, and beckoned them graciously forward. The closer they came, the more they felt Eleanor's witch-like beauty hang in the air like a spell. Her plucked eyebrows reminded the Archbishop of a lizard, black eyes glittering beneath. The Archbishop resisted an impulse to cross himself. He decided to overlook the niceties.

'I regret to inform you, the King died at the Château de Vincennes two days ago. An epidemic of dysentery. His body is now on route to Calais and Dover for burial in the Abbey.'

The effect of his words amazed him even more. Eleanor raised her clasped hands above her head as if about to brain someone. Humphrey jumped to his feet and went into a Caesar-like pose, one arm outraised as with an invisible toga, bandy legs and pot belly shaking underneath. Humphrey was obviously in the grip of deep emotion. Suddenly he crumpled onto his throne and began to weep, noisy, slurping tears. The hideous insincerity of it made the clerics cringe. Eleanor, meanwhile, was muttering prayers as if they were a curse.

'No,' wept Humphrey. 'Not England's glory. O royal brother, Conqueror, saint!' He couldn't keep it up. His dry sobs turned into barking coughs. Eleanor quieted him with a stroke of her hand. It was her turn now.

'Is that the royal seal?' She pointed at the documents.

'The dispositions, just about to ask. Well?' Humphrey demanded.

'Your grace, you have been appointed Lord Protector of the Realm.' Eleanor uttered a faint ecstatic cry.

'This is from the Duke of Bedford.'

He handed Humphrey an ebony baton chased in silver and gold, a falcon with talons outstretched on one end.

'Your baton of office.' Humphrey was speechless with self-importance – as Bedford had foreseen.

'During the minority, a new Grand Council of the Realm . . . '

' . . . of which ye, Duke Humphrey, are head,' hissed Eleanor, by now beside herself.

'Of which the Earl of Warwick,' the Archbishop corrected, 'the Cardinal Winchester, and the Duke of Bedford have joint control, with yourself, of course, your Grace.'

Humphrey couldn't quite take it all in. This was some kind of deadly insult from the grave. The monster. To his own brother! He felt rage glowing inside.

'Who has control of the babe?' demanded Eleanor, crouching like a cat about to spring. Silence. The Archbishop's moment had come.

'My Lord of Warwick and Lady Warwick.'

Humphrey and Eleanor turned to stone. The Archbishop laid the official documents on the table, making the sign of the cross over them. The Archbishop noted that Humphrey's face was beginning to turn puce. Eleanor was holding onto him. The

Primate of England gathered up his skirts, turned abruptly, and strode out of the chamber with his Deans.

Humphrey exploded. The cooks in the kitchen heard the demented yells. In the vegetable pantry, one of the scullions cut off the tops of turnips and hid them under his jerkin. He would scatter them about after midnight, as ordered. He didn't know where the money came from. All he cared was that it came regularly, he believed, from the same mysterious monk that he met in a tavern in the town of Troyes.

63

Hopcyn crouched lower. He was being watched by a thousand glinting eyes. The ferns and bushes around him teemed with the dark forces of the Otherworld. *Annwn* was still out to encircle him. He ran upwards until, ahead of him at last, he saw in the blood-red moonlit clouds the grim outlines of the Dolmen of Unease. Under the capstone, he saw that someone had rested on the pressed grass, someone who had survived. Owain, yes, he knew it was Owain. A faint yellow rimmed the horizon. At last, it would soon be dawn. The evil flashes began to fade like fireflies. But still blue emanations came from within the stones. He felt a thousand shades panting to escape, to speed after him, to live again within his very soul. Hopcyn felt a strange sense of sudden calm, then he tensed, gripping his brow. He gazed over the gravestones, awaiting the warp-spasm. Just below the surface, the stones began to glow outwards until a deep, unearthly blue flooded the tombed graveyard. The spasm fell like a great ring of light over his vision, and in one great flash it sped into the clouds in ever widening pools of blinding illumination. What was the shape shimmering out there. He felt himself at one with all becoming, the quick and the dead. Was it *Afallon*? The serenity that knows no end?

'Am I dead?' he wondered. 'Only the dead see *Afallon*.'

Above, the stones floated up like feathers and danced in the upper air. From a monolith, a figure arose. From every pore and strand of hair poured unending streams of golden light. Yes, the Opalescent Ones of *Afallon*. He was being vouchsafed a miracle. The figure beckoned. Hopcyn felt himself rise above the ground in immeasurably gentle flight. The Opalescent One spread out his arm. At once the trees, the hills, the mountains opened out into a single gigantic plain of light, the whole moving under winds in perpetual harvest, the Land of Apples, the Meadows of Midsummer, the Place of Eternal Youth. Yes, this was *Afallon*. Plain upon endless plain filled the black vastness of space, the interstices of the distant stars bathed in endless light. The Opalescent One pointed. At once Hopcyn heard a muted, multitudinous, silvery rustling, like a million beech leaves whispering in a night wind in a dream. And now swam into his sight row upon infinite row of quivering silvery wings like the gossamer wings of massed butterflies, pausing and settling as at the dawn of creation. With every shivering motion those wide whisperings reached out with the light into the boundless stars. Stunned with joy, Hopcyn understood that he was witnessing the vision of *Annwn* itself, the spirits of the dead gathered in a single sweeping, immense communion. The Opalescent One pointed again, and the whole illimitable host of wings rose up momentarily, silvery souls whispering to silvery souls, before settling down again into the cavernous, unfathomable peace of the Otherworld. For all of humanity, the bard Hopcyn was witnessing the grand choiring of the earth's multitudinous departed spirits singing in flight. An overpowering love for all the souls of all of the dead of all the ages of the world filled his being, and he fainted for the very love of *Afallon*.

64

The Monk reined in the horses abruptly as they galloped into the stable yard of the Court of Good Shepherds. The darkness could not conceal the wholesale destruction. Isabelle's glorious Garden of Eden had been reduced to broken piles of half-burned rubble. The remains of the dovecotes, bowers, tigers and lambs littered the grounds. No panthers snarled and no turtle doves cooed from the high eves. The outhouses and stables had been torched. Charred timbers pointed to the sky.

The scene was the same inside the palace, each room having been systematically sacked. The floor of the spacious kitchen was covered with holed and dented pots and pans, its empty fire-places piled with damp ashes, and the whole area running with rats and mice. Isabelle's inner sanctum was a sodden mass of ripped tapestries, crushed statues and fragments of smashed marble, breasts, toes and hands. Isabelle noted with satisfaction, however, that some phalluses were still intact. The firebugs seemed to have stopped here to rest, eat and pack up their spoils.

The Monk had commandeered an upturned cart in the nettles by the back entrance. He unloaded the corpse. The King lay in a box from the gardener's shed, his winding sheet made of rough hessian and his catafalque a two-wheeled hand cart. The Monk cleared a space in an empty alcove and curtained it off with tattered remnants of tapestry. He set up a table and chair in a corner for Isabelle. A bucket by the table caught the water dripping through the ceiling. They had pressing work to do, and little time in which to do it. Isabelle intended to squeeze the last ounce of royal power out of the King, even if he happened to be a corpse.

Isabelle sat in the stiff-backed kitchen chair. The table top in front of her was covered with documents, parchments, the King's royal seals, sticks of sealing wax, large signets with the royal coat of arms, both French and English, small bags of nobles, quills and ink, a dozen blank safe conducts, letters of reference, indentures with the King's signature, ready for either signet, all lit by the flickering light of two altar candles.

'Take your pick, your list of credits, here and in London. Help yourself, whether I'm alive or dead,' she said, but the Monk hung onto her hand.

'My little curled up potato peeling,' she kissed him, 'you stayed to the end.'

'Not the end, Madam,' he whispered, 'we'll have fun yet.'

'Of course, funs, that's life, ja?'

The monk had carried out a search of the palace and had rooted out the chef and a scullion from the concealed passages in the kitchens, where they had taken shelter. They explained that they had received a flying visit from the fiendish *Ecorcheurs*. The rest of the servants were still in hiding in the hills. When the Monk presented the survivors to the Queen, they cheerfully offered their services. They were at once rewarded for their fidelity with five gold nobles each, enough to last them for the year. She still fed their families and they still worshipped her. Isabelle decided to use them as messengers along her usual courier route on the estate. She would win through yet. Her newly appointed messengers eagerly awaited their new orders.

Soon a steady stream of state papers was being passed to them. As Regent, Isabelle could forgive debts, award titles, confirm sinecures, remit taxes, sell off properties, call in favours, convert securities into cash, arrange bank guarantees, put jewels into pawn, take others out. This was no folly. It was business as usual. Most of the royal commands would arrive before the news of the death of the sovereign. And she still had a day's grace until the new King recovered the kidnapped corpse of his father, along with the seals.

She added her signature and sealing wax to the ever growing pile of royal messages.

'Make sure that these copies are safely lodged. You know the safe houses. Here, the supporting affidavits, especially the Dukes'. Watch the *godons* at all times.' She paused. 'Bloody fools. Holy Henry included. Except one, who could fuck like the devil, at least' She shook herself. 'Yes, well now, these bankers' drafts – only into my Katty's very hands, understand. Give her all my love, lots.'

The Monk nodded dumbly. He had a terrible feeling these might be his last orders. He would carry them out to the death.

'Death's thirsty work,' the mourner-in-chief commented, as if reading his thoughts. The Monk dispatched the Chef in search of refreshment.

'None of that horse piss wine, though!' she shouted after him.

The chef returned almost immediately, breathless, pointing behind him. A faint chant of plainsong came to their ears.

'What's that unholy caterwauling?' demanded Isabelle.

'*Te deums* for the dead.'

'The Dauphin . . . ' said the Monk.

' . . . the King, you mean.'

'He has a heavy escort, Ma'am,' added the Chef.

'Are we surrounded then?'

'Soon,' said the Monk.

'Men-at-arms!? Tear each other to pieces, then say sorry over the bits. Hall of the Worthies? Hall of the Worthless on the lot of them! I am still his Keeper! Hear me?' she yelled to the outside. 'Come on, I know you're out there, bastard pig!'

The new King, Charles VII, shrank back into the shadows

behind the great doors, sagging on their hinges against the wall. The familiar, dreaded voice momentarily paralysed him. He wiped his nose on the back of his hand, and managed to control a sniff.

Isabelle motioned. The two messengers filled their pouches with the last of the messages.

'You, my poor robbed crotch, your new ordainment.' She handed the Monk a document affixed with the Papal seal. 'I hereby declare you to be Father Abbot of Fleury, protege of the Cardinal, ally of the English, my secret messenger-in-chief, go and come as you please.' The Monk fell on his knees and covered her hand with kisses.

'Just have funs,' she said, 'in memory of me.' The Monk stifled a sob. The plainchant grew louder. The Monk gave a last salute, and the messengers led by their new Abbot, descended into the cellars and the concealed passages.

Isabelle swept the table bare. She ground the royal seals under her heel. She doubted if Charles had brought new ones. Her orders could not therefore be countermanded. It all seemed tidy enough. She had done her best.

Outside, the new King was trying to summon up his courage. His friends had rallied to him, hadn't they? All members of the escort were personally sworn to him. The Maid was on his side. The courtiers of the *Bal des Ardents* had old scores to settle with the Bavarian whore. That would help. Besides, with two monarchs dead within weeks of each other, rich pickings were going free. There would be many fresh petitioners. The new favourites outside now flapped over the living like the *Ecorcheurs* over the dead. And Isabelle was caught in their talons. They would do for her.

The plainsong stopped just outside. She could hear the shuffling of sandals on the flagstones. Bunch of stupid monks. But where were the Men-at-Arms? And what orders had they received? That was her main worry.

'Hear that, Well Beloved?' she shouted at the corpse. 'You will soon make your last journey to your Maker from my Court of Good Shepherds!' She crossed over to the alcove, and brushed aside the bits of tapestry. She fell silent at the sight of the corpse. Had he ever been so small, so unsexed? Had he ever once been inside her? His body seemed to be shrinking away before her very eyes. Already his face was that of the Lord Death. Like a dried up dog in the stables no one had bothered to throw on the rubbish tip. She found her tear ducts were as dry as the corpse's. Her sackcloth had finally found its ashes.

She had one last little job to do. She reached inside the box and eased her husband's personal signet off his little finger. She polished it on her sleeve, then secreted it in the folds of her dress. She grasped the handles, and trundled the cart into the room. At the table, she looked up. The new King stood there, quivering, having finally plucked up the courage. He recoiled when he saw the contents of the cart.

'Poor father!' Tears coursed down his cheeks.

'In sackcloth, ja.'

'You kidnapped him.'

'Just borrowed him.'

'Heartless witch!'

'Whore, please.'

'He is my father.'

'You exaggerate, pig.'

'He is, I tell you.'

'Help yourself then, if you need one so badly.'

'All the signs say I am anointed King.'

'Then wipe your nose, you disgusting sight.'

'The Maid's voices say so.'

'You'd doubt your own mother's word for that of a mere virgin?'

'Yes.'

'What is it you want, you twisted bedstead? Come on.'

'Say he is my father.'

'No.'

'Say it.'

'Again, No!'

'Please.'

Isabelle just shook her head, smiling.

'He's dead,' continued the new King

'Exactly.'

'Say it!'

Isabelle's hand shot out and grasped the King's tunic. She twisted it so that her son's head was an inch from his father's.

'Look, see. Nose, chin, mouth, see. Not a bit like his!'

'The same,' panted the King of France. 'Nose, chin . . . ' he mouthed, slobbering at his mother, ' . . . the same.'

Isabelle released him and straightened up, spitting, 'I'm damned if either of you looks like anyone I ever knew.'

'I'm taking him to St Pol.'

'Let him rest here for the night.'

'I'm taking him.'

'He won't be any trouble.'

'Your days are done!' Isabelle was taken aback. For a moment he had again sounded like a real Wittelsbach.

'I too am a man.'

Well, she would show him who was still mother. She gripped the handles. Charles pushed her away. Isabelle clung to the coffin. Charles grabbed the bottom end and heaved. Isabelle pulled in the opposite direction. A tug-of-war started. The King's signet ring suddenly clattered onto the floor from her dress and skidded across into a corner.

'My father's signet!'

'Out of my way!'

'You'd rob the dead!'

'He robbed me!' Isabelle shook her fist at the corpse, 'and I'll flatten you just as you did me!'

Isabelle pushed her son aside, and scrabbled for the ring on her hands and knees in the shadows.

'Hah, got it!' she finally shouted in triumph.

When she turned, she was just in time to see her son disappearing with the cart through the open entrance. She hurried after him. As she came to the doors, two Men-at-Arms of the King's new personal bodyguard stepped out, barring her way. They were wearing the livery of the hated *fleur-de-lis* of France. Isabelle tried to thrust past. The guards unceremoniously shoved her back with their lances crossed, then stood sentinel, strictly watching her every move as they had been ordered to do.

The *benedictus* started up again. The late King had indeed embarked on his final journey on this earth. Isabelle slumped down in the chair. A bird in an iron cage again. First by her husband, now by her son. And this time her prison was in the ruins of her very own beloved Court of Good Shepherds. But, she swore, she was far from finished yet.

65

Owen came to slowly. He first heard a distant scratching sound. He opened his eyes. A dim light seemed to come from higher up. He felt his limbs. Unhurt. But he had lost his sword and dagger. He saw that the strange glow came from a tunnel dead ahead. To his immediate left rose a huge rock fall of massive slabs and boulders up to the roof of the cavern. The whole area seemed to glitter whitely with a myriad reflected sparkles. Owen closed his eyes briefly, and looked again. Then he saw them, dozens of skeletons splayed out, seemingly intact. Many wore bassinets and helms, still holding sword and spear. Owen moved forward, clambering up the slope. The mass of rock began to slide. Earth and stone pattered down from the roof. Owen paused. The tremors stopped. Close up, Owen saw gashes in the helms, sword blades broken and rusted, severed thighs, gashed skulls, smashed breast bones and rib cages. He picked up a lance. It crumbled in his hands. Then, at the top, he made out a glinting of gold thread. He froze. He saw the outline of a standard propped among the rocks, a gold dragon on a white background. Glyndŵr's own personal standard! In a flash, he knew. This was Glyndŵr's last redoubt, his final resting place, the ultimate cave of the sleeping heroes of Wales, awaiting the call to lead the *Cymry* to freedom. But where was Glyndŵr himself? And why was he, Owain Tudur, an obscure Welsh squire with no following, wanted here,?

That uncanny scratching again. From behind a shadowy boulder in front of him, rose the Sin Eater. He raised his inky, venomous wings, chittering, and scratching his fingers against the rock. His marble eyes gleamed as he looked on Owen, running his tongue over reptilian lips. Owen saw his long, stick-long fingers gleamed like polished metal. The Sin Eater picked up a holed helmet.

'This once sheltered proud Glyndŵr. Now dead spinners refuse.' He tossed it aside. He held up a buckler. 'This once held the sun. Ashes now scorn it.'

Owen moved down the rocks. The Sin Eater advanced on him, smashing the relics of bone and lance.

'Cavalcades of dust. Glyndŵr's a barren enchantment now. Look on me. Incest of patricide. Infanticide of sodomite. Demon lust of matricide. All are within me. I came too late for their wickednesses, but not yours, *y Mab Darogan*, founder of noble houses. Let me eat the abominations of an unborn hero, my black banquet on this Samhain night. Let me place this yeast of Satan on your breast, so when the sun comes up all your mortal iniquities will rise into the bread, and I will feast at dawn on a living legend, and be at one with the sable, sin-crammed immortals of *Annwn*.'

Owen retreated towards the tunnel. The Sin Eater crouched towards his prey, raising his stick-like steel-tipped fingers.

The shattering peal of a leper's bell broke the silence. King Leper leapt out from behind a boulder. He stood stock still, arms raised, between the devil and his victim.

'Keep back, Owain!'

'The white death!' chittered the Sin Eater fearfully, retreating up among the rocks and bones.

'Tomb vulture! Coffin leech! Hell hound!'

The Sin Eater reeled before King Leper's onslaught.

'I'll close your rushing lids of death! Now, ye Sin Eaters of the world, come, view this quenched alabaster!' He ripped open his leper's cloak, exposing his pallid, lumpen breast. The Sin Eater scrabbled backwards.

'Have dark audience of me! Come, O most apocalyptic

obscenity, make mouths over me!'

His bell pealed out again. The Sin Eater glanced at the the tunnel behind King Leper.

'Prepare yourself, you Sin Eaters of the World, prepare yourself for King Leper, Prince of Disease!'

The Sin Eater dropped his nauseating clump of dough, and tried to bolt past King Leper. King Leper engulfed him in his cloak, and hurled him to the ground, pressing his molten chest down over the Sin Eater's nose and mouth. The Sin Eater struggled frantically, like a bat trapped in a net. The chittering came in strangled gasps. His heels began drumming on the earth. With one final despairing burst of strength, he spread out his webbed arms, then clutched, enclosing King Leper within his wings. His gleaming fingers stabbed fiercely downwards. The razor-sharp talons sank deep into King Leper's straining back. Blood burst from the wounds, but still King Leper did not ease the deadly weight. Sounds as of rushing bat wings, came from the Sin Eater's mouth. He stiffened and finally fell silent, drained of all evil. King Leper rolled from the body, blood pulsing from his wounds. Owen at once cradled his dying brother's head in his arms, stroking his brows, kissing his face. A faint trembling filled the air. It became stronger, as if some huge force was pressing down from above.

'Go, Owain,' whispered King Leper. 'Samhain is over, your destiny is freed. Go.'

'What is my destiny, brother?'

'The whole family of Wales.' The entire vault of the roof was violently shaking. 'Now go!'

The cave bucked and shuddered. Soil and shale spattered onto them. Skulls, skeletons, weapons clattered down the shifting rocks.

'Go!'

Eyes streaming with tears, Owen gave his beloved brother one final embrace, and dashed into the dusty tunnel mouth. At that moment the great arch of the roof split into a dozen gaping fissures, and with a thunderous, drowning roar, the fatal darkness fell, shrouding every saint and sinner in the neutral aeons of eternity.

66

Owen burst out of the mouth of the tunnel into brilliant, blinding, morning sunshine. Birds sang in the bright air and breezes ruffled the feathers of the pigeons in the tree tops. No trace of the nightmares of Samhain remained. The bonfires had died out, the smoke dissolved into the morning mists. The whole world seemed to be sleeping the sleep of the innocent.

Owen looked about dazed. All he could see was King Leper's eyes closing, and the evil filth of the Sin Eater lying dead at last. His brother was gone. He, Owain, was the last of the family now. Brother greatheart. Gone. Owen shook convulsively with grief. He knelt and prayed to the old gods. He knew King Leper's spirit had joined his ancestors in the teeming Otherworld. His destiny was done. Yes, Owen knew it was his turn now. To bear his destiny, to follow fate, to carry the whole weight of Wales and the Tudors. He straightened up, his direction clear at last. But he would miss the greatheart at his side.

He looked up the slopes of the hillside rising before him. Above, he could see the crags of King Arthur's Seat. The meeting place. Owen set out, scrambling upwards at speed. Half way to the crags, he saw a pillar of smoke rising into the air. A signal from Hopcyn surely. In ten minutes, Owen, Hopcyn and Agnes were embracing each other.

'Agnes tracked me down,' said Hopcyn, looking behind Owen, knowing there was no King Leper. He had already bade farewell to him.

'King Leper is dead,' said Owen.

Hopcyn nodded.

'He saved me. The Sin Eater, too, is dead.'

Agnes hugged him again.

'Brother Greatheart.'

'He freed your fate, Owain.'

'You knew?'

'Yes.'

'I know the way now.'

'We shall all miss him,' said Hopcyn. 'Bless him forever.'

They were silent for a moment.

'Now, Owain, tell us what happened last night,' said Agnes.

Owen told them about the warriors in the river bed, the Lantern birds, the ancient graveyard, the blue stones, the Triumph of Death, and the harridan at the river.

'The Hag of the Ford,' said Hopcyn, 'has slipped through to the day.'

'But Samhain, King Leper, the Sin Eater, it's all over now.'

'Agnes has got news too,' said Hopcyn.

'Yes?'

'Henry the King is dead.'

'What?'

'Lying in state, in the Abbey.'

'But how?'

'Dysentery, at Bauge.'

'Even Henry. A tough nut. Damn sieges. Won't be another command like his. I saved him. Destiny again. I fit into it somewhere, I know it. They must give me a fighting command now.'

'Henry confirmed you Captain of the Queen's Guard.'

'No!'

'And Clerk of the Queen's Wardrobe.'

'I shall not take it.'

'Owen,' said Agnes, 'you have got your manor and estates in Pembroke back, haven't you?'

'Yes.'

'And the last of your distant kin in place?' added Hopcyn.

'Yes.'

'The Tudors are rising from the ashes,' said Hopcyn gently. 'King Leper prepared that way for you, too.'

'And that way,' said Agnes, 'lies in the direction of the Queen's court.'

'Yes,' said Owen, 'you're right. And I must follow it for King Leper.'

'We must go poste haste to London, and Baynard's,' said Agnes. 'Catherine has sent for us.'

For a moment Owen felt a warm sense of urgency. He suddenly needed to see Catherine.

'She has need of us, too,' said Agnes with a smile. 'And Warwick has ordered you to report direct to him.'

'When?'

'Yesterday.'

'Come on!' They mounted up and travelled back along the path they had taken the previous night. It seemed a century ago, and in another world. The place where they had parted was a picture of sylvan peace. Just below, they paused at the edge of a shady glade, carpeted with thick layers of leaves and dotted with sturdy, scrub oaks. Hopcyn noted the clearing formed a near perfect circle. He felt a slight spasm. He reined in. The image was there. Indistinct. Bright red. Danger.

'Stop,' he said, and at once dismounted.

'Why?' asked Agnes.

'Walk the horses. Here, by me, Owain.'

Owen dismounted next to the nearest oak and moved over to join Agnes and Hopcyn. At that instant, a hooded figure hugging the far side of the tree, as flat and clinging as the bark itself, detached itself and spun in a circle. As Owen passed, she thrust a dagger at his breast just above the heart. Owen felt the breath knocked out of his body and fell flat on his back. In a second, Hopcyn had hammered the figure to the ground. Agnes ripped off the hood. The Hag of the Ford leered, spat and hissed in their faces. Hopcyn glanced at Owen. He seemed stunned, but unharmed, struggling to sit up.

'Hold her!' Hopcyn unwound his belt and bound her hands behind her back. The Hag writhed like one demented. 'And close her filthy mouth!'

'Let me,' said Agnes. She parted the witch's waist length hair behind, wound it round her throat, and passed it once again around her mouth, tightening it into a heavy knot which she thrust into the reptilian mouth. She undid her belt and tied the Hag's legs.

Owen was swaying, but standing, examining the knife cut in his tunic. It was identical to the cut in the tunic in the river. A little blood oozed out, but there was no flow. Agnes ripped open the cloth. The chain mail underneath had held. The point of the knife had snapped off in the hooks.

'Just a nick,' she said. Hopcyn pulled out the blade tip.

'So,' growled Hopcyn, 'let us see now.'

He knelt and raised the Hag's head. His multi-coloured gaze stared with a white-heat intensity into the witch's eyes. He brought to bear every hellish image he had ever beheld, in life and in death. The Hag shivered, averting her head.

'Do we kill her here?' asked Owen.

'No,' replied Hopcyn. 'Her spirit would haunt you for the rest of your days - which is what she wants.'

He walked over to an oak, and banged on it with the hilt of his sword. He did this to a second, third and fourth tree. The fourth produced a short, heavy echo. Hopcyn clambered up into the boughs.

'Owen,' he called down, 'see that trunk?' He pointed to a fallen trunk, thick as a man's body and about half as long. 'Bring it over here.' Owen did as he was requested.

'Now lift up the Hag. Up. Lift.'

Hopcyn grabbed her and lifted her high by the hair, and held her there for an instant. Then he dropped her bodily inside the hollow tree trunk which opened below his feet. He looked down into her baleful, satanic eyes. They were beginning to shade over.

'The trunk.'

Hopcyn raised the trunk above the trapped hag. Before he dropped the upright log like a huge plug into the aperture, he saw her eyes had changed to marble black, solid as any Sin Eater's. The heavy clunk echoed through the trees. The Hag was sealed in. Hopcyn got down.

'No, Owain,' he explained, 'we cannot kill her. We have to transform her. The oak there is sacred to the old gods. They will never release her spirit. She is now transformed into a wood demon, for eternity. And you are freed indeed.'

'I should have killed her.'

'Some things only a bard can do.'

'Thank you, Bard Hopcyn.'

As they rode out, a mad, thin, keening wail arose. The crows and rooks in the trees wheeled away in fright. For centuries, no bird would perch or sing among the leaves of that glade. The leafy circle remained frozen in unnatural, deathly silence, even at the yearly birth of Spring. But every Samhain night, the one-legged Lantern bird could be seen, pecking its hideous red feasts and shrieking its sepulchral cry as for a lost mate. But none ever came.

67

Outside, the day was appropriately dismal. The skies were scudding with grey and black clouds. Inside, the Abbey of Westminster was hung with the panoply of death. All the hangings, the banners, flags, pennants, altercloths and tapestries were bordered with black. The myriad altar candles were black, with black wicks. Even the bells of the Abbey were shrouded before they were tolled. The multitude of mourners below moved like massed crows across cold pavements, rising and settling, as they stood and knelt. Catherine, the mourner-in-chief, was in black too, with a black veil and even her kerchief was the same shade.

In the newly constructed St George's chapel, Catherine stood at the side of Henry's grey tomb, fit resting place for a national hero. The tomb was made of two-inch thick slabs of stone – the final walls of Jerusalem for Henry. On the top reclined a moulded full-length silver-plated replica of Henry, the head in solid silver. Catherine had permitted the silversmiths to use the leather image of Henry. She shivered. The likeness was uncanny, lifelike. She half-expected to hear his familiar voice call to her. Though the painted eyes shone, they stared ahead robbed of all sight. Henry was indeed gone, his cleaned bones reverentially laid inside the cold sarcophagus. Catherine had been at pains to observe Henry's every last wish. Within his bones now rested the Welsh Agincourt arrow. The black altar bells tinkled. Time to depart. The black-robed priests and monks, holding black candles, led the way out, chanting their doleful requiems and masses.

Everyone knew this was more than just a day to grieve the loss of a husband. Catherine would mourn the loss of her babe as well. Her Demoiselles, Joanna and Joséphine, in black silk dresses from head to foot, waited outside in the funerary carriage. Along the streets, the windows were hung with black linen cloths and flags. The coach was black and the horses shone like ebony. Between the Demoiselles sat the upright figure of the Countess of Warwick, out of the same stern, superior mould as her husband. On her lap sat the baby King. The Countess felt only sympathy for Catherine. As a mother herself, she knew what Catherine was going through. She deferred to Catherine, but knew that, she, too, had to do her duty. Sadly, she realised that this was the last time the young mother would dandle her own dear babe in her lap.

The procession slowly wound out of the spacious doors of the Abbey and lined up on the pavements in farewell. Catherine was ushered, with all the ceremony due to a Dowager Queen, into the black, padded seats of the closed carriage. The Countess tenderly handed the babe to Catherine. The cheers from the waiting crowds were muted, out of respect and genuine sadness. So young to lose all. The people mourned not only a great King, but his youthful widowed Queen as well. Catherine was only twenty.

The carriage set off at a slow stately walk through the streets. Once away from Westminster, the pace doubled. Catherine was anxious to have it over and done with. The destination, Baynard's Castle, was where Catherine was to bid farewell to her baby son and, according to Henry's last instructions, give him over officially into the care of the Countess.

Catherine was pale but determined. She would not let Henry or herself, and certainly not her own son, down in any way. She would do her duty, however much she longed to keep her son, the only fragment left of her first little family. She smiled tremulously at the babe in her lap, and resisted the impulse to cover his little face with kisses. His healthy, shining face was in contrast to her own sombre pallor. The little King was dressed in a short velvet gown, in black, trimmed with black fur, and on his head, a turned up black velvet cap. On it rested a shining golden miniature crown, the only note of sunshine in the whole procession. In his right hand, he waved a toy sceptre, surmounted with a small cross. He loved the sound it gave. It was the royal rattle. Dear little Henry, Catherine thought, was proving unusually sensitive. He sometimes gazed around with a filmy, uncomprehending, look, as if he were watching from another world. Catherine's heart bled. She knew where she had seen that look before – on her dear 'Well-Beloved' father's face.

Soon, with the grey turgid Thames on one side, the turreted donjon of Baynard's castle loomed into sight. The walls rose high and grim, more of a fortress than a castle, and surely never intended as a home. But Catherine's apartments were at the back, overlooking acres of parkland, glades, woods and meadows. Lilacs grew in wild abundance there. She couldn't wait for the spring. But first, the dreaded English winter would have to be faced, and faced without the consolation of her firstborn. Out of diversity had come disunity. She stopped the thought. She would never be bitter. At least the nuns had taught her the futility of that.

The carriage drove into the court yard of Baynard's and stopped at the steps up to the main entrance. Catherine kissed the babe for the last time. Little hands clung to her fingers. Steeling herself as she felt sobs rising in her throat, she gently laid the babe in the Countess's waiting arms, lifting away the curling, little fingers. Although the babe didn't cry, he never lost that far away, puzzled look. Catherine quickly mounted the steps, followed by Joanna and Joséphine. At the top, she turned and motioned the coachman to leave. She blew one last despairing kiss as the carriage disappeared under the archway into the lowering evening murk.

Catherine hurried into her own apartments. In her bed chamber, her heart finally gave way and she wept without stop. But as she listened to the comforting counsels of her old friends, she realised, come what may, that her babe would have need of her one day. It was her duty to remain calm and healthy. She was soon, with her Demioselles, trying to eat her first meal since the previous day, and going over the sad events of the last, dark, twenty-four hours.

The destination of the carriage, now going at a brisk pace northwards, was Warwick Castle, the seat of the all powerful Beauchamp family. 'The King makers' were capable, aristocratic, and avowed champions of *courtoisie*, absolute serviteurs of the ruling family. That family would have need of every ounce of strength, for everyone knew the days of a minority were strewn with plots, conspiracies and murder most foul. And that dread prophecy of Windsor, though never mentioned, still hung over the court like a cloud and a curse.

68

As Catherine was settling into Baynard's that night, an emergency meeting of two of the main members of the Grand Council was in session in the White Room of the Palace of Westminster. The Earl of Warwick, guardian to the King and now Lord Chancellor of England, was debating the recent civil disturbances with Cardinal Beaufort of Winchester.

Cardinal Beaufort had a bluff, hearty exterior, with an appearance that matched his character – square-jawed, broad-faced, with a florid complexion, curling eyebrows, a shock of grey hair and a cheerful voice. He was in fact a tough-minded born intriguer with an uncanny knack for the main chance. He was a brilliant business man. His wealth was immense and never seemed to get in the way of his religious duties. He was popular in Rome, and even had the ear of the Pope himself – for they were two of a kind. Winchester was one of the worldly prelates which infested the Papacy, and brought it into the lowest disrepute. This was, however, the best qualification for becoming a leading member of the College of Cardinals. Although the Cardinal was descended from the old Duke of York, he sided with law and order, the party of business and profit, wherever it was strongest, and this happened to be on the side of Henry and the Lancastrians. He was condemned as a traitor by the Yorkists, but his wealth, power and consummate abilities, kept his enemies at bay.

In front of them lay reports from the Constables and Sheriffs of London and the home counties. They told of the ever increasing clashes between the red and white factions, clashes which were becoming bloodier by the day. They had summoned the Duke of Somerset, a leading Yorkist, who was waiting in an antechamber, fuming with an earful ready for these arrogant Lancastrians. Humphrey had declined the invitation to be there, which was a mistake. The two could issue decrees in the name of the whole Council, decrees that could limit the rapidly declining power of the Lord Protector himself. There was no quorum, a detail Humphrey had overlooked.

Winchester did not seem over worried.

'Minority always equals anarchy,' he observed.

'The reds against the whites,' said Warwick.

'And Humphrey against everybody.'

'Do we confirm his title, "Protector of the Realm"?'

'Why not? It has a fine hollow ring. And there is no quorum.'

They signed and sealed the documents.

'The quorum are the laws we sign here.'

'Now about these army pay returns. Highly irregular.'

'Let's request an audit. Just to put the wind up him.'

'Done. But these intercepts . . . '

' . . . he's still got Captain Dark in his pay.'

'Do we show we know?'

'No, better let him have those. We'll re-imburse the Queen, and keep an eye on Isabelle as well.'

'These sums on his Palace. Outrageous.'

'That's where the pay chests go.'

'Just express concern. And keep these pay rolls in a safe place.'

'Now the Anti-riot laws. A curfew, with no drawn swords or daggers, or cudgels within ten miles of the City. Confirmed?'

'Confirmed.'

They signed and sealed the documents again.

'Now let's inform Somerset of our new measures.' Warwick personally ushered in the sullen Somerset.

'So sorry to keep you waiting, my Lord. Good to see you.'

'Greetings my Lord,' said Winchester. 'You should come to the capital more often, and bring York with you. He's much missed stuck up there in the north with his castles.'

'We would, were it not for your troops.'

'They are England's troops.'

'They are Lancastrian troops.'

'Like the Yorkist ones then,' said Winchester.

'Please,' soothed Warwick. 'We must remain united if we are to keep our Empire in France. Even now Burgundy is flirting with the Dauphinists.'

'How can we be united if we Yorkists are denied power?'

'Nobody is denying you power.'

'You are squeezing us out.'

'We are squeezing you in.'

'United! That was Henry's last command. We will follow that to the death!' Warwick reinforced his words with a rap of his knuckles on the table. Somerset was thrown by the iron tones.

'I . . . I too condemn these clashes. They are not on my orders. My retainers feel personally insulted. They too were at Agincourt, they deserve their just rewards. They can't help venting their anger. And this title, 'Lord Protector', that should have gone to a Yorkist. You Lancastrians have taken all the plum positions yet Humphrey still sets his men against mine. He always starts it.' Somerset had recovered his nerve. 'If there are divisions, they are of your own making.'

'Ha,' he thought, 'that's rubbed their noses in it.' Although Somerset was short and slim, he was a noted sword fighter. His thin, sharp features hid a vicious but shrewd intelligence. He was no rival for Winchester or Warwick, but he had the courage of persistence, a keen eye, and his determination always came as a surprise to friend and foe alike.

'And Henry's claim is not in the direct line,' he went on.

Warwick raised his hands.

'No dynastic squabbles, please.'

'Whatever you Lancastrians say.'

'You claim through royal bastards,' returned Winchester. Somerset's sudden rally had surprised him too.

'The bend sinister's claim is just as valid, as William the Conqueror proved once and for all. And you, how can you side with the Henrys, my Lord Winchester?' But Winchester answered.

'No problem, nephew, for a Cardinal.' He continued with a question. 'Is it true, my Lord?'

'Is what true?'

'You're chasing Queen Catherine.'

'She is only twenty,' replied Somerset. So this was what they were really worried about.

'She is still in mourning,' said Warwick.

'That's what I mean,' smiled Somerset. 'Only twenty.'

'We are her guardians, my Lord Somerset.'

'Do you deny me an interview with her?'

'Until the official period of mourning is over.'

'And how long will that be?'

'As long as the Council decides it to be.'

'Is that final?'

'It is the law,' said the Lord Chancellor. 'You may go now. And take your retainers with you.'

'The new anti-riot measures, my Lord Somerset, will be most strictly enforced,' said Winchester. 'Take a copy.'

'And if I find just one of your men left in the capital tomorrow,' added Warwick, 'you will not see him for a very long time.'

Somerset snatched the document from his hand, and marched out. It was as he had expected. He would retire gracefully for now. Such selfishness, such stupidity. Who had any respect for the laws of mourning, anyway, when a whole

Kingdom was at stake. He'd show the whole pack of those greedy Lancastrians. Just a question of time. He had set a little trap. He had ordered groups of his men to change into the livery of Duke Humphrey, and had stationed them in inns and ale houses along the roads into the city and in bawdy houses around London bridge.

'Well, there goes a cool fool,' said Warwick, as the footsteps died away. 'Far too cool.'

'Everyone wants to get into the Queen's bed,' said Winchester.

'Everyone wants to get into her crown.'

'So Henry put her safely to sleep in Baynard's.'

'I think even Somerset would stop short of scaling the walls.'

'Well, thank God, Humphrey's not on the loose.'

But even they had underestimated Humphrey's mindless genius for infinite mischief-making.

69

The Gardens in front of the Palace of Placentia were teeming with Humphrey's retainers. Bonfires and a thousand bobbing torches lit the scene. Humphrey's men were celebrating the retreat of Somerset's troops. Captain Dark had done his work efficiently. He had struck hard at Somerset with night ambushes and attacks, and the occasional murder when the getaway was clear. He had also interrogated a prisoner whose livery was the falcon, but whose dagger was for York. Humphrey had listened with glee to Captain Dark's counter plan. But once the curfew order had been received the good Captain, like any faithful soldier, retired in good order.

Humphrey had prepared a lavish welcome for his 'lads', who in reality were nothing more than his despised rabble. It was politic. Row upon row of food and beer stalls were set up. Bear-baiting pits were dug. Stages had been erected for non-stop pageants of St George, and reconstructions of the Duke's last charge at Agincourt, the one which had of course secured English victory. Jugglers, mummers in grotesque masks representing monkeys, lizards, unicorns, devils, and acrobats tumbled and whirled everywhere. There were even tents with displays of cheap and cheerful bawds. And it was all for free. And to top it, on Captain's Dark's insistence, Humphrey had arranged for the distribution of largesse. Newly minted groats flowed almost as liberally as the beer. Humphrey had granted the Captain a special bonus, for he had also succeeded in stopping the turnip tops, and the words 'sausage fingers' had vanished from the palace walls – at least, for the time being.

Yes, everyone listened to the Captain, for he had a hundred daggers to hand.

With hundreds of his retainers getting roaring drunk outside, Humphrey had broken no law. These were private festivities within the purlieus of his own domestic dwelling place. The fact that they were armed to the teeth meant nothing. It was all perfectly legal.

Humphrey strutted up and down in the Long Room, bewigged and bandy-legged. His baton of office rarely left his hand. He listened with a smile to the baying mob. How easy they were to manipulate, just like women. Eleanor followed, looking up in rapture at him. Both wore their royal robes and coronets. Only Captain Dark and two of his assassins were permitted entry. They alone supervised every detail, and were sworn to absolute secrecy – for the Long Room had been re-christened the Throne Room. The twin seats of majesty were now in permanent position on the dais at the end of the room, as was the Palace of the Caesars to one side. Only the sinister gallery of wax heads was hidden from view. Around the thrones was a veritable forest of St George's pennants, and Humphrey's pennant crest of the striking falcon. A table in front of the dais was littered with reports, maps and documents. Flames from a roaring fire in the immense canopied hearth threw red shadows across the walls. Eleanor's plucked brows gleamed like a lizard's in the warm glow.

She wanted to get Humphrey down to business so she started on the subject closest to his heart – the succession.

'I thought the babe looked peaky.'

'Sick!'

'Fay too.'

'Bloody loony, like his granddad!'

'Like a foundling.'

'Like a bastard you mean, like his dad.'

'So pale.'

'Get the Witch onto it.'

'She be onto it already, my lovely.'

'Tell her to hurry.'

'She not done us too bad up to now, right?'

'True.'

'To business, my lovely.'

'Not too much, I'm tired.'

'What if the Queen don't accept our Lady Ann de Burgh?'

'Our spies, our eyes. She'd better.' He brought his baton down like a club.

'Well, Lady Ann be a sharp one. Now this request of our Agnes for more payment?'

'Denied.'

'No, my darlin'.'

'Why not?'

'She be young.'

Humphrey held his baton like a prick, and guffawed.

'So?'

'Suitors.'

'What? Who?'

'Somerset.'

Humphrey's face darkened.

'Devil dukes again! Who told you?'

'Calmly now! Agnes.'

'We'll teach that rat a lesson. And tonight!'

'Pay Agnes then?'

'I suppose.'

Humphrey seized another document from the table.

'I'll give them curfew!' he shouted, and threw it into the fire. 'And this about no drawn swords?' He pointed dramatically to the mob outside. 'Tell that to them! And this request for audit! Bloody cheek. I am the audit here. Into the flames!'

He picked up another document.

'Queen Isabelle's request to attend the lying-in-state of

Henry – denied! Queen Isabelle's request to visit Baynard's – denied! Catherine's request to visit her father's last resting place – denied. Queen Isabelle's bank drafts. Diverted! On what grounds? – defence of the Realm. Justification? I am Lord Protector – Bedford's only Regent, and he's absent anyway.'

He swung around.

'Listen to that cheering!'

'Captain Dark be a real angel, my love.'

'I protect my own.'

'And this report here?'

'Enough for now.'

'Paymasters rolls.'

'Stab in the back!'

'Complaints. Thy expenses for Placentia.'

'An insult! Work of national importance; shrine to England's greatness! Listen to our patriots out there. That gives the lie to all these lies!'

He scattered the papers and strode over to the balcony windows, flung them open and stepped outside. Ecstatic yells greeted him. He held up his hand for silence.

'We won another brave victory for England today! From Paris to London, our Empire will last a thousand years!'

Wild cheers rose up.

'To the victors! For Humph . . . Harry, England and St George!' He gave the 'V' sign, punched the air with his baton, and shouted 'The iron fist!', which was the war cry for the night.

More outbursts split the air. Choruses could be heard above the crowd, carefully orchestrated by Captain Dark. 'Iron fist! Humphrey for King!'

Humphrey held up his hands protestingly, backed into the room and closed the windows, panting as after an orgasm.

'Ye heard 'em,' said Eleanor. 'Ye have the common touch.'

'Iron fist! Humphrey for King!' The chanting outside grew in a loud crescendo.

'They fair dotes on thy greatness, and so does I!'

'Beer guzzlers and ape shitters, but they'll do the trick.'

'Ye be the king in fact, my lovely, the power behind the Council.'

'And they'll all soon have a taste of it!'

Eleanor drew the alcove curtains, and slid open the panel of the travelling chest. Between Humphrey and the throne, only two heads remained, Bedford's and baby Henry's. Eleanor raised the needle above the baby's waxen image.

Let 'em sicken, let 'em die,

Humphrey be King, and Queen be I!

She plunged the needle into the wax. Humphrey winced, then relaxed. Only two to go! From outside the bonfires leapt up, and the babble rose in waves into the night.

'Iron fist! Humphrey for King!'

The whole mass seemed spoiling for a fight. They were right. At dawn, Captain Dark had orders to march on Tower Bridge and on London Bridge – in defence of the Realm, of course.

70

Owen stood at ease in front of Warwick in the White Hall of Westminster. He had been given a rousing welcome by his companies of Welsh archers. Warwick had personally accompanied Owen inside to the headquarters room.

'Captain Owen, it was the King's last wish.'

'But, my Lord, I was to receive a fighting command.'

'This order supersedes all others. The Dowager Queen must be protected by our best men. You know how rowdy things are in the capital now – Duke Humphrey, York and Somerset. Up and down the country, it's the same. Do you know, Captain, we have more guards around the Abbey here than in Notre Dame in Paris. Sorry to hear of your Leper's death. A good man. What about his network?'

'Disbanded to the Lazariums. Still have three at Baynard's.'

'Keep them there. Frighten off Humphrey. Matters not going well. Unity, we must have unity. And this Maid's getting the people on her side in France. We released details of Charles' possible bastardy, but it made no difference. Now he's got a clever mistress and he listens to her every word. La Tremouille she's called. Got one thing that's making us bleed. She knows good men. The King's new generals, Etienne de Vignolles, Constable Richemont of Brittany, and this bastard Dunois of Orleans – they seem to love their royal bastards over there – all of them are Tremouille's choice, and all with victories behind 'em now. Then this virgin in soldier's armour, most unnatural. Burgundy's playing a doubtful game too. Adds up to a mess of trouble. But all that's as nothing unless we have unity at home.

So never mind the problems over there, Bedford's been informed and is on the way to London. As Regent, he has the final word in the Council. Together, we'll settle these rabble-rousers once and for all.'

'Who takes over from Bedford?'

'Our brave Talbot from Wales.'

'A natural soldier,' Owen acknowledged.

'I know you Welsh hate these Marcher Lords, but you trained them to fight at least.'

All these left-handed compliments, thought Owen, all I want is a command of my own, like Talbot.

'And there are dependable commanders like my Lord Huntingdon and Sir Gilbert Umfraville, Willoughby. But we do not have an inexhaustible supply.'

A loud clatter of footsteps came from the stone-flagged corridor. Winchester hurried in surrounded by his entire staff and the commanders of his Retainers, all fully armed. Winchester had even strapped on a sword over his clerical robes.

'Alarm, gentlemen, alarm. Welcome, Captain Owen. Your companies are on alert too, I see. You'll have a fighting command quicker than you think. My Lord Warwick, I encountered messengers on the way back. Bedford has landed and is on the road from Dover.'

'Excellent.'

'And Humphrey's moving the mass of his Retainers on to London Bridge.'

'What?! Has he gone mad?'

'No, he's always been that way.'

'This is against every ordinance of the Council.'

'He's pleading "defence of the realm", that is, war on the Yorkists. A showdown with Somerset, for Humphrey's own ends. But of Somerset's men, my messengers could see nothing.'

'We must stop this dangerous imbecile now.'

'Agreed. These are the measures. Had no choice but to act at once.'

Warwick nodded.

'Go on.'

'All my Men-at-Arms are assembled outside, my Retainers too. I have sent out scouts north and south of the river, with orders for all garrison commanders to raise drawbridges and prepare to repel besiegers. Your archers, Captain Owen are now waiting outside, all mounts ready. You are to ride at a gallop to London Bridge. You are to occupy the two towers at both ends. You are to install archers at every slit, with two reserve lines on the battlements. You are to reinforce the main gates on the Southwark side, with chains and whatever else you can find. You are to hold your position at all costs. Humphrey must not be allowed to break through the bridge defences and into the City.'

'Are you sure of Humphrey's line of march?'

'Nothing is sure with that fool, but I think we've covered most routes. So, gentlemen, we move off now. Captain Owen, hold that bridge.'

Owen saluted and hurried off, elated. A fighting command at last.

As Owen and his archers approached the danger area, they noted that the houses were shuttered and the shops barred. The streets were empty except for marauding dogs, sure signs of trouble ahead. Owen clattered onto the bridge, unopposed. They had beaten Humphrey to the punch. From the Towers, in the dim light of dawn, they could see Humphrey's host, its torches gleaming, but not moving. Providentially, Humphrey had halted to re-group. Beneath the hundreds of St George banners and falcon pennants, many of his men were still too drunk to walk, let alone fight. Many had been left inert in the grounds of Placentia, sleeping it off. The rest kept going with promises of rich booty in the City.

Owen at once set to work. He strengthened the huge gates with chains and bolts, then built a makeshift but solid barrier behind it, made of bales, boxes, building beams and merchant's carts commandeered from the inn yards close by. The archers were then installed in the towers. They were to remain concealed until they received the order to shoot. They could not make out the next bridge for it was still concealed in the morning mist.

As Humphrey's mob moved off, Warwick and Winchester galloped up with reinforcements. They joined Owen on the battlements of the Southwark tower. As the sun rose, Warwick examined the mass advancing along the south bank with a trained eye.

'About a thousand I'd say. Slow as old women. Booze, no doubt. Well armed.'

'Two thousand were reported. Where are the rest?'

'And where's Somerset's rabble?'

As the mass turned into the road leading directly onto the bridge, the mob saw the barrier. With a roar of rage, they broke into a run, drawing their swords, pennants streaming in the winds, yelling,

'Iron fist! Humphrey for King!'

When the mob were clambering onto the barriers, Owen gave the order to shoot. Howls of panic went up. Showers of steel-tipped arrows, at the rate of twelve a minute per bowman, at once cleared the barrier. Further showers drove them back to the shelter of nearby houses. Shocked at the fierce opposition, the dead and wounded remained unaided in the open. The mists were now dispersing.

From the top of the Tower, they could now make out Humphrey, in savage mood, standing on a dais in his 'war chariot', as he liked to call it. He was in his fighting armour, still with his baton. When he saw his adversaries, he waved his two-edged battle sword in defiance. He choked with rage when he recognised Owen.

'Mad dog. Destroy him here and now,' growled Warwick.

'But still Protector of the Realm.'

'Look! Have we beaten them off so easily?'

'No,' said Owen, 'look.'

He pointed in the direction of the upstream bridge. It now stood out clearly in the sunshine. Columns of smoke were rising from it. Humphrey's second company of men had taken it, as planned, and were now attempting to burn down the wooden structure. Yells and screams rose and fell in the morning wind.

A messenger thrust his way onto the battlements and handed Warwick a scribbled report from the Governor of the Tower.

'Humphrey's column captured the bridge, investing the walls now, aims to force the Keep. Governor's counter attacking . . . ' he pointed, ' . . . even now! There!' Two squadrons of horse suddenly burst from the raised portcullis of the Tower and charged down the bridge, scattering Humphrey's men before them. The yells floated over the waters. At the same time, more and more clusters of Humphrey's men tumbled off the bridge until none remained on the Tower side. The cavalry then sealed off the two ends of the bridge. In a final effort, after the cavalry had drawn off, Humphrey's repulsed forces clambered into waiting boats to attempt an amphibious assault on the far bank. Owen shouted down his orders. A company of archers detached itself and ran to the water's edge. Under the showers of deadly arrows, the unprotected open boats were soon abandoned. The remnants of the second column was now in full retreat to join Humphrey's defeated riff-raff further downstream. Humphrey stood arms akimbo on his war chariot. Next time, he vowed, those three on the tower would be the first to go.

'Done for,' said Warwick, relaxing.

It was at this moment that Somerset's leaders gave the word to go over to the attack. They emerged in yelling hordes from their lairs along the river banks and inns. At once a general melee was joined, with bodies of men colliding ferociously, going down in gutters already awash with bodies. In ever widening pools of blood, more and more bodies floated down the river. Humphrey was determined to have the victory over somebody. Somerset's men were getting a frightful beating.

Warwick and Winchester and his troopers watched the mayhem in solitary silence. No one felt inclined to cheer. After all, many of the fallen would be sons, cousins, brothers. Humphrey's little 'revenge' had turned into a murderous fratricidal battle. His 'Defence of the Realm' was complete.

71

Catherine stood in the main Hall of Baynard's. In attendance were her Ladies-in-Waiting, Adéle, Joséphine and Joanna.

The loss of her baby had plunged Catherine into profound depression. She had retired early on that first night, too sorrowful to talk to anyone. She had remained like that for days but, one night before she went to sleep, she had dried her tears, paced her chamber into the small hours, steeled herself, and made up her mind. Whatever the loneliness, whatever the loss, whatever the dangers, she would, like her mother, never give in. She would make Baynard's into a real home for her friends and for her family, even if they were dead or dispersed. Although she'd had enough of the black accoutrements of official mourning, she would continue to wear the accustomed black, but at the same time, and by every means possible, introduce as much colour into her daily life as possible. With this sudden access to decision and maturity, she fell into a deep sleep.

Next day, she awoke refreshed. To her immense surprise, she could hear footsteps rushing to and fro, shouted orders, and a cheerful bustle coming from below. Without calling for her Demoiselles, she investigated for herself. In the great Hall, she was confronted by the full staff of her household. To her delight she discovered they were mostly French and Welsh. They had been stealthily installed during the small hours.

Elated by her decision of the previous night, and by the apparent reward it had just earned, she felt composed enough to go on a tour of inspection. She quickly realised that the great hall building itself was detached from the main battlements and, though connected to them by narrow corridors, stood independently within the open bailey of the castle. The rectangular building had been continuously added to, so that the extended wings were a rabbit-warren of house-sized rooms with large windows opening onto the grounds behind. Her own private quarters, or solarium, were connected with the stable yards hall below by narrow enclosed, turreted staircases. Private exits and entrances ensured discretion for any visitor. The whole construction was compact and convenient, as if it had been carefully planned.

The stables, too, turned out to be recently renovated with a new stone-built archway, and a second smaller portcullis protecting the courtyard. When she inspected the stables, she found the water troughs full, with plenty of hay in the lofts for the horses that were steaming and stamping in the stalls.

Her whole new dwelling place resembled a miniature Keep, but with all the comforts of home. She suspected her guardian angel was her brother-in-law, the Francophile Bedford, more of a friend than an in-law. No ordinary *godon* would have taken so much trouble over a mere foreigner, let alone a 'froggie'. What was wrong with the English, she thought, that they made every other nationality into some kind of dirty devil? – especially when the *godons* themselves usually turned out to be the dirtiest devils of all.

The Ladies were delighted with the surprise they'd had a part in playing. Looking round the hall, Catherine loved the way they joined in her own delight, like a family, like sisters!

The walls had been re-plastered and painted a light, pleasing green. At the head of the hall, the raised dais and high table were lit by a projecting oriole window blazing with brightly coloured glass. The old-fashioned central hearth had been tiled over and the louvre in the ceiling covered. Three of the new hooded fireplaces with chimneys, had taken its place.

Fires could now burn merrily, without half-choking people with smoke.

The 'screens' area, the buttery, the kitchen with its well of fresh spring water, were fully stocked with utensils, and the pantries were full.

Catherine's solarium on the second floor above the dais was also freshly painted blue, including the central supporting pillar. Her curtained, four-poster was spacious and crackled with clean linen. Lumps of the new 'sea-coal' had been placed in warming pans to heat the bed.

Catherine clapped her hands with pleasure at every new discovery, and her Demoiselles laughed along with her, pleased to see the sadness so completely lifted from her brows. Joanna, who loved dancing, pointed up at the gallery.

'Harps! A little music for our re-union, Owen and Agnes . . . '

'And I will need a new set of dresses! – although, of course,' she hastened to add, 'I shall continue to wear black.'

Now why did I say that? she impatiently asked herself.

'And they're bringing the new guard Chaplain. He's called Damascus!' They all laughed. What odd names these Welsh gave each other.

In the minstrel gallery, Catherine had come across eight huge chests packed with new tapestries, displaying the happier miracles of Christ – the *Annunciation*, the *Changing of the Water into Wine* and, as if an antidote to the *Triumph of Death*, the *Raising of Lazarus*. She clapped her hands again as she saw the royal *fleur-de-lis* arms of France woven at the corner of each scene. Other chests were crammed with the finest linen draperies, which could also served as hangings. The bare spaces on the walls were now draped over. The colours exuded a warm, bright, even intimate atmosphere.

She now saw why her mother loved building her fabulous nests. But whereas her mother liked it out of pure extravagance, Catherine enjoyed it out of making the most out of the least. But both planned for one thing in common – comfort.

Catherine moved over to the high table on the dais. Her correspondence was piled up there waiting for her – soon to become a daily chore.

The brilliant Adéle, skilled in calligraphy, Latin, English and French, supervised all of Catherine's correspondence, personal and official. Joséphine, with her innate sense of order, saw to the running of the household and the domestic accounts. Bubbling, vivacious Joanna took care of the social side, including court protocol, audiences and interviews. Agnes had a roving commission with the added responsibility of household security. All four had been working together in harmony since Troyes. Soon, they would be re-united.

That day, Catherine's Demoiselles never ceased to be amazed. From their dear old childhood friend of the nunnery, to a virgin Princess of eighteen at Troyes, she had developed, overnight it seemed, into a mature mother and responsible Queen. But during that decisive night, Catherine had understood something else. After the report of the Battle of the Bridges, she knew why Henry had split up their little family. Neither she nor her baby would be threatened at the same time. And situated as they were, either in Warwick or Baynard's, they would always have time to react. Her grief was much lessened by the knowledge that her babe would always be safe. Yes, she thought, he certainly knew 'what was going on the other side of the hill.' Henry's hill by now was death itself.

Again, Catherine embraced her friends.

'Thank you. Thank you all. I will be re-united with my babe when he is seven. Until that time we will remain united ourselves, and prepare for his coming.'

The ladies bowed, Catherine was now indeed behaving like a queen.

The whole guard and household had been stunned by the news of the Battle of the Bridges, as it was now called. The

Guard cheered when they heard of Owen's part in it. Catherine detested Humphrey more than anything else for his insult over the subtlety at the coronation feast. The fact that Owen, a member of her own household, had taken part in Humphrey's discomfiture filled her with intense satisfaction. It was definitely poetic justice, the best there was, she concluded. She longed to ask Owen for details. When was he coming?

'I'll write to Bedford. No, I might thank him personally, if these messages are true.'

'He's convening an emergency parliament.'

'Let's hope Humphrey chokes on it,' remarked Joanna.

Catherine picked up another letter.

'This Lady Ann thing. Duke Humphrey again, where is she now?'

'I've installed her above the screens area,' said Joséphine.

'She won't like the cabbage smells,' smiled Adéle.

'Exactly,' Joséphine agreed.

'She is the Duke's spy, of course,' said Catherine.

'How do we get rid of her?' asked Adéle.

'She has shown herself so arrogant, like her master, I think she'll manage to do that all by herself. She'll be in attendance most evenings, so watch for the least offence. Then she shall go.'

'These letters from Somerset, the Duke of York?'

'No reply. Plead mourning.' Again her Ladies were surprised at Catherine's incisiveness.

'My requests to the Council to receive my mother and visit my father were turned down by a single member of the Council, acting on his own. Bedford must put a stop to that. Make a note of it.'

'And your monies and pensions are not getting through from France,' said Joséphine.

'Agnes's reports go direct to Bedford. Patience. And thank God I am used to living on very little.'

She looked around,

'Here I am living in the lap of luxury.' Yes, she thought, in spite of the glories of Henry's court, this little court of hers was infinitely more glorious, for it was a home, although a home without a babe – as yet.

The four friends settled down to further business.

72

Agnes stood in the private guest quarters of the Mitre Inn in Greenwich High Street. It was midnight. The room was lit by a bronze lantern. On the table was a bottle of the best Bordeaux wine, two glasses, and a small pile of gold nobles. The figure pacing up and down was wrapped in the voluminous folds of a travelling cape and hood. She clutched a small vanity case. Eleanor's reptilian black eyes glittered with anger as she again confronted Agnes. This woman was undoubtedly the most mercenary she had ever met.

'She lacks even for bread, ye said?' She added a few coins.

'Her French pensions're not coming through, yes.'

'What about Bedford's money?'

'Not half enough. Everyone's strapped.'

'Copies of her accounts?'

'That'll cost.'

'Don't ye try my patience!' Eleanor declared.

'In future, ask your Lady Ann then.'

'Don't ye get high and mighty with me!'

'Her information isn't worth a groat and you know it!'

'Here!' Eleanor banged a small purse on the table.

'That's a beginning.'

'So Catherine took sick?'

'She lost her husband, her country, her baby, and now her freedom – hardly surprising.'

'Her own fault. How sick?'

'Took to her bed.'

'A good sign.'

'Wept for days.'

'Even better. And the babe, peaky?'

'Yellow.'

'Jaundice! His Grace will bless you for this, you'll see.'

'Settle up first.'

'Not a farthing more.'

'Someone's sniffing around.'

'Who?' Agnes remained silent.

'Dang you!' Eleonor spilled out more coin. 'Who?'

Agnes counted.

'These are just quarter nobles. The full number if you please.'

Eleanor banged down another small purse.

Agnes smiled. As long as the purses were small, she knew that more would keep coming. Eleanor was paying out the promised sum in driblets, her usual practice. She was too greedy to notice she'd been rumbled.

'Who?'

'Somerset.'

'What! But we just smashed him!'

'The "iron fist"!'

'And that Welsh clothes peg was smashed too. Whole world knows!'

'Somerset's revenge then.'

'How?'

'Stab in the back. Through Catherine.'

'You sure?'

'No doubt of it.'

'You got proof?'

'Copies of his letters. Signed and dated.'

Eleanor avidly read through them.

'The snake! Finish him next time. Catherine's reply?' Agnes waited and Eleanor hastily added to the growing pile.

'Pleads mourning.'

'Snubbed him?' Agnes nodded and Eleanor continued. 'Fine for now. Every letter, mind, copies. Here, the Mitre Inn.'

'Not for long.'

'What now, me girl?'

'Queen's picked clean.'

'So?'

'I'm moving on.'

'Ye'll stay where you are!'

'With a pauper? Never!'

'Be money the only thing in thy life?'

'I certainly hope so.'

'No more.'

Agnes prepared to leave.

'Tell that to His Grace.'

Damn, thought Eleanor, Humphrey'd given the order. Best give it all over to the bitch. Eleanor changed her tune.

'Ye don't come often enough here, me dear.'

'That's because ye don't pay often enough, your Grace.'

Eleanor dipped into her vanity case and slammed down the last, much larger, purse. Agnes hefted it in her hand.

'The full amount!' grated Eleanor, baffled. How had Agnes known she'd brought the total sum.

'Alright. I'll stay. Same payment next month.' Reluctantly, Eleanor nodded.

'Let's drink to it then.' Agnes poured out a glass each. Agnes sipped. Eleanor slurped, then wiped her lips with a kerchief, as if doing the washing up. Old turnip top never lets you down, thought Agnes, with a knowing smile. Eleanor's black eyes gleamed. What was the minx grinning at? Agnes raised her glass.

'Humphrey for King!'

'Ah, yes!' Eleanor exclaimed involuntarily. That was more like it. At once she felt less furious about the money. Agnes was sharper than she'd given her credit for. She was backing the winner. And, after all, wasn't that just what she, Eleanor, had been doing all along as well?

Eleanor raised her glass and slurped, feeling very pleased with herself.

73

Yes, thought Owen, as he jogged along by the river in the warm sunshine with Hopcyn nodding at his side, Henry's last campaign was fought from his death bed – for Catherine and the babe to win through in the end. A solid start too, because Humphrey had received a right royal bloody nose. Other claimants might not now be so bold. And Bedford had taken over. Owen smiled. And Bedford's 'surprise' – he could just see Catherine's face. The wise Regent of England had certainly got Catherine over on his side, and with the expenditure of very little cash. But more importantly, he had given her what she most wanted, a home. There was no harm in having the French Queen Dowager behind him when things were going so badly at the front.

'Paris is a rock,' Bedford had summed up, 'and as long as Paris stands, so will the Treaty of Troyes.' But with the taste of blood still in his mouth, Owen doubted whether the Yorkists or Humphrey would ever see it that way.

'Go now, guard the mother of the crown. That is your fighting command.'

Owen had given the order of the day to his Captains. They knew what to do. They'd worked together since Agincourt. The defence of Baynard's was set up in a few hours.

'Thinking thoughts?' asked Hopcyn, yawning in the sleepy afternoon.

'Thank God for Bedford, Catherine's safe now.'

'You trounced her *bete noire*.'

'Bedford advises a less strict mourning.'

'Very wise, she's just lost her baby.'

'And no mother, father or brother.'

'Or partner.'

'I know how she feels.'

'You do?' asked Hopcyn slyly.

'And they'll never let her out of England.'

'The Dauphin's surprised us all, Isabelle included.'

'These sieges. Bedford's calls them "points of diminishing returns".'

'If Bedford can't keep Burgundy sweet, England's out.'

'Wish King Leper could see that,' said Owen.

Hopcyn's horse brushed against a bush of wild dog roses. A host of butterflies rose into the air.'

'Look,' said Hopcyn, 'they say they're the souls of the departed taking flight.'

'Let them take my love to King Leper then.'

'They will.'

'So, I'm free?'

'It was the Hag's last bid – for the moment.'

'More battles ahead?'

'Keep your sword sharp.'

'Done.'

'Owain, what's it like killing Englishmen?'

'Not bad, Hopcyn, not bad.'

'Humphrey's saying he smashed you on the bridge.'

'Quite painless, Hopcyn,' Owen grinned.

'Damascus reminds me of Eustace.'

'Damascus is prettier though.' Owen's grin was even broader.

'Damascus is my cousin.'

'Never had a Chaplain who was a Pythagorean.'

'Don't worry, it's smothered in gospels.'

'And where are Agnes and old Damascus?'

'Coming up.'

'Agnes alright?'

'Ask her,' said Hopcyn reining in his horse. 'Here they come.'

Damascus and Agnes cantered leisurely into view. Agnes leaned over and embraced Hopcyn.

'Alright?' asked Owen. Agnes patted her bulging saddle bag and said.

'Humphrey's donation for Baynard's.'

'Thought you'd fallen asleep,' said Owen.

'Agnes didn't, I did,' answered Damascus.

'And where was that?'

'In the eye of the light and in the face of the sun.'

'Where there was the least of self,' added Hopcyn.

'We'll just have to take their word for it,' smiled Agnes at Owen.

'So, you two, you're Pythagorean cousins then?'

'We believe in Jesus of Galilee,' replied Hopcyn and Damascus in unison.

'None of this nonsense about reincarnation . . . ' said Hopcyn.

' . . . or this stuff about transmigration of souls,' added Damascus.

'Well, don't do it in the street and frighten the horses.'

'Are we on punishment, Captain?'

'You're still my blue-eyed boys – for the moment. And Damascus, doff your bardic robes before we get there, comb the honeysuckle out of your hair, and put on sober clerical garb, alright?'

'Cross my heart.' They all laughed.

They lapsed into drowsy silence. Fine, thought Owen to have communion in silence. Perhaps Pythagoras was right, as Hopcyn had once quoted, 'The greatest love is the longest silence.' Another shower of butterflies danced about their heads. God, thought Owen, suppose Hopcyn's right about that as well! Since his vision of eternity, Hopcyn felt the warp-spasms weaken. It was as if that single glimpse was for a lifetime. But the three suns still haunted him.

'There they are,' exclaimed Joanna, pointing from the window in Catherine's solarium down at the four travellers in the courtyard. Joséphine and Adéle gazed with admiration at the tall, striking green-eyed Captain.

'My!' Joanna enthused, 'that's what I call a real figure of a man! Doesn't even have to try!' With a sudden beat of the heart, Catherine looked out with them. Owen had dismounted, and stood squinting up at the great Hall. The Guard poured down from the battlements and soon stood at attention, ready for inspection. When Owen had finished his tour of the ranks, they gave three rousing cheers for the recent victory. They had no doubt that their doughty Captain had engineered it. Catherine could hardly restrain herself from joining in. Owen again looked up at the hall, as if searching for someone. A burst of sunlight flooded the rooftops and lit the space where he stood. Owen's whole being seemed to glow. With dawning apprehension and terrified delight Catherine felt that same tingling as when she had stood before the window of Isabelle's hall near Troyes. It spread over her whole body. She shrank back, pressing her hands to her breast. She turned and hurried to her bedchamber. She had to get control of herself. For Catherine and her Demoiselles had decided to prepare a surprise welcome for Agnes, Hopcyn and Owen, and the whole household, that very weekend.

74

Humphrey was furious. He had arrived too late for the parliamentary proceedings. He paced the floor of the debating chamber of the huge hall of the city of Leicester, where Bedford and the Council had conspiratorially convoked the parliament. Thank God, he had brought a strong escort with him. He had heard there were new laws banning arms. Somerset's men had shied stones at them as they passed into city, but Humphrey had instructed his men to keep their weapons concealed until they could use them with impunity, preferably at night.

Humphrey was also irritated by the long journey. Why come all this way when parliament could so easily have been held in Westminster? Why had they done it? Was it because the Council feared the universal support he, the Lancastrian champion, had in London? Were they intimidated by his tremendous victory over Somerset at the Battle of the Two Bridges? Had he put the wind up the mighty Bedford? Proof surely who was winning, and who was the greatest power on the Council – he himself, of course, with his baton. The natural leader, the born Caesar, Lord Protector of England, Humphrey of Gloucester.

Humphrey glowered covertly at his brother. Bedford was going over the minutes of the recent deliberations, signing copies of the new ordinances. His hooked nose seemed to sniff out every page, looking for errors, correcting inconsistencies. Bedford was not as intimidating as Henry, nor could he impose an instant silence with a haughty look, but he was a substantial presence, and not to be contradicted when the basic interests of the family were threatened, as they were now.

Muttering to himself, Humphrey flourished his baton at frequent intervals, at nobody in particular. His mutterings however came to an end when he was addressed.

'I see that yourself and her Grace now constitute a quorum on the Council,' Bedford observed, looking directly at his brother, scarcely able to conceal his dislike. Humphrey raised his baton, saying.

'I am Lord Protector.'

'And I am Regent of the Realm, I outrank you. Any future meetings will be held in the White Hall of Westminster, under my official seal. Understood?'

'This is not fair.'

'It is the law. Now about this appalling fight at the bridge . . . '

'I saved the nation from the Yorkists, from Somerset.'

'What both of you did was treason against the King.'

'Somerset murdered sixty of my men.'

'And you murdered eighty of his.'

'And Winchester, Warwick, and that Welsh clothes peg joined in on the traitors' side – when I had Somerset in the palm of my hand! Infamous! Warwick holds the baby King to blackmail, I tell you. And Cardinal Winchester, our damnable uncle, what don't I know about him! Plans to kidnap the king, move him from Warwick to Winchester . . . '

'Arrant lies and nonsense! And stop waving that stupid baton under my nose.'

'And remember Winchester's plot against our father . . . ?'

' . . . let's not go too deeply into that, shall we?'

'What about his Southwark properties?'

'What about them?'

'The most notorious brothels in London!'

'And the most popular with your men.'

'Know what the brothel signs outside are now? A Cardinal's hat!'

'And just what sign's outside your house, a butcher's cleaver?'

'But he's a Cardinal, what an example, living off immoral earnings, it stinks of hypocrisy!'

'You, along with Warwick and Winchester and all other members of the Council will follow my final decisions, and observe Parliamentary law, as voted for yesterday, in full session. Remember too that I am Keeper of the Privy Seal. No act can become law without that. I am now keeping that seal under lock and key until such times as the majority of the Council agree on changes in the law. Like these.' He pointed at the list of new ordinances.

'Why wasn't I informed of all this?'

'You were too busy celebrating your London Agincourt.'

'I resent that.'

'If you hadn't been duly appointed by our late brother, Humphrey, in his last will and testament, I would strip you of your pitiful pretence of authority right now, and send you back to the London rabble you profess to love, but actually despise, for suitable punishment. If you understand nothing else, understand that!'

You would too, you swine, thought Humphrey, ignoring the insults. He flourished his baton, strutted like a peacock, but backed down.

'Now to the ordinances. First, no naked blade to be drawn within two miles of the royal baby's residence, wherever the baby might be. Two, everyone entering the City of London to lodge their weapons at regular collecting points. Three, no one to appear on the public highway in daylight with weapons of any kind.'

'But Somerset's men are carrying clubs.'

'Clubs, bludgeons, staffs are also banned.'

'They're still carrying brickbats in their bag-pipe sleeves, I saw them with my retainers outside.'

'Brickbats too have been banned.'

'Have they?'

'Of course. Didn't you know this is the Parliament of Bats?' Humphrey missed the grim humour completely.

'Well,' Bedford went on, 'your own stone throwers are being arrested even now by the constables and sheriff's men. Now a final word – our Empire in France is under threat. The costs of the campaigns now outstrip the profits, though we still possess huge territories, notably Normandy. There are fewer and fewer donations, fewer and fewer volunteers, our expeditionary forces are scraping the barrel. The Commons want to keep all monies in England, and are beginning to refuse to grant supplies. If this goes on, we will have to hire Swiss mercenaries or beg Burgundy for the use of his troops, and Burgundy is now lukewarm. The Exchequer is desperately short of cash. We are at war! Do you understand? We must not make the same mistake as the French under the mad King, and tear each other to pieces with factional disputes. The French King – the Queen Dowager's brother after all – grows stronger by the minute. Now listen, brother, I swore to Henry that I would observe the Treaty to the letter, for unity, for our dynasty. "Secure England," our brother said, and I will! Above all, remember this, if anything happens to that baby, I am next in line, and you will have to answer to me! You can go.'

Humphrey turned like a whipped schoolboy, clutched his baton and slunk out of the hall. He mounted his carriage in safety, without jeers or cheers. The peace and quiet made him uneasy. He would have to put an end to it, or people might think that his arrogant, jumped up brother had got the better of him. His rabble wouldn't have that either. And there was no room for losers in the Palace of Caesars.

75

Owen and his little group had been amazed at the life and colour in Catherine's new Court. But in all the bustle of activity there was an underlying sense of order. People knew who was in charge. Baynard's was already taking on the character of its owner – organised, defiant and determined. And the Welsh guard were everywhere discreetly in place.

'It's a safe home for my child,' Catherine explained to Agnes, as she showed her around the hall, 'tomorrow or in seven years. The walls may keep me in, but they keep out the world as well. I don't intend to live like a nun. "Life is funs," my mother is right about that. I'm fond of my staff, except for that awful Lady Ann. My people here speak a language I fully understand, and one I don't understand at all.'

'We'd be glad to teach you Welsh,' smiled Agnes. She paused. 'And how is your son?'

'Don't hesitate, Agnes. We must always talk of him, that is normal. I have weekly bulletins. Lady Warwick is most understanding. My baby is flourishing.'

'Strange, Henry taking that curse of Windsor so seriously.'

'Well, nobody else did.'

Just two short years, thought Agnes, and she is a woman.

The household hummed smoothly and in friendly fashion, with laughter from every quarter. There was only one false note, that being the presence of the overbearing Lady Ann de Burgh. She was thoroughly put out by her quarters above the screens. She had already descended on the staff below a dozen times ordering them not to shout or laugh when she was 'in residence'. She also insisted they spoke only English to her. In the mornings she constantly complained about sleeplessness, although she slept ten hours a night. Twice she had been late on attendance on Catherine. When Joséphine had upraided her, Lady Ann had called her 'a nag, a nuisance and a foreigner, who was ignorant of superior English ways', and flounced out. She poked her nose into Catherine's solarium without permission, and had even tried to bribe a cleaning maid for information. Lady Ann was the only person at Baynard's who was not aware of the fact that she, the spy, was being spied on most of all.

Catherine carefully avoided asking about Owen at first, although she believed she had now got her feelings under control. She confided her plans to Agnes about the secret welcome for the coming weekend. It was to be for the whole household.

'. . . to bring us together. I will have to live with my household – now, and for years. I don't have to go to bed with the local heroes.'

Agnes wondered at the odd choice of words. So did Catherine.

'How is the most detestable man in the world?'

'Humphrey believes you are *desolate*, going into a *decline*.'

'Dangerous work for you, Agnes.'

'My Lord Bedford cut him down to size.'

'How is my best friend and ally?'

'Like you here, Catherine, in charge.'

'Yes, he's fair, wise, and speaks French like one of us. And he warned me – it mightn't be too bad here.' They laughed.

'He's keeping both Kingdoms under control, but what about his family?'

'King Leper is dead.'

'I am sorry. He was a remarkable friend. What about his lepers?'

'Owen and my Lord Bedford take care of them now.'

'And how is our dear bard Hopcyn after his adventures in Wales?'

'We are both happy, Catherine.'

'And our new friend, the chaplain?'

'They're cousins, Damascus and Hopcyn. The only difference is that Damascus has same-coloured eyes.'

'One of the few things Henry didn't quite know how to face up to.'

They laughed again. Yes, reflected Catherine, she could think quite dispassionately about Henry now, it was as if a gulf lay between them, and the name of that gulf was 'love'. She didn't know why but she had to screw up the courage to ask,

'Could you tell Captain Owen I want an inspection of the grounds and outer fortifications. I intend to get to know every inch of my new home. And to bring an escort.'

An hour later Queen Catherine was riding together with the Commander of the Queen's Guard, which was protocol. What was not protocol were her feelings. She was sure enough of herself to accompany him in the presence of an escort, but the thought of being alone with him thrilled her and, at the same time, filled her with dread.

Catherine saw that the gardens had been ploughed and manured, and row upon row of fresh vegetables sprouted. The small orchard had been pruned, and was covered with budding apple blossom. Foresters were still at work in the glades, copses and knolls, the sound of their axes filled the air. Dead tree trunks were sawed up for firewood, the underbrush cut and cleared, and a new nursery of seedling trees laid out. Bedford had thought of everything, Catherine reflected. Bless him. She saw that lilac trees grew in abundance everywhere. It was as if the other trees could not do without such beauties at their side.

'Wonderful lilacs,' Owen said involuntarily.

She nodded, trying to look directly at him, but again her

eyes avoided his. What's wrong? Owen wondered – until he realised that he was doing the same.

'Captain Owen,' she said, 'I want to show you something. Bring up the escort.'

She pointed at a little dell in the distance. There, wild lilac trees stretched up as wide as apple boughs, each branch plumed with purple and white blossom. Their fragrance wafted on the breeze to where they rode. Owen cantered after her. Catherine dismounted and thrust her way through. She held up her hand. Before them lay a ruined chapel. The walls were fissured but still solid. Some surviving window panes glittered between the mullions. The roof was covered with ivy, but when they entered the dim interior, it felt as warm as on a summer's day, as if protected from the cold and damp by the roof of spreading blossom. An earthen floor and simple square altar of stone stood before them

'This will be my retreat within my retreat,' said Catherine. 'I have given orders for it to be restored.'

'I won't have to worry about your safety here,' said Owen. 'It has an air of extraordinary peace.'

'I knew you'd say that!' she exclaimed, and lapsed into silence. Thank God the guard were still nearby.

'I love this little dell. I will ask Damascus to bless it.'

'Yes . . . '

' . . . I'm sorry to hear of King Leper,' she blurted out.

'Yes. I miss him.'

'An extraordinary man.'

'He was my brother.' She looked fully at him.

'I am so sorry, Owen.'

'Four others . . . in the Welsh wars.'

'Terrible.'

'King Leper died saving me.'

'He loved you.' There was a catch in her voice.

'The last of the line.'

'So you are alone?'

'My fortunes, thanks to this command, are restored. I have a number of distant kin in place now on the estates I bought in Pembroke, *Penfro* we call it, my Welsh base now. But *alone*? Yes, I suppose, though the Tudors are blossoming among the lilacs.' They exchanged open smiles, hearts beating apace.

'I have to see my Captain of Engineers,' Owen broke the spell.

'Is everything alright?'

'Yes . . . there's a secret supply tunnel which runs from your quarters to the stables, then up to the turret in the long wall not far beyond. The sight lines don't converge. There's a blind spot. We'll have to enlarge the turret. And Surgeon Samuel and his wife, midwife Megan will soon be joining us.'

'The surgeon for deaths and the midwife for lifes!'

'Well . . . ' Owen wasn't sure whether to laugh.

'Greet them for me. They are welcome.'

'Excuse me.'

He pushed his way through the fragrant green and purple shadows into the daylight. He realised his knees were trembling.

'Alright, Captain Owen?' the head of the escort, his chief engineer, Idris, asked.

'Have you given the order to re-build the turret?'

'Yesterday, as you said. Any further orders?'

'Yes. Detach two of your men. Have them cut as many of these lilacs as they can carry. Take them to Lady Agnes, for the solarium. And don't let the Queen see you.'

'Yes, sir.' What was his commander up to? Why, no! He glanced at Catherine as she emerged from the glade. 'She looks pale,' he thought, 'our captain wouldn't be doing . . . that, would he? She, a Queen twice over? Mother of a King?' Well, well, there'd be plenty to talk about in the armoury tonight.

As Owen and Catherine rode back, it was as if both were

waiting for something of tremendous import to happen, and that both were beginning to recognise what it was, but neither of them, nor fate, seemed ready yet to pick the burgeoning blossom, like the lilacs now being plucked in the dell.

76

The great Hall was aglow. The rushlights and candelabras were changed every hour, so the light would remain constant. There was a nip in the air so piles of logs burned in the hooded fireplaces. Flickering flames threw the shadows of the guests onto the bright walls. A certain decorum was still in place. This was Catherine's first appearance before her whole household. She still insisted on wearing black, but this merely emphasised her youth, liveliness and beauty. Catherine was determined to get her life at Baynard's off to a good start.

'Well begun is half done,' she remembered was one of Hopcyn's favourite sayings.

The usual benches had been placed along the walls, but Catherine had also introduced tables and chairs into the area, something that Lady Ann highly disapproved of. These were meant only for the nobility, not for mere servants. The senior officers of the garrison and the chief members of Catherine's staff and household, had tables closest to the high table. Catherine sat at the centre of the long trestle table on the dais, her personal attendants behind her, and her Demoiselles to the right and to the left of her. Lady Ann sat at a corner, the farthest seat from Catherine. Owen and his Commanders sat at a separate table closest to the dais, with Damascus in full priestly garb. Hopcyn sat, with Catherine's permission, next to his beloved Agnes.

The atmosphere was of someone firmly in charge, but someone with the uncommon qualities of humility and kindness, most unusual at any time, let alone in a royal Court. Everyone present, from the humblest scullion to the most senior

Demoiselle, soon became expansive and cheerful under such a genial regime. Catherine was a rare Queen indeed.

Lady Ann stirred uneasily. These peculiar foreigners. What was going on? Hopcan, or whatever his name was, with the mad eyes. Lady Agnes with her flaming unnaturally red hair. The pasty faced Valois. Lady Ann had checked up on the weird Damascus, and had been astonished to discover that not only was he a fully anointed priest as well as a noted theologian and scholar, but he had also been, for a time, personal chaplain to the Archbishop himself. Owen of the pock-marked face, she reluctantly admitted, did have a certain animal appeal. But what a motley crew, dancing, laughing, and even singing in the Queen's presence. Humphrey and his lads would have soon put them in their place.

Hopcyn and Agnes had recruited the musicians, who were now comfortably installed in the minstrel's gallery. It seemed that the entire garrison could play a musical instrument, especially the portable Welsh harps. The many harps merged melodiously with the three-stringed square fiddles, and the elegant lutes. Droneless bag-pipes added deeper but still mellow tones. The long trumpets were hung with armigerous pennants, the *fleur-de-lis* of France – a little touch that pleased Catherine. The dancing pipe and tabor players had clapper bells on their hoods. The cymbals, matched in pitch and loosely tied together, and the kettle drums, added touches of drama when needed. The humble triangle tinkled away pleasingly in the background adding its own, distinctive miniature charm. Hopcyn had been appointed Master of the Queen's Music and kept an eye on the musicians, who watched for his every signal from the gallery.

Catherine had been astonished at the musical expertise of even the most lowly Welsh soldier. Her own French servants were not half as gifted. However, they excelled in dance, and they were soon teaching the captains and troops the niceties of the more graceful steps, the measures without which a court was never complete.

'Yes,' commented Catherine to Joséphine, 'however poor we were, we always had an Italian dancing master. They were the best.' She watched Agnes trying out a measure without much success. Catherine rose from her chair and crossed over to her friend.

'No, Agnes, like this,' she demonstrated. 'The feet never leave the ground. A gliding, sliding motion, like this.' She moved with such grace, the hall was momentarily stilled. She looked around with a smile. 'Thank you. That was the *basse-danse*, Agnes. Forget the skips and leaps of the *haute-danse*, that comes later. Now, stand like this, the man on the right here, holding the lady's hand, the man's other hand resting on the hilt of his sword, this side . . . '

'But I have no sword,' joked Agnes. 'Come on,' she beckoned Owen. 'With your permission, my Lady. Owen, do your duty.' Owen rose, appalled.

Agnes had 'dressed' Owen that night, knowing what suited him best. He had on a short, crutch-length, blue doublet with loose, fur-lined sleeves, an undershirt which curled up at the neck; across his hips, a low-slung girdle with a silver buckle. His legs were encased in blue hose, with thigh-high soft leather boots, turned down at the top. Everything, in short, that brought out his athletic figure and emphasised his striking green eyes. His abundant hair Agnes had painstakingly washed in fresh rain water, and it now hung in natural waves down to his shoulders. Catherine took this in at a single glance. Before the crowd, Catherine could only look him full in the face. Her heart turned over, her whole body went hot and cold. She swayed, and at once pretended it was part of the dance. With the last vestiges of her self-possession, she managed to control herself.

'Yes, Captain Owen,' she heard herself say, 'not the high kicks, but like this – serene, slow, a chorale.' Owen followed her, step for step. Another silence settled over the packed hall. Surely, such a shining, beautiful couple had never graced this ancient hall before.

'And when you finish, Captain Owen, you bow to your guests, and to your partner.' Owen executed a perfect, graceful bow, one of the things Agnes had insisted he learn. Spontaneous cheers and applause broke out. Catherine's bright-eyed flush was put down to the excitement of the dance. She took her seat again, scarcely able to tear her eyes away from the handsomest man she had ever seen. Even Lady Ann was taken aback by his beauty, and felt the first stirrings of desire. Damn! These animals, she thought.

Hopcyn nodded. The musicians struck up a bold *haute-danse* as lively as any reel. Owen, now joined by Agnes, executed a few high leaps and kicks, again to generous applause. The couple approached Catherine's chair. Owen, hardly aware of what he was doing, again executed a high kick. This time, his descending right foot hit the dais step, and he stumbled. In a second he was sitting lop-sided in the very lap of the Queen. He felt her arms about him, as if helping him not to fall. She felt the tingling which started from her crotch, up to her breasts, then her throat and face, and nearly fainted again. Owen hastily detached himself. Covered with confusion, he bowed, stammering words of apology. It was at this point that Lady Ann decided to make her move. She would be revenged on this beast in heat, and on the others. She marched across to where Owen was standing, and confronted the Queen.

'Your Majesty,' she declared looking down her nose at Owen. 'I think you should be informed, as a stranger over here, that this person comes from a wild and barbarous clan of savages who are inferior even to the most common English soldier. Let him be banished to the stables where he belongs!'

A hissing intake of breath filled the hall. The stupid woman had insulted one of the Queen's own personal staff, and in her own court.

Catherine rose to her feet. Her imperious, icy, anger filled the hall.

'I hope you have noticed, too, Lady Ann, that I also am a "barbarous foreigner", but let me assure you, I see no difference between the people who inhabit these islands, except by their good manners and bright minds, both of which you most conspicuously lack. You have insulted one of my guests to my face and in public. No, my Lady, it is for you to be banished. You are hereby dismissed from this, and any other royal court, I will see to that.' A hundred eyes burned upon the shamed Lady Ann as she hurried out, head bowed, almost sick with humiliation. Catherine turned to Hopcyn.

'Master of our Music, please all of you continue these celebrations. I beg your indulgence while I retire. It has been an honour to be among you.' She inclined her head graciously, and left for her apartments directly above. Owen felt utterly wretched. His incredibly idiotic error had been responsible for all this. He bowed in apology to the assembled company, and excused himself with aching heart and burning cheeks.

Although hushed by the unpleasant event, the guests were elated by the fact that the loathed Lady Ann was on the way out. Moreover their Queen had acquitted herself with exceptional dignity and firmness. At that moment, there was not a single person there who would not have died for Catherine.

It was past midnight when Agnes received a sudden summons. She was to present herself at once at the Queen's bedchamber. When she arrived, she found Catherine half distracted, pacing the room, wringing her hands, compulsively smelling the innumerable vases of lilacs. A fire still burned in the fireplace.

'Agnes,' she started, 'I can't sleep. That was a horrible scene. Such an insult. And from one whose kin killed Owen's own family. Poor Owen. My fault. I should have got rid of her much sooner. My conscience. I must apologise. Yes. Now. I just cannot sleep. Please send for Captain Owen immediately, I don't care what time it is.'

Agnes hurried off. She shook Owen awake herself. He had been dozing in a chair, still fully clothed, unable to rest properly, going through the scene and his stupid part in it, again and again. She told him that he was commanded to the Queen's presence. She pretended not to know what it was about. Is this the end, wondered Owen. This is one hill, he thought, that I cannot see the other side of. At the same time Agnes's own heart was going pit-a-pat. Could she trust her instincts? Was it really going to happen? She ushered Owen into Catherine's room. One look at the expression in Catherine's eyes told her.

Agnes hurried off at once to the quarters of the Demoiselles. They would all now have to keep guard over the door, by strict rota. Agnes was determined that Catherine should have the one true love of her life. With Joséphine, Joanna and Adéle, Agnes at once announced that Catherine was unwell, and was not to be disturbed. Then, like the rest of the world, they could only wait.

'Owen, please forgive me.' Owen was stunned.

'But it should be me asking for forgiveness.'

'I should have got rid of that woman much sooner.'

'That stupid fall, my fault. I didn't know what I was doing.'

'Neither did I.'

'Did I hurt you?'

Catherine instantly decided. Now was the time. Without hesitation, she seized it.

'Yes,' she replied, 'you did. Here.' She pressed her hand to her breast.

'My heart. Feel it, Owen.'

She drew his hand towards it. In a sudden, rushing embrace, they found their arms round each other, hugging warmly, then frantically.

'My love, my love,' she murmured. 'I want you. You, Owen.'

'Catherine, my love.' Kisses rained upon kisses. With every caress, they grew closer and closer, getting used by the passing seconds to the already strangely familiar feeling of love, of adoration, of passion, as if it was unfolding in their hearts for the first, the second, the hundredth time. Love for them was a sort of half expected birth, a burst of instant, dawning, endless affection, tying them together, changing them forever.

Catherine stepped backwards to the drawn curtains of the four-poster, pulling Owen tenderly with her, never taking her eyes off him. She fumbled trying to undo the brooch on her gipon, under her outer velvet dress. Owen helped her, and as she discarded her clothes, so she helped him to take off his, until she lay back on the soft bed, naked, gazing up with adoration at his tall, muscular figure. Owen hardly aware of his own nakedness, stared down entranced at one of the most lovely forms he had ever seen. He sank into her waiting arms. They clasped each other, closer and closer, moaning, kissing, Catherine sometimes weeping with the relief of pent up desire that had been suddenly released. Catherine's tongue explored every inch of his body, and Owen responded, his own mouth sinking down her belly, into her cleft, feeling her giving herself with all her being to him. Catherine dimly realised it was this which had been hiding under the surface of her nights with Henry, a gulf which Owen was now filling, a gulf rapidly disappearing under the onrush of real, newly borne love. Her hands flowed over his muscled back, thighs, legs. She too let every kiss discover again and again every part of him. She spread her thighs open and lifted her legs high as he bore down onto her with every increasing lust, but a lust that mingled, then united, with an overwhelming, irresistible affection. She wrapped her legs around his waist as he pulsed into her, at the same time smothering his face with kisses. His body moved in rhythm with hers, seeming to know exactly what to do to bring her to the very peak of pleasure. They both moved swiftly in unison to their first climax. It crashed through their consciousness simultaneously. They collapsed at rest, clinging to each other in shattered, ecstatic closeness. As Catherine opened her eyes, she saw the shadows of the flames leaping on the curtains of the bed, and smelled again, now very differently it seemed, the blossoms of love that Owen had spread before her. She burst into tears of relief, delight, bewilderment, and love.

'Owen, Owen,' she murmured again and again, holding his head so she could gaze into his eyes, without holding back, openly, as if trying to make up for the times she had avoided his look. She caressed his chest.

'So hard on the outside,' she kissed him, 'so tender on the inside. My leather lamb.'

At first Owen had been too overwhelmed to speak. Finally he murmured,

'You are my affection cup. I pour all my new love into you.'

As the fire faded that night, she knew with absolute conviction, that come what may, she had experienced one of the greatest gifts life had to give, a love without bounds, limitless because it was returned in ever increasing measure. She clasped him to her arms, the kisses mounting, again and again. They did not hear the dawn chorus, nor did they rise until hunger drove them to it. Love satisfied, she thought, transcends everything. The words of a poet quoted by Hopcyn, as in another existence, had said, 'Love is the last light spoken'. Yes, she felt that she now knew the meaning of each of those beautiful words.

Owen knew, too, with a similar certainty, that his destiny was here at last, in his very arms. He had been blessed with the greatest love of his life, whichever way it chose to take him. Happily, he surrendered himself to his revealed fate, and again embraced his Catherine's whole, true, unwounded heart in his strong, tender arms.

77

Bedford was retiring after a victorious campaign in Brittany. The hated Scots and troublesome Bretons had formed an alliance. They seized the 'English' town of Pontarson and, in memory of Henry V at Montereau, massacred the inhabitants. Bedford moved with all speed. He invested the town at night, and dispersed the enemy into the hills. The Celtic alliance, for the moment, disintegrated. Bedford then received an urgent message. His presence was desperately needed at the interminable siege of Orleans which was, once again, turning into a profitless stalemate. This was especially humiliating after the recent reverse at Patay, where the Maid had her first great victory against all the odds. Bedford again turned his weary horse's head towards the road to Paris. After a forced march two days later, he rode into the allied lines at the head of his troops. He made his way at once to the English held Tour des Augustins, a twin turreted bastille that sat square on the stone bridge on the southern side of the great Loire river. On the far side rose the still unbreached walls of the proud city of Orleans, its four impregnable gates still intact. Bedford joined his main commanders on the turrets. They were Sir William Gargrave and Sir William Glasdale, both of them being veteran commanders, and the brilliant Salisbury who was the winner of innumerable artillery duels. They surveyed the battleground. Bedford noted the other bastilles dotted in a gigantic defensive circle around the city north, south, east and west, on both sides of the river. Some were held by the English, some by the French. Some changed possession within hours. Out of cannon and bow shot, the opposing sides could view each other clearly. Smoke shot, camp fires, drums, bugle calls and shouted orders rose on every side.

Bedford spoke:

'Obviously, gentleman, the key to Orleans are the bastilles, and the key to the bastilles is the fortress we are now standing on.' He glanced below at the fast flowing waters of the river.

'How many sorties from the French?'

'Hundreds.'

'Our losses?'

'A few at a time, but after eight months, my Lord, we are being bled dry.'

'The French just call up replacements from the surrounding countryside,' added Sir Thomas.

'I know. What's your garrison in the tower here, Salisbury?'

'Four hundred Men-at-Arms, one hundred bowmen.'

'Reinforce them, Salisbury, that's not enough.'

'That includes the reinforcements, my Lord.

Bedford gestured towards the huge *fosse*, or ditch, protecting the end of the bridge behind them. A French held bastille rose on a hill not far away. Salisbury followed his Commander's eye.

'Don't worry, we've driven them back every time,' he reassured his commander.

'And our rear's quite secure,' added Sir William.

'Well, gentlemen, we can't stay stuck here forever.'

'I suggest a massive bombardment of the walls, bring up our cannon at night,' suggested Salisbury.

'But, my Lord,' objected Sir William, 'look there, sir. The French engineers have blown a gap in the bridge. We'd have to get over that before we could sortie against the city, however successful the artillery might be.'

'Yes,' Bedford said, rubbing his chin thoughtfully. 'And Dunois, *the Bastard of Orleans* I hear they call him. How is he doing?'

'He knows what he's about,' said Salisbury. 'And so does the new Maréchal de Rais. That's why we're still here.'

'And this frightful, blasphemous so-called Maid?' Bedford asked tightly.

Salisbury had been waiting for this. He knew how much Bedford hated her.

'Slips from bastille to bastille at night . . . '

' . . . led a dozen sorties . . . ' added Sir William.

' . . . and not even wounded,' said Sir Thomas.

'They say when she passes, murderers fall on their knees and confess.'

'Superstitious rubbish!'

'Our troops my Lord, are nevertheless, somewhat in awe of her.'

'We will have to change that. Limb of Satan!'

'Look!' shouted Sir William, pointing behind them as trumpet blasts filled the air. 'They're going to have a go at the *Fosse* again!'

But Salisbury spotted something else. He ran over to the shelter of a short turret on the far side. Something was developing in that quarter as well. He peered through the steel grille of the window opening.

'They're trying to throw a gangway over the gap.' Sir William joined him.

'And look!' Salisbury pointed down at two sailing boats sweeping towards a point just below the tower, on the rapid current.

'Alert!' shouted Salisbury, pointing below. 'Lay the cannon on those boats!'

Attracted by the shouts of the familiar voice, not more than fifty metres away, the French bombardiers on the quay opposite, set their pieces and fired. Their first ball hit the centre of the steel grille and sent a hundred sharp splinters in all directions. Sir William was impaled through the lungs by an iron bar. A section of sheered metal sliced up through Salisbury's jaw, taking half of his face away so his brains spilled out. Both died instantly. The

316

French cannoneers cheered the hit. When they learned that they had disposed of one of their most formidable adversaries, the Governor of Normandy no less, they fired off a derisory salute of honour, for it had been from Salisbury that they had first learned the bloody art of gunnery. Bedford picked himself up, ears ringing, spattered with the blood of his two best generals. Meanwhile, Sir Thomas was shouting orders to repel the attackers on the *fosse*. In spite of the showers of arrows, they attacked with *élan*, and were trying to get the scaling ladders in place against the walls. After fierce hand to hand fighting, the French were repulsed. This was the closest they had come to success so far, and the English troops were rattled. They had good reason to be. As the French streamed back, a familiar figure appeared at the gates of the French bastille, and the Maid herself galloped out, leading a force of reserves. An uneasy silence settled over the English defenders. The Maid rode her usual black charger. She was encased from throat to feet in unblazoned armour, and carried her personal standard bearing the image of Christ, the Virgin, two angels, the *fleur-de-lis* of France with the words, *Jesus* and *Mary*. This was the first time Bedford had actually confronted the detested she-devil in battle. He examined her face in detail under her open visor. She had a plain, potato face topped by brownish pudding basin cropped hair, and a square jaw. He could see that she was solidly built and was indistinguishable from the hundreds of other soldiers. But the way she carried herself with such absolute assurance, as if born to the task, was dangerous and unnatural. A great cheer went up from the French. Her charisma was unmistakable.

She galloped up to the edge of the *fosse*. Every soldier followed her back. She flourished her battle axe and, as she raised her arm again, Sir Tomas saw the opportunity.

'Fire!' he ordered his nearest archers.

The Maid reined in abruptly and nearly tumbled off. A wild cheer went up from the bowmen. They could see that one arrow had penetrated the armour and protruded from her shoulder. As she turned and charged back to the bastille, the French troops streamed after her. The attack petered out. Bedford saw at once that her presence on the battlefield was worth double the number of the fighting troops there. She was abnormally formidable, especially for a girl of seventeen. But was she done for? It would be ample revenge for Salisbury and Sir William. The defenders, who had come as attackers, relaxed. It would soon be night and there was no time to prepare for another sortie.

The Maid was resting on a bench in the courtyard of the bastille, surrounded by her worried followers. She was eating slices of white bread dipped in red wine. When she was ready she reached up and gripped the arrow, which had penetrated about four inches into her flesh, and slowly drew it out without a murmur. Whispers of awe went up. She then doused the wound in wine, pushed in a swab against the wound, clasped her hands and prayed. The whole company followed suit. A cheer went up again. Another miracle. But the Maid knew the arrow was armour piercing and had lost much of its force when going through the metal plates. Being armour-piercing, it had no barb and could therefore easily be drawn out – provided that it hit no vital organs. The wine would prevent infection. But the Maid saw also that her wound offered a golden opportunity. She glanced up. It was almost night. Yes, the *godons* would be standing down now, cooking their supper. She knew a night attack was coming on the gap in the bridge. If she put in a rapid, sudden assault on the *fosse*, would the bridge attackers join in when they saw her leading another unexpected attack? Jeanne calculated with absolute certainty that they would. Envelopment of both flanks. Perfect. She now pleaded, implored, begged, and even prayed for the Captains to prepare another assault. At first they refused. It was against all current siege practice. There was only a little daylight left. There were no reinforcements. The objections continued until Jeanne offered them a view of her wound. That couldn't have been done at first either, she argued. The officers yielded. The Maid was right again – it had truly been a miracle of healing.

Bedford was still in the turret organising the removal of his two comrades-in-arms. He had ordered the bodies and fragments of bodies to be carried below to the vessel tethered behind one of the piers for all such emergencies. The two veterans would be sorely missed, but Salisbury was irreplaceable. What of Normandy now? he bitterly wondered. As he took a last look round before making a tour of inspection, his view of the twilit area was further obscured by sudden billows of drifting smoke. He leaned out over the battlements. Through the smoke, he could see belching flames licking up from a point below the tower.

'Damn!' Yes, poor Salisbury had spotted the danger! Fire boats had been loaded to the gunwales with sulphur and pitch! The fierce flames had climbed the wooden sections of the bridge, and were now creeping up the sides of the tower itself. Through a drift in the smoke, Bedford saw the French engineers frantically working to bridge the gap with heavy planking. Sir Thomas had also seen the danger and at once launched a gallant charge against the engineers. As his troops raced towards the enemy, the flaming bridge collapsed under their feet. Every man perished, if not by fire, then by water as they sank into the swift currents below.

Bedford ordered his gunners to blow the wrecks out of the water. But the flames were leaping higher and higher. The choking troops were running below before the fires could reach them, leaving their posts unmanned. When the Maid judged the panic was at its height, she ordered the attack. She herself led the all-out charge across the open space. It spilled over the lip of the *fosse*, and carried straight up to the now thinly defended, smoke-shrouded battlements. The few defenders recoiled in alarm. The Maid, still urging on her men, seemed totally unharmed. Was this another miracle? Perhaps God really was on her side. The attackers were inexorably growing in number. The defenders were being pushed down the turret steps into the yard below.

The French forces on the far bank saw the Maid's banner bobbing on the battlements. Without waiting for orders, they at once joined in the attack, as Jeanne had foreseen. With a supreme effort, in spite of the flames, the engineers finally succeeded in throwing the plank bridge across the open space. The infantry charged across, passed unchecked under the arches of the tower, and burst into the bloody melee in the courtyard. The defenders were surrounded. They threw down their weapons and raised their arms in surrender. It was alright fighting the French, the Burgundians, or whoever they were ordered to fight, but it was madness to fight against God. Not only were the garrison beaten in a fair fight, their morale had also been broken. And that, Bedford realised, was far more serious.

Bedford made his escape in the only surviving boat to the English-held banks higher up. With him went three wounded archers, and the shattered remains of two brave captains and fellow countrymen. Bedford recognised that Orleans was the most devastating loss of the entire campaign, indeed it might signal the end of the campaign itself. And it could all be laid at the door of a virgin-whore, the *Orleans pucelle*, whom Bedford called 'the Limb of the Fiend'. By English hook or crook, he swore, she would have to be silenced.

The siege of the great city was over. The English at once started their withdrawals. The Maid was ferried across to the cheers and bravos of the victorious soldiery, the flags of the *fleur-de-lis* still fluttering in triumph over the unbreached gates. A few moments after she had landed, the Tourelle des Augustins went up in a gigantic sheet of flame. Another sign, it seemed to the prisoners, that the Maid was indeed at the right hand of Jesus. Moreover, it seemed the same to the French, for what the whole of their army had failed to do in eight months, the Maid had accomplished with a single regiment in a few hours. By popular acclamation, the Maid was placed at the head of the procession which wound its way into the Cathedral for the universal service of thanks. As Jeanne raised her banner before the high altar, all the bells of all the churches of the city rang out together. Glorias and magnificats were sung in the streets, in the squares, on the rooftops. Every inhabitant of the city of Orleans, indeed of the whole of France, joined in the celebrations. And these were just the first.

78

Humphrey was spotted before he even disembarked from his barge moored at Baynard's quay. The alarm was raised. From tower to tower, from captain to bowmen, Owen's emergency plans went into action.

In spite of Eleanor's soothings, Humphrey was uneasy. Was it Lady Ann's abrupt dismissal? She had mentioned other suitors, all part of the Yorkist conspiracy no doubt, like the Earl of March Edward Mortimer, who was the most recent claimant to the throne. What else were they hiding here? His suspicious mind scurried like that of a ferret in search of a rabbit.

The infant King, too, was growing apace. Precocious brat, thought Humphrey, too big for his baby boots already, always wearing his little crown. He was unnaturally wise and unseasonably pious. If he wants sainthood, thought Humphrey, I'll give it to him. Yes, hurry it all up, see what could be flushed out. Good timing too, after the debacle at Orleans. All part of the Yorkist plot with this blasphemous 'Maid', of course. What was Bedford up to being humiliated again. By witch or virgin, it made no difference. Damn, he thought for the hundredth time, that Governorship of Normandy was rightfully mine, not bloody Willoughby's. He thought of the enormous revenues from the Duchy. I'm surrounded by greedy bastards, he swore. Passed over again, is it? Not for long. Salisbury lost his head for it, he smiled. Bet Burgundy had a quiet chuckle over that. Agnes was still useful. If what she reported was true, then Catherine was a recluse, while the rest of Baynard was a cesspit, in every sense. He'd find out for himself today.

As Humphrey's horses were being led down the gang plank, Catherine's Demoiselles, lead by head cook Megan, were busy reducing the living quarters of Baynard's to a shambles. The cheerful tapestries were rolled up and stored away. Greasy pots and unwashed utensils were rushed from the kitchen to the great hall and portions of uneaten food were scattered about. Clogged week old rushes from the stables were strewn on the floor paving. Among the empty bottles and spilled wine, were boxes of overturned perfume and face powder, giving off an odour reminiscent of low brothels. A leaking barrel of brandy was set up in a corner, with a table for Damascus and Hopcyn. They took their places, swigging, suitably drunk, singing incomprehensible songs in Welsh, dressed in unwashed threadbare clothes especially saved for the occasion. The door to the nursery was left open, so the shrieking garrison kids could set up a yowling. Dirty baby bed linen filled two wooden buckets by the door, adding yet another foul odour to the already poisoned air.

In the courtyard, pigs were released from the piggeries, horses from the stables, chickens from their roosts, dogs from their kennels. Garbage was carelessly thrown out from the kitchen for the released animals to fight over. From the kitchen came screams as kitchen maids fought off randy scullions and cooks. Leftover scraps were burned in the stoves, and stinking billows of burning meat assailed the nostrils of anyone who crossed the yard. Megan was becoming the cook of their nightmares.

In the guard room, drunken troopers, deserted by their Captains, played cards, helmetless in dishevelled uniforms. Weapons were piled haphazardly in corners. The portcullis was lowered so it stuck half way. A sentry was asleep in his box by the archway. There was not an officer in sight.

When Humphrey and his troop cantered into the yard, they had to crouch low over the horses' necks. Once inside, and suitably irritated, they were greeted by the sight of a drunken guard pissing against the guard room wall, and another puking into the horse trough. The riders had to dismount and kick their way through the excited, scrambling animals. Smoke drifted over the entire area. Yells and drunken laughter came from every side.

Now Humphrey knew. A glance told him all that he wanted to know. Simple. A woman's domain would be in absolute chaos. Orderless and unchecked, it amounted to total misrule. Rags and ordure were the order of the day. A half-crazed recluse, with faithless, greedy servants and soldiery did the rest. And of course, not a sergeant or corporal in sight. Obviously making hay with the wenches in the lofts. He didn't blame the smelly rank and file, for they were just feathering their nests, and there was nothing wrong in that. But a bit of discretion. Useless trying to beat any discipline into the heads of these sots and tarts. Yes, Agnes's reports were confirmed only too disgustingly.

Humphrey strode into the hall and instantly recoiled, wrinkling his nose in revulsion. His horrified look focused on the two Welsh loons at the table, who could clearly hardly sit, let alone stand. Hopcyn stared back blearily, brandy dribbling down his chin. Damascus was talking to himself in that strange, barbarous tongue of theirs. A crescendo of shrieks came from the nursery. Humphrey winced. Death to all brats. He nearly puked at the smell from the buckets. Damascus slid to the floor and puked quietly, even demurely, onto the smelly floor rushes.

Humphrey addressed Hopcyn, although he doubted it would do any good.

'Hey, twang-twang, where's old clothes peg?'

'Inshpecting, I exchpect.'

'Inspecting what?'

'People, I shppose.'

'Whores or brandy more like.'

'And where is the Queen?'

'At her devotions.'

'Where?'

'In the chapel.'

'How long?'

'About two months.'

'Like her milksop son,' Humphrey guffawed. 'Where's the Chapel?' Perhaps he should take a look at it.

'Next to the old Lazarium.'

Humphrey backed off. Not there. So, he thought, she now lives in a pious, human pigsty. Leprosy. The disease of dirt. What a fate. He'd seen a few lepers loitering about the landing stage. He'd give the order to clear them from the area on the way back. Disgusting objects.

Agnes now appeared at the nursery door, suckling a baby at her ample breasts. Humphrey blanched at the sickly odours of baby milk and shit. He sniffed at her again. Was it possible someone had recently tupped her? The babe opened its gums and shrieked. Humphrey couldn't take his eyes off her tits. What a waste.

'A beautiful day, your Grace.' She seemed quite sober.

'Remind me to look at it sometime.'

'Can't you smell lilacs?'

'I can smell dungheaps.'

'I hear the milksop's very bright.'

'Nothing to do with me.' He was still fascinated by her tits.

Joanna and Joséphine erupted into the hall, biting, scratching, tearing each other's hair, both obviously the worse for wear. Agnes and the others didn't seem to notice. Still struggling, the two Demoiselles disappeared behind the screens in the direction of the kitchens.

'Daddy, Daddy!' a child's voice nagged from the nursery.

Humphrey winced again. The garrison children. Still here. Should be kept in the stables.

'Someone's got to look after them,' said Agnes.

Hopcyn raised his fuddled head, slurring,

'Tell the little bastard Daddy's busy!'

'Story, Daddy, story!' came the voice again.

'Keep the bastards in order, woman! We're busy!' he roared this time, swigging from the bottle again.

So the twang-twang was now fathering bastards. Savages! Agnes handed Humphrey a document.

'What's this?'

'A petition. From Captain Tudor.'

'No! For what?'

'A posting to France.'

'No, I said.'

'But he's wasting away here.'

'Exactly.'

'Please.' She went on her knees before him. Humphrey felt a thrill at the posture. At least someone knew about court protocol.

'Sire,' she added. Humphrey swelled. Better. Agnes was worth her pay after all. 'Any message for the Queen?' she asked. Humphrey looked around.

'I needn't have bothered coming,' he spat.

The babies yowled, the pigs squealed, the chickens clucked. Stale ale stank in his nostrils. The baby shat itself again, burped, and screamed. And twang-twang was staring at him again with those mad wizard eyes of his. He felt uneasy prickles creep up his neck. He turned to go, saying,

'What any one of you has to say to any other one of you, is, thank God, beyond me!'

As he boarded his barge, he looked back at the black bulk of Baynard's. A witch's coven, surely. A cesspit and a lazarium, created by the pious squalor of a lunatic, froggie queen. He longed to cleanse it all by fire. But time was pressing. The witch would have to hurry it all up again. Time. He touched the hair at his temples. That morning he had found more grey hairs. He would wait no longer. He refused to grow old in the service of a puking baby. Time for action. But as for Baynard's, let the whole poxy, degenerate crew sink in their own pig-swill.

79

Humphrey couldn't get rid of the feeling that his chances were slipping. Baynard's might have been nicely scuppered by the Witch, but Bedford still clung to power, and the infant King to his crown. The Witch would have to stamp out those persistent heads or, as Humphrey threatened, he would cut her off without a penny, black arts notwithstanding. He stamped and swore for action. Eleanor could tell the fool would brook no delay. She departed next day for Suffolk, officially to visit her ailing father, but coincidentally to dice with Satan over Humphrey's inheritance.

'Don't ye worry, my lovely, leave it to thy Queen of Darkness!'

In the deserted village of Eye, an accursed spot where the Black Death had removed every living being a few years earlier, intermittent moonlight filtered down through the scudding clouds. The single road through the village was overgrown with gorse, knot grass and briars. By the old, now overgrown, village green, the church rose gaunt and dismayed among its ruins. Dusky yews spread deeper shadows. Owls hooted in the empty belfry.

Within the crumbling walls of the nave, below the empty space of the fallen roof, obedient to the Witch's call, were the sixty full members of the coven, all in pointed black hoods, black silk robes, and black leather sandals. Members, both male and female, wore nothing underneath. In place of the old blessed font, a square black stone altar had been set up. An inverted cross, also painted black, rose from the polished surface. Directly in front of the cross, made out of gallows oak, was the image of the beast, carved into the likeness of a snarling black cat whose eyes glowed of its own accord as the ceremony reached its climax. By the beast stood a black chalice, for Christ's blood, and a painted black platter with wafers, for the host, Christ's body. Two reeking hessian bundles lay between the talons of the beast. A billy goat was tethered close by. The Witch now spat on the cross, raising the chalice which was charged with urine and menstrual blood, along with the body of Christ which was disintegrating particles of decaying meat. As the first communicant knelt to taste this unspeakable devil's offal, the Witch began to chant the dreaded *maleficium*, the unholiest invocation on this Sabbath to Satan. As she finished, the Beast's eyes glowed, the Witch tore the cross down and threw it into the centre of the congregation. It was spat upon a hundred times, then chopped into a thousand splinters. The Witch drained the foul brew to the dregs. The platter and chalice were smashed on the remains of the cross.

The Witch now offered up the hessian bundles to the Beast, for they contained the dismembered remains of two recently murdered babes whose flesh had also adorned the platter. Mixed with the rotting flesh were a dozen wax heads, small replicas of the heads in the hideous chest at Placentia. Writhing maggots dropped from eye sockets and mouths, invoking the living heads to share the same fate. Still chanting the *maleficium*, the coven moved off, bearing the smashed utensils and the fragments of the inverted cross, until they reached the sides of a newly dug grave. Into this pit went the cursed remnants, the slaughtered babies last. The grave was filled in and the earth trampled down, then urinated and defecated on. Afterwards, the coven wound its way back to the altar, still chanting. The Witch lead the goat to the altar, reached down underneath its belly and masturbated the animal to full erection. She then removed her garments, and lay back naked on the altar, thighs spread apart. The goat, out of long practice, sprang up, placing its forehoofs on either side of the Witch's thighs, and lunged forward with its penis, plunging it deep into the Witch. A foul groan of perverse pleasure went up. As the goat rode its lust to its first frantic climax, the coven howled, ripped off their clothes, and went into a delirious orgy of their own, each waiting for their turn with the goat. The beast's eyes glowed yellow and red. It was content. And so was the Witch. No one had ever survived the dreaded full curse of the *maleficium*.

Behind the tilting tombstones of the cemetery crouched the Monk, Abbot of Fleury, relishing the dread acts he was witnessing. He crouched lower as the voices rose higher. He knew that if he was caught, he would be torn into a thousand pieces, like the cross. As the second *maleficium* rose higher and higher, he found himself fervently praying, and for the first time in his life he meant every word.

80

Catherine and Owen were picnicking in their favourite dell. The lilacs were again in bloom. The full years passed as swiftly as the sun itself. Summer was threatening to arrive early, and the day was calm and balmy. The little chapel had been renovated, the roof restored, and the stonework cleaned and renewed. The windows glowed with new, brightly pigmented glass. Two rows of pews were in place. An altar of elmwood was erected before the ancient cross carved into the wall. As in winter, the air inside the chapel was warm and mild, in a sort of perpetual full bloom, a little miracle that comforted everyone who stepped inside the front porch at any season. A beaten path now led from the fields and trees outside, directly up to the front porch. The lilac trees canopied the whole chapel like a perfumed snow-white cloud. This sacred place now rested at the heart of a secret, the secret of an untold, enduring passion, and of a new dynastic birth.

After that first night, so long and yet so short a time ago, the entire staff and garrison had closed ranks in an involuntary gesture of unity and dedication to the new, ravishing secret. Surgeon Samuel was there when needed, and midwife Megan took care of the garrison births. The outside world had become an unwelcome guest, to be discouraged at all times; the future, a distant prospect where present love dispelled all coming fears. The Welsh Guard were the outward guardians, the Demoiselles, the inner sentinels of the hearth. All worked in uncanny unison, each watching over the other, wherever they happened to be. Plans for every conceivable emergency had been drawn up, each person with his assigned place and role.

Catherine and Owen lay on a blanket in the sunny glow near the chapel. Blue skies spread above the trembling leaves. Catherine stroked Owen's cheek and ran a hand over his chest.

'My leather lamb. Yes, you are.'

'And you are my love, the only one, my little affection cup.' He kissed her, and looked down at her curved, swelling belly.

'The three of us,' he said, 'and now, the fourth.'

'I want your children more and more. Look at little Jasper, the happiest of us all, never mind the times and dangers. Two at first, three's a family, and four a blessed family.' She laughed. Her face glowed. She looked as young as she had been when he had first seen her at Troyes.

'Yes,' she went on, "This little one will be the family we never had in our childhood, Owen.' Owen nodded, feeling the happiness flow into his heart from hers.

'Do you still miss Henry?'

'Yes. But God, or destiny as you call Him, decided to recompense me twice over, so how can I complain?'

'Jasper has your charm.'

'And your energy.'

'We'd better stop before we make the child impossible!' They laughed.

'But yes, you're right. I am worried about Henry.'

'The Countess of Warwick couldn't be a better guardian.'

'I mean, Owen, he is very much like my dear late father.'

'The Well Beloved, and so will Henry be, you'll see.'

'Do you love me?'

'The greatest love is the longest silence, so what can I say?'

'Say what the blackbirds say. Listen.' The long melodious trills filled their ears.

'*Sweet songs for sweeter spirits*, as the bards say.'

'I love you old pagans and your Isle Abounding with Beauty.'

'But we lost *Afallon* to the Saxons.'

'Like our Eden of France, you'll get it back one day.'

'Yes. But it will take much longer.'

'You think Humphrey's out of the way now?'

'He's making civil war on your suitors, new and old, from York to Somerset. And crowning himself every day. Keeps him busy.'

'My uncle of Bedford's the best leader you have.'

'And your own Jeanne's the best general you have.'

'Mother doesn't care who wins.'

'She's probably right in the end.'

'Eustace loves it though.'

'But all that's on the outside.'

'The world's gone away!'

'Only for a while.'

'But that *while* is our heaven.'

'And our secret.'

'How long must we hide it?'

'As long as it lasts. Agnes will take on the birth again. And Samuel and Megan will be there.'

'Why do you look so . . . thoughtful? Come on.'

'Humphrey. We must put him off for good.'

'How? You've got a plan?' Owen nodded. 'How then?'

'By letting him know what we're up to here. Listen.' Owen talked her through the plan. She embraced him. Yes, it was dangerous, outrageous even, but it would do.

A gust of wind shook the blossoms down onto their heads, and they made love again, gently, pleasantly, to the song of the blackbirds.

81

Hopcyn was entertaining the Monk in the main hall. Bottles of the Monk's favourite Claret littered the table. He was at his devotions. He sipped, sighed, and made the sign of the cross over the wine.

'My congratulations on your elevation,' said Hopcyn.

'Being an Abbot's not bad. Opens a few cellars. Good health.'

'Cheers! And what else have you been up to?'

'Lazariums.'

'Charitable work. And the lepers?'

'Nicest people I've met here. Two weeks in this land is enough. I tell you the *godons* over here fight nastier than the ones in France. What's the matter with them? They eat like pigs, drink like swine, pee in public and shit on the highways. If it wasn't for their wars overseas, they'd die of disease over here, dirtiest dogs in Europe. Albion's an open air *vomitorium cum jacques*.'

'You must tell Eustace that one.'

'Eustace said it first. From himself, to you, with compliments.'

'*Vive la France*! How is he?'

'Uglier than ever.'

'Poetic justice, such beauty. Please give him this little triad – the three things that must be most understood in poetry: the Little, the Great, and their Connectives.'

'A sweet one. That'll keep him busy.'

'For a lifetime or two. So the Maid's trouncing the *godons*.'

'It's the end, Hopcyn.'

'She'll free France through fire.'

'You've seen it?'

'Yes.'

'Must be true then. *Santé.*'

'*Iechyd.*'

'I heard Master Humphrey dropped in here.'

'And out again.'

'Keep an eye on him.'

'We are.'

'His ignorance and thievery are typical.'

'Don't worry. How's our *wunderbar* Isabelle?'

'Mourning her Court of Good Shepherds.'

'And her delightful son, Charles VII, of France?'

'He plans to have himself crowned.'

'A big step for a young man. It will cheer up the Queen. What is Charles's attitude to Isabelle?'

'His attitude is he doesn't want her within a thousand miles of himself.'

'So the Maid knew instantly who he was, even among all his courtiers.'

'He is a bastard no longer, so Isabelle is under diplomatic confinement.'

'Does the King of France or of England actually know they've got brothers?'

'Not at the moment, Hopcyn. And keep it that way.'

'By Gwydion, Eustace and I had a time at the signing at Troyes, remember?'

'A masterpiece of theatre. "Funs" as Isabelle says.' For once, he forgot, and his voice came out as soprano.

'Funs,' Hopcyn repeated, but affecting the Monk's hoarse baritone. They both laughed.

'To business then, just a bit. I have Catherine's money here, in gold louis. Bank drafts on the Florentine bankers.'

'Still paying her dowry, amazing.'

'Said she would never let Catherine down. And she isn't.'

'What does she say about her grandchildren?'

334

'Messages of love. Danced when she first heard. Happy her Katty hadn't left it too late, and that a Wittelsbach had bedded one of the most beautiful men in the world.'

'I'll tell Catherine that.'

'Why?'

'Because she agrees.'

'Now, here are the documents, signed and witnessed. And open safe conducts, promotions . . . '

'Is that the royal seal?'

'Copied directly off the Troyes Treaty, by Isabelle herself.'

Hopcyn closely inspected it, whispering;

'By Gwydion, it's perfect.'

'No problem. French seal's even better. A work of art. My humble opinion – as a man of the cloth, I mean.'

'If you're not careful, Father Abbot, you might well turn into a Christian.'

'Not while I'm in your company, my friend.'

'Tell me now, how is Isabelle?'

'Coughs too much. Put on a lot of weight.'

'Sorry to hear that, my friend.'

'She is still my Queen. When can I present my letters to Catherine?'

'When she's back from the Chapel.'

'Not as pious as son Henry I hope.'

'No, just went riding again.' They laughed.

'*Santé*!'

'*Iechyd*!'

82

At midnight, dressed in her travelling cloak and hood, Agnes was again ushered into the private chambers above the Mitre Inn. This time she was there at Eleanor's express request. As the door closed behind her, the Duke suddenly stepped out from the shadows. Agnes jumped.

'Nearly made you pee yourself that time, didn't I?' He lit the lantern on the table. Agnes suppressed a laugh when she saw that he was still carrying his baton.

'Surprised to see me?' he asked, trying to be silky.

'Surprised and delighted, your Grace,' she returned, succeeding in silkiness. 'Where is her Grace?'

'Suffolk. She'll be here anon. You looked a bit different at Baynard's, put the shits up me. That baby!' He wrinkled his nose in disgust.

'Well, we all look a bit different at Baynard's.'

'Barnyards more like!' He honked, trying to sound like a pig. 'Now, to business.'

'What about Mortimer and Suffolk?'

'Nothing new. We watch the Yorkists like hawks.'

'Does Bedford watch them too?'

'Ha! He's been trumped by a virgin!' he waved his baton. 'As governor of Normandy, I'd have soon stopped the rot!' He threw down a small bag of coins.

'What's this?'

'Your payment.'

'No, it is not.'

'Your reports tell us nothing.'

'Of course they do,'

'They are nil reports.'

'They are expensive reports.'

'Not a groat more!'

'Then I'll leave the Queen's service.'

'You will stay where you are.'

'The new suitors. Suppose she gets married?'

'Council's prepared a law against that.'

'When does the law come into force?'

'Why?'

'I want payment up to that date.'

'There's months yet, so stay put. Got to say it, your greed's almost as big as your tits,' he guffawed.

'There's never enough time for money. And forget about my tits. Her Grace promised the full amount.'

'I am in charge here.'

'If I ever left the Queen's service, I'd have a story to tell.'

'Are you trying to blackmail me?'

'I'm glad we understand each other.' Agnes upended the coins in the bag onto the table. 'See that? In a few minutes you'll multiply that ten times over.'

'Rubbish!'

'And then ten times again.'

He banged his staff on the table, shouting. 'No!'

'Dowager Queen's taken a lover.'

'Impossible!' He had bitten.

'Possible.'

'Treason!' His anger mounted.

'Calm yourself, your Grace.' Agnes was at her silkiest best.

'I'll have his head! Who is he? York, Mortimer, Suffolk, Somerset?'

'No, no, no, and no again. Think of her mother.'

'A scullion, stable lad?'

'Lower than that.'

'Alright, full payment!' He threw the heavy pouch. 'Now tell me who he is!'

'He is . . . a Tudor.' Humphrey was dumbstruck. He finally squeaked again,

'I'll have his head!'

'No titles, no lands.'

'Let me think.'

'You smashed him.'

'So?'

'Let him dip his fingers in her pie.'

'Why?'

'He is nothing. No threat. You are next in line.'

'But the other suitors?'

'If they get near her, I'll spread the dirt.'

'I like it. No one would touch her.'

'The shame. A Tudor!'

'Saw it all along, perfect trap! But suppose she gets pregnant?'

'Get rid of it. Her midwife's a witch.'

'That's a burning offence.' Still, he liked the idea.

'Use that too.'

'It would work.'

'This way you stay second in line.'

'It's watertight.'

'One last thing . . . '

'Go on.'

'Did she grant you an audience when you called?'

'I didn't need one.'

'She is a recluse.'

'We all know that.'

'Why is she a recluse?'

'Alright then, go on!'

'She's sickening.'

'For what? Go on.'

'For . . . the Tudor.'

'What do you mean?'

'The Tudor is tired of her.'

'I don't believe it!'

'That's why he wants a posting.'

'They'll stay where they are, both of them. Like cornered rats, and poor as church mice, scotched by God, tearing each other to pieces. Just right again. Take the money.'

'You did it, your plan. Don't worry, it will be your day soon, Sire.'

'Yes.' His hand strayed over her breast. He tried silky again, but only managed to croak, 'I always wanted to fuck you.'

'Women are so attracted to you.' God, the woman was on heat.

'I know.'

'When a man's on top of me, I pretend it's you.'

'Your hair, down there. All bushy and red and foxy, I bet.' He licked his lips. Agnes thrust her belly towards him.

'Your Grace, your understanding of womanhood is above that of ordinary men.'

She let his hand grope down to her belly. When he felt the bulge, Humphrey recoiled.

'Not again!' he exclaimed in dismay.

'You can still do it.'

'No, thank you.' He moved away.

'Who's the father?'

'Haven't decided yet.'

'Ha, I like it.' He looked down at her body. 'What a waste.'

'Then I'd better go. But I'll save it for you for next time.'

'Of course you will.' Agnes gathered up the money. 'Farewell, my Emperor!' And she was gone, carrying more subsidies for Baynard's.

He paced up and down in excitement. Yes, it had been a good day. Agnes was ripe for him as well, and for once, worth every penny. When Eleanor arrived, her eyes were gleaming.

'Let 'em sicken, let 'em die . . . my lovely. She's done a *maleficium* on 'em.'

He felt a chill, but even this was good news. He told her about Agnes's revelations. Eleanor agreed, Baynard's was neutered now. She asked about the Tudor in great detail. That night as Humphrey puffed and panted his way on top of her, in her mind's eye, Eleanor pretended it was the handsome green-eyed Tudor.

83

Charles VII of France stood at the high altar of the recently completed Cathedral of Rheims, 'one of the seven wonders of France,' as Eustace had christened it. Charles was dressed from head to foot in sumptuous coronation robes. La Tremouille, his number one mistress, had made sure they reached the floor, thus covering the King's spindly shanks and legs. The throne stood behind him. It was covered in silk with the *fleur-de-lis* in blue and silver, and the woodwork in gold inlay. The artisans and craftsmen had been hammering, carving, fitting masonry and raising gargoyles for months. The twin spires of the two magnificent towers had been completed and soared up majestically on both sides of the vast entrance. The wide doors had been covered with huge panels, again decorated with enormous *fleur-de-lis*, timely and frequent reminders of the revived puissance of France. All the stained glass panels were in place in the immense roseate windows and in the clerestory of the nave. Saints, evangelists, apostles, kings and queens, heroes; all gazed down in aureoles of blazing light that shimmered on the polished floor. As Charles listened to the tedious prayers in Latin, he counted the window figures. There were twenty-nine apostles, twenty-five haloed saints, twenty Kings and Queens all orbed and sceptered, fourteen bishops and archbishops, and ten of the greatest worthies with Geoffrey de Bouillon, the premier chevalier of France, in the lead. But the apostles, Charles noted, won hands down. Well, thought, Charles, I have but a single saint, Saint Jeanne, and she is half devil they say, so I will have to rely on myself in the end.

In spite of himself, some shadows of the past flitted across his memory – the poverty of St Pol, his father's awful fits, the terrible *Bal des Ardents*, the confrontations in the loathsome Court of Good Shepherds, the vile struggle over his poor father's remains, and most despicable of all of Isabelle's acts, the theft of the royal signet as his father lay in his coffin. That was the one act that gave him the resolution to face her down and to confine her, as his father had also done, under lock and key. Yes, that had been the beginning of the exorcism.

The refurbished two hundred year old organ, which was the oldest in France, boomed out once again in celebration rather than lamentation. The great concourse of nobles, the Clermonts, the Vedons, the de Lavals, from duke to knight with attendant Marshals, Generals, bishops and archbishops, filling the crammed benches all arose in his acclamation. The Duke of Burgundy was absent, but soon even his voice would rise in praise of the new-crowned King. The English alliance was fast fading. Grouped round the King were the acknowledged heroes of the hour. There was the Duc d'Alencon, the senior duke who had ceremoniously knighted Charles *maréchal de Rais*, and who was Commander and First Admiral of the navies of France. Also there was Dunois, the heroic 'bastard' of Orleans. All eyes, however, were focused not on these worthies, but on the fabled creature who had been standing at the side of the King throughout the ceremony, Jeanne d'Arc herself stood upright in her unblazoned armour holding high her personal standard, her whole being radiant and entranced.

The Abbot of the Cathedral bowed and approached the King, the golden flask of sanctified oil borne before him. The anointing was brief, with but a few drops of the holy oil invading the royal scalp. The crown was raised high and placed on Charles's blessed brows. A hum of approval went up. Charles had excelled himself. Throughout, he had sat straight-backed and immobile, as instructed by La Tremouille, giving himself added stature and dignity. He smiled briefly at her, not three metres away, sitting at the front in one of the royal seats of honour. She was now a recognised power in the land. Charles sniffed but, again as instructed by La Tremouille, raised the French kerchief that he now carried in the sleeve to his nose in a brief but elegant gesture. It was again noted with approval.

As the prayers started, Charles's mind strayed back. How far he had come! And all so sudden. It was the Maid, in part. True, she had picked him out unhesitatingly. But he wondered how he could have even doubted his legitimacy, or ever relied on peasant Jeanne's weird 'voices'. The Ogre, his dreaded mother, had shrunk to the size of a prune. Similarly, he asked, why had he ever been intimidated by her – a dropsy-ridden hag who, like the English, had had her day? Yes, as her chains tightened, so his had loosened. He thought of Catherine. What was his partner in hunger doing now? He longed to see her, and for her to see him now too. He felt a sudden surge of affection for his father, not out of being a fellow monarch but for having been a companion in suffering under their common persecutor, Isabelle.

He glanced at La Tremouille. Trust is there, he thought, she trusts me to be as treacherous as I deem expedient, and I trust her always to know which side her bread is buttered on. But there was also another precious element in their relationship – La Tremouille not only knew how to make him come in four minutes flat, she could do it four times a night! After such multiple certainties, the old fears and phobias seemed to dwindle and vanish. Charles stirred on his throne, scarcely able to sit still.

He stole a quick glance at the holy shadow by his side. Was she a devil as Bedford and the *godons* thought, or an angel as the French believed? After life with his mother, he had learned one thing about women. There was a bit of the devil in every one of them, and they had to be watched at all times.

The Maid now turned and, with raised banner, led the King and his exalted entourage down the aisle to the booming triumphant organ. This time, thought Charles, she might lead, but after this I will see to it that I am always at the head of things. Yes, the new King was beginning to come true. Charles had no doubt on this special day, and in the future days, that the sun was shining down on him at last, and through him on France. *Vive le roi! Vive la France!*

84

In the English Headquarters in the main square of Rouen, at the ironically named Joyeux Repos Hotel, the Cardinal of Winchester and Bedford were conferring over the continuing military and political crises. On the table in front of them lay open maps, each bearing its own disastrous story.

'With Salisbury gone, Normandy's wide open, though Willoughby's doing a good holding job. But this message from Humphrey, is he serious? Demanding Normandy as his, by right.'

'That's not the only thing he thinks he's first in line for,' remarked Bedford. 'Fights more in the stews of London than in the fields of France. Damn reds and whites. Cutting each others' throats. That's what we English call, "covering our rears". Well, my brother can stick his staff of office up his own rear for a change. He's not going to come over here.'

'It's the loss of revenues, the Commons won't vote our supplies again.'

'Exchequer's on the brink of bankruptcy, so I can see why they want to hang onto what they've got left. But these towns here, Chalons, Rheims, and now Troyes, the treaty town itself – another omen of the Maid, no doubt. If these losses continue, Paris will be cut off and our escape routes to the coast with it.'

'With the reinforcements you raked up here,' said Winchester, 'and with the forces I've brought up, we're back in the business of attack. But where are Sir John Fastolf and Talbot?'

'They should be here by now. Talbot's still the main

bogeyman of the French.'

'Well, the bold Duke of Burgundy certainly isn't. Holding back in every engagement now . . . '

'Backing the winner, it's called. And Burgundy's getting seriously legalistic over the terms of the Treaty.'

'It's that damnable Maid, the virgin-whore. A limb of Satan in men's clothes . . . '

'Must be displeasing to God.' Bedfords hatred of her nearly choked him.

'That didn't prevent God from favouring her at Orleans.'

'I know. I was there. And these dangerous fables about her too. The miracles and voices – birds burst into song when she passes. Clouds of butterflies, the protective spirits of the dead, accompany her into battle where doves hover over her head. Rubbish, but . . . '

'How about this this one – heard it this morning – she squeezed the hands of a dead child, and it yawned and woke up.'

'Bad for morale. Our men are as superstitious as theirs. And now our lads are developing doubts about our right to be over here at all. Reports of deserters running up and down the Normandy beaches looking for boats to get home, or joining the brigands in the hills, or these filthy bands of *Ecorcheurs*. It is a fact that Henry is King of France by divine right.'

'The Maid claims divine right too.'

'I tell you, these voices are nothing more than demons of her own derangement. And she's destroyed the last chance for Henry's great crusade for Christendom. She is an apostate, a heretic and a witch!'

Again Winchester was mildly surprised. Bedford was far more religious than he, a high cardinal. But then, he reminded himself, the old King, brother Henry and the boy king all had a streak of religious fanaticism in them. Winchester decided to change the focus of attention and ventured.

'What we need is another Agincourt.'

'What we need is something to rally our cause.'

'Like a coronation.'

'Is it safe to bring the King over here?'

'We've still got enough troops to bring him in.'

'But have we got enough to take him out?' Bedford was all too aware of the dangers.

'He's the only rallying point we have.'

'In Paris?'

'That would be a victory in itself.'

'Is he strong enough?' Although Winchester seemed sure of success, Beford could apparently only see disaster looming.

'His constitution's fine, it's his mind that isn't . . . well.' Winchester carefully chose his word.

'What does he think of the plan?'

'Swears he'll do it in memory of his sainted father.'

'What about his sainted grandma, Isabelle?' Bedford was clutching at straws.

'He prays for her too.'

'What news of Catherine?'

'Well out of it, practically a recluse.'

'Well done, brother Henry, he saw to that.'

'I'm very fond of that little princess.'

'Aren't we all? She's the only innocent in all this.'

'She deserves better.'

'Yes. Well, coronation it is then. Notre Dame?'

'Yes, orders drawn up.'

'Keep our fingers crossed, I suppose.'

A clatter of footsteps came from the corridor. Sir John Fastolf burst in, in bloodied fighting armour. Bedford and Winchester jumped up in alarm.

'Sir John! What has kept you?'

'And where are your attendants?'

'Driven back, my Lord.'

'Didn't you counter attack?'

'My men were taken prisoners.'

'And where is Talbot?'

'Driven out of Beaugency . . . '

'And . . . ?'

' . . . Taken prisoner too.'

'Damnation!' swore Bedford, 'you should have counter-attacked, however few!'

'Your orders, my Lord?' asked Sir John.

'Sir John, you are hereby stripped of your most royal order of the Garter!'

'I protest, my Lord. I fought to my last breath. Remember Troyes.'

'To my dying day. You are dismissed!'

Fastolf retired fuming but not disgraced. He knew Bedford spoke out of weariness and exasperation.

Dying days indeed. Yes, Bedford must feel it, thought Fastolf, even if the coronation happens, and even if brave Rouen and faithful Paris stay with him, he must feel what we are all beginning to feel. The most righteous causes have their endings, and surely the coronation, he reflected, did not represent a new triumph at all, but a last, desperate set back.

85

Agnes and Hopcyn were in the royal bedchamber sorting out suitable loose gowns for Catherine in the coming months.

'Come on Daddy,' urged Agnes, 'tell us a story.'

'Can't you see I'm too drunk, children.'

Agnes held up four dresses.

'That should be plenty.'

'A little old-fashioned for the Court, but perfect for a recluse.'

Hopcyn began bouncing on the royal four-poster.

'I've got a poem for you.'

'Alright, Daddy, go ahead.'

Hopcyn stroked the bed, and recited.

'This is the place of the girl of the white wave
With her and I delighting in desire,
Licking the sweet lips of the girl,
Feeling and fondling will I ever be
For the smiling gem below the brushwood.
Stroking her belly will I ever be,
Caressing the thighs of my lovely love
In a rage of desire for my golden mistress,
Full as the waters of the lake
Giving so freely of her marvellous body to me.'

'For me, Hopcyn?'

'Every word. Agnes, from today, I want no other but you.'

'Fine with me.'

'And you?'

'Fine with me too.'

'Let's celebrate then.'

'How?'

'By taking our clothes off.'

'Look,' shouted Hopcyn, 'I wave my bardic measure to my love!'

'By Gwydion,' said Agnes, 'it groweth by the second.'

'Hang on to the corner post and bend down.'

Hopcyn entered her from the rear.

'By Gwydion,' he groaned, 'this velvet glove's got my measure. Smooth as a daisy.' He thrust, twirled, hurled, howled, slid and bounced into her, opening and closing her buttocks, caressing her belly and her nipples.

'I can do without raiment,' he gasped, 'I can do without gold. But however old, I can never do without this!'

'Let's do it when we're one hundred and one,' moaned Agnes, hanging onto the post.

'Now, now now!' they shouted in unison as they came. Afterwards, sleeping in each others' arms in the royal bed, they knew that this was the come that had decided them to be faithful thenceforward to each other, for always. And they were.

86

In the quarters of the Demoiselles, Joséphine, Adéle, and Joanna were sorting out Agnes's selection of dresses.

'Yes, they'll do,' said Adéle.

'No trouble,' added Joanna.

'Where's Agnes?' asked Joséphine with feigned innocence.

They all laughed, then set to work widening and lengthening, sewing and cutting. Agnes re-appeared, patting her hair into place.

'You look breathless,' said Joséphine, not so innocently.

'I'm no angel,' responded Agnes, 'thank God. But Hopcyn and I have decided, you can have the entire Welsh guard to choose from now on, including the three intrepid Captains.'

'Wonderful!' They crowded around, hugging her.

'Tied the knot.'

'Why not? Tired of looking around.'

'And as for Idris, Huw and Ifan,' laughed Joanna, 'we know them better every day!'

They finished dress after dress, then started on Agnes's maternal gowns, each suitable for different stages of the pregnancy. Agnes was used to the role now, as were the Demoiselles. None of them considered the danger of what they were doing. None were afraid of betrayal, although no oath had been taken. The whole was a sort of spontaneous conspiracy, a kind of secret, irresistible union of love, with the Gallois/Gallics holding it together, and the Saxon safely out of it for once. It was as if Baynard's had been built just for that. Catherine had insisted that the Ladies visit their own homes and families in the normal way, and Agnes briefed them on the rumours they were to put out about Baynard's, that reclusive House of Sorrows. Owen also ordered the Guard to take leave on a regular basis, and pass on their information in a similar way. As time passed, all rumours confirmed what the conspirators wanted the world to believe, that the Castle was a hermit's retreat, and the main actors and actresses in the play, were playing a game where happy families, little children and passionate love had no place at all. And so the secret lived on.

87

Even the weather now seemed to be in alliance with the French. After a dozen battles and postponements, Bedford was finally constrained to fix the date for the coronation for mid-winter. Nothing wrong with that. But it turned out to be the worst winter in living memory. Snow fell every day. The countryside, picked clean by the various armies and by the bands of brigands, was bare. After the food sources dried up, the big freeze set in. Vines and woods were being destroyed by frost. At night, the pine trees exploded in the sub zero temperatures. No food at all arrived at the markets of the capital. Bedford managed to scrape together twenty barges of provisions for the populace, which he sent up the Seine under heavy guard. It was a drop in the ocean. It lasted a few hours. People were freezing to death in the streets. Houses were torn down and used as firewood. The English troops joined in. They too needed warmth to live, let alone fight.

The boy King, his entourage and long supply train, were now launched into this new arctic land of blizzards and starvation. Due to Bedford's careful planning, it made good progress. The route and staging points had been carefully worked out by Bedford himself. Under snow-laden skies, the coronation procession was now drawn up outside the historic Porte de Saint Denis. The English regiments were strung out for miles, chilled to the marrow.

The boy-king was brought out of the comfort of his closed carriage. He was enveloped in a thick woollen cloak, and mounted on a placid Arab mare, specially selected for the occasion. He would lead the procession through the City to the Cathedral. Henry had borne up surprisingly well under the horrendous conditions. He spent much of the time praying and seemed to enjoy the enforced privacy of his carriage. He wore a permanent expression of slight bewilderment mixed with child-like determination. He would not let any one down. He would do his duty, with the help of God. On his golden Plantagenet hair, was now placed a golden filigree coronet.

Henry had taken a great liking to his uncle Bedford and obeyed his every word. Standing beside the King, just inside the Gate, Bedford motioned forward the Paris delegation of welcome, the Councillors of the French Parlement, the city Provosts and Constables, the bishops and nobility, all uniformly clothed in thick, grey winter capes. All had responded to Bedford's call. Not only was he still the Governor of Paris, but he was also the best they had ever had. He had made the citizenry, merchants and nobility prosperous. If their Governor wanted to crown a King in their greatest Cathedral, it was alright with them. However, they did have one reservation. They remembered only too well the insult the boy's father had paid them on his own triumphal entry into the city. After presenting Henry with the traditional welcome gifts of gold, they quickly retired to the rear of the column without another word. Not a promising start, but Bedford felt he couldn't blame them. He urged the procession forward.

The starving population had turned out in large shivering numbers, mainly in the hope of some generous concessions to mark the occasion, such as remission of taxes, a public holiday or, as they all prayed, free distributions of bread, flour and wine. When the boy King and his court pulled up at the great doors of Notre Dame, even a few feeble cheers were raised. The expectant, famished crowds were still in good mood.

Before the high altar, Bedford had erected a dais so the little King would be visible to the whole congregation. The steps up to the throne were painted sky-blue and studded with inlays of *fleur-de-lis*, in silver and gold. The Cardinal of Winchester had finally decided to conduct most of the ceremony himself, including the holy anointing. This upset the Bishop of Paris, whose job it really was. His Grace retired, muttering, to a back seat. Bedford had been unaware of the change in his instructions, and felt a sense of unease. He had also given instructions not to linger over the ritual, but to speed it up before they all froze to death in the unheated gloom of the huge arches. It was already ten below zero. The crowning went off without further mishap, although the prayers, holy oaths and glorias were drowned by the stamping of feet, the clapping of gloved hands, coughings, expectorations and huge exhalations of breaths. Once outside, the royal cavalcade moved off swiftly to get out of the swirling snow and icy blasts. Bedford's planned grant of a free share of the little stores of food that still remained would have to wait. As the carriages were disappearing, an irate Bishop of Paris appeared, shaking his fist at the departing troops. The Catherdral's most valuable plate and gold chalices had been 'liberated'. The Bishop issued a public plea for their restoration. This fell on frozen as well as deaf ears. Gold could still buy bread. Yes, thought, the Bishop, Deschamps is right, these *godons* are no better than a swarm of locusts, and the king's *joyeuse entree* was a criminal farce.

The coronation banquet was to be held at the Palais des Tourelles, Bedford's own headquarters, the safest, warmest and roomiest building available. But Bedford, for once, miscalculated. The Guard laid on for the crowds in the square and the royal party in the Great Hall, proved inadequate. More men were summoned from the barracks. The square was now packed, and the press was pushing the spectators into the hall in ever increasing numbers. The Guards were heaving back the crammed citizenry, but they were moving inexorably forward towards the banqueting tables. They watched with mounting hunger pangs as the servants entered, bearing precious dishes of meats, vegetables, soups and sauces. The odours were greeted with uncontrollable groans. However, the people gazed in astonishment as the seated French notables first glanced at their food, then pushed it away angrily. The victuals weren't fresh. They had been pre-cooked and heated up for the occasion. Only dogs ate pre-cooked food. It was a culinary catastrophe. Although this error was beyond Bedford's foresight, the disgusting repast was regarded as yet another insult. The starving mob, however, had no such scruples. In a single blind rush, they made for the piles of food. The guard closed in around the royal party. The mob now went into a feeding frenzy. Every morsel of food disappeared in minutes, then the platters themselves, the tureens, knives, forks, anything of value. The reserve guard arrived just in time, charging through the mob and causing further panic, but managed to surround the King. He was escorted out, quite composed in the circumstances, hands together in prayer, but a wet stain was spreading down his hose. He was escorted to the barracks close by, where a change of underwear and further prayer soon restored his customary puzzlement. Extra weapons were distributed from the armoury and Guards stood sentry at every door and window.

Outside, the mob had taken over. They pillaged every room of Bedford's palace from cellar to attic, stripping them bare. Every moveable object disappeared. The mob then started on the business of keeping warm. They tore down staircases, doors, floors, wall panelling, and tapestries in gigantic bonfires on every floor. Soon the building itself was in flames. The mob moved on to the next building and the next. The riots spread from district to district, until the whole city seemed to be going up in one gigantic conflagration. Even Bedford's most disciplined Men-at-Arms could do nothing. Bedford and the praying boy King, Henry VI of England, also just crowned

356

Henry II of France, stood by watching their beautiful city go up in flames. In spite of this new disaster, Bedford swore to himself,

'I will be true to the end.'

He paused. For the first time since his arrival in France, he realised he had used the ominous word 'end', in its terminal sense.

88

Catherine insisted on the marriage.

'Without a marriage we are not a recognised family,' she insisted.

'Our love, my love, needs no recognition. It is here, there, all around us.' He pressed his heart and hers.

'Look at my brother, didn't he always long for "recognition", a real mother.'

'But Jasper and Edmund know who their real mother and father are.'

'I want the boys to live inside the law.'

'The boys will be taken care of by the King, their brother.'

'This new law of Humphrey's means I will soon have no choice.'

'We don't know it will become law.'

'I want the marriage for the little one here,' she pressed her belly.

'Are you sure?'

'Of course. Why do you ask that?'

'Well, look at me I . . . have no titles, no estates . . . '

'Well, I do look at you, and I see the most beautiful, tender, strong man in the world.'

'But . . . '

'No "buts". Those are your titles. And you love me?'

'Yes.'

'Love is the best title a woman can have.'

'Crowned with love, is it then?'

'That's better.'

'But the Council will . . . '

' . . . no more politics today. No alliances, treaties, coronations, officers of state. No, a real wedding, like those out there in the little towns and villages. Just us, husband, wife, children, us, our family.'

'My darling Catherine, I'm more in love with you every day, you know that?'

'Yes, Owen, I do know it – because it's the same for me.'

'Affection cup.'

'Leather lamb.'

Hopcyn stood over piles of documents on the table in the main hall, sipping wine. He felt easy inside himself. The visions had taken on a benign glow. No more Sin Eaters, Hags or accursed glades. King Leper, Master of Last Reassurances, including Owen's life, bless you! He thought of the time he saw eternity that night and the souls of the massed dead. Other worlds, he thought. Still the vision of the three suns returned from time to time to trouble him. But recently he'd had a recurring vision, of Jasper and Edmund enthroned. But that would be a story for the future. Now the present destiny was Owen's, the son of prophecy, and it was taking its irresistible course. And a happy one now, come what may. Concentrate on the day, he thought, sipping the wine. Yes, this was the turning point, the rest of the world would unroll in its own way, like time itself, but at Baynard's this was the pivotal hour.

Damascus entered carrying tied up bundles of letters, ready for delivery.

'To practical matters,' said Hopcyn.

'Exactly,' said Damascus, 'the dye is cast.'

'All copied?'

Damascus's lean face beamed with satisfaction.

'All,' he said.

'No gaps?'

'I think only in perfect circles.'

'So?'

'There is no loophole here, in canon or in civil law. Birth and marriage certificates all dated, signed and counter signed. Paternity attestations, sworn statements, my ordainment, legal status, Inns of Court, notarised descriptions of all documents, witnessed again. Listed destinations, alternative addresses, forms of receipt. You name it, there's a law for it and we've got the lot. And all to be delivered at the same time by selected messengers, with reserve messengers if needed.' He leaned over the documents like a genial crane before adding,

'As I said, a perfect circle.'

'This madness for legality's one of our best allies.'

'What God has brought together, let no man break asunder.'

'Exactly. And how is our son of destiny?'

'Our trembling lamb, you mean.'

'Nothing as fearsome as the altar of marriage.'

'*Iechyd da!*'

'*Iechyd da!*'

They drank to the sacrificial lamb. It was also Damascus's and Hopcyn's job to escort Owen safely to the chapel. Owen wondered into the Hall, like a stranger entering a room for the first time. He looked at his two friends, as if trying to find the right words.

'A trifle pale, I told you,' said Hopcyn in a stage whisper.

'A little speechless, too.'

Owen hardly heard. His left leg trembled involuntarily, and his mouth kept running dry. He remembered standing in the light of the windows in Isabelle's great hall. That was when he knew.

'Boys,' he said, 'I think I'm falling in love all over again.'

'Well, it's a real man who can admit it,' said Damascus.

'In the eye of the light and in the face of the sun,' added Hopcyn, 'you can stop trembling now.'

'Careful, it'll be your turn soon enough.' Hopcyn's heart

turned over. Yes, it was a distinct possibility.

'You leave the visions to me, friend, and I'll leave the marriages to you.'

'One up to me though, Hopcyn.'

'True enough!'

'Time we wended, boys,' said Damascus, struggling into his priestly robes. 'I don't want to be in these for too long.'

The three friends made one more toast to each other, linked arms, stepped out into the sunlight and made their way along the beaten track to the shady, tranquil chapel.

Agnes and the Demoiselles had helped Catherine to choose her wedding dress. She was unable to wear the fashionable, tight-fitting, gipon, so Agnes and the Ladies had designed a special gown in voluminous plain white silk, embroidered with gold *fleur-de-lis*. Gathered high under the bodice, it tumbled in folds to her feet, discreetly concealing the curves of her body. Up around her slender, swan-like throat, the silk curled up into a high collar. The white veil was thrown back from her face and held in place with a light, silver coronet. Around her neck, hung her father's little gold crucifix.

Catherine stood at the chapel altar. Behind her stood Agnes and the three Ladies. Behind Owen stood Hopcyn, ready to prop him up if necessary. Damascus reared up above the group like a smiling genii.

The sun had blessed them again. After the recent shower, the lilac blossoms had spread their fragrance throughout the dell and inside the chapel. The blackbirds seemed to be singing in chorus. Butterflies rose with every gust of the breeze, as if silently witnessing the great love being blessed below. The birdsong suddenly faded, and they felt a slow, otherworldly peace descend on the place, like a shaft of dawn sunlight falling on a dusty floor.

Agnes had devised a little ceremony of her own and Hopcyn to end the wedding. As it drew to a close, Damascus proffered

Owen and Catherine their earliest pledges of love, their exchanged kerchiefs. These they now bound round each others throats, the *fleur de lis* and the red dragon, then embraced for their first married kiss, the Leather Lamb for his Affection Cup. As they walked arm in arm out into the sunlight again, both felt the new fullness of a family enfold them, about and within. They knew that they were looking out together onto a new world, which, whatever were the pains to come, had granted them a moment of true peace and of love, indeed a portion of eternity on the earth itself, however brief.

Love, felt Hopcyn in his bard's heart, had changed her very name that day, to the Lily and the Dragon.

89

Bridges were vital for the English to operate in northern France. Bedford was now confronted with a battle for the bridges on the great Loire river at the all-important town of Compiegne, a staging post on the route to Paris. Compiegne had followed the lead of many other towns in the region, and had declared in favour of the Maid. On the other side of its main bridge stood the fortifications of Margny, an English held bastille.

Jeanne had come up early to survey the new battlefield. Yes, she decided, conditions were just right for one of her classic thrusts – a sudden attack on an unsuspecting garrison with an escape route, a bridge, behind her to retire along if need be into the safety of a friendly town with well-defended gates and walls. To reinforce the defence of the gates, the Maid had stationed an extra force of crossbow men in boats moored below on the river, so any attacking force would be caught in a crossfire. Margny, she thought should fall like all the others.

Jeanne let the first assault. The attack was quickly beaten back. Unbeknown to her, Margny had been reinforced during the night by Bedford and a small force of Burgundy's troops. After a second attack, her men were soon in wild retreat. A sortie by the English caught the rearguard of the fleeing columns. After failing to stop the rush onto the bridge, the Maid turned to fight alongside the rearguard, to give the rest of her men time to get back through the gates. This she succeeded in doing, but as the enemy pressed closer and closer, a panic ensued inside.

'Close the gates!' terrified voices rang out, although the

order had never been given. The huge gates slammed shut. The Maid was left on the far side, battling against the enemy, until she was dragged off her horse by an obscure bowman and forced to yield. The bowman owed allegiance to the Bastard of Vendonne, who, in turn, owed allegiance to the Duke of Burgundy, who owed allegiance to the Duke to Bedford, and Bedford, finally, to the boy King. It was, therefore, a most notable English triumph.

When the news was brought to Bedford, he at once uttered a prayer of thanks. This was a direct judgement of God, who had cut off this limb of Satan. The Maid was now exposed as an ordinary mortal, subject to the usual fortunes of war, like any common soldier. Not only was she shown to be false, so were her miracles, her voices, her butterflies and her doves. They were mere transient tricks of the Fiend. Yes, Bedford thought jubilantly this time, the Lord has rewarded the just. He at once wrote of to the doubtful Burgundy,

Our cause is the just cause. The Maid has been shown to be an impostor. And not only that, isn't the so-called King himself, Charles VII, also shown not only to be an impostor, but a murderer, blackmailer and kidnapper as well.

It turned out to be another mistake. Burgundy circulated the letter around the French court. The insulting words stiffened the resistance, and inclined Burgundy even more to the winning side. Although it was no Agincourt however, the morale of the English enjoyed a rare boost. But many troops disagreed with the perpetual blackening of the Maid's name. Perhaps, after all, she did hold communion with Christ. And she fought as fiercely as any man. She was a worthy opponent.

Negotiations for the full possession of the Maid dragged on for months. All the legal nicities of the allegiances had to be observed. Burgundy eventually accepted the Maid from the Bastard of Vendonne for a cash payment of eight thousand pounds. Now it was a question of persuading Burgundy to sell her to the English, as his feudal superior. With the payment of a further eighty thousand, Bedford finally had her under lock and key.

But other more sinister negotiations had been going on. The Vicar General of the Spanish Inquisition had also been holding his own investigations into this consort of Satan. He wanted her tried immediately on charges of apostasy, heresy, sorcery and witchcraft. The Bishop of Beauvais, a faithful ally of the English, also thirsted for revenge. The Maid had recaptured his Bishopric from the English, and had left him impoverished. He longed for the return of his lost revenues and also thirsted for revenge. Bedford agreed to appoint him Chief Prosecutor. With the Vicar General at his side, they made a deadly pair.

In her first French prisons, the Maid was treated with respect, even veneration, but as she was shuttled from jail to jail, her confinement became more and more brutal. When Bedford, the Inquisition and the good Bishop of Beauvais, finally got their hands on her, matters changed drastically for the worse. She was at once plunged into the deepest cell, her ankles fettered, her hands manacled, and an extra chain wrapped tightly around her body. The ends of the chains were attached to a huge immovable beam. Fear of her possible escape had turned into paranoia. She was lifted into a cage built inside her own small cell, and attached to the bars, with an added chain around her throat. The Maid was in such close and barbarous security, it only emphasised the greatness of the threat she presented. Bedford's biggest coup was proving to be his greatest weakness. But there was a still greater one in store for him – the Maid's ascent to heaven.

The Duke of Bedford, next in line and legal representative of King Henry VI of England, who was now also King Henry II of France, was constrained to sit through the tedious and terrifying months of the trial. With the Maid still suffering the savagery of close imprisonment, the judges finally brought in the verdict. It contained a degree of malignancy which even went far beyond the poor Maid's alleged conspiracy with the devil. The Chief Prosecutor for the Crown leaned forward, pointing at Jeanne in the dock. She stood imperturbable, her appearance very little changed from the moment of her capture, in spite of all the physical and mental torments she had endured. But this, at least, was the prelude to the final torture.

'Jeanne d'Arc, who calls herself "La Pucelle", liar, pernicious deceiver of the people, sorceress, blasphemer of God, presumptuous disbeliever in the faith of Jesus Christ, boastful, idolatrous, cruel, dissolute, invoker of devils, apostate, schismatic and heretic, you are herewith found guilty as accused, and are sentenced to death by burning. You will therefore be taken to the duly appointed place of execution, namely the Market Square of the city of Rouen, on Wednesday the 30th of May, there to suffer the supreme penalty by fire at the stake for your most heinous and manifold sins. Take her down.' Jeanne was just nineteen.

Bedford brought in regiments of extra troops, fearful that Jeanne's many friends and allies might try a last minute rescue attempt. She was hemmed in closer than ever, right up to the moment of her ascent onto the scaffold. The Market Square was packed with troops. Shoulder to shoulder, they lined the walls of the square. Around the scaffold area, they stood in serried ranks, arm in arm. Special flying squads covered every exit and entrance, and the best shots among the bowmen were stationed along the roof tops. All had been issued with an extra battle-axe as well as the usual short sword. Bedford was determined that not even a miracle would save his *bete noire*, the shining Maid.

90

Staring gloatingly out of the windows, in special apartments directly overlooking the scaffold, stood Humphrey, Duke of Gloucester, second in line to the English throne, and his gracious consort, Eleanor, Duchess of Gloucester. They had both come for the burning. The Grand Council had been unable to deny them a place among the exalted witnesses to the event. A balcony gave out from the room, with a sweeping view of the area.

'There be thousands now,' commented Eleanor. 'They still be comin' in.'

'Yes, the stink,' replied Humphrey, holding his nose.

He was still aggrieved over the reception he had received from the troops. Earlier that morning he had marched out onto the balcony to address his faithful 'lads', he had raised his arm and shouted, 'The Iron Fist!' and pointed at the scaffold. An icy silence had greeted his words. Indeed, although he could hardly believe his ears, there were even growls of dissent. What had further enraged him was the shrieks and yells of derision and hostility from the legions of whores. These 'filthy harpies' seemed to have been specially orchestrated for the occasion, throwing up their skirts, and giving the 'V'sign. Some of them had even been plying for trade among the troops. Humphrey had beat a hasty retreat, muttering in disbelief. What was the world coming to? He had not been out on the balcony since.

'She put a curse on 'em,' commented Eleanor.

'Not for long.' Humphrey said, thirsting for revenge.

They looked down at the milling, expectant crowds. There

was an occasional curious hush, as if everyone were expecting something special to happen.

'Wish they'd hurry it up,' said Humphrey. 'I'm getting hungry.'

Humphrey was not alone. The piemen and street vendors were doing brisk business. A good execution sharpened the appetite. Humphrey pointed at them.

'See! All the fun of the fair. These froggies! I tell you, even a good English coronation's wasted on this rabble.'

'Bedford be out of his pea brain. Paris peed on 'im,' said Eleanor causing Humphrey to guffaw.

'And that milksop, forgot his potty. Mama's boy, 'cept he's got no Mama!' They roared with laughter.

The sinister skeleton of the scaffold rose high above the heads of the onlookers. The single massive finger of the stake, cut out of gallows oak, stood up stark and straight, pointing towards the sky. The base beneath, in which the stake rested, was constructed of heat-resistant brick and plaster. Piled high around this, and on the scaffold itself, were tied bundles of thick, dry faggots, drenched in combustible oils and sulphur. Sacks of charcoal were in place to pile onto the faggots once they were truly alight. They would glow to a white heat and incinerate anything within yards.

The Executioner now marched to the scaffold to make his last inspection. Howls of fear and loathing cut the air. The Executioner started. Strange. He wished he'd had his trusty axe. Much more dependable. And the folk in the square. Different. Weird. As for the witch, she'd burn like any common tart. He adjusted the black cloth face mask which covered his entire head. He tested the chains hanging from the stake and inspected the faggots. All was in order. He stood by, torch ready. At the given signal he would light it from the glowing brazier at his side.

'About time!' shouted Humphrey, pointing as the Maid

appeared. 'Like a rat out of a garbage heap!'

The Maid was led out by a whole procession of worthies, a priest walking directly behind her in case she recanted. She was hemmed in by a phalanx of guards as if she was a dangerous murderess.

The Maid appeared calm and controlled, for all her ordeal. Her strong, short, body, moved deliberately and surely as she made her way to her English 'doom', or French 'martyrdom'. Her gaze was fixed on the sky. For a moment, her face was suddenly illumined by a shaft of sunlight. A sigh of awe went up. Many could hardly believe they were really going to burn this innocent, sainted, fearsome virgin. Some of the English soldiers hastily crossed themselves.

'Damn traitors,' said Humphrey. 'I'll have their balls afterwards.'

The Maid was dressed in a snow-white gown which reached to her feet. It showed every line of her short, strong figure. On her head was a tall, conical witch's hat, with words on it.

'What's 'er hat say then?' asked Eleanor.

'It says, "boaster, blasphemer, immoralist, invoker of devils, sorcerer, idolator, apostate, heretic",' said Humphrey with relish. 'What they said in court.'

The Maid had reached the foot of the steps leading up to the scaffold. She looked up at the looming stake painted black for the occasion. One of the English guard reached down, bound two sticks from the faggots together into a rough cross, and handed it to Jeanne. With a murmur of thanks, the Maid clasped it to her heart and mounted the steps. The crowd hushed. Humphrey felt a chill in the room. He shivered and looked over his shoulder. But it was only Eleanor there, smiling thinly, enjoyably.

The Maid now stood with her back to the stake, still holding the cross. In silence, the Executioner now first bound her tight with rope, then with lengths of chain, which would hold her in place after the ropes had burned through. A priest stood close at her side, in case she recanted at the last minute.

'Recant! Recant!' shouted numbers of the spectators.

'Suppose she do?' asked Eleanor.

'After all the trouble she's caused? Never!' said Humphrey, 'Or I'll have her guts for garters!'

The Maid held the cross tightly, still looking up into the sky. She began to pray quietly. The Executioner waited, looking at the Captain of the Guard who was looking at the Duke of Bedford, prominent among the assembled notables. Bedford nodded. The Captain raised his hand. The Executioner dropped his torch onto the brazier. It flamed up. The Executioner moved around the pyre of faggots, lighting them at short intervals so they ignited almost simultaneously. With a sudden 'whoosh' the flames flared up in a widening circle. The Maid was still praying, although she could not be clearly heard. When a moan rose from her, many of the watchers fell to their knees and clasped their own hands in prayer. Although her lips were still moving, only a single distinct word was heard, and that was 'Jesus'! The cracking flames drowned out the rest.

The Maid began coughing, then choking on the greasy pillars of smoke. Her head drooped onto her chest. Around her thighs, the naked flames now flared up in a single searing sheet, and engulfed her upper body. The Maid was now completely shrouded in billowing black smoke, through which the flames gleamed white hot, as her body was consumed.

'There she goes!' shouted Eleanor, caressing him.

'What a relief!' responded Humphrey, pressing her hand to his crotch.

Half the square was now on its knees. Humphrey noted with indignation that many of the English troops were actually weeping. What a nation of milksops! Had England really sunk to this? He'd have a word with the Sergeant-at-Arms afterwards. Meanwhile he grunted in anticipation as Eleanor

370

sank on her knees before him.

Afterwards the troops got drunk with the whores in the inns around the Market Square. The Executioner, still in his mask, second cognac bottle in his hand, was clearing up the Maid's final remains. He was in a state of drunken, superstitious terror, for he had clearly seen in the Maid's last moments, the word *Jesus* appear written in smoke above her; then a dove had descended and hovered over her head. He tried to banish the images with drink, but it was no good. Then, as he scraped through the ashes, he found the innards of the Maid and her heart. He nearly fainted. To his horror, he saw they were fresh, bloodied but intact, not even scorched by the flames. In a fit of terror, he ran and hurled the dreadful things into the waters of the Seine. For the first time in his life he felt terrified of ever doing his filthy job again. He got crazy drunk with the tarts until he collapsed unconscious. When he awoke, he found he could never again mount a scaffold, however much money he was offered.

Her burning was not Jeanne's last miracle on earth, for it was not only her own heart which had survived, but the heart of the whole of France.

91

In the safety of his palace at Rheims, far from the cruel scenes at Rouen, Charles VII sat on the side of his bed in his night-shirt with, the cunning, ruthless La Tremouille. Arms resting on his thighs, he sniffed lugubriously. La Tremouille passed him a kerchief. He took it gratefully and wiped gracefully. La Tremouille smiled her approval. Charles was learning better than she had ever thought. Sometimes he even appeared less than ungainly, manly even. But Charles at the moment was in need of mild reassurance.

'Whatever they say, you did not desert her in her hour of need,' said La Tremouille.

'It wasn't me who handed her over to her enemies.'

'The whole world knows that.'

'She was captured in a fair fight.'

'Before the whole army.'

'All the rules of chivalry were respected.'

'No one can argue with that.'

'Everything was done according to the law.'

'In open court, for all to see. What could be fairer?'

'She could never win back France.'

'Only you can do that.'

'Those miracles, just pretence.' He paused. 'I suppose I could have exchanged her for Talbot.'

'One of France's most fearsome enemies, never!'

'Or Normandy.'

'Normandy is part of your ancient Kingdom.'

'Or demanded a King's ransom.' He giggled.

'Your Exchequer is filling nicely at the moment.'

'Her hat said it all, "apostate, heretic, blasphemer" . . . '

'I'm a woman, she was no saint, I can tell you.'

'No woman is a saint,' declared Charles. La Tremouille remained silent. She knew his hatred for his mother only too well.

'*Limb of the Fiend*. For once the *godons* were right. Now let's have a look at those Exchequer returns.'

'Do we have to, tonight?' she asked, sliding her hand up his night-shirt.

'No,' he gasped, 'we haven't.'

When it came to the bottom line, Charles didn't care if the Maid was dead or alive. All the reassurances he needed in life had been vouchsafed him at last, which left the rest of the world, as well as himself, out on their own. It was the way God intended things to be, so why whine? God's will, as the Maid had learned to her cost, was God's will. Both he and La Tremouille were only too aware of that fact.

With a groan, he fell back onto the bed, his night shirt riding above his belly. On the day of the burning of the Maid, the first of Charles's four climaxes was magnificent. Yes, the saviour of France was solidly back in the saddle. But in the fullness of time, it was the King who died. Jeanne lived on.

92

Also pacing his apartments, not far from those of King Charles's, was the rash and restless Duke of Burgundy, he of the thirty-two mistresses, all still installed in style, and available at any time. But even they proved little comfort in these trying times. Which side was he to jump on? Whose wagon should he ride? How the English hung on! How Bedford always managed to wriggle out of the most devastating losses, and keep the factions down at home, was beyond him. No doubt the French King's star was rising, but so was that of the new English boy-King's. Burgundy was getting increasingly impatient with the territorial claims of the English, especially when they couldn't hang on to those territories themselves. It was a question of revenue, he knew that, but he wasn't going to pay for the English armies. And he was fed up with taking orders. Henry this and Henry that. And their hypocrisy, what with Henry V with his crusade, and the present Henry with his prayers. There was also that stupid prig, the Bishop of Beauvais, burning the Maid while chanting *Te deums*. And what a waste that had been. Properly handled, they could have exchanged half of France for her. The sum he had received was derisory. Should have burned her myself, he thought, to teach them a lesson and kept the money.

Well, Bedford was now making the mistakes, not Charles. Henry's coronation had been disastrous, and he could see that Bedford's personal vendetta against the Maid would also turn out to be costly. Well, if the *godons* were on the way out, he'd better take out some insurance. Yes, Charles had surprised everyone, especially in his choice of commanders. The King had learned to delegate, even to the competent, something he himself had never dared to do. Moreover Charles had very few mistresses, little taste for luxuries, and rarely overspent. These were lasting qualities, not ones that were liable to fade overnight. Bedford was growing weary, and still had a minority with which to deal. That would last too. Yes, further emissaries to the French court, he decided, and more gifts and offerings of good-will were in order. Burgundy knew that the Bishop of Beauvais had informed Bedford of the conciliatory moves he was making to the French court, and that their relations as a result had become 'quite cordial'. But so what? There was now no Henry V to press home the point on the rash Duke, namely that he would be lost without the English alliance. The English might sometimes have to rely on Burgundy for supplies and revenues, but Burgundy had to rely on them for his very existence. Without England, Burgundy would be rapidly out-gunned, out-supplied and out-fought, while the English even if defeated, could retire intact to their sea-locked fortress. The Duke was flirting with the very power which would destroy his little empire in eastern France, that being the French themselves. But Burgundy never sought, nor heeded advice, and he wasn't going to start now. He'd had enough of taking orders.

93

Meanwhile as part of La Tremouille's special celebrations for the continuing victories, Charles granted an audience to the seemingly permanently enraged patriotic poet, Eustace Dechamps. Hopcyn's nickname, King of Warts, had stuck, like the human wen it described. Eustace carried the sobriquet proudly. He enjoyed the idea of having been re-named by a fellow poet.

Charles remembered Eustace, too, as one of the few who had remained faithful to his afflicted father through the grinding, squalid days of poverty. Charles was also aware that Eustace had also stuck to his accursed mother, in more senses than one, but he had long overlooked that strange dalliance. Moreover, Eustace had been one of the few who had invariably stood up to the English in public, and in danger of his life. Eustace had confided in Charles how he and Hopcyn had 'arranged' their drunken eruption into the Treaty Hall of Beaurevoir. Eustace had to tell and re-tell the story, and was often invited to re-give his daring, venomous speech from that day.

But now Eustace was concluding the exhortation he was saving for a later special occasion, the final expulsion of the *godons* from France. His long, hirsute arms flailed, frequently knocking on the floor. His bristling face, half-ape, half-boar, with skin thick as leather, was too ugly not to stand fascinated by it. His hunched back gave him the look of a huge, epileptic tortoise. It was the passion and truth of his words, and the beauty in his eyes, that made people forget the unbeatable ugliness of the man.

'Out! Out! Out! From the Rhone to the Seine, from Calais to Marseilles, our people have been put to the sword, or fled into the hills to live in the caves like wild animals. I myself have seen the fertile fields of La Belle France, from Champagne to Acquitaine, abandoned to scrub and briar, made into deserts, and become the dens of brigands and the vile *Ecorcheurs*. And you, you murderous *godons*, with your greed and your love of violence, the guilt lies entirely with you. You are worse than the plagues of Egypt, more destructive than the barbarous Turk, more bloodthirsty than the heretic Saracen. Now, go, go with your benighted King. Take your ignorance, brutality, and cunning home with you, and continue practising those virtues of yours on your own people, as you have so well begun to do. And at the end, may this new Saxon barbarism sink in the sea of its own self-abasement and gore!'

Wild cheers greeted this garbled piece of poetic blood, thunder and hatred. But it well suited the temper of the times. Eustace was anything but exaggerating.

'Sire, permit me to add that I may have sounded a little desperate when I wrote those words, but that was only because those times had not been put to rights as these days have, by your own wise, courageous and heroic deeds.'

Charles nodded, pleased with the compliment, which he knew perfectly well was half hollow flattery, but half genuine truth as well – in about the right proportion, he thought. Only saints tell the truth, and not even then, often. He bitterly reflected that women were created to be the farthest signposts from truth on earth as was humanly possible.

Eustace wound up.

'I salute you, Sire, the man chosen of God, to lead this Kingdom back to prosperity, freedom and civilisation. It is you, Sire, who with Godfrey of Bouillon, now stands at the head of the Hall of Worthies of France. The Kingdom salutes you.' The entire court rose in acclamation.

Yes, Eustace was better than the Saints any time, thought Charles, and far more entertaining.

But Eustace, former lover and courtier of the Court of Good Shepherds, was a master of half truths, a professional survivor who knew exactly when a lie could serve as a truth, and a truth as a lie. The trick was in the timing, when to use it, and just as importantly, when not. But in his heart of hearts, he grieved for the person he knew was the real redeemer of France, the blessed Jeanne, the warrior-virgin-saint, the Maid of Orleans. It was she who should not only be sitting on the throne of France, Eustace knew, but enshrined with the saints and heroes in Notre Dame.

Charles rewarded Eustace with golden louis, and again confirmed him in the offices granted by his father. The King had the ballades and exhortations printed and circulated. Soon they were being shouted from the rooftops by all the town criers of France. But in the quiet of his own home, Eustace prayed and wept for the true saviour, Jeanne d'Arc, the Maid of Orleans.

94

The effects of the burning of the Maid, the good will overtures of Burgundy, the continuing string of French victories, spelled the beginning of the end of English rule in France. Burgundy had come out publicly against the Treaty of Troyes, but had not yet torn it up. His jurists and theologians were finding nit-picking holes in the original articles, enabling Burgundy to plead that the whole treaty lacked all legal basis in the first instance. Burgundy now made a positive proposal of peace to the French King. He agreed to a meeting of conciliation with Charles at the town of Arras, and did not even bother to inform his oldest, and most faithful ally, the Duke of Bedford.

Bedford, meanwhile had returned from Paris. He had contracted a debilitating fever in the capital, where typhoid, cholera and dysentery had broken out. He was failing as rapidly as his brother had done after Corbeil. The indomitable Bedford fought for his life in the apartments of the Joyeuse Repos, trying to shore up the ruins of his royal house's English twenty-year rule in France. He lay in bed, head propped up on pillows, shivering, straining and aching in every bone, the fever raging. His beak of a nose protruded from a face as narrow and emaciated as a bird's. His stools had turned white. His body weight fell dramatically. He soon recognised the symptoms which Henry, his brother, had suffered.

Wise to the last, he called in his secretaries. Things would have to be tidied up before the end. His personal physician confirmed Bedford's own diagnosis. There was nothing to be done. They all grouped around the bed, ready to carry out their master's last orders. Bedford ordered his personal chaplain to arrange masses for his soul, just as his brother had done.

'Any further news from Burgundy?' he still spoke distinctly.

'Nothing, my Lord.'

'Does he understand our alliance is the key to his survival?'

'I used all your brother's arguments, my Lord, and added yours.'

'To no avail?'

'He lost his temper, my Lord, said it was the last time he'd ever even take the trouble to ignore orders from the English.'

'He may be right there. Anything else?' The secretary paused before answering,

'He declared the treaty null and void, lacking all legal foundation.'

'Did he officially announce his withdrawal from the treaty?'

'No, my Lord.'

'One more try then. Tell him that I, or my representatives, are perfectly prepared to concede territories, even Normandy itself. But I hold to the original articles of the treaty, and the King still holds to his French titles, as sole rightful heir, as declared by Queen Isabelle in St Michel Cathedral. I pledged my word of honour to my brother to uphold the articles from that moment, to my death, and I do so now.' He was momentarily wracked with pain. 'But leave the way open for negotiations on all other matters, however difficult. If these most constructive overtures are rejected, then we can see no other alternative but not to send any further delegates. Be sure to use the most courteous French. See that a copy is leaked to King Charles.'

The secretary nodded. He could hardly believe the great, undefeated Duke was dying before his very eyes.

'Now, as to my burial, I do not want to follow my brother in this. That is, I do not want to have my bones boiled and sent home.' He smiled faintly. 'It has always pained me that we had to fight against such a great and civilised country as France. I have loved my time here, and found it a privilege to be among such a learned race, however hard we fought against each other. To show my enduring respect, I direct that my body stay in France, to rest here in the Cathedral of Rouen . . . ' His voice faded. His whole being seemed to sink in upon itself. The chaplain leaned over, and listened at his lips. He straightened up.

'What did he say?

'*Vive le roi.*'

'Which one?' No one ever quite discovered.

The nobility of Paris were moved to compose an epitaph on their great governor's death.

'Noble in birth and worth, wise, liberal and beloved, we say farewell to a most respected and admired lover of France.'

At the court of King Charles, the pugnacious Eustace called for the destruction of the tomb and the removal of its occupant. For once, Charles demurred.

'The Duke was the only man I know among our enemies who cared one jot for our country. He is also one of the very few men I know who kept his word to the death. Would that I had more men like that about me. I count it an honour to have him rest in French soil. His tomb stays where it is.'

95

The boy King, sixth in the line of Henrys, the second of France, was reading a communication from the Duke of Burgundy. It was written in learned, legalistic Latin.

'Look,' pointed Henry, 'Burgundy no longer calls me his *sovereign*. What has gone wrong?'

Henry was sitting in the high chair in the White Hall, in conference with his leading councillors, the Earl of Worcester, Archbishop Chichele and Cardinal Winchester. He had wept bitter tears when he had learned of the death of his favourite uncle, 'Johnny', the one he most trusted and would have wanted as a father. He ordered all the bells of all the churches on Bedford's estates, and his own, to be tolled every day for three months, and paid for one year's worth of monthly masses for his soul. The King's Councillors, for once, gave their complete approval. They, too, grieved the loss of a great companion and wise adviser. At least the King's extreme grief was a true echo of what they all genuinely felt.

Henry's temperament was causing concern. There were the outbursts of tears and long introverted silences but, worst of all, the sudden slides into endless prayer. This meant that no business of state was conducted for dangerously long periods. Yet there wasn't a vicious bone in the boy's body. He looked on everybody with a sort of universal benignity, as if he was already an enshrined saint. No one doubted his extraordinary intelligence, yet they were alarmed at his obsession with unnecessary detail and his inability to see to the root of a problem. He would weep over the loss of a favourite pet, but would greet the loss of a city like Paris with a faint smile of bewilderment. In one of these moods, when pressed to get down to daily business, he would say,

'Why try to order that which God has already ordained?' and slip to his knees and pray.

'Yes,' said the Cardinal to Warwick before the session had started, 'he's more a monk than a monarch. He prefers translating the gospels to translating events.'

And today they had very pressing business indeed. Henry looked over the maps spread out on the table, and traced his finger over the lines of lost roads, towns and cities. Not only were strings of towns around Paris itself and the Loire now committed to the French camp, that very morning much more dangerous setbacks were reported.

'Look,' he said tearfully, 'Harfleur and Dieppe gone today. A tragedy.' It was worse than a tragedy, it was a military disaster. These were the ports of entry for supplies and reinforcements. The English armies were now in very real danger of having their lines of communication cut, and then of being chopped up in small pockets. Warwick, Chichele and Winchester had adopted Bedford's policy. They offered to send a full peace delegation to Arras and suggested, as had Bedford, the possibility of surrendering the rest of Normandy in return for the re-affirmation of the Treaty of Troyes. But they all knew that at best this was salvage operation. The end of their power in France was near.

'We must keep our Empire. After all I was crowned there. By God's right. We promised, like uncle Bedford. Why can't we keep united?' Winchester and Warwick exchanged uneasy glances.

'It's the Yorkists, isn't it?' he said abruptly. Yes, thought Chichele, he had spotted the basic English weakness.

'Our reinforcements fight in the streets, don't they, instead of fighting over there.'

'True, Sire, but we have laws to deal with that.'

'The ordinances are inoperative,' he declared, using the long latinate words he sometimes favoured.

'But what to do about it?' asked Warwick.

Henry had correctly diagnosed the problem but then promptly backed away from it. At least, he's not praying, thought Chichele, near despair.

'Where is my mother?'

The three knew that Humphrey had been blocking the correspondence between Henry and his mother. At least they had been able to put a stop to that.

'It's my uncle, Humphrey, isn't it?' he said, as if reading their minds. 'His striking talons, the whites and the reds. My uncle regards the Yorkists as more dangerous than the French, doesn't he?'

That is the nub of the problem; now do something about it, thought Warwick. But Henry moved off on another tack.

'I want to see my mother.'

'She is perfectly happy at Baynard's,' said Warwick.

'Uncle Humphrey keeps us apart, doesn't he?'

'Humphrey does his duty as he sees fit,' said Winchester.

'Well, it's not as I see fit.' They waited for a definite order against Humphrey, but none came.

'Why doesn't she come to see me?'

'Sire, your gracious mother is also the sister of the King who has recently robbed us of many of our rightful possessions in France. With this anti-French feeling around, it might be dangerous for her to travel.'

Henry could easily have ordered five regiments to escort her to Westminster, but he merely commented,

'I suppose she'd better stay there then. But I do not ever want to see my uncle Humphrey here in court, ever.'

'Sire,' pointed out Warwick, 'he is still Protector of the Realm.'

'What he is after our dear uncle's death, is next in line, isn't it. That's why he watches me and mother like a hawk.'

Warwick took the nettle in both hands.

'Then, Sire, order his house arrest.' Henry didn't even hear. He slipped to his knees, saying,

'Well, I'm not even going to pray for him.'

This evidently was the limit to poor little Henry's line of action. The jumbled prayers tumbled from his lips out of control. The Councillors sank to their knees. The paralysis was complete. Warwick glanced at the mass of unopened documents on the table, as chaotically scattered about as the conditions they attempted to describe. And none but Henry prayed so hard and so fruitlessly, for the peace to end it all.

96

Humphrey had placed Captain Dark and his guards at the door of the Long Room in the Palace of Placentia. He had ordered bonfires lit in the grounds and laid on free beer and entertainments.

But Humphrey and Eleanor intended to celebrate this death in private. Remnants of a banquet were scattered over the table and floors, fragments of food and countless empty bottles. A hundred candles and torches burned in the wall sockets. A roaring fire blazed in the hearth. The walls were covered with new tapestries that were not meant for the public eye. They included splendid images with the crest of the talon, but this time with the French King in its grip, better than any of Humphrey's old subtleties. Somewhat prematurely, the talon was surmounted with a royal crown

The Palace of the Caesars stood centre stage. The niches for Humphrey and Eleanor were now occupied with plaster statues of themselves, Humphrey holding his baton, in pose imperial.

The line of wax heads were on display on the table, the boy King's head scored with countless new jabs. The heads were subject to streams of abuse and spittle. Humphrey and Eleanor danced in a frenzy around them, spitting and shrieking, holding sloshing glasses of wine. They were both quite naked. The flames threw their demented shadows onto the red talons of the walls. Again they sank back onto their thrones on the dais.

'We done it, lovely.'

'And John got buried over there . . . '

' . . . like the devil Maid.'

' . . . traitors to the end!'

'And thee!' Eleanor rose and plunged a needle into the boy King's head. 'Thy days be numbered!'

'For St George and the Iron fist!' Humphrey roared, and gave a ferocious 'V' sign at the heads.

Eleanor glared at the head of the boy King.

'*Maleficium* on ye!' she spat.

'The great whore of Baynard's . . . '

'Milksop!'

'Expose her!'

'Yes! Send the saint into a decline!'

'Give him a heart attack!'

'Lovely, my lovely!'

They danced and shrieked again around the heads. From outside rose a bellowing chorus of,

'Humphrey for king! Humphrey for king!' It was Captain Dark's nightly claque for Humphrey. Humphrey grabbed his baton, bandy-legged, pot-bellied, bald as a coot, the English hero posed like a Roman, and emptied a bottle of wine on his head so it ran down his body to the floor mingling with the vomit there, forming a stinking pool for him to stand in - the once and future king. Eleanor circled him skreeching her incomprehensibly tuneless version of whatever it was she sang, and then grabbed him and dragged him to the floor. There, they fell on each other's genitalia, slobbering, sucking, gobbling like two foul porkers in a manure heap. The falcon had truly landed.

97

Without the firm, fair and guiding hand of Bedford, matters in Paris rapidly got out of control. After the frightful winter, the famine and the disease, the revived French monarchy and its fresh victories, which had been blessed rather than cursed by the Maid's hideous end, and the continuing mass English desertions, the new Governor of Paris, again the reliable and seasoned campaigner Lord Charles Willoughby, could do little with the slender resources he had to hand. Willoughby had quickly replaced the doubtful Burgundian commanders with loyal English officers, sharpened up discipline, and scoured the provinces for replacements, but it was all too little too late.

The victorious Bastard of Orleans at once recognised the feebleness of the English resistance and, following a rapid march, set siege to Paris. The English garrison was strung out, the walls thinly defended. The Bastard quickly penetrated the gaps and soon gained a foothold inside the gates. He now advanced street by street, aiming at the heart of the city itself, the Cathedral of Notre Dame. The English retreated before him, trying to find a way out, but the city had become an armed camp. Every house was against them, miniature bastilles, barricaded, shuttered and dangerous. The English bowmen and Men-at-Arms tried to hold the streets, but were fired on from all sides, and from the rooftops. The barred doors prevented them from clearing out the enemy. They took to shooting indiscriminately through the window slits and shutters, causing innocent casualties among the children and the old, which only reinforced the determination of the remaining defenders to fight on. The citizenry organised into armed groups and, in concert with Dunois, began cutting off the streets with heavy chains and impromptu barricades, bottling up the English troops, now helpless without an overall command. The small remaining garrison of Burgundians studiously turned their backs on the battle.

Lord Willoughby recognised that the situation was untenable. He sued Dunois for a cessation of hostilities. The honourable Bastard was surprisingly generous in his terms. Willoughby was to surrender unconditionally, but his army was permitted to retain its arms, keep its remaining cavalry intact, and take the last of its supply wagons with it. Lord Willoughby accepted with alacrity. He had expected a massacre, something he had engaged in himself on more than one occasion. But the canny Dunois knew the only way to get the *godons* out post haste and once and for all, was to allow them the means to do so. They would need food, horses and wagons. The sooner they reached the channel ports the better, and the fewer the French losses – and any loss was now superfluous anyway, for the English were out for good. Slowly, sullenly and suspiciously, the last English troops marched out under the gates of St Denis where they had entered so triumphantly nearly fifteen years before. Above the gates this time fluttered a solitary flag. It bore the royal arms of France.

The delirious Parisians lined the route. Eustace turned out his whores in battalion strength. These patriotic harpies shrieked at their former clients, now transformed into devils, giving the hated 'V' sign, which the bowmen of England wished had never been invented. Eustace clambered onto the roof tops and ran along them like a gorilla possessed, a bag of garbage in one hand. He pelted the dispirited troops with their own leftovers. At the gates, he emptied the last of his garbage, and then the last of his bladder onto the departing heads below. As the last of the English disappeared into the distance, Eustace recited the whole of his special exhortation. The cheering, yelling mob took up the chorus, 'Go! Go! Go!'

That night, the citizens of Paris did not even bother to lock the Gates, they knew the English would not be back, ever! England was done with *pacification* on French soil.

98

In the neglected Court of Good Shepherds, not far from the bonfires of the celebrating, liberated city of Paris, Isabelle lay dying. Her strong body was swollen and misshapen from the ravages of dropsy. The sole companion of her last hours on earth, with whom Isabelle had never had sex, was the renegade eunuch of the Papal castrati choir, her faithful Monk, the Abbot of Fleury. Her ever respectful ally and friend of the English, he had set up her bed in one of the small alcoves.

Her bedside table was littered with quills, ink, sealing wax, sealed packets of letters and small silk bags of golden louis and nobles. Uneaten eclairs and stale pots of beer stood by untasted. At the foot of the bed, was a shrouded statue, the Monk's last surprise.

Isabelle awoke and groaned. She was perfectly aware of her approaching end, but her mind was as clear as her best Bavarian brew. She smiled at the Monk, crouching by her bedside wringing his hands. She laughed softly. The Monk perked up. He loved Isabelle's quips and death-bed jokes.

'Fancy the great whore ending her days in the arms of a eunuch!'

The Monk doubled up in hoarse giggles.

'Never die for balls,' she added, 'especially tennis balls.'

Yes, it was mad, lovely.

'And my Katty makes me a grandma. Even better.' The Monk nodded ecstatically. Isabelle continued. 'Yes, I didn't let her down, and she, not me either. Owen, the only envy I have of her, bless her! To business, my crunchy little beetle. The letter to my grandson, Henry . . . write, on the outside, "A grandmother sends her loyal and most tender greetings. To my merciful and most benign grandson, Henry, King of France and England" . . .'

' . . . that should please him!'

'Now, "For his Majesty's eyes only".' The Monk scribbled away.

'Put it with the rest.' She paused. 'My budless little blossom, what is dying all about.' The Monk shook his head expectantly.

'Dying is life crying, "Business as usual"!'

The Monk whimpered with pleasure.

'Yes, we all come in through the same hole, and we all go out through the same, as well.' The Monk lowered his head and sobbed fearfully.

'What are you afraid of? Come on, you can tell your great little whore here.'

The Monk whispered his secret fear.

'What? The dead stink! Is that all? Well, no more than the living, my little worm!' The Monk chuckled, reassured. Time to unveil his last surprise.

He whipped the sheet off the statue. It was the discus player, with impressive erection intact. The Monk had uncovered it in the weeds and nettles outside the kitchen door.

'Ah!' gasped Isabelle. 'For a second, I thought I was in paradise!'

The Monk covered her hand with kisses.

'My thanks. Such funs, my little one.' She paused. The Monk waited. 'Tell me, why did god create man?' The Monk shook his head.

'It wasn't God – he'd gone for a piss. It was the cook.' Again the Monk shook with delight. Isabelle was surely right. No God could have created the dreadful beast, man, but a cook might have managed it – just!

She clutched her crook and drew the Monk towards her, crooning,

'Chick, chick, come to mother.' She embraced him and kissed him full on the lips. His head fell on her breast and he wept. She raised him up, comfortingly.

'Now, listen, my chick. As I said, no mourners. And remember to tip the gravedigger.' The Monk nodded dumbly. He was the gravedigger. Isabelle suddenly sat bolt upright and licked her lips.

'Eclairs!' she said. Her wide eyes locked on the phallus of the discus player. She smiled her old smile, then fell back onto the cushions, dead. The Monk sobbed. His heart was breaking. The true love of his life, never mind the lack of balls. He desperately searched for a prayer for the terrible occasion, but all he could come up with was,

'*Merde! Merde! Merde!*'

Still sobbing, the Monk trundled the late Queen of France and great Princess of the Wittelsbachs, in a wheel-barrow to her selected last resting place, her favourite bower, where the innocent violets blew. A freshly dug grave awaited them. The Monk buried her still in her night-gown, with utter tenderness, watering the soil with his tears. When he had finished, in a final salute of love, he stuck her crook over the grave. In time, it too fell down and rotted back into the earth, leaving no sign that a Queen had ever been there. But in the spring, Isabelle wore a crown more glorious than any in life, a circlet of brilliant, eternal violets.

99

It was close to midnight. The moon shone directly overhead. The clouds hung low, grey and black. Owen and the Demoiselles stood at the foot of Catherine's bed. Catherine was sleeping peacefully. Midwife Megan had administered a tincture of laudanum. Catherine's face was serene and composed, although sweat stains covered the pillow. Catherine had been in labour pains for two days. The contractions had come at perfectly regular intervals at first, as had happened with both Jasper and Edmund. But the baby refused to budge. Megan was getting increasingly worried. She had called for Surgeon Samuel, to have a second opinion.

Shouts of laughter came from the nursery nearby.

'No, I won! I killed you!'

'No, you didn't. You're dead!'

'Joanna, Joséphine, go and tell them to be quiet, will you?' said Agnes quietly. The Ladies hurried out. Agnes watched the calm face of the sleeping Catherine. How she had strained and struggled.

Footsteps clattered on the turret steps. Surgeon Samuel came in directly from the courtyard. He had also witnessed the previous two births, but at both those times, Megan and the Ladies had managed perfectly well without his services. There had been nothing then which had indicated that the next birth would be a difficult one.

Megan gave him an outline of the problem. They exchanged worried glances. Samuel proceeded with his examination. He straightened up. What Megan had suspected, they both now knew was fact.

'The baby is facing the wrong way,' he said.

'Is she going to be alright?' asked Owen, biting his lip.

'She's fighting hard and that's the first thing,' said Samuel.

'She has a very strong will to live,' added Megan.

'Is she strong enough to travel?'

'She could be moved, yes, but only in the next few hours, and only on a litter.'

'So we couldn't go to Pembroke as planned?'

'We've got about two days before the real crisis.'

'Couldn't you, well, help the baby to move?'

'Yes, but the baby could be . . . damaged.'

'But would it be alright for Catherine?'

'She might be hurt too.'

'What is your advice, Samuel?'

'Let her sleep.'

'Yes, sleep and rest can work wonders,' said Megan.

'She'll have another struggle soon, the baby might come of its own accord, I've seen it before.'

'So, all we can do is pray.'

'As long as she can sleep, there's still a chance.'

'I'd like to be alone with her for a moment,' said Owen. Adéle, Megan, Samuel and Agnes quietly left.

Owen looked down with sinking heart at the person he loved most in the world. He could not lose her now. He was fighting to keep up his hopes. But the hopes would slip down into the depths, and then rise and fall with Catherine until he felt ill and giddy. Megan and Samuel had given some comfort. Catherine could not get better care, and she was surrounded by friends who were willing her to win the desperate struggle. He stroked her cheeks, so radiant, even in such pain. Sensing he was there, she slowly opened her eyes.

'Owen, lovely man,' she whispered.

'I'll always be here, my love.'

'I just saw my mother.' She smiled. 'Laughing.'

'Such funs.'

'Such life. Owen, we've been blessed. Jasper, Edmund.'

'No problem before. Why now? Why?'

She reached up and stroked his hair.

'When I think of us, our family, the pain's bearable.'

'Our lilac days.' He cradled her in his arms.

'Lovely man,' she murmured again, and slipped off into sleep again. Owen gently laid her back onto the pillows, his whole being bursting with the grief of what might happen. Therre was a cruelly cutting flint lodged in his heart. But she was sleeping again. Surely if she could sleep so deeply, and appear so lovely, she had to get better, she had to live.

The outside world was beginning to crowd in on Baynard's. Catherine mourned her favourite brother-in-law. He had been like a rock, both in England and France, errors notwithstanding. She had blessed him many times for preparing this home for her.

In the streets of even the smallest village, the reds and the whites were again marauding in ever increasing numbers. Humphrey was flexing his muscles. He constantly tried to diminish the influence and authority of Warwick and Winchester on the Council. He was blocked at every turn. But his mindless persistence was wearing everyone down. Humphrey switched his bullying tactics to Baynard's, threatening audits and military inspections. He also began stirring up anti-French feeling in the area, so people became more aware of the enemy in their midst, however reclusive.

The boy King was also becoming insistent. Why had his mother not visited him? Were his messages getting through? He wanted her presence in court. He had no other close family, he complained. To jog her memory, he sent her a delightful little bejewelled crucifix.

The Countess of Warwick, too had pressing questions about

Henry's education, future development and supervision. Her brother Charles VII in Paris also sent invitations to visit his reinvigorated court in the triumphant capital.

Catherine's suitors were becoming more importunate. The removal of her dear brother-in-law had thrown her into much greater prominence. She would be a great catch for either the reds or the whites. Her Yorkist admirers, Somerset and Suffolk, sent emissaries more frequently. A Yorkist marriage would knock the Lancastrian ambitions of Humphrey on the head. Catherine could well be the key in the hotting up dynastic dispute. Roger Mortimer, the young Earl of March, was growing fast, and was now old enough to press his own claims. A grandson by an elder brother of the old King, his legal closeness to the throne could not be denied. In two months, traffic had tripled at Baynard's, so had the rumours, alarms and speculations. The old disguise was wearing dangerously thin.

Agnes took the children upstairs to say goodbye to their mother. Damascus and Hopcyn sat at the high table in the hall in their travelling clothes. Captains of the Guard, Huw, Idris and Ifan were present, fully armed in every day clothes, without a crest. They were grouped around a map of London. It showed the City and the surrounding area to the west, outside the walls. Hopcyn was passing on Owen's last orders. An air of finality hung over every action. Just after night had fallen, Humphrey, with a heavy guard, had been spotted pushing off in his barge from the Palace of Placentia. He was making rapid progress towards Baynard's, with oars muffled. This present alert seemed somehow terminal. Everyone felt it. The only person who refused to accept that Baynard's was in final crisis was Owen himself, upstairs with the sick Catherine.

Hopcyn traced the route on the map.

'Here are we. There, the road north to Hendale Cross, there. Now, first safe house, in the Market Square, there, the Queen's Head. From there going west, you come to the river Lugg, right across our path. Once over the river, the route home to the west, is wide open. Right?' It dawned on them all. They really were going home. The great adventure was over at last.

'A hundred hiding places in Pembroke, of course, for the boys, and . . . for . . . ' he paused, ' . . . Yes . . . but the danger spot, here.' His finger stabbed on the map. 'Hendale Cross. 'Now you, my three Captains, will leave in small groups, let your weapons be seen, it's like an armed camp out there, but no crests. Re-group before the town, then straight through to the west road. At the river Lugg, here, rising up the slope here, is a wood, Winwood. That is our rendezvous. Clear.' They nodded and he went on. 'The order of march home to Wales is Dragon Company One, Two, etc. Again in small groups. Squads of five. As soon as you arrive at Winwood, the rest of you set up camp lines, but be ready for a rapid move out. Now, drawn up your week's rations? Good. We haven't got enough mounts, so you'll have to double up. But there should be enough time. After Owen's broken out, for all our foot soldiers to reach the wood. Clear? Ifan, you wait for the boys, they'll be down in a minute. They'll double up with you and Damascus. Good luck, may Gwydion go with you.'

They embraced. The Captains hurried out. A few moments later, the sound of hoofbeats told Hopcyn that Dragons One and Two had left. The first part of the plan was in operation.

Hopcyn hadn't mentioned Catherine. And no one had asked. Everyone knew that Catherine wouldn't be able to travel with them. They knew Owen was making his last agonising decision. They would be ready to follow him at a moment's notice, whatever that decision was.

'Everything looks ready for a mighty old fight,' said Damascus. 'Humphrey will surely offer a reward. There'll be bounty hunters, too, the wolves!'

'They'll have the hardest fight of their lives, against Owen,' said Hopcyn. 'And don't forget, we'll be there too.'

'The happiest years of my old life are unravelling,' said Damascus, his genial nature for once cast down. 'That's life – and it's too bad,' he added with a despairing look upstairs.

'Damn!' exclaimed Hopcyn, at last stating the unstated. 'Suppose Catherine really can't go with us. Whole plan's based around her.' But in his vision of visions, he knew the truth.

Sounds of stamping horse and jingling harnesses came from outside. Captain Ifan ran in.

'The falcon has landed, ten minutes at most. The boys. Now!' He ran out.

Jasper and Edmund sat on their mother's sick bed, cuddling up on either side of her. Owen sat with them, holding her hand, unable to take his eyes off Catherine's face.

Agnes stood at the foot of the bed. What a lovely little family, she thought, each special in their own way, each as loving as the next. Agnes heard Ifan's warning voice from downstairs.

'Please,' she begged, 'the boys must leave now.'

The boys gazed questioningly at their father. Owen looked stricken.

'Boys,' said Catherine playfully, 'your holidays, don't forget!'

The boys jumped up and down in excitement.

'To the seaside,' they sang in unison.

'Now give us a last kiss, then you go off with Agnes.'

'But what about you?' asked Jasper, faintly alarmed.

'I'll be staying on here for a while.'

'But why?'

'Well, who's going to prepare supper?'

They nodded. Of course. They understood. Catherine threw back the covers, and sat on the edge of the bed.

'You see,' she said, 'I'll be getting up now. A hug.' She hugged them so hard, they gasped, then laughed. All part of the holiday, no doubt.

'Now off you go.' In a daze, Owen kissed and embraced them. Agnes took their proffered hands.

'And don't forget, do what your father tells you to do.'

'Yes, yes . . . '

'Promise.'

'Promise!' rang out, again in unison.

Downstairs, Agnes handed the boys over to Damascus. No one dared mention Catherine.

'By the seaside!' the boys sang again.

'Come on, boys,' said Damascus, 'forget that silly old carriage. You are going mounted up behind me and Captain Ifan. Come on!' His eyes twinkled.

The boys shrieked with delight and Catherine, hearing the laughter, swayed. Owen tried to help her back into bed.

'No, no, got to get up now.'

'You are coming with us.'

'Owen my, darling, we all know I am going nowhere.'

'I am not leaving without you!'

'You are, my love.'

'You can't face this alone.'

'I have got to, and so have you.'

'Humphrey is on his way here.'

'I am still the King's mother.'

'Hurry, Owen!' Hopcyn's urgent voice came from the stairs.

'Owen, my love, our love will live, our family will live, as long as the boys are safe.'

'I should be here with you.'

'Your destiny, Owen, our name, the Tudors.'

'My destiny is here with you.'

'Let our family live.'

'You are so beautiful, my affection cup.'

'Leather lamb. Do this for me!'

Agnes burst in with Adéle, Joséphine and Joanna.

'You must go now. For the boys, for our love. Go, my love!

400

Owen! Take him, Agnes!'

Owen allowed himself to be half dragged outside, his gaze never moving from his beloved's face. When the door closed, it was like a black curtain being pulled down over his heart. He tried to turn back, but Agnes pushed him downwards. Shouts of alarm and horses neighing came from the yard. The portcullis was being drawn up. The enemy was at the very gates.

Catherine stood up. She saw the tears in the eyes of her faithful Demoiselles.

'Now, I must do my part to keep what Owen and I have made. Help me to dress. The court gown, please.'

As Humphrey and his Retainers clattered into the yard, the hoofs of Owen's troop of horse were fading in the distance.

Humphrey jumped down from his horse. He looked around.

'Where's everybody?' he growled, prowling around. 'Place is deserted.'

He ordered his men to search the stables, battlements and guard room. Empty. He made for the great hall. What in the hell was going on? He burst in through the door and strode into the hall, glaring wildly. He came to an abrupt halt.

At the high table, lit by a single candelabra, sat the Dowager Queen, in her most elaborate court gown, a silver coronet on her head. She seemed to radiate an unearthly, self-possessed beauty. Her three Demoiselles stood in attendance behind her, as if at a formal audience. Joanna spoke.

'Her Majesty, you're Grace, is ready to receive you. You may approach.'

Humphrey slowed to a halt. Who did these haughty whores think they were? Yet he bowed, in spite of himself. Catherine's shining presence seemed to demand it.

'Her Majesty would like to know,' continued Joanna, 'on what authority you enter these premises in this most discourteous way?'

401

'On the King's authority,' Humphrey answered. Why did he feel so unsure of himself? Joanna consulted Catherine again.

'Her Majesty wishes to remind you that you are talking about her son, and in the last communication she received from his gracious Majesty, he did not mention your name or that you had been granted free access to her private quarters, or do you venture in uninvited?'

Were they trying to set him up?

'No, no. King's business,' he blurted.

'And her Majesty wishes to remind you that you must come uncovered in the presence of royalty.' She motioned to Humphrey's cap. Again, he hastily took it off.

Catherine calculated that Owen and her sons were now well clear of Baynard's.

'Where is your guard?' demanded Humphrey.

'On manoeuvres,' replied Adéle.

'At this time of night?'

'Of course.' He stared hard at her. Were they mocking him?

'And the rest of your staff?'

'On leave,' said Joséphine.

Captain Dark entered and whispered to Humphrey.

'What!?' he exclaimed. Captain Dark left. Humphrey turned with a malicious smile.

'Your Majesty, my troops have taken over guard duties. Your own have deserted you. I will have the lot of them arrested, don't you worry.'

'On what grounds?' asked Adéle innocently.

'Desertion.'

'But her Majesty dismissed them.'

'On . . . my charges, then, if need be. Whatever.' He could smell a rat, however self-assured these stupid, lying women were. He swaggered closer demanding, 'Where's Twang-wang and old Clothes Peg.'

'Your insolence passes all bounds!' Catherine's icy voice

held a fury that made him quail.

'And you will regret it sooner than you think,' added Joséphine.

What was that supposed to mean, he wondered. He frowned. What was happening?

He waved his baton at Catherine.

'I am Lord Protector. I still have my staff of office.'

'You are in danger of losing both,' she replied. He stirred uneasily.

'I'll get to the bottom of this.'

'So will the King.'

Were they actually trying to browbeat him?

'Where's Lady Agnes and her bastards?'

'They are not bastards, your Grace,' said Catherine calmly. 'I suggest you visit Lambeth Palace, Archbishop Chichele has matters of grave importance to convey to you.'

'Chichele?' he queried. Catherine got to her feet, so Humphrey could see the advanced state of her pregnancy.

Humphrey gaped, his mind in an instant turmoil. He pointed speechlessly at her belly. The French whore! Pregnant!

'But . . .'

'No "buts" about it, your Grace,' said Joanna.

'Treason!' he gasped out.

'The nursery here is full,' added Adéle.

Suddenly it hit him between the eyes. Bastards! Who was first in line?

'Conspiracy!' he shouted, with a thrill of fear. 'Baynard's is now under my command. No one moves without the Council's permission. My Guard will keep out all unauthorised persons! Captain Dark!' He rushed out, scarcely able to drag his eyes off Catherine. No, no, he thought. Pregnant!? Some scullion. Next in line? No, no! Bastards. No marriage. Banned. Illegal. Against the law. All wrong. He'd arrest the Archbishop as well, if need be. As he galloped out of the archway, he, too, felt the world was somehow closing in on him, but with hidden daggers in the shadows. And for once, he was right. He swore out loud that he'd take care of the lot of them!

100

Eleanor helped Humphrey up off the floor of the Long Room, purple and panting. His world was falling about his ears. His previous triumphs had faded into nothingness. He was exhausted. The pains in his chest were excruciating. Eleanor's efforts to calm him had been of no avail, his rage had wracked him. She knew everything depended on what action they now took. The table and floor was scattered with hastily opened documents, certificates, maps and fragments of broken seal.

'The Tudor. Father-in-law to the King! Yaaaaa!'

'Now get a hold of thyself. Thy power is still great.'

'Yes!' The thought stopped him momentarily. 'It is. They'll see.'

'Now, think. How can the marriage be legal?'

'Look at the date, woman! By two days, two shitty days.'

'Dang, ye should have passed the law when I said.'

'You and your damn witch, lot of good . . . '

' . . . it bain't over yet.'

'Not good enough! Bloody Winchester. Archbishop's lapdog. "Father-in-law to the King!" Warwick's words. Bastards! Prove it. I am next in line! Yorkist King. French take-over. Plots. To murder the King. Murder me. Kill Tudor's bastards before it's too late. Not a priest. False witnesses. Archbishop devil. Of course it can be faulted! I fault it!' He scrabbled on his hands and knees again among the documents, tearing them to pieces, grunting, spitting, gnashing his teeth.

Eleanor managed to drag him upright once more. She thrust him onto the throne and dashed a jug of water into his face. The shock of the water restored a vestige of self-control.

'Calmly, my lovely.'

'Alright! But don't talk to me like that!'

'Think slow, think deadly,' she cooed as she wiped his face. She gave him his baton. He clutched it like a drowning man.

'Somewhere in there, ye still be next in line, I swear.'

'Why are they doing this to me? Is God testing me?' He snatched up Eleanor's hand-mirror and gazed into it.

'Look in there,' he said, pointing at his image in the mirror. 'What do you see?'

'The brows of a king?'

'I know that. Look again.'

'The very top of majesty.'

'Yes, yes, woman. The lines, the lines.'

'Thy worry lines, is it?'

'At bloody last, yes, the worry lines, for my people, my England. And look.' He lifted his wig and showed the greying tufts above his ears. 'Found 'em this morning. Growing old in the service of my people. And they do this to me. By St George, has my own country let me down?' He burst into tears of self pity, and slipped to his knees.

This will not do, decided Eleanor, get the fool off the floor and moving again, or the crown is lost. She grabbed him by the collar and shoved him back onto the throne. Before he could object, she seized the great seal and shook it under his nose.

'Ye still have this.'

'They want it back.'

'Ye got to take thy chances.'

'I know that. What to do?'

'Caesar burned his boats and thou still be that Caesar!'

'I'll crucify them!'

'That be the spirit. Now, slow. Think o' the Tudor. Now, raise thy ire. Slow. Now hold it!'

Humphrey gritted his teeth.

'That be it! This time, think! What do ye see?'

A look of bestial spite came over Humphrey's face. His eyes fixed on the bloody image of his own revenge.

'Ye witches and demons, give me an oak, a noble oak, an English oak, an oak hundreds of years old. And hew a block out of it, a square block, and polish and polish it 'til it shines like a mirror. Then when that Tudor's head rests on it, he can look into that glass of wood, and, behold that axe rising, then falling. Thunk! Slicing into his own damn neck! Chop and chop and chop.' Humphrey wielded his baton like an invisible axe.

'Perfect!' hissed Eleanor. 'Ye be that Caesar still.' He paused.

'But what to do, woman?'

It was now or never.

'Use the seal, my lovely,' said Eleanor.

'Yes, yes . . . but how?'

'Declare under the King's seal, official, that Tudor be an outlaw.'

'An outlaw? Yes!'

'And Hopcyn, and the priest.'

'Outlaws!? Perfect. I was working on it too, my lovely.'

'O' course ye were.'

He grabbed the seal and parchment and scribbled away. Eleanor melted the wax. Humphrey pressed the Great Seal onto it.

'Now send copies direct to the sheriffs of the boroughs and shires before the Council gainsays it. The Clerk can copy it. Then return the seal.'

'Damn Warwick. Archbishop. Yes. Outlaws. Done!'

'And, my lovely, put a price on their heads, thy own personal price, they know thee hath the wherewithal.'

'Yes! Yorkists, murderers, bounty hunters, all after that . . . codpiece!'

'Five thousand gold nobles.'

'No. I mean, too much.'

'Last chance, lovely.'

'Alright.' He mopped his brow. Outgoings exhausted him too, especially ones in hard cash. Eleanor scribbled in the reward. It would be with every town crier in London before morning. Humphrey leaned back.

'My lovely . . . '

'No more,' he begged.

'That Tudor be a foxy one. A hundred hidin' places 'tween 'ere an' Pembroke. Got to lure him out, so thy hunters can pounce.'

'Yes, yes, of course. Go on!'

'Offer all three safe conducts back to Wales.'

'Safe conducts? He furrowed his brows. 'Let me think. Would the Tudor believe it?'

'He'd have to test it.'

'Yes . . . But why?'

'Cos he got the bastards in tow.'

'Of course!'

'He wouldn't desert 'em.'

'Chop! Chop! The iron fist! That would do the trick!' He danced a jig among the torn documents. At last, thought Eleanor, she had again managed to bring the fool round. One more bit to go.

Eleanor seized a map, and traced a finger along Owen's route.

'Come here, me lovely,'

'Where'd Captain Dark lose 'em?'

'Hendale Cross. Here.'

'Concentrate there then. Keep Captain Dark's men across the road to the west. Block every route. Now, last thing, me lovely, suppose, the Tudor and the babes separate? Obvious thing to try, right?'

'Of course.'

'Where'd he try to hide?'

'Well, where?'

'Who just insulted ye?'

'The damn Archbishop!'

'And where do he live?'

'Lambeth Palace, by God!'

'Get thy men down there. Churches be sanctuaries for babes, too.'

'Damn right. You see it now.'

'And tell Captain Dark, his first job be to cream off the babes, and . . .'

Humphrey wielded the invisible axe again,

'Yes, yes, yes! And then . . .'

'. . . Ye still be first in line!'

'I think I've solved the crisis yet again.'

'O course, I knew ye would, me lovely.'

'But, wait, what about the French whore?'

'Don't ye worry, I got that worked out too.'

'Prison?'

'And she pregnant? Never.'

'The Tower. It was treason.'

'No.'

'Come on then.'

'To atone for her sins.'

'Damn well think so.'

'Penance.'

'Why?'

'Cos the King would approve.'

'Yes! Silly saint can't argue with that, can he? But where?'

'A nunnery.'

'Brilliant!'

'I knows a dreadful cold and mortal place where the holy sisters be carved out of stone like statues over tombs, a place of frozen crows and hangin' ice, close to the Hounds' Ditch, bounded by bogs and fens, disfamed for fevers and strange ends. It's called the Abbey of Last Martyrs. And if anyone be that, it be the whore! And the King will pray for her!'

'He will, bless him!'

'And ye will be that king.'

He fell into her arms. She was, he felt, almost as magnificent as he.

101

The Abbess was astonished when Humphrey's Retainers arrived with their charge. Who would venture out in this fog and at this time of night? When she discovered who her illustrious penitent was, she was taken aback. She was also profoundly worried when she saw the extreme condition of the royal patient. Why travel when she was in such a state? But the King's seal was authentic. The Retainers who had brought her all bore the crest of the talon, that of Humphrey, Duke of Gloucester, the King's uncle. All very disturbing. But it was by the king's will, the seal said so. She installed Catherine in the only spare, bare little cell, lit a fire in the damp fireplace and piled the cot with the thickest sheets and blankets she could find.

On receiving his orders, Captain Dark had no compunction in seizing the royal carriages and transferring Catherine, under warrant of the seal, into the comparative comfort of the closed carriages. Catherine bore it all with stoical calm. Captain Dark's Cavalry escorted the Demoiselles to their own homes, but only after Catherine had insisted they went. Agnes, though, had slipped off and was nowhere to be found. Catherine was still under Samuel's medication, and slipped in and out of dreamless sleep, relieved beyond exhaustion by the escape of her beloved husband and sons. She had achieved this against all the odds. She blessed her friends and the Welsh guards who had made such relief possible. She felt as if she herself had escaped. The Duke would never catch up with them, Owen was far too resourceful and Hopcyn far too cunning.

The trip lasted four hours. The last hour over flooded, rutted roads shook her into full awakedness. But only once did she cry out in uncontrollable pain. Then her lips compressed, determined not to give them the satisfaction of seeing her in agony again. When they arrived at the Hound's Ditch, near the Abbey of Last Martyrs, the babe trapped in her womb was shifting, and now made strenuous attempts to come into the world. Every effort to push made Catherine feebler and feebler. The Abbess, herself a midwife, saw at once there was little she could do to aid the birth or the poor tortured mother. The crisis came a few hours later. It nearly tore Catherine in half. The baby was born dead and the haemorrhaging wouldn't stop. The Abbess herself nursed Catherine, at first changing the swabs and dressings every few minutes, then at longer and longer intervals. The Abbess well understood her patient was fading fast but, by the Mother of God, she thought, never had she seen a more determined fighter. Then, without consulting the Retainers who were still at the gates, she sent urgent messages to the King.

Catherine came out of her coma-like sleep, and wept when she was told the baby was lost. It had been a girl, and Owen had always wanted a girl,

'The image of you, my darling,' he had said. And where was Owen now? And her loving friends? She gasped in agony as the pain shrieked silently through her body again. As the night drew on, with the fire guttering in the grate and the shutters banging in the wind, she clutched her father's little crucifix, and fell into a feverish sleep. She was immediately wracked with terrifying dreams; the dance of the cannibals with her father as flame and glass; the picture of the *Triumph of Death* with its sweltering visions of blood and demons. Out of these seemed to rise a figure in cloak and cowl, the face obscure, but the voice familiar. It seemed to creep towards her bed. She gripped the crucifix tighter.

'Where is the Holy Mother?' whispered Catherine.

'Under my protection.'

The harsh voice echoed in her ears.

'And my children?'

'Under my protection too.'

'And Owen?'

'Owen also.'

'Who are you?'

'I am Lord Protector.'

'What is it you want?'

'What I'm getting.'

'Why are you here?'

'For more.'

'No.'

'Pity about the girl.'

'The King's sister.'

'The King has no sisters.'

'He has brothers.'

'Swear they are false.'

'No.'

'Swear the priest is false.'

'No.'

'Swear conspiracy.'

'No.'

'Your family will be free.'

'It is already free.'

'I'll set you free too.'

'Too late.'

'Then die!' the voice hissed. Through throbbing lids, she made out the cowled shape bending over her, the breath on her face, then an arm holding high a sharp-pointed needle, aimed at her head. She thrust out the crucifix. With dim shrieks, the figure seemed to melt and flow into itself, like a river of wax, and disappear into the dusky folds of night, down into the fiery furnace forever.

Catherine shuddered, and dipped into dream again. This time her whole being was invaded with a golden glow. She heard Owen's voice, felt his arms around her, light kisses on her cheeks, murmuring, reassuring, soothing her. And this time she knew it was no dream, her Owen really was there, he would always be there shining in her heart, he would never be far away, in this world or the next.

102

The 1st, 2nd, and 3rd Dragon Companies were encamped in Winwood above the slopes of the river Lugg in three columns, as ordered, ready to move out at an instant's notice. Evacuation of small groups to the west had already begun.

Their pursuers, a variety of retainers from the various factions, as well as criminals and bounty hunters, hesitated to attack a fully armed guard of veterans. They held off, but pursued them tenaciously from a distance, always on the look out for a very valuable Captain accompanied by two children. Owen had not been spotted when he had reached Hendale Cross. He was now sheltering in the Queen's Head, overlooking the square. Agnes had ridden in at a gallop shortly after the three had arrived, and had taken over control of the children. They had been right to disperse the group.

Owen learned of Catherine's fate at the hands of Captain Dark, and where Catherine had been taken. He knew he had to move rapidly now to forestall any further punishment of his beloved, faithful and innocent wife. Action now!

They turned to the sudden commotion outside their windows. They saw the town crier mount his stand in the middle of the square. He shouted out the words in a stentorian voice:

'Be it known that the renegades Evan Hopcyn, Damascus Jones, priest, Owen Tudor, former Captain of the Queen's Guard, are fugitives from justice, for crimes and treasons against the royal person, and are hereby declared outside the protection of the King's law. Be it also known that safe conducts will be granted should the fugitives surrender into the hands of the sheriffs. If they reject this royal clemency, their capture, dead or alive, will be rewarded by his Grace, Humphrey, Duke of Gloucester, and the fugitives shall be subject to the extreme penalties of the law. By order of the Grand Council, given this day under the Great Seal of Henry, the King!'

The watching group exchanged looks of dawning comprehension. So that was why the pursuit had been so hard. Greed, as well as murder, was in full pursuit. Owen glanced around the Square. He noted the crests of at least four royal factions, as well as heavily armed private individuals. More were arriving by the minute.

'They'll be starting their house to house searches soon,' said Hopcyn.

Owen returned to the table. He had formulated a plan. Everything was now submerged to the urge for action. Owen needed to have that awareness of intent, that clarity which was of the essence. It would mean risking everything, but it also meant that everything else was subordinated to the new plan. It dulled the pain of memory and the sadness of separation. It helped the grief over Catherine's fate, the terrors of the future for the boys, the family, even for love itself. Humphrey's mad dream wasn't going to let him rest so it would be action to the end for Humphrey as well. But Owen knew that his diseased ego was eaten away. The boys had escaped. Owen prayed they would be welcomed in the place he would send them.

Agnes entered from the bedroom.

'Boys alright?' asked Owen.

'Think it's part of the holiday.'

Damascus and Hopcyn looked at Owen. It was his decision.

'Change of plan,' he said. 'We do it and we do it now. When we go out of that door, we disperse to our destinations, the columns will wait our return in Winwood, you know where they are. Horses ready?' Hopcyn nodded.

'Damascus, how many men out of uniform?'

'Twenty.'

'All armed?'

'Fully.'

'Ten to go with us, ten with you, Damascus.' He unrolled the map. 'Agnes, you go with the children . . . here.' Hopcyn looked and whispered,

'Taking a chance.'

'They're still looking for a Captain with two boys, not a mother with her sons. Agnes is briefed.'

'Damascus, you and your men leave last. Let Hopcyn and me get a good head's start. Follow from a distance. Along this route.' Damascus nodded.

'Hurry,' said Hopcyn from the window. 'Drawing up in ranks, searches starting.' They heard hammering on doors.

'Now go. Agnes, kiss the boys for me.'

It was no time for words. Agnes embraced them and hurried out.

'And where do we go?' asked Hopcyn.

'To our one friend at the moment.'

'Who?'

'The Archbishop of Canterbury.'

'Lambeth Palace?'

'Yes.'

'It will be well guarded.'

'He is our only ally.'

Yells and the shattering of wood came from the houses on either side.

Eleanor had calculated correctly. Owen did ride west. She was also right that his second destination would be Lambeth. But she never dreamed, until it was too late, where Owen had sent the boys.

103

Owen and Hopcyn stood at the back entrance of Lambeth Palace. Light streamed through the upper windows. Owen and Hopcyn drew back into the deeper shadows of the garden. Damascus and his men were in reserve, on the far side of the wall. Owen motioned Hopcyn forward. It was time. They had to make contact with the Archbishop. Owen looked again. Why the lights? It was well past midnight. As they reached up stealthily to push open the back door, it was flung violently open. The Archbishop himself stood framed in the doorway. Behind him loomed the figure of Humphrey. Hopcyn looked around. From the darkness of the trees, stepped Humphrey's Retainers, swords drawn.

'I am sorry,' said the Archbishop. 'The Grand Council is in full emergency session.'

'Where are these safe conducts, your Grace?' asked Owen.

'You will have to wait,' said Humphrey, smiling triumphantly. 'Clothes peg!' he suddenly spat out. The Archbishop looked baffled.

'What, my Lord?'

'Never mind. You are prisoners.'

Owen addressed the Archbishop.

'I hope you will inform the King.'

'I have already sent to His Majesty.'

'That will not help either of you,' growled Humphrey, beckoning his men forward. From the high wall, Damascus watched and listened.

'My men will take over now.'

'My Lord,' said the Archbishop, 'I would remind you, you stand on consecrated land, the land of the church, and you are now under canon law. I am witness to the fact that these two fugitives have been captured here. They will be treated with the respect due to our ecclesiastical law. And I hereby order them both, Captain Owen Tudor and Evan Hopcyn, to be taken to the prison of Newgate, and held there under the King's pleasure.'

Humphrey could do nothing. But once inside the prison, then God, let alone the Archbishop, would not be able to help them. Humphrey stood back. The Archbishop's Retainers took over and marched the two out. Damascus clambered down from his perch. He gave his orders. At high speed, his troopers galloped off, Damascus in the lead.

The Archbishop, with a look of contempt, turned from Humphrey, and swept off to the council chamber.

Humphrey turned to the scar-faced Captain, still standing there.

'Get two squads down to the prison.'

'What are their orders?'

'They have been briefed.'

'When do I get my reward, your Grace?'

'Later.'

'Now.'

'You didn't get the bastards.'

'The bastards were not mentioned in the warrant.'

'Just carry out my orders!' Humphrey stamped inside, shouting for wine. As he watched him, Captain Dark drew an imaginary dagger across his throat.

Humphrey congratulated himself. He had captured a King's father, and in doing so had saved a King's ransom! Most cunningly done. Eleanor herself couldn't have arranged things better.

104

Owen and Hopcyn, heavily guarded, were at first conducted to the deepest cells. However, Damascus had been the first to arrive. He flourished one of Isabelle's fake seals under the Jailer's nose and swore him to state secrecy. He was to listen to no other except himself, for not only was he the King's private envoy, but also personal chaplain to the Primate of England, as the papers proved. These fakes also guaranteed freedom of movement to the holder, instant access and suitable reward. Damascus gave the Jailer five freshly minted gold nobles as a token of the King's respect. Damascus ordered the fugitives to be plunged into the deepest cells until both the Archbishop's and Humphrey's Retainers had left. The Jailer was bewildered by all these high connections, but the fat bribe banished all further puzzlement. He was their man. As soon as the mob of Retainers had departed, the Jailer ceremoniously transferred his prisoners to the chambers reserved for prominent, fee-paying prisoners, overlooking the street and main gate.

Humphrey had meanwhile left, well pleased with his remarkable solo success. He imagined Eleanor's face as he made his report on the night's work, Owen having been taken and the threat to the throne contained. He had also dispatched his own personal Company of Guards, the Talon Company, to Hendale Cross with special orders. Every eventuality had to be catered for. He patted himself on the back. Wait till that little plot had run its course. The only blot on his night's victories had been the truculent, demanding insolence of Captain Dark. Getting too big for his boots by half, muttered Humphrey, but he knew how to take care of him.

Captain Dark seethed at the ingratitude and cavalier treatment, especially over the delayed payment. The escape of the bastards had been Humphrey's blunder. He should have mentioned them in his warrant and reward proclamation. Once again, he had been the instrument of the Gloucesters' good fortune, but was not permitted to share in any of the spoils. He vowed that this would be the last time. His purplish scars glowed as he contemplated the best means for revenge, his sole consolation.

Owen and Hopcyn paced the wooden floors of their rooms. It was more like an ale-house parlour than a prison. On arrival, as arranged, Hopcyn had demanded a priest for their confessions, which was the irrefutable right of all prisoners. The Jailer cheerfully acquiesced and sent for the influential Chaplain, as the Chaplain himself had instructed. Hopcyn and Owen now awaited Damascus's arrival. Owen felt that desperate need for action, no matter what.

Owen shouted and banged his mug on the table. The Jailer came running. The first thing that met his eyes was a small silk bag of gold, with some coins spilled on the table.

'Where is the priest?'

'With the condemned prisoners, sir.'

'Well, hurry him up!'

'On his way, sir.' The Jailer scooped up the coins, pulled his forelock and hurried out. If this keeps up, he muttered with a prayer, I'll be a rich man in the morning.

'We've got to be on the move in the next thirty minutes,' said Owen. Clattering footsteps came from the corridor.

'Here's our man,' said Hopcyn.

The Jailer bustled in. Behind him followed the lean, crane-like figure of Damascus, an amused smile on his lips. His height and the priestly robes gave him a lofty authority.

Owen and Hopcyn fell to their knees, hands clasped in

prayer. The jailer made to leave. Damascus stopped him.

'I will hear your confession, too. Jailer.'

'But, sir, I . . . '

'Kneel you wicked sinner!' boomed Damascus, making the sign of the cross over him. The Jailer knelt. It was the last thing he remembered doing for two days.

'Horses at the back,' said Damascus. 'Come on. Through the Governor's quarters, then the back gate. Careful, there's a guard house. Streets are full of Humphrey's men.' He handed out daggers and short swords from under his cassock.

They ran down the corridor, slipped in through the door of the Governor's quarters, and broke out into the yard. A small guard room stood at the rear entrance. As they made for the gates, they were challenged. In the brief fight, one guard was killed and another wounded. Damascus held open the gates. They ran to the tethered horses and the four waiting Welsh guards. But the alarm had been given. The Retainers came running around from the front of the prison. At the same time, the hue and cry was raised. The pursuit would be taken up by any citizen who chose to follow.

'Change of plan,' gasped Owen as he mounted up. 'Damascus, try to draw them off. Hopcyn, follow me.'

'Where to?' shouted Hopcyn.

'Sanctuary. The Abbey. Main doors!'

Damascus and the Guard turned their horses east. Owen and Hopcyn dashed to the south, still followed by a stream of Humphrey's men, not put off the false scent. There was too much money at hand.

105

The road to the Abbey lay open before them. It would be a wild desperate dash, as their pursuers raised every household they galloped past with shouts and yells. As still more joined in, their chances of outdistancing every pursuer became slimmer and slimmer. The whole of Westminster seemed to join in the chase. With their enemies only fifty yards behind, the towering bulk of the Abbey loomed into view. Without slackening speed, Owen pointed at the main doors. They galloped full tilt at them, threw themselves out of the saddle, sprinted to the doors, grasped the two huge iron rings, and yelled so everyone in the vicinity could hear,

'Sanctuary!' Their pursuers, now only twenty yards or so away, paused, dismounted and formed a semi-circle around the two fugitives. Owen and Hopcyn clung to the rings. As long as they didn't release their hold, they couldn't be touched. Sanctuary was sacred and it was blasphemy to break it. Owen and Hopcyn could now shelter safely inside the Abbey itself. They had only twenty-four hours while they were immune from the law. After that, they had the choice between giving themselves up for trial, or be hunted down and possibly strung up by the mob.

'Sanctuary!' they yelled again as Humphrey's men began to inch forward. They heard the bolts inside being pulled back. The doors opened and they fell inside. The doors were slammed shut and the bolts pushed home again. Owen and Hopcyn picked themselves up. They were confronted by the Abbot himself.

'Captain Owen and Master Evan Hopcyn?' he calmly asked.

'How did you know?' asked Hopcyn, astonished.

'The fame of your exploits, I assure you, has travelled ahead of you.'

'Damascus?'

'He has just left. For Hendale Cross, I believe.'

The Abbot seemed unusually well informed as well as sympathetic.

The Abbot addressed Owen directly,

'Are you indeed the father of the Dowager Queen's children?'

'If you ask it, then you know it's true.'

'I wanted to hear it from your own lips.'

'The Archbishop!' said Hopcyn.

'Yes, I have copies of all the relevant documents.'

'The marriage is valid,' said Hopcyn.

'As the whole world is learning,' he motioned to the outside. The heavy doors were now being pounded with fists and sword hilts, but no effort was made to open the doors. 'And they all seem to want a share in it.'

'Humphrey's men want to cut our throats,' said Hopcyn. A sudden wild cheer went up from the mob.

'We appreciate that,' said the Abbot, remarkably self-possessed through it all. 'You seem to have done a favour for certain high persons, Captain Owen. Humphrey is no longer next in line. But you, I'm afraid, are now in the direct line of fire.' A Monk padded up to the Abbot, whispered, pointed, and returned to his post by the door.

'The good Duke had just arrived. He wants a parley. It is his right. But he enters here only on my sufferance. None of his retainers, of course can come near you, for the moment. But what might happen after twenty-four hours, I have no means of telling. Now, sit behind the screens over there. No one will see you there. I will conduct the Duke in. But first a little chat with him.'

The Abbot turned on his heel and made his way sedately to the main doors, his sandals slap-slapping on the paving. The Monk slid open the bolts, and the Abbot stepped outside. Hopcyn and Owen took shelter behind the darkened screens.

'He's giving us a chance, Owen. What do we do?'

'Scout out the back. Through the vestry. Go, go.'

Hopcyn darted off. Owen waited, hoping for action, dreading thoughts of Catherine flooding him. Voices were raised outside the main doors. Owen recognised Humphrey's voice, braying in anger. The Abbot's certainly keeping him waiting thought Owen. Hopcyn scuttled back.

'Got it!' he gasped. 'Remembered . . . from the coronation . . . two doors down the cloisters.' He was getting his breath back. 'Into the cemetery, path runs down directly to the river . . . Quay's empty, no boat.'

'Have to take that chance,' said Owen. 'Here they come, if I'm not mistaken.'

The Abbot stepped inside, leading the portly, restless figure of the Duke. They could hear his furious breathing from where they crouched.

'Wait here, your Grace,' he commanded. Humphrey tightened his lips. He was not going to be ordered about by a mere priest. He loosened his sword, and tried to follow. The Abbot turned on him.

'You will wait where you are. You will speak from where you are. If you approach once inch more, I will declare sanctuary broken.'

All this God stuff, thought Humphrey. Damn cleric! But Humphrey dutifully shuffled to a halt. The Abbot approached the screens.

'Parley with his Grace the Duke of Gloucester,' he announced in a loud voice. 'Be it known that you are still in sanctuary.' He lowered his voice. 'After the parley, I will keep his Grace engaged for five minutes. Just five minutes, no more.'

'There is no boat,' whispered Hopcyn.

'There will be,' murmured the Abbot, and returned to his place at the side of the fuming Duke.

'Show your faces!' Humphrey shouted.

Dead silence.

'Cowards!' Hopcyn put his finger to his lips.

'Is it personal combat you want,' Humphrey challenged. 'I am ready!'

'I thought we were already engaged in that,' returned Owen.

'Your Grace,' said the Abbot, 'you will respect these cloisters. This is a parley. If it is only abuse you want, I will have to terminate the proceedings.'

'These are felons and murderers,' insisted the Duke.

'Offer what you have to offer, and leave,' commanded the Abbot.

'You have safe conducts back to Wales. Take them while you can.'

'It's safe conducts out of here we want,' said Hopcyn.

'I'm not talking to you, mad-eyes,' shouted the Duke, 'it's old clothes peg I want.'

'I take it the parley is over,' said the Abbot.

'No!' Humphrey clung on. 'Declare they are bastards!' he shouted at Owen.

'I know of no bastards,' replied Owen.

'I am still Lord Protector. Your last chance. Declare the priest false . . . '

'No!' Owen and Hopcyn spoke in unison.

'The marriage null and void . . . '

'No!'

'I will guarantee safe conduct out of here, and to the West.'

'No!'

'What God hath brought together, let no man break asunder,' added Hopcyn, for good measure. The reply drove Humphrey into a fury.

'I will have your heads on a block!' he roared.

'Quiet!' the Abbot broke in. 'You are not at your witch's den of Placentia now!'

'What do you mean?' asked Humphrey, taken aback.

'This parley is now terminated,' the Abbot announced, and walked to the main doors, followed by the protesting Duke.

'What did you mean?' he asked again.

'Have you not spoken to the Archbishop, your Grace?'

'Those documents? Forgeries, lies, treasons, conspiracy. By those two murderers!'

The Abbot escorted the Duke to his horse, and insisted on saying a benediction over him. That's all I need, thought Humphrey furiously, a bloody blessing while murderers get off scot free.

'I will wait here until the cock crows, and then blood will flow, you'll see, you'll all see!' Humphrey burst out.

Ten minutes later, Owen and Hopcyn were rowing steadily with the current of the Thames, the Abbey receding behind them in the darkness. After twenty minutes, Owen stood and pointed. Their destination hove into view.

106

Agnes looked down at the deathly pale face of the friend she most cherished in the world. The last bucket of swabs and bandages had been taken away. The haemorrhaging had steadied to a thin, deadly trickle. The sight of Catherine so wrung Agnes's heart, she could hardly bear to look at her. She had been in such a deep sleep when Agnes arrived, she thought Catherine had fallen into the final coma.

The Abbess herself was hushed and reverential. She had come to recognise a truly brave fighter, and was as saddened as Agnes as the life slowly faded before her very eyes, from the still lovely, royal person in her charge. Catherine's inner being was slowly slipping away from its bodily casing. Her life guttered, rising one moment, then dipping off into the shadows. Yet at the bright peaks, her whole face seemed to be illuminated from within by a near miraculous youthfulness. The Abbess crossed herself and said her rosary. Something extraordinary was happening, something for the ages.

A lantern gleamed on the bedside table, piled with last messages, documents and Catherine's will. All had been signed and witnessed by the Abbess. The little jewelled crucifix gleamed on the wall above her head. Two crucifixes for her last moments, one from her father and the other from her son, the members of her family she had been most deprived of. The Abbess, in spite of instructions to the contrary, had arranged for messages to be sent directly to the King. The story of Catherine and Owen was now spreading like wildfire. And here, still young at thirty-five, her life nearly extinguished, lay the other partner of the amazing story.

Catherine's eyes fluttered. She moaned quietly. Her eyes suddenly opened wide. She made out the form of her friend.

'Agnes!' she reached out, then dropped her arms, too weak to hold them. Agnes hugged the wasted body.

'The boys? Owen?'

'Out of harm's way.'

'Owen saved them?'

'Yes.'

'He understands why he had to leave?'

'Yes, yes . . . ' It was all she could do not to break into unceasing sobs. She gripped the edge of the bed. She had to be in control for Catherine's last moments.

'No one can touch the King's brothers.'

'You were right, Catherine'

'Joanna. Adéle . . . ?'

'With their families.'

'I've left legacies . . . '

'I'll take care of it, don't worry.'

'Now, my appeal to Henry. There.' With a feverish access of strength, she whispered out her last letter to her son.

'My sovereign Lord and most dear son, when I first looked upon you as you lay in my arms, you filled my heart and soul with joy. God had blessed me with the family I so yearned and prayed for. But, when only a year later, you were taken from me, how I wept, and how alone I felt without you, especially when your dear father was also wrenched from me. But through all this sorrow, you always remained my first born and dearly beloved son. I write this, my dear boy, on my death bed, the last bed I shall know on this earth. I beg you from the fullness of a faithful heart, not to think too hard of me. I beg you, too, in the name of Jesus who dwells in us all, to forgive Owen, my dear husband, who has brought nothing but kindness and love into my life. We are helpless when love strikes into our hearts. I beseech you to look on us both with mercy, we could not help our love. And I beg you too, cherish my two sons, Jasper and Edmund, your own brothers, testament of your mother's deep love. Soon I shall pass away from the face of this earth, as naked and desolate as any sinner. My dear son, I beseech you, preserve this little family, unite it with yours, which will remain, so we can endure together as a family, the death we have to endure alone. I commit my dear sons, your brothers, to your most royal, tender care. I kiss my father's crucifix and think of you, in Jesus. I ask lastly, that my body rest in my Lady's Chapel of Westminster, where you and I spent our last day together . . . '

' . . . ssh' Agnes smoothed her brows. 'I will deliver it myself.'

'Bless you.' She gazed into the distance, smiling. 'Remember the dance. Owen, like a little boy. In my lap.'

'We all loved it.'

'I fell in love, so much, so wonderful.'

'You were lovely together.'

'Still a little family.'

'Yes.'

'We've won.' She smiled radiantly.

A searing pain tore through her body. Above the agony, a cloud-like calm seemed to fill the room, a floating, springlight with the fragrance of lilacs in bloom. Catherine saw Owen's face stooping over her, reassuring her, covering her face with kisses. An intense bluish glow rose from her breast to her throat and face, filling it with a radiant, unearthly youthfulness, yet leaving the shell of such beauty, empty of breath, drained of life. Catherine of Valois sighed happily with her Owen at her side, and died. Agnes fell across the body of her friend and wept uncontrollably until dawn.

107

Owen stood in utter stillness by the window, Agnes's terrifying message in his hand. Hopcyn guided him to a chair. Owen moved like sleep walker. He felt that the piercing, all embracing, grief could only be assuaged by death.

'No, no, no . . . ' were the only words he had spoken since midnight when the terrible news had arrived.

'Owen, Owen . . . ' Hopcyn again tried to rouse him out of the wrack of his irredeemable loss.

'This is my death too.' He spoke at last.

'Not of the family.'

'I can only join her.'

'She does not wish it.'

'I deserted her.'

'You saved the boys, the family.' He looked around and shivered. 'You feel it?' Hopcyn nodded.

Yes, he felt it too. Everything was shrinking, as if Catherine's love and affection had left a vacuum around him whilst other, lesser feelings were contracting, leaving the air dry and loveless.

'I must join her.'

'It is not your destiny.'

'I saved only myself, now I must . . . '

'You saved her.'

'My Catherine is gone.'

'Then save her memory.'

'How?'

'Think of her. Closely. Her hair, shoulders, breasts. Feel

them, touch them. Kiss them. The lilacs, smell them. The butterflies, the blossoms, embrace them. Now.'

Owen collapsed in tears. At last. Owen had broken out of the shell of his grief.

'Now, you must be her. Be her love, her family.'

'The boys, yes . . . '

'She lives on in them, in you, in all of your love.'

'Yes, yes, yes . . . '

Hopcyn cradled his friend's head in his arms, caressing him, soothing him, just as Catherine had done.

After hours, it seemed, Owen finally fell asleep.

At least, thought Hopcyn, he had been drawn away from images of his own death. Any absence, any pause in the intense sorrows, would begin the infinitely small, first cure of life reasserting itself, of carrying on, of letting the dead bury the dead. And it was just in time, for the next day, Hopcyn knew, Owen would fight the most crucial battle of his life.

108

Owen sat on a bench in an ante room of the Palace of Whitehall. The Court of the King's Bench was in full session, with the boy King himself presiding.

Both Owen and Hopcyn were arraigned together. The exact charges were now being worked out. Owen now waited, the first of the accused to be tried.

After Hendale Cross, Owen had decided on the boldest of manoeuvres, this being to throw the boys, and himself, on the King's mercy. After being cornered by Humphrey in sanctuary at the Abbey, from which there had been no permanent escape, this had been the only move left. It was fraught with dangers and imponderables. Would the King's Councillors support him? Would the marriage be recognised? Would the reds and the whites get to him first? Were there assassins about? At least he had survived the first shocks.

Agnes had informed the King of his mother's death. After that, everything had changed. It had affected the King as much as Owen. But Owen, with his friend Hopcyn, had pulled himself around. He knew now that not only was he fighting for himself, but for Catherine and the boys as well.

In another ante room close by, Humphrey, Duke of Gloucester strutted about, but with shaken confidence. Recent events had thrown the victories of the previous day into turmoil. Owen and Hopcyn, just murderers and traitors in his eyes, had been arrested, but they had been kept in honourable confinement, and now even doubts had been thrown on the charges of murder and treason. What had gone wrong? And not only that, after his triumph with Eleanor, he himself that same morning had received a summons to appear before the court. How dare they? Wasn't it obvious the conspiracy was still in place. This was simply a continuing effort to deny him his rightful place as next in line. So obvious. He did feel a certain uneasiness, however, over the death of Catherine, but he convinced himself with the reassurances of Eleanor, that he really had nothing whatsoever to do with it. The journey hadn't killed her, that was just a deliberate, vicious rumour. It was the fault of his enemies. He, the Lord Protector, had ordered it for her own safety. But he had received reports that someone had poisoned the King against him on account of this accidental demise. Typical, he thought, those swine still at it, Warwick, Winchester, Chichele. He swished his baton like a club. He'd show the lot of them – he himself, St George, hero of the iron fist.

Humphrey's summons had mentioned certain irregularities in his military accounts, something he had long rejected and forgotten. What trumped up charges had they this time, he wondered, for there was not a shred of evidence. He'd soon prove that. His own Retainers were already brawling in the streets, showing what they thought of the accusations. And these very street disorders, too, were being held against him. Hell, Humphrey thought, everybody did it, including the murderer Owen and the loon Hopcyn. Damn cut-throats!

He glanced down at his ill-fitting hose, surcoat and shoes, all in black and donned in haste, at the King's bidding. He hated black. It filled him with foreboding. To his added consternation, his beloved Duchess, Eleanor, was unexpectedly ushered in to join him. She too was dressed in black. With her pale complexion and pointed nose she resembled nothing more than a black-eyed, evil little ferret. She rushed over to Humphrey and embraced him.

'What in the hell are you doing here?' he asked, pushing her away.

'I got a summons after you left.'

'Bloody insult! Trying every dirty trick. Getting at me through my family now. Disgusting. Damn Yorkist devils!'

'Where be the bastards?'

'Who cares?'

'What about the Tudor?'

'Ran away, didn't he?'

'Catherine dead done for him, I heard!'

'Who's fucking who now?'

'The worms!' They both guffawed. He swished his baton again, but not without a worried frown.

The King and his Councillors were again going over the charges and indictments, examining every word of the statements of the accused and their defence. Damascus had exerted every ounce of his forensic skill. Henry followed the legal nicities with keen appreciation for the rare skill of the jurist. From time to time, he paused and snuffled, blowing his nose with his kerchief. His face was stained with tears. He had taken the death of his mother exceptionally hard. He had instantly ordered daily masses for her soul, and instituted a most rigorous form of mourning, everything in black, the furnishings, the furniture shrouded with drapes, or re-covered, interminable periods of fasting, endless sessions of prayers, chanted hymns and requiems. The little jewelled crucifix Agnes had returned to him, Henry now wore around his neck, occasionally stooping to kiss it, dabbing his eyes after each kiss. Catherine had left the crucifix in his care, for Edmund. His mother, he now saw, had been as pious as he, and he had never known until it was too late. A pall of gloom and sorrow hung over every word and action, while a feeling of doom, death and punishment permeated every corner.

Catherine's expulsion from Baynard's had unloosed a veritable avalanche of documents, each set delivered simultaneously to a dozen high clerics and councillors, from the

Lord Chancellor, Warwick, to the King himself. The only people who had been strictly excluded from this mass of public information were the Duke and Duchess of Gloucester. The King, Warwick, Winchester and the Archbishop were now going through some of the most outrageous falsifications, seditions, treasons, lies, briberies and thefts they had ever been informed of. But one of the documents, tied in black crepe, contained some of the most horrifying statements any of them had ever read. The King, pale as an egg but fortified by an absolute faith, had insisted on pressing on. It was a successful excursion for the boy into the real world. Warwick, as Lord Chancellor, only wished it would extend into the realm of politics. Then, perhaps, they would have another Henry V, with real sainthood thrown in as an extra. But again, he felt pity for the young King who had already sat so often at the graveside of life.

Henry again read his mother's last appeal, managing to stifle the usual floods of tears. If the King had any doubts about Owen's role in the affair, this appeal from the grave removed them. He saw, with his quick and precocious understanding, that the lovers' acts, however outrageous they seemed, had been done out of real love, the love he had only associated up to that point, with Jesus. After reading the appeal for the first time, he had at once sent for the boys. When they had come into his presence, he had seated them and gazed at them both, enraptured and puzzled. From being a virtual orphan himself, he'd suddenly come into the possession of a family, fully equipped with a father and two brothers. This softened the blow of his mother's death. The boys would be ever loving memorials of her. But all three at first were still in a state of shock over their common loss. They wept dolefully every time Catherine's name was mentioned. The Countess of Warwick finally had to conduct Edmund and Jasper to their quarters, so they could recover. The King placed a heavy guard around his brothers. After reading the recent reports, he knew there was deadly work going on. He was not going to lose his new family to bloodthirsty intrigue and factious disputes. His Councillors, meanwhile, were revelling in Humphrey's dramatic change of fortune. The so called 'bastards' had put an unbridgeable distance between Humphrey and the throne. He was now definitely out of contention, having been reduced to his old elementary role of bully, troublemaker, thief, miser, satanist and killer. Warwick could see something like resolve stirring in the King's face. Yes, a settling of accounts was on the books, but would it last long enough?

Archbishop Chichele tidied the documents into neat, classified piles.

'I think we are ready now, Sire.'

'So be it.'

They took their places. The King abruptly held up his hand. Warwick groaned inwardly. Henry's resolve had lasted but a minute or two.

'Sire?' he asked.

'My sword of state, the small one.'

Chichele bowed and moved off. Why did Henry want the sword now? The sword was used only for investment ceremonies, knighthoods and ennobling.

'And call in my brothers.'

The two boys were quickly presented by the Countess. Henry greeted them like old school mates brought in from the playground to play. Henry beckoned for footstools, and motioned for his brothers to kneel.

Without more ado, he proceeded to dub them, having obviously worked out in advance just what titles they should have.

When he had finished the little ceremony, he whispered,

'Rise and be recognised,' and there was no doubting the gladness in his voice.

437

As they stood, the two boys were now ready to take their places with the most powerful in the land. Jasper as Earl of Pembroke, and Edmund as Earl of Richmond, had been granted prize plums in the royal gift, with considerable revenues combining both wealth and status. At a stroke the two boys were now ranked above the 'common' nobility, and only just below the royal dukes.

Henry's Councillors were genuinely impressed. Henry had fenced in the throne, reinforced the royal prerogative, and protected the boys. The factions would be enraged at the elevations, for it brought the boys as close to the crown as their own royal masters. Humphrey's machinations had received their death blow.

But looking at the three boys now standing together, Chichele saw it was family affection which had moved Henry as much as politics. With a final hug for them, Henry watched them fondly as they were escorted out. What strength of character had failed to achieve, family affection had.

The Councillors felt reassured. They bowed. The King's Court was truly in session.

At the guarded door of the ante room stooped Humphrey and Eleanor, straining to make out what the King was saying. They could hear his piping tones, but the words eluded them. The King was whispering. But his tone, for once, seemed clear and self-assured, not the usual namby-pamby whinings of a milksop. Humphrey and Eleanor straightened up uneasily. What was going on?

'Why all this secrecy?' asked Humphrey. 'After all, we are family, I am his uncle.'

'The King be against thee over Catherine.'

'Nothing to do with me.'

'The Nunnery . . . '

' . . . that was your idea.'

'You gave the order.' Her desperation made Humphrey bristle.

'Don't talk to me like that!' he squeeked.

Humphrey's commissary clerk entered. He bore messages from Captain Dark. Humphrey's last orders had been carried out after all. Excellent. Humphrey looked at the clerk. Yes, why not, promote him over Captain Dark's head. That would be a fitting punishment, a mere clerk over a fighting commander. Humiliation. Perfect. He dismissed the clerk. All was going well on the outside.

'Ssh!' They both listened intently at the door again.

'Call Captain Owen Tudor!' the voice of Warwick came over.

'Damn clothes peg! Coward! Justice at last!' The sound of marching footsteps echoed in the hall. They halted at the Bench.

'Captain Owen Tudor, Clerk of the late Dowager Queen's Wardrobe, before the Court of The King's Bench, to present his plea and petition to the King.'

'The noose, at last.' growled Humphrey. Eleanor grinned wolfishly.

Henry stared down with admiration at the striking, martial figure of his 'father' before him. Owen was in plain costume, black hose, a black brigantine jacket, black under shirt, thigh length black leather riding boots. He had also been permitted to wear a black-hilted ornamental dagger. There was no denying his charisma.

Owen knew from the moment he had woken on this day that here would be his crucial battle. Hopcyn had shown him the way. Now he gathered his strength, determined that his family and Catherine's memory would survive, whatever happened to himself.

He returned the King's long, admiring gaze with confidence. He had a definite feeling that Catherine was at his elbow. The King leaned forward. He seemed to sense it too. They exchanged sympathetic looks. They shared a common loss, and wore a common colour too, the colour of grief.

Warwick now spoke.

'Firstly, as to the charges of murder and treason. These have been reduced to causing affray and disturbance.' Owen's plea of self-defence and wrongful imprisonment had been accepted.

A buzz of speculation arose from the court. This amounted to royal clemency, if not public forgiveness.

'What!' exclaimed Humphrey.

'But my lovely . . . '

'He murdered a jailer!'

A chill ran through Eleanor.

'Them polecats, Warwick, Winchester . . . '

'I'll get 'em right now.' He seized the door handle. Eleanor hung on to him. Hell, she thought, the simpleton's going to throw it all away in one stupid burst of temper.

'No lovely . . . ' she begged, wishing she could kick him in the balls.

'I'll show 'em! Iron fist . . . let me go!'

'Contempt of court,' she gasped. 'Prison!' He paused, panting.

'The court will now hear the plea and petition of the defendant, Captain Owen Tudor.'

As Owen began to speak, Eleanor muttered the words of the . It had to work. And now.

'Let 'em sicken, let 'em die . . . ' she began.

'Shut up, woman!' hissed Humphrey. 'Listen.'

Owen's voice was firm and steady. He came straight to the point.

'Sire, when I first came into the presence of your dear mother . . . ' he paused for a second, and then plunged on, 'I came not by stealth or deceit, nor for preferment or profit, as my enemies put out. Look at me now, I boast no titles or vast estates. I came, as I say, on the direct orders of your most sainted and puissant father.'

Warwick nodded. The word 'sainted' was well chosen.

'And I took up with a profound sense of gratitude, my

promotion to Clerk of the Queen's Wardrobe. I had no notion of love or any feelings of passion for your most pious and exalted mother, but only a burning desire to do my duty. Sire, who can foresee when love strikes? Who can contain it? Who can say when love exactly entered our hearts? But when it did, Sire, it was as irresistible as the tides of the moon. We were helpless against it. And we experienced a love which was pure, simple and honest. Sire, it saved us. It was our sacrament to life itself. And we were as astonished by that love as any child who sees the stars for the first time. We were grateful to God, from that moment on, for that rarest and most precious of gifts – love. Your mother revered mother church with a whole heart, as you do Sire, having been brought up by the holy sisters of mercy in her childhood. As our love blossomed, she experienced agonies of conscience. She longed, Sire, for our union to receive the sanction of the Church. I could not resist her, Sire. Nor did I wish to. I am certain that after her most sad departure from this life, she now stands before her Maker as pure and unstained in death as she was in life.'

Tears glistened in Owen's eyes. The King burst into prayer amid a flood of tears. The whole court slipped to their knees, praying too.

'Damn! The viper,' whispered Eleanor.

'The verdict, the verdict?' demanded Humphrey, beside himself again.

'Die, die, die . . . ' muttered Eleanor.

'Hang 'em both!'

The prayers faded. The voice of Warwick came over.

'The decision of the court in the matter of Captain Owen Tudor is . . . '

Eleanor and Humphrey tensed.

'Banishment.'

'Banishment?' Humphrey repeated, stunned.

'Better'n nothin' I suppose,' said Eleanor weakly.

'Rubbish!'

'The said Captain Owen be banished from the purlieus of the City of London . . . ' continued Warwick.

'Hell, no!' Humphrey couldn't believe his ears.

'For a period of no less than a month.'

'A month!' Humphrey's jaw was limp as the terrible voice pressed on.

'Captain Owen Tudor, you are herewith released from outlawry, and are declared to be under the protection of the King's law, as before.'

Humphrey slumped onto a chair, as if from a physical blow.

'A travesty! Travesty!' he repeated again and again.

'You are free to depart with your companions, who are bound by the same conditions. Have you anything to say?'

'Sire, may I dare ask, after this most merciful decision, about my dear sons. May I be permitted to visit them on my return to the City.'

'I am sure Jasper, now Earl of Pembroke, and Edmund, now Earl of Richmond, would want me to grant this request. It is so granted.'

Owen paused. Ennobled! And so soon. Yes, this time he had seen the other side of the hill, his awareness of intent had been right. The boys were now safeguarded by both title and favour. He had carried out Catherine's last wishes. The family was intact. Owen's voice rose in gratitude.

'Your mercy, Sire, is even now being praised in heaven.'

Excellent, thought Warwick. Winchester, and Chichele, nodded, well fought. A fine victory. Captain Tudor had scattered the enemy to the winds – for the present.

The footsteps of the guards faded as Owen was led out to his freedom.

109

Humphrey felt a numb, mounting incomprehension and fury.

'No! No! No! No!' exploded Humphrey, like poisonous gases bursting from a rotting corpse. 'Not ennobled. No!'

'Calmly now.'

'Bastards!'

'Time to think, my lovely.'

'I'll give the order! My lads are ready.'

The fool would spoil any chance they still had.

'The throne is mine!'

'The first of the Caesars, o' course, my lovely . . . '

'Don't call me that!'

He made for the doors again. Eleanor hung on. He tried to shake her off. The doors were suddenly thrown open. Warwick stood there, in the robes of the Lord Chancellor, barring his way. Armed guards flanked him.

'Against all the laws of England, you will pay for it!' blustered Humphrey. 'I will not stay. A travesty!' He turned to leave. Warwick motioned to the guards, who blocked his exit.

'What madness is this?' shouted Humphrey. 'I will not be treated like a common criminal!'

'You have been summoned to answer certain charges . . . '

'Lies, old lies!'

Eleanor tried to sidle past. She too was pushed back by the guards.

'And you too, Eleanor Cobham, have charges laid against you.'

'This is the biggest mistake of your lives!'

'If you do not moderate your temper, my Lord, the jailers will do it for you.'

Humphrey gaped. Eleanor nudged him. He closed his mouth. With a chill, he understood that the Lord Chancellor had meant it.

As they entered the court, Eleanor paled. The King's dark, wounded eyes followed them. He could hardly look at Eleanor. He fingered the crucifix the whole time she was in his presence. Warwick motioned them to halt. They now stood bowed before the boy whose head they had so often cursed and execrated. They cringed for he was still the temporal authority of divine right on this piece of earth. Warwick launched into the charges without any of the usual preliminaries, as if to finish off as soon as possible a particularly unpleasant task.

'Be it known that you, the accused, Humphrey, Duke of Gloucester, did prefer your own private interest and peculiar profit before that of your comrades, your regiments, your King and your country; that you did, after the campaign of Agincourt, pillage the King's booty, his baggage train, his war pavilion, even removing the furnishings therein.'

Humphrey flared up.

'My fair share, stolen by my brother.' He had evidently overlooked the fact that the alleged "thief's" son was even now sitting on his father's throne in judgement over him. Warwick continued.

'Furthermore, that you did divert military funds for your own purposes, namely the Palace of Placentia at Greenwich, and did make wrongful confiscations and take war chests of army pay, in specie, and later transferred these treasures to Greenwich, and by these depredations you did cause discontent and disaffection among the rank and file, putting the expedition at considerable danger. Further, that you did subvert the army pay rolls with publication of false accounts, with inflated expenses, invented figures, having two sets of books, one private, the other public . . . '

'Old stuff!'

'Were discredited years ago,' added Eleanor.

'Here are our Exchequer accounts, audited and corrected down to the last groat. And here,' Warwick lifted up a sheaf of papers, 'are copies of your own private accounts.' Eleanor and Humphrey stared horror struck as Warwick held the offending accounts under their eyes. 'You will note, Your Grace,' he continued, addressing Eleanor, 'that many are signed and dated by yourself.'

'They are forgeries,' burst out Humphrey.

'And that they are witnessed, signed and dated by the Abbot of Fleury, faithful ally of the English. He had no reason to lie, being another clerk in your own employ, and the Queen of France herself. Herein is conclusively revealed the scale of your frauds, thefts, briberies, extortions, secret gold shipments, and concealed banking facilities. All sealed with the crest of the talon.'

Humphrey looked at Eleanor, snarling,

'You used my seal!' His hands reached out as if to strangle her.

'Your Grace?' Warwick's voice sounded a warning and Humphrey lowered his hands.

'You said so, my lovely,' Eleanor protested, clutching his sleeve.

'Hands off me, sausage fingers,' he hissed, jerking his arm away.

'Come to order, your Grace.' Humphrey's breathing eased with difficulty.

'Now, in another particular of corruption, the papal annulment of your marriage to Jacqueline of Hainault, that you did corruptly offer a bribe to the Cardinal della Rovere to secure the said annulment. And that this inducement was a precious stone from the King's own hoard.' He held up the brilliant, walnut-sized pendant. Warwick continued. 'This is the

445

signed statement from the Cardinal himself, affixed with his college seal, the bribe returned with his condemnation.'

Humphrey was dumbfounded. Where had all this come from? Who had engineered it all?

'The whores, don't believe the whores,' he muttered distractedly as Warwick pressed on relentlessly.

'Further, again out of private malice and inward grudge, you did declare heinous treasons against the King, in this wise, *Humphrey for King! Humphrey for King.*'

'I told you to shut it up,' he shot at Eleanor.

'Stand by me, my lovely,' she begged.

'Nothing to do with me.'

'I adored only thy greatness.'

'You adored only yourself.' He moved away.

'You will both come to order,' snapped Warwick. 'And guilty, Eleanor Cobham, of further betrayals of the King by putting this most treasonable verse abroad.' He addressed Humphrey, '*Let him sicken!*' He then turned to Eleanor, saying, '*Let him die!*' Addressing Humphrey again, he said, '*Humphrey be King,*' and lastly he speared Eleanor with, '*And Queen be I!*'

Eleanor narrowed her eyes to slits, a black film fell across her vision. Humphrey stood immobilised, frantically trying to get his brain to work. Warwick plucked the baton from his nerveless fingers, and snapped it across his knee.

'You are hereby formally expelled from the Grand Council of the Realm.'

'Nooooo!' The cry came as from someone in the grip of terminal agony. 'It was all for St George, England, my people. I swear it!'

'The three things, your Grace, you hold most in despite, as these documents so abundantly prove. So spare us any more false oaths. Now, I want you to note, in particular, my Lord, that these copies, have been witnessed and countersigned by the Lady Agnes, faithful companion of the late Queen Dowager,

God rest her soul.'

In a flash it came to them both. There was a conspiracy. Lady Agnes and Isabelle. And the turnip top spy at Placentia. That's where the copies had come from. Then full realisation hit them. Agnes was not only a double spy, she had also been in the pay of Henry, the dead King. That was how he knew their every next move. They had a glimpse of the living hell they had prepared for themselves and were now trapped in. They understood with hideous clarity that all their schemes and stratagems had been futile, doomed from the start. Humphrey knew it was no longer a question of being first in line, but of simple survival.

'*Maleficium!*' shouted Warwick suddenly. He turned to the King and asked gently, 'Sire, can you bear to hear it all again?' The King nodded dumbly.

'Then let the prayers begin.' Warwick signalled, and the chamber was filled with the murmur of a hundred prayers, from cloisters, screens and altars.

'Did you, Eleanor Cobham, Duchess of Gloucester, in the village of Eye in Suffolk, ever hold communion with one known as The Witch of Eye?' A tick started up in Eleanor's cheek. No words came. Her tongue seemed cleft to the roof of her mouth. Warwick beckoned. Two guards entered carrying a large travelling chest between them. They set it down nervously. Warwick motioned to them. They lifted the lid, recoiled at first. With sweat breaking out on their foreheads, they lifted out the image of the snarling cat-beast. A thrill of horror ran around the court. Those present hastily crossed themselves. Many held up crucifixes against the beast.

'Eleanor Cobham, are you privy to the blasphemy here, in that the true cross was spat upon before this Fiend here, and then smashed to pieces?' Eleanor lowered her head. 'And that the fragments were thereafter defiled with urine and excrement, while *Maleficium* was chanted? Do you have any knowledge of this?' Eleanor remained silent. 'And that these heads,' he rolled out the miniature heads of the royal family, 'were pierced with needles, to bring the curse of Satan, and death down upon them?' Eleanor was mute. 'This head above all.' He held up the wax image of the boy King, who swayed, then steadied himself. A hissing as of serpents filled the chamber. It seemed to come from the beast. They all crossed themselves again. Humphrey looked more and more terrified. Warwick picked up a bible, as if in self defence. 'You knew nothing of any of this then?' Eleanor did not react. 'And that, further, the witch thereafter held congress with animals, that is, he-goats and rams, at the high altar of the Fiend.' Humphrey blanched. Beyond his ken. Why was he forced to listen to such foulness? 'And that this report,' went on Warwick, 'is witnessed and confirmed by the Abbot of Fleury, with two other independent witnesses. Now,' he demanded as he confronted her for the last time, 'Eleanor Cobham, who is this Witch of Eye?'

Absolute silence reigned. Humphrey stared at her with dawning horror.

'Eleanor Cobham, is it not the truth that you, yourself, are this Witch of Eye?' Again, silence.

'Do you deny you are?' Eleanor's eyes were blank. 'Then the court will take your silence as assent.'

'Not my doing! Under her curse, the witch!' blabbered Humphrey, hardly able to look at her. Eleanor remained still as stone. The Archbishop stepped forward.

'Eleanor Cobham,' he asked, 'do you repent?' Still there was no response. Warwick turned to the King, who nodded, fearfully.

'This is the verdict of the Court. You, Eleanor Cobham, Duchess of Gloucester, are hereby found guilty of witchcraft and of *maleficium*. You are condemned to do penance in three public places in the City, on three separate days, in a witch's peaked hat, with all your sins writ down on your back for all to see. Thereafter you will be sent into perpetual banishment and close confinement in the King's Castle on the Isle of Man. There, never to receive visitors, nor the consolations of the church, nor holy sacrament, even up to the point of death. And after that event, your body will be conveyed to some secret place for burial after midnight, by the public executioner, and every trace of your last resting place will be consigned to the dust of death forever. Nor do we cry "mercy!" for there is none without repentance, and now the Fiend alone will enjoy his own in the flames of eternal damnation. The sentence to be carried out forthwith.'

'Out, out!' yelled Humphrey, pointing accusingly at Eleanor, who at last came to life.

'I became the Witch for thee!' she beseeched, but Humphrey turned his back on her. With an animal whine of self-pity, he sank to his knees before the King.

'Mercy, Sire.' Eleanor, flushed with rage at the rejection and abject plea, screamed,

'Don't ye turn thy back on me!'

'Mercy, Sire.' He was pathetic.

Eleanor erupted like a screeching cat. She circled her once Caesar, clawing and spitting at him.

'Pig!' The guards held back in fear.

'Then let thy head melt into the flames of hell!' With a quick movement, she plucked a needle from the coifs of her hair and plunged it into Humphrey's scalp. Humphrey howled with pain, and scuttled away, clutching the wound and his torn wig. Blood trickled between his fingers.

'Secure her!' shouted Warwick! 'Take her down!'

The guards dragged away the hissing, spitting witch.

The trial was over. The King, still clutching his crucifix, slid to the floor in a dead faint. He was at once surrounded by worried Councillors. The Archbishop made the sign of the cross over him.

Poor Henry, he thought, he may have recovered a family, but if he is not already mad, then what he has seen and heard today will one day surely make him so.

From the distant corridors of the palace echoed the crazed words,

'Let him sicken, let him die . . . ' This time the Witch of Eye was not cursing the boy King.

110

News of the downfall of the vaunted leader had not yet penetrated to the streets. Humphrey's Retainers still milled about the public highways. Mortimer's men were in aggressive mood and brawls were breaking out on every street corner. Somerset's men were also on the loose and getting the worse of it. Somerset himself arrived at Hendale Cross to reform his shattered columns.

Fully armed once again, and with a fresh Welsh poem in their hearts, Owen, Hopcyn and Damascus spurred out of the City before dawn, first making certain that their disguises were firmly in place. It was clear that Humphrey's reward still stood, and would remain so, until either his humiliation was made public or rather, as Owen suspected, until he was dead. Owen knew that he had reduced the chances of both the red and white factions to the throne. The ennobling of his offspring had first been greeted with disbelief, then outrage. The dynastic picture had, overnight, been turned upside down, and all this due to the deceptions of a common Welsh stallion, who had somehow managed to dishonour a lonely widow and defenceless Queen. Behind these turmoils, the King was a fixed bastion, but he was still hardly more than a child, and the fight would now be even longer and more arduous. Instead of attending a triumphant marriage, given the time scale, the contestants might well be attending each others' funerals.

Dawn arrived with a curious, sinister purplish glow on the horizon. The air around the sun seemed to sparkle as if millions of crystal particles had suddenly been released. Hopcyn stared at the vaulting canopy of light with dismay. This was not a good portent. He felt the first stirrings of a warp spasm.

A group of Retainers jostled past, not wanting to challenge what were obviously two heavily armed veteran mercenaries.

If this mob keeps growing, thought Hopcyn, there's going to be pitched battles. What is it, he wondered, that makes an Englishman so restless if he isn't bashing someone. Bash, bash, bash – that's the history of the English.

'Be straight, not superior,' Bedford's words came back to him. How many of the English, he wondered, would ever understand those wise words?

Damascus and Agnes had been dispatched ahead to the Winwood encampment, with orders for the three Captains to begin crossing the Lugg for the road home. All that was left for Owen to do was to reinforce his victory by linking up with the remainder of the Dragon Companies in Winwood, and pushing westwards to Wales and home. And only four weeks stood between him and a free return to visit the boys.

Owen had recovered from the near total paralysis of grief, for he now knew that Catherine's 'awareness of intent' had been right. She had correctly foreseen what was happening on the other side of the hill. He had not deserted her, but had carried out her last wishes to the letter. His own subsequent decisions had led directly from Catherine's, and they had worked out, too. Not only had the boys been saved but, by some miracle of the new King, they were now also sheltered a mere arm's length from the crown itself. Owen felt that Catherine was near, and although he longed for a glimpse of her, he knew that she would be smiling, at the boys and at the husband who had been faithful to her to the end.

When Owen and Hopcyn galloped into the main Square of Hendale, it was a bedlam of retainers, pushing and fighting their way to the Westgate. Apart from guarded supply wagons and reserves of stacked arms, a scaffold had been erected on one side of the Square, guarded by a mixed bag of retainers who glared at each other, although they maintained their ranks. An executioner's block was also in place, shrouded in black cloth. Owen noted that Somerset had set up his headquarters at the Queen's Head Inn, and judging by the comings and goings of messengers, some sort of battle was imminent.

Owen and Hopcyn fought their way across the area and finally forced their mounts through the press at the gates. Once outside, they saw the reasons for the melee. The Retainer army was streaming down to the river, forming up in three columns, under the command of Somerset, who had more men in the field than any other. He now surveyed the field from his war pavilion in the rear of his right column. The river was dominated by his little force, and the road to the west was effectively blocked. The enemy was obvious - the remnants of the Dragon companies still encamped in the woods.

'Make a dash for it!' shouted Owen. 'Still time before they get everything in place.'

With a mad gallop, Owen and Hopcyn charged through the straggling lines, plunged into the river ahead of the unformed troops, and hauled themselves up the far bank. Shrieks and yells rose from the Retainers. The two galloped to the wood. Just inside, under a spreading beech, their headquarters had been set up. Damascus and Agnes, along with the Captains Huw, Ifan and Idris, were waiting. To the cheers of the troops, they all embraced. News of the ennoblings had travelled fast in this direction at least. Their Captain had once again won the victory. He would he win this one too. They noted with unease, however, that their Captain was dressed from head to foot in black. They knew that this was out of respect for Catherine and had been commanded by the King, but never before had anyone been led by a Captain dressed in the colour of death.

'Thank God,' said Idris. 'We got most of the people over, then they began blocking the road. Since you needed an escort, we withdrew the last of our men and encamped here to wait for you.'

'Let's have a look.'

They stood at the edge of the wood looking downwards towards the river.

A strange haze surrounded the sun, shrouding the early morning light with a mysterious glow. When is the sun going to break through? thought Owen. Hopcyn shifted worriedly.

The Lugg presented a barrier, although it was fordable in places. Somerset's forces were out along the banks looking for the shallowest spots. Groups of Retainers had already crossed and were forming up, again into three columns. The slope upwards to the woods was steep, but nothing that infantry couldn't manage if taken steadily, and with cavalry to back them up.

'How many men do you estimate, Idris?'

'About one hundred in each column.'

'How many have we got?' asked Owen looking around.

'We can put out about fifty against each column.'

'Mm,' grunted Owen. 'Two to one. What's our cavalry?'

'Twenty five horse.'

'Put them with my column. We'll concentrate there, turn their left flank. You boys push the centre and right columns back into the river. Then cut across to join me in a breakout out to the west road, with our cavalry covering our rear. Any questions' The three Captains nodded. They knew what they had to do, but they also knew the odds, and they were not stacked in their favour.

'Right. Your men in three columns, you on the right, Idris. Huw and Ifan in the centre, I'll lead the left. Do it fast, before all their men cross over. Friends, Captains, whoever breaks through first will lead the way out. No stopping for wounded or stragglers. Now, for St David and Home!' The shout was taken up by the men as they hurried to their posts. After all the years this would be their final fight with Owen, and it would be a fight for their lives.

Owen now turned to Agnes, Hopcyn and Damascus.

'You three,' he embraced them in turn. 'You know my love for you, we have seen and done great things together, and the greatest of these was our friendship, and our love for Catherine.' They bowed their heads. 'But Catherine told me to go, and so must I tell you, too, to go. As soon as we engage, take the first crossing not too far out on my left flank, make for the north, then circle around east and make south for London and the King. Warn him and the Council of developments. And, arrange for Catherine's burial, your last task for both Catherine and myself. Will you promise that?' They were silent for a second. 'As Catherine would have wanted,' he pleaded. They nodded, speechless in their misery. They knew Owen was right as Catherine had been, too. He embraced them from the saddle, and wheeled to take his position at the head of his men.

The three cantered along inside the wood, rapidly putting distance between themselves and the fighting columns. They reined in, watching for the Welsh columns preparing to move down onto Somerset's troops.

It was at this moment that the skies opened and the sun moved out from behind the clouds. Shouts of awe went up from all sides, for the sun was followed by a second, and then a third. The three suns hovered in the purple haze, with glowing, sparkling haloes over each one. Then the whole scene shivered like a mirage. The three suns flickered and disappeared behind the clouds. This frightening phenomenon was followed by a shower of crystal-like hailstones, each one red as blood. This most unnatural event left both sides praying, crossing themselves and prophesying the sinister omen in their favour. But Hopcyn knew. It was the day of the three suns, the day of Owen's death. He shook himself out of the final warp spasm. Within a mirror of wood, he had beheld Owen greet Catherine, and the meeting had passed the bounds of all previous joys.

Owen raised his sword, pointing forward. The Captains raised theirs in salute. The three columns debouched into the open and charged down onto the opposing forces. Almost simultaneously, the three columns met head on. The enemy archers dropped volley after volley onto heads of Owen's men and followed up with a charge with short sword and dagger. But Owen's impetus had broken the head of the Retainers' column. The enemy disintegrated and streamed back in retreat across the river, pursued by Owen's victorious men. Owen shouted for his followers to turn, but, intoxicated by the triumph, they continued their pursuit in small, dispersed groups. Owen turned to see how his centre and right were faring. The central column had been stopped in its tracks. They were fighting to the death, but slowly being pushed back up the hill. Dead and wounded littered their tracks. Even as he watched, he saw his extreme right flank gather for a counter attack, and charge a second time. The attack splintered, and was driven back in confusion. Idris was killed. The survivors plunged into the press and, in hand to hand combat, were cut down one by one. Somerset saw that his left was victorious, and ordered this group to turn and attack Owen's retreating centre. With this reinforced weight, the Welsh column disintegrated. On the right, Owen's own column was still strung out, trying to rally to his shouts. Somerset saw the opportunity. He unleashed his cavalry. Running before the lances, Owen's men were slaughtered by the lances. Owen was toppled by a charging horse and pinned to the ground. The order, 'No quarter!' was given. Retainers began finishing off those who had surrendered or who still lay wounded on the ground. Owen was hauled to his feet. Somerset strode up to him. Without a word, he pointed towards the town. No chance of ransom. Owen smiled, So it was to be Somerset. Let him and Humphrey go to war over the reward then. They'd fight to the death over it, as he had today. Whichever direction Owen looked, it was Englishman spilling

Englishmen's blood. Nothing wrong with that. He shrugged, and followed his baying captors.

Hopcyn, Damascus and Agnes watched, sickened, from the town battlements. The drinking and brawling had already started, as they had anticipated. The Retainers charged into the square, dragging Owen behind them. The Executioner, in his mask, had taken up his position by the block. Its surface gleamed with reflected light. Owen stood at the bottom of the scaffold steps, gazing up at the block. Yes, thought Hopcyn, he had seen it, and he had hidden it, now he must confront it. Gwydion and the old gods had given over the lamentations to the ancient bard.

Owen mounted the steps firmly and unhurriedly. Three suns, he thought. Why not? One for Catherine, one for myself, one to share between the boys! The Tudor family would shine tremendously. He smiled at the idea. As he stepped onto the scaffold, he was composed, his green eyes glinted, his shoulders squared. Yes, it was his last day on earth, but as he looked around, he felt the impotent rage of his enemies seething in the square below. This was the greatest victory of all. What he had won, he knew, could not be undone. Yes, he thought, looking at the Executioner, this head which once rested in the lap of a queen will soon rest upon your deadly block. He nodded, handed over his scarlet cloak, knelt, spread out his arms to keep a balance, and said clearly, so the whole square could hear, 'In the name of Catherine, St David and Wales, now strike!'

His eyes stared down into the oak, polished until it shone like a mirror. For a moment, Catherine's face faded into his vision, beckoning, closer and closer. As he reached out to touch her, in one blinding flash, her face and all the light of all the suns of the earth were extinguished forever. To savage drunken yells of rage and revenge, Owen Tudor's body rolled down onto the scaffold, blood pumping out of the neck arteries. His head had fallen and lay face upwards in the waiting basket, the lids unclosed, eyes still gleaming green as emerald.

To vent their rage, the mob discarded the corpse at the foot of the scaffold for the dogs, and as a warning to all who would defy them. The mass of blood-sated Retainers now embarked on an orgy of drunkenness and destruction, which lasted long into the night. When the moon was high, Hopcyn, Agnes and Damascus crept out to retrieve the body. But someone had got there before them.

From the shadows on the wrong side of midnight, crept the mad woman of Hendale Cross. She had glanced briefly into the basket but had become instantly entranced. There before her lay the most beautiful man's face she had ever seen. She fondled the hair, caressed the cheeks, lifted the head out and placed it in the centre of the scaffold. She hurried off to the Church and returned with water from the font, and candles from the chapel. She washed the head, wiping away every vestige of blood. True, never had she seen such beauty in death or in life. As she cleaned, she whispered words of love, covering the lips with kisses. She then arranged the candles in a circle, lit them and sat within the flickering flames, looking into the green eyes, talking to the head like a risen lover.

She was still murmuring words of adoration when Hopcyn came to reclaim the remains.

111

Humphrey had lit every torch and candle in the Long Room. The fire in the hearth blazed up once again. Humphrey was obsessed by the idea of purification by fire. He was determined to drive out the demons he was convinced had been responsible for bringing down this curse on his head and causing his downfall. Fire was the vast red cave into which he was shovelling all the poisoned fabrics of his life. Added to his insane rage was the fact that the floor had been littered with turnip tops, the work of that damnable but elusive spy. He had yelled for Captain Dark to locate and execute the devil, but the good Captain had failed to put in an appearance.

To move more freely, Humphrey had discarded his clothes. He now lashed out in all directions, as naked as the day he was born. He paused, panting, dripping with sweat. In his hand he clutched a newly sharpened battle-axe. Around him for the whole length of the hall was pile upon pile of smashed and lacerated debris. He had chopped up every inch of his Temple of the Caesars and stamped the plaster statues underfoot. He had dismembered the two thrones and ripped up the upholstery. The secret travelling chest was in splinters. He had placed the royal heads in a row on the table, from Clarence, Winchester, Bedford to the boy-King, and occasionally stopped to spit and piss on their faces. He had dragged out Eleanor's 'royal' gowns, slashed them to shreds and pounded her coronet flat. He was now hysterically tearing down the talon tapestries, shredding them and piling them by the fire.

He finally strode over to the heads. It was time for the

executions! He raised the axe high and, with a yell of insensate rage, brought it down onto Henry's head, splitting it neatly in half. Humphrey gasped in ecstasy. Next was another Henry and Clarence and Bedford, until he came to the boy king, the cream of the crop. Quivering with excitement, he brought down the axe with every ounce of strength he had left. He hit the head square on the crown. It promptly exploded, smothering his hands, face, belly and genitals, with a mixture of menstrual blood, urine and excrement, packed into the head by Eleanor months before. The accumulated gases rose like a miasma, choking Humphrey, who clutched the edge of the table and vomited over the smashed, squashed wax. The appalling stench sent him reeling, stomach churning. He retched and retched until the wracking, dry heaves nearly brought up his liver. Eyes bulging, purple face swelling, a sudden shower of needles seemed to pierce his chest and shoulders from the inside. A numb spreading agony shot down his breast and arms. The fires around him blurred, his knees buckled as the pain struck again and again. He grasped at the table, knocking over the candelabra which tumbled to the floor onto a pile of shredded silk coverings. The silks flared up. The flames leapt onto the next pile and ignited. The underside of the table was now alight. The trail of flame reached the wall and caught the remaining strips of hanging tapestries. Soon a dozen fires were blazing, each feeding the other, spreading irresistibly.

Humphrey was paralysed. He could make out the path of the conflagration but was nailed to the spot by the engulfing pain. He tried to scream, but his lips scarcely moved. His cries became internal, infernal, dumb shrieks smothered in never ending agony. Bits of debris from the burning fabric danced across his vision, and burning gobbets of material settled on his bare face and body, inflicting still more torture. He screamed his silent screams again. The main doors were suddenly thrown open. A few seconds later he made out the shape of Captain

Dark bending over him, but he could not see the look of gloating triumph on the scarred face. The Captain straightened up. Yes, the flames had caught nicely. But he would still have enough time to strip every chamber, cellar and attic of every article of any value. That he thought grimly was not only payment in full, but an added bonus as well. Humphrey's eyes expressed terrified incomprehension. The Captain couldn't be leaving. No, no! Tears slid down his cheeks, the last living vestige of a dying monster.

Captain Dark hurried out. He would have to organise his Retainers double quick and get every cart and wagon in the stables ready. Then to London to disperse the booty. All under cover of darkness. Perfect. This was to be a double killing.

The heads on the table were now melting. Ever thickening streams of red wax ran to the edge of the table. Humphrey could make out the advancing, leaping progress of the fire. He could finally behold his tormentors, the furies and devils of hell, leaping up in the flames, screaming at him in triumph, stooping ever lower over his unprotected, nerveless flesh. ·The eyes of gleaming cat beasts glared at him through the curtains of flame. He opened his mouth and screamed as the swooping talons pierced his heaving chest again, this time tearing his heart out. A heavy stream of wax ran over the edge of the table and poured down over his open eyes, into his mouth, plugging his upturned nostrils. The flow increased as the royal heads melted away to nothing. The mass congealed for a second, and Humphrey's sightless eyes stared up through a block of blood-coloured wax, the last head in a line of kings. A few minutes later, the flames exploded across the ceiling, a fitting and final canopy over the tomb of a would-be demented and departed emperor.

Captain Dark was exultant. He had not only cleared out the main chambers, he had been able to locate Humphrey's accumulated booty in the cellars. The wagons were now drawn up, packed and sheeted down, to the last inch. The wheels creaked and groaned under the burdens. Every man worked with a will. This was better that any murderous brawl. After this it was luxury and ease for the rest of their lives. Captain Dark kept a careful eye on the progress of the fire. It seemed to work with them. As they cleared one room, so the flames would take over. Any evidence would go up in a pall of smoke. The only missing link was the commissary clerk, but this was a mere detail. The mass of Placentia's treasure was now his. It was he who was unstoppable, as his crazed, greedy Caesar melted into the anonymity of flame.

The Retainers excitedly boarded the carts and whipped the horses into motion. In good order, the column rumbled and creaked down to the closed, main iron-wrought gates. Here they dismounted to open the barrier for the last time. It was at this moment that Warwick gave his archers the order to shoot. From the trees, bushes and walls on both sides of the gates, shower after shower of arrows rained down. Captain Dark fell in the first volley, with an arrow through the throat cutting the wind pipe. He died drowning in his own blood. Warwick gave the further order, 'No quarter'. This was one body of bloody retainers which had committed its last crimes and murders. After ten minutes, a pall of silence settled over the convoy, punctuated by the screams and groans of the dying. A burst of distant flames sent a faint glow over the scene. Warwick sent the commissary clerk to check the wagons.

Warwick and Winchester looked on at the burning palace. Neither moved.

'Yes, all there,' reported the commissary clerk, hurrying back. 'Pay chests, Henry's loot, a King's ransom, the lot.'

'Why did you inform us, Clerk?'

'Had a job to finish, my Lord.'

'You won't accept any payment?' asked Warwick. The clerk pointed at the conflagration and said,

'That is my payment.'

'Who are you? You sound cockney.'

'Welsh. Born in Eastcheap. Parents prisoners here in the Welsh wars. Duke Humphrey hanged my Da. Mam died in a brothel. Home to Pembroke after this.'

Warwick nodded. No alarm was ever given. All three, with one accord, gazed on the inferno of Placentia as it was devoured by cleansing flame, before its final descent into the eternal black abyss of Satan.

112

Catherine lay in my Lady's Chapel in the Abbey of Westminster. The boy king had vowed to respect his departed mother's wishes to the last. Masses were being said for her in every chantry and chapel in the land. The requiems filled the vaulted roofs of the Abbey twenty-four hours a day.

Catherine's body lay in a closed coffin on trestles in front of the little altar of My Lady's Chapel. At midnight, a second coffin, again at the King's direction, took its place alongside Catherine's. Agnes, Hopcyn and Damascus stood at the foot of the coffins, heads bowed. They had brought Owen with them to be with his beloved at the end.

Owen's face in death was as it had been in life, strong, broad-jawed, strikingly handsome. Around the last, frightful wound of this son of destiny, where his neck had been severed from the body, Agnes had bound Catherine's voluminous, silk, *fleur-de-lis* kerchief.

Agnes kissed the cold forehead. Never would such a story be told again. Bless you, my poor, dear, loving, lost friend.

Damascus and Hopcyn gave their final kiss as well.

As Damascus looked down on his two friends, he said the final words of the great geometer of the world.

'In the eye of the light and in the face of the sun, the Three Great Reincarnations of the Isle Abounding with Beauty – Owain Tudur, Catherine of Valois, and their family.'

Hopcyn recited the ancient prayer;

'Receive this great son of Cymru and his love. Be blessed with Gwydion amidst his everlasting stars. Rest in his long, high home, and be re-united with each other's spirits in the shining fields of *Afallon*.'

Damascus knew Owen had been 'in the world' before, but he knew too that Owen would be on earth again.

'Destiny does not die,' was his last message to his friend.

Agnes slid open the lid of Catherine's coffin. The three friends gasped in astonishment. Catherine's body appeared to be in the first flush of youth, red cheeks, rosy lips, skin still glowing with life. As they looked, Owen's dragon kerchief around her neck, seemed to lift and flutter in an invisible breeze. They shivered in awe. It was as if Catherine was waiting, breathless, for some ecstatic entrance, for some last loving call from her beloved. It seemed that their love had denied the dreadful, icy, immovability of dissolution.

Hopcyn felt the warp-spasm building up, then burst into his mind's eye. It was the vision of a crowned child, with the crest of a lily and a dragon. As the image faded, a rushing sound came from above, as of a myriad, tiny, rustling wings. The glimmering outlines of the Opalescent Ones shone into sight. They hovered above, beckoning. A rush of colour rose up from the breasts of Owen and Catherine, irresistible, unearthly, and floated away, embodied, through the vaulted and transparent roof, through the opened canopy of the sky, up until they flowed into the vast spaces of eternity to join the huge, whispering, choruses of the earth's small and mighty, still undimmed, spirits. And as the lovers moved into the fields of immortality, the stars blinked a multitudinous welcome, and clustered to form for a flash of a second, the form of a lily and a dragon, Owen and Catherine, now never to be apart in the shining shadows of the everlasting arms.

'Yes,' sighed Hopcyn, as he gazed on the miracle, 'the poet to come is right. "Love," indeed, "is the last light spoken".'

Epilogue

After the battle of Bosworth in 1485, Jasper Tudor's son and Owen's grandson, became King of England as Henry VII, the first of the great Tudor monarchs.

Like his grandfather, Charles VI of France, Henry VI of England suffered prolonged bouts of insanity during his long reign. He was eventually murdered.

A most extraordinary fate awaited Catherine. Years afterwards, when her coffin was opened for her entombment beside Henry V, her body was found to be in a state of near perfect preservation. It was put on public display in Westminster Abbey at a penny a look. In 1667, Pepys recorded, 'Today, I kissed the lips of a Queen!' This Queen was Catherine. Her remains were not finally interred until 1803, almost four hundred years after her death. It was, indeed, as if Catherine, against the cruel passage of time, had kept herself beautiful for the return of her true love, Owen.

An author's response to history is, by definition, tinged with a touch of the fanciful. In the case of Owan Tudor, the fanciful cut short his life by twenty and more years. But many would argue that he died with Catherine in any case, and who would have it any other way?

Dedwydd Jones is from West Wales, educated at Haverfordwest Grammar School, Latymer Upper School, the London School of Economics and the Warberg Institute of Classical Studies, London University. Former Fellow in Drama, University College, Cardiff. Variously a postman, bargain basement towel salesman, forest labourer, insurance inspector. Two years in tank transporters. Captain of the Berlin Army 1st rugby XV, his highest achievement. Taught English in Paris, Brussels, Berlin, Barcelona, Mallorca, and Lausanne. Mainly a dramatist, over 26 productions, from Cardiff's New Theatre to London's Mermaid, Swiss radio and the Edinburgh Fringe. Most recent plays: *The Man in the English Lunatic Asylum*, *The Man in the Welsh Lunatic Asylum*. The 'enfant terrible' of the Welsh National Theatre movement, with numerous articles and *Black Books* to his name.

The Lily and the Dragon is his first novel.

He now lives between Bedford, Carmarthen and Lausanne. Three lovely daughters, Awen, Caryl and Caroline.

LITERATURE FROM WALES

- **THE FRENCH THING**
  A novel by Chris Keil to the backdrop of the western Welsh agricultural crisis and livestock exporting.
  ISBN: 0-86381-768-8; £7.50

- **THE LILY AND THE DRAGON**
  A historical novel after Agincourt by Dedwydd Jones.
  ISBN: 0-86381-752-1; £9.50

- **BIG FISH**
  by Jon Gower
  Lively, entertaining short stories.
  ISBN: 0-86381-619-3; £6.95

- **RARE WELSH BITS**
  by John Williams
  A strange and compelling melange of tales.
  ISBN: 0-86381-700-9; £4.50

- **GREAT WELSH FANTASY STORIES**
  Ed. Peter Haining
  ISBN: 0-86381-618-5; £6.90

- **CAMBRIAN COUNTRY**
  by David Greenslade
  Creative essays on Welsh emblems.
  ISBN: 0-86381-613-4; £5.75

- **THE LITERARY PILGRIM IN WALES**
  by Meic Stephens
  A guide to places associated with writers in Wales. 266 places; 415 writers.
  ISBN: 0-86381-612-6; £6

ANTHOLOGIES FROM WALES

- **WALES A CELEBRATION**
  An anthology of poetry and prose. Ed. Dewi Roberts
  ISBN: 0-86381-608-8; £6

- **FOOTSTEPS: an anthology of Walking in Wales.**
  Ed. Dewi Roberts. *ISBN: 0-86381-774-2; £5.50*

- **SNOWDONIA, A HISTORICAL ANTHOLOGY**
  Ed. David Kirk; *ISBN: 0-86381-270-8; £5.95*

- **AN ANGLESEY ANTHOLOGY**
  Ed. Dewi Roberts. *ISBN: 0-86381-566-9; £4.95*

- **BOTH SIDES OF THE BORDER**
  An anthology of Writing on the Welsh Border Region. Ed. Dewi Roberts
  ISBN: 0-86381-461-1; £4.75

- **GREAT WELSH FANTASY STORIES**
  Ed. Peter Haining
  ISBN: 0-86381-618-5; £6.90